The Many Half-Lived Lives of Sam Sylvester

The Many Half-Lived Lives of Sam Sylvester

MAYA MacGREGOR

ASTRA YOUNG READERS

AN IMPRINT OF ASTRA BOOKS FOR YOUNG READERS

New York

Sincere thanks to Lydia K. Valentine for her review of and input regarding the manuscript, helping us to ensure that all readers can connect with our story and feel genuine representation.

Heartfelt gratitude to Noemí Martínez for their helpful feedback on Sam's story.

Quotation on page 76 from Jack London, *The Call of the Wild* (New York: The MacMillan Company, 1903).

For information about permission to reproduce selections from this book, please contact permissions@astrapublishinghouse.com.

This is a work of fiction. Names, characters, places, and incidents are products of the author's imagination or are used fictitiously. Any resemblance to actual events, locales, or persons, living or dead, is entirely coincidental.

Astra Young Readers
An imprint of Astra Books for Young Readers,
a division of Astra Publishing House
astrapublishinghouse.com
Printed in the United States of America

Library of Congress Cataloging-in-Publication Data is on file
Library of Congress Control Number: 2021050226 (hc)
Library of Congress Control Number: 2021050227 (eBook)
ISBN: 978-1-63592-359-9 (hc)
ISBN: 978-1-63592-570-8 (eBook)

First edition
10 9 8 7 6 5 4 3 2 1

Design by Barbara Grzeslo
The text is set in Sabon LT Std.
The titles are set in Futura Std Light Condensed and Khaki Std 1.

For my queer family. Whether you can come out yet or not, you belong.

CHAPTER ONE

The first time I see the house, it's as it swallows my father.

I count to three—Dad's strategy for doing things I'm not ready to do—and make myself look up.

The sound of something rattling in a hastily packed box behind me has stopped. I've carefully kept my eyes on my phone, scrolling Tumblr, but I can't avoid it anymore. I sit here watching motes of dust drift in the slanting afternoon light.

The front door is even ringed in red like a mouth. Not a bloodied mouth, nothing monstrous. Nor are the two dormer windows at the top in any way aggressive. They droop. The house looks like it *tried* but that it had found whatever it tried just too hard, and it quit.

I can kind of relate to that. New house. New city. New school. Again.

I hope I do better than the house did.

"Sam!" Dad sticks his head out the door to holler. "You've gotta come see this place!"

He's so excited about it. I've seen pictures, of course, but he insists they don't do it justice.

I push a lock of lavender-swirled hair out of my face and open the car door.

Outside the wind is chilly, and I'm amazed that I can smell the ocean. The salt tang to the air and the brisk winter wind wake me right up. I shouldn't be surprised to smell the sea; it surrounds Astoria on all sides. There's even a damn palm tree in the yard next door. Aren't we fancy? I like it. There's no one around, but it's Wednesday afternoon, so I guess people are still at work. Just as I think it, I see a person with a backpack covered in She-Ra and Steven Universe patches and Pride flags turn the corner onto our new street. I'm pretty sure I feel their eyes on me as they look over their shoulder, and I hurriedly turn away, even though I want to know if I saw right—I thought I saw the telltale pink-purple-blue of the bi flag. I don't want to get my hopes up. Maybe I didn't see what I thought I did; it was just a glance. I'm used to being the only queer in the room (the only one who was out, anyway), and in Portland, I was still too terrified to even register that wasn't true anymore.

Tapping my thumb against my iPhone's screen, I trot up the few steps to the house. I close my eyes on the top step. The floors over the threshold are dark hardwood, maybe walnut. Even from here, I get a whiff of newish paint, the smell fading but not gone. The foyer's mostly offset by pale light coming through the windows. The house is oriented north-south, and I wonder what it'll be like in the golden hour if the sun ever *really* comes out here.

I can see it behind my eyes, all warm orange turning the dust motes to sparks instead of sparkles.

"Sam!" Dad calls my name again. He's upstairs, from the sound of it.

I open my eyes and let the house swallow me too, stepping over the threshold.

The house echoes around my footsteps. It's a strange sound, like I'm descending into a cave. We have zero furniture. There's supposedly a truck from IKEA coming in the next day or so, but for now, my feet on the stairs feel heavy, so heavy their thumps should be heard by the ocean and its waves three streets away.

I put one hand on the banister as I climb the stairs, and my trepidation grows. Like the sea wind or a wave at the change of the tide, it washes over me and retreats, slipping back into the deep.

At the top of the stairs is Dad, leaning on the railing. He's a smidge taller than I am, around six feet. I'm still not used to seeing him without his locs surrounding his warm brown face, always in contrast to my pale white skin and naturally dirty blond hair that is more half-hearted wave than Dad's gorgeous tight coils. He cut the locs off for his new job. I said I didn't want him to cut them. He said they were heavy and giving him migraines with extra pressure under his hard hat (plus his hairline's receding, and he's self-conscious about it), and then he chased me around the apartment after I buzzed his head. The downstairs neighbors pounded on their ceiling to tell us how much they appreciated *that*.

He laughed at the time, but I think Dad had more mixed feelings than he let on, and the silliness was him trying to hide it. He's worn locs since I was little, and while I know it was his choice and his reasons, I think he felt the weight of more than hair once it was done.

"Did you see the palm tree?" I ask. It feels important that he knows it's there. Palm trees are vacations and sun-drenched shores, and this move is neither of those things, but the tree seems hopeful anyway.

"I did, I did." Dad grins at me. "Not quite a tropical paradise, but I thought you'd like it. Come see your room."

I follow, trailing my hand along the banister. It looks like it's been freshly sanded and re-varnished, the same dark wood as the floor. My fingertips stick slightly on the smooth surface. I think if I bent over, I could see my face in the glossy reflection.

He's giving me the biggest room. He insisted that he's too lazy to climb stairs to get to bed, and his smaller room has an en-suite, which just means he gets his own bathroom. And when I walk into my new room, a little shock goes through me.

The room is huge. The windowsill directly ahead of me spans both dormers, almost a window seat, and is a solid two feet deep. The upper bit rises straight along the outermost edges of the windows and then curves inward to meet in a little point like the peak on top of an ice-cream cone.

Walking to one of the walls, it's almost too bright to look at. It's white. White-white, not eggshell or cream. It looks and feels hastily done. There's even a seam visible. Dad would be mortified if his crew did this. I rap my knuckles on it, and a hollow sound greets me.

When I touch the paint, I take a step backward, the way I saw a kid do once at the IGA supermarket when he called a woman *Mom* and when she turned around, it was a stranger. A thrill buzzes up the length of my spine, an echo of the premonition I hadn't even articulated in thought enough to consider being right. Someone *did* cover something up here.

It's not the sound of the hollow echo that startles me, but the feel of it. Like instead of wood, my knuckles touched an electric current—or the ghost of one. I fight the urge to pick at the seam, to dig into the wall to be able to touch whatever is waiting behind it.

"What do you think?" Dad gestures around with a flourish as I spin around to look at him. He had his back to me and must've missed my movement. "You're going to be Emperor Sam up here."

I rap my knuckles on the wall again, harder this time, trying to ignore the way it sends little shock waves zipping up and down my fingers. Yep, definitely hollow. I want in there. I can't figure out what's waiting if I can't touch it, and this crappily

4

done wall is in the way. Dad watches as I circle him, knocking on each wall. Sometimes I knock a few times, listening to the variations in sound. I find a rhythm. Hollow at hip level, fading into shallower sounds in both directions, then back out to hollow again. Dad doesn't say anything. He's used to me by now.

"You can be yourself here, kid," Dad says.

I think he means what I'm doing right now—knocking on walls like the weirdo I am. I wonder if what he says is true. For one glorious moment, my universe expands like his words sparked a Big Bang. I could be me. Really me. For the first time. Maybe figure out who the hell that even is.

The moment contracts as quickly as it expanded. I pull my hand back, and I tap my fingernails hurriedly against my palm, stimming.

"There're shelves behind the walls, I think," I tell Dad.

He gives a little start at my words, then looks around. He's used to me not responding to emotional things, too. Walking over, he knocks lightly on one panel, and sure enough, it gives that same hollow echo a little too deep for it to just be regular drywall and beams. Like I said.

"Huh," he says.

He doesn't question, but he does look at the wall a bit closer. He gives an offended sniff at the shoddy crafting of that wonky seam and mutters, "Previous owner's attempt at DIY, maybe." After a moment, he beams at me. "It'll be a good project for us to open them up. If you want."

He looks so eager that even if I didn't want to, I'd agree. Besides, now that he's seen that seam, I wouldn't be surprised to wake up with him fixing it in the middle of the night. It's going to drive him nuts.

I return his smile. "Damn right."

"Don't say *damn*."

"Darn tootin'."

"That's worse. Say damn."

His phone goes off downstairs, playing "The Imperial March" from Star Wars.

"Uh-oh. BRB." He lopes out the door and thumps down the stairs calling at me, "Sam! No neighbors to yell at us now!"

"So you say!" I call back.

I haven't seen him this happy in I don't know how long.

I trail my hand around on the wall, feeling the uneven paint and that thrill just out of reach. My fingertips buzz against the paint like I'm touching one of those lightning balls you find at novelty shops. I can almost see where the drywall bows a bit between the shelves beneath it. There's something there, something for me to find. And this room is *mine*.

New town, new house, even a seemingly new dad.

I hope to hell it goes better than last time.

. . .

I pass the time waiting for Dad to return by lying flat on my back in the middle of my new room, staring at the ceiling and trying not to scratch at my still-new sleeve tattoo. The tattoo was a deal when I turned eighteen. Dad said I could get one if I passed pre-calc, but I think it was also his way of giving me agency over my body after what happened in Montana. And I don't think even Dad knows what it all means, the designs I chose, even though he went with me to all my consults and listened to me talk to the artist. I'm not even sure I know what *all* of it means. The top half from my shoulder to elbow is watercolor, the aurora borealis. Throughout the colors are black designs. A bird molting feathers that bleed into ink splotches. A constellation. A tree that becomes roots that become a fan of swords at the crook of my elbow. Elbow to wrist is more water-color, but this time water-water, like colors of water. A raven swimming at my wrist, wings splayed. They're all familiar images to me, even if they dissolve like the northern lights in the sky when I chase them. Trying to figure out weirdness is an ongoing thing in my life.

Like this room.

Something about the room unsettles me. Not in an Amityville way. Something . . . else.

Lying there alone, for a moment I'm suspended. It feels like this place wants something from me. Probably just my "vivid imagination," or whatever my teachers called it before Dad got me my proper autism diagnosis. Or my histories, which my therapist in Missoula said were autism-related special interests. You know, like that show with the autistic kid who knows every single Pokémon. That's not always what it looks like, obviously. We're not all the same. For me it's finding the stories of teens who died too young. Some of my tattoo is for them. That I can never tell Dad. I didn't even want to tell my therapist; I just had to explain my histories started before the attack, not after, since she naturally assumed it was me almost dying that made me obsessed with teen deaths. Nope.

I swallow as the scar on my neck twinges.

Dad comes back so quietly even I don't hear him until he scuffs his foot on the doorjamb. He stops in the doorway, and I meet his eyes without lifting my head from the floor. After a moment, he walks over. He lies down too, bumping the top of his head against the top of mine.

"Bad news," he says.

"Was it the furniture people?"

"Yep."

"Are they bringing us a stampede of un-potty-trained puppies?"

"Nope. How would that possibly be bad news?" Dad throws his hands in the air as if I've said something outrageous. "Stampeded by puppies is a life goal."

"Puppies piss and shit all over, and not cute little poop emojis. But puppies are cute! And I guess hardwood's easier to clean than carpet."

"Sam," Dad says, "practice not swearing before we go meet your principal tomorrow."

"Fine, fine." The floor is still nice and cool against my back. My hands explore it, palms down, fingers finding the cracks between the floorboards. "So what's the real bad news?"

"Holiday season holdup. They're coming a few days later."

"So you're saying we've got plenty of time to knock down some walls before they get here."

I can feel his quiet chuckle because it shakes his head against mine.

"Yeah, that's what I'm saying." Dad's quiet for a moment. "You still okay about the new school thing again?"

He says *again* because it's the second one this year. It's not a normal thing for us, moving.

This time I'm quiet, long enough for Dad to go, "Sam?"

"Yeah, I'm okay." I mean, okay as I can be. I don't need to say that out loud for him to know what I mean.

"The principal sounds very supportive," he says. "And Oregon's not Montana."

"I know."

I do know, but kids are kids and teenagers are teenagers, and that's the same anywhere you go, especially these days when all sorts of ugly are ready to stamp all over our progress toward ever-elusive equality.

I feel it then, that tightness in my throat that comes with the mention of Montana. More than just my scar getting twitchy. My muscles tighten around my eye, and I don't try to stop the movement in my face. It's just me and Dad here. I ball my hands, pressing my nails into my palms in quick flutters.

Dad scrambles up behind me. I look at him upside down.

"Come on," he says. "We're gonna unload the car. And then we're going to set up our egg crates and sleeping bags, and then we are going to go for a walk to see . . ." He pauses to stare at me melodramatically. "The *ocean*."

I can't help the small bounce I do. Dad is good at this. Giving me direction, expectations. Especially because tomorrow will be stressy, and even he can't tell me how it'll go.

Dad notices the bounce and grins wider. He has learned to tune himself to my frequency.

He keeps me busy for the rest of the day and into the night, and we explore Astoria from the stretch of sandy beaches and slate-gray water (I love the hypnotic sound of the waves, real waves, not just my white noise machine) to the small downtown with tourist shops that are sleepy and unrushed since it's the off-season despite the Christmas lights everywhere.

By the time I lie down on my egg crate in the too-echoey room, I am actually exhausted enough to fall asleep immediately for once.

I don't know how falling asleep is for the rest of the world, but for me, it's like stepping into a tunnel of silver-white mist with the aurora behind it. That's the one part of my tattoo I get in full. Colored lights flicker through this tunnel, and I'm here.

I'm present. I know what lies beyond the mist, even if I can't touch it. I can taste it.

Some nights, most nights, that's all there is.

Not tonight.

I'm back in Airdrie, listening to my old principal tell Dad that they don't have enough evidence to expel the kids, just like the cops said they didn't have enough evidence to bring charges against them.

He says, "I'm sorry. It's not as simple as accepting Sam's word that she recognized the Barry boys and Sherilee Tanner. We need evidence."

My dad is still, so still I can feel his fury. I can't talk because my throat is swollen. I want to open my mouth and scream until my jaw unhinges and I can eat this principal whole. The way he says "the Barry boys" as if he's not their uncle makes me want to vomit.

"This was a hate crime," my dad says softly. "And you will use my child's correct pronouns."

Dad's the only Black man in a white-as-a-blizzard town, and everything he does here is quiet, soft, because to everyone around us, his very existence is loud, even as the white folks here proclaim how they're not racist. How *could* they be when they haven't run our interracial family out of town and *besides*—and I've literally heard people say this—they can't be racist when everyone is white, right? We stayed because Dad loved his mountains and his job; our ten acres in the foothills of the Sapphires were his sanctuary. Until they couldn't be mine.

But Dad. His words hold the intensity of a supernova, and I love him for it. The principal's mouth starts moving, but I don't hear a word he says.

I'm seven years old again, and it's the first time I ever see Dad. He comes into the foster home with the social workers, and when I see him, I know. He looks at me, and something ignites in me, something fierce and bright and everything at once. I know he doesn't just see a ragged little white kid with shaggy dishwater hair who people think can't talk.

He looks at me and my Led Zeppelin shirt and my hair in my face and he saves me. In that moment, something in his shoulders loosens, something in his face softens. He takes me out of that place and the first thing I ever say to him on my eighth birthday is *thank you*.

I'm sixteen, and I'm not Sam Sylvester. I reach for my name but I can't find it, even though I think I should know it. It feels close, present like the scent of the sea in the wind and as unattainable. I'm surrounded by books and David Bowie's voice and laughter that lightning-zings back and forth between me and someone I can't quite see. They are backlit with the sun, the outline of curls the only clear thing in the haze. Golden light pours through double dormers, and the room is filled with hazy giggles that fade as soon as they began. I swallow and cough. And then that laughter turns to a gasp, my gasp. My throat is itchy and tight, and I fall to my knees and I can't breathe. I can't breathe.

Light fades from my eyes into red and purple flashes.

· · ·

"Sam! Breathe!"

I gasp a breath big enough to drain the room of air.

Dad has me, my arms crossed over my chest, holding me in a tight cocoon. The back of my head throbs. I gasp again. Then again.

11

"Hey, Sammy, it's okay, it's okay." The hall light is on, cutting a golden swathe into my room.

I flail for a moment, my brain belatedly processing Dad's words.

"Breathe in," he says, and I do. "Breathe out."

I do that too. He breathes with me. This is a ritual we've repeated far too often. This is why I will never understand how people think family is as common as blood. To me, family is breath; it's trusting the person beside you to demand your right to air in a world that would take it from you. It's the vulnerability of feeling someone's chest move in a careful rhythm to give you your own back. Dad and I both know this fear for different reasons. His mom died of lung cancer when he was a kid.

Slowly, he releases his grip and lowers me to the floor. I'm all the way off my little egg crate pallet, and at first I think it's the floor's fault that my head's throbbing, but then I see Dad wince and rub his cheekbone.

"Shit, D-Dad, your cheek." Alarmed, I scramble to sitting position. My chest is still full of my rattling heartbeat. I try another slow breath.

"It's okay, Sammy. I've had worse." He waggles his tongue through the hole where his eye tooth was—it got knocked out before I was born, and he wears a plate during the day. "I'll live."

I swallow, trying to keep my heart from swinging on my uvula. This was worse than the other ones, and he knows it.

"What time is it?" I ask. The sky's still dark, but that means nothing in December.

"No idea." Dad sits back and leans on his hands while I check my phone.

"It's five to seven," I say.

"Do you want to talk about it?"

"The time?" This time I'm being purposely literal, but Dad doesn't smile.

"Sam."

I don't answer.

"Okay," Dad says, and with him, I know he means it. Some people say that to preface them changing tactics. Not Dad. "Want to see if we can find a decent breakfast place?"

I nod at him. Sweat drips between my shoulder blades, tickling. This time I help him up off the floor, and he mimes a broken back.

"Skull emoji," I say wryly. "I'm going to shower. Meeting's at nine, right? Do we have time?"

"Half past nine, and I hope so—be quick. I'll meet you downstairs in thirty."

I have to go downstairs myself to grab my toiletries and clean clothes. In the shower I wash quickly, scrubbing my face and throat as if I can wash away the dual-nightmares. One was me. Sam. I lived it last year.

I collect stories of kids who died before nineteen—when I was younger, that seemed like the threshold between childhood and adulthood. Kids who got sick, kids who got killed, kids whose own brains told them to die. I feel like someone should remember them.

That dream—that had to be the one from Astoria, from the eighties. Kid named Billy Clement, though I couldn't recall his name in the dream. I try not to let myself think about him. It's too weird.

My special interest happened before my attack. *She* used to tell me I was morbid, but I just thought somebody should know the stories of kids who don't get to grow into adults. I thought they deserved to be seen the way Dad saw me.

I dress myself methodically. Black boxer briefs made of softest modal, a binder Dad had made special for me, tattery jeans, long silky tank top, long cowl-necked sweater with a jagged asymmetrical hem. Black eyeliner and a smudge of silver at the edges of my eyes. Dad insisted I get new things when we left Montana (I'm half-surprised he didn't set my old stuff on fire). I did the shopping at thrift stores, but Portland had that market cornered. I think Dad was a little surprised at the direction I took, but looking like a badass makes me feel safer. I used to just wear old band T-shirts and jeans, but now every piece of cloth I put on my body is a choice. Girding myself in armor for the day.

I shop by touch before looks, but I'm good at finding the exact right thing. The softness of the sweater, the beaten-to-pliable texture of the denim, the intentional constriction of the binder—it's all for me. No one else. I throw a little pomade onto my hair and toss it around until it waves the way I want it to, the lavender and pale green and silver-gray strands weaving together. They fall down over my right ear and expose the shaved left side of my head. I run my fingertips over the stubble, enjoying the sensation. Dad's going to have to buzz it again soon on both sides and probably touch up the dye before school starts in January. He does construction management for a living, but I sometimes think he missed his calling as a hairdresser.

Dad finds us a diner and I get an enormous Belgian waffle covered in strawberries that are probably more sugar than fruit. Dad gets biscuits and gravy with a side of hash browns.

"Want some carbs with your carbs?" I ask him over the rockabilly music playing too loudly on the speakers.

"You're one to talk." He holds up his coffee mug, and I reach out with my orange juice. "To new beginnings."

"To new beginnings," I echo, clinking my glass against his mug.

Halfway through my waffles, I get that low-belly slip and remember what today's about. Remembering my therapist telling me to pay attention to what I feel in my body, I let myself feel it for a moment, but all I really feel is silly. Is this anxiety? If Dad notices me poking at a strawberry with my fork, he doesn't say anything. Eventually I choke the rest of my breakfast down, sopping up some liquified whipped cream with my last hunk of waffle.

I don't want to do this again, this whole *meet the principal* thing.

This time Dad seems to sense it.

"If it doesn't work out here, we'll work something else out for your senior year."

My head jerks up from where I'm staring at my smeared plate. "What?"

"If public school is too much, we'll figure something out. Homeschool or something. You could probably even pass your GED if you needed to, but I'd rather we try for your diploma. That'll make things easier for you in the long run."

Holy— "Dad." I stop. What's that thing he always says? "We'll cross that bridge when the Pope—"

"—Don't finish that one." His smile's only half-wattage, but he stopped me from saying *shits in the woods* out loud. "I just wanted you to know it's on my mind."

CHAPTER **TWO**

Astoria High School is set back from the road behind a line of trees that stands like sentinels to guard it. I like the trees. The building itself is red brick, and it gives me a jolt to see that the parking lot is full. School's not out for winter break yet.

Dad parks in a visitor spot and turns the engine off. "Doors open on three, okay?"

I nod. He counts.

"One. Two. Three."

I open my door and get out, pulling my sweater tighter around me. The arms are long enough, which is saying a lot since I'm almost six feet tall. I put some thumb holes in it myself with silver embroidery thread. The wind outside is cold, but it's so much warmer than Montana that even after the last eight months in Portland, it feels warm to me.

I follow Dad into the school just as the bell rings out through the hallways. Not good. Within seconds, students pour into the corridor, and pretty much every eye lands on me and Dad. Almost all the kids are white, though this school is way more diverse than Airdrie. I'm about the same height as Dad, but we look nothing alike, and I'm not sure that's even why people are staring. Maybe it's my hair.

The school feels too warm. It's as if each person's gaze makes the atoms between their eyeballs and my face start hopping around.

I look at Dad. He's got Concerned Face on, and from the way he's fiddling with his car keys, he's three seconds away from turning around and heading right back to our furniture-less home to knock holes in my bedroom walls or curl up on the barren floor with a box of strawberry Pop-Tarts even though we just had breakfast.

I see his Concerned Face way too often these days.

That's it. I make a decision. For Dad's sake. There's a scrawny kid standing just to my right, not even making an effort to disguise that he's staring at me.

"Principal's office?" I ask, too loudly.

"Uh, down the hall to the right," he says.

"Cheers."

I march in that direction. My boldness fades with every step, but as soon as we get there, Dad tells someone we're there to see the principal, and she bustles us right into the office, where the principal herself greets us. She's short and white, and she's wearing an expensive-looking—to me, anyway—blue-and-green sweater in jewel tones. And jeans. I like that. Her jeans have a distressed knee, and the effect pleasantly looks like she's not trying too hard. My mental alarm goes off to remind me not to stare. People don't like it when you stare, as I've learned the hard way.

"Mr. Sylvester," she says to Dad. She shakes his hand. "I'm glad to finally meet you. Margarie Frankel."

"Please, call me Junius," Dad says.

She turns to me and smiles, reaching out a hand to me. *Social introduction script, activate.* Dad's talked to her already on the phone, but this is the real test. Maybe if I tell myself the pressure's all on her, I'll actually believe it enough to make my hand stop quivering when I try to lift it.

"I'm Sam," I say, looking at the spot right between her eyes for a moment before looking away again. Here goes nothing. "My pronouns are they/them."

Principal Frankel looks startled at that, but she recovers almost instantly. "It's a pleasure to meet you, Sam," she says. "My pronouns are she/her."

I look at Dad and don't have to say anything as I manage to shake the principal's hand. *This is hopeful.* I can almost hear him thinking it. His eyebrows are raised halfway up his forehead. I should be happy. Concerned Face has given way to Hopeful Face.

I always get it just a little off. I introduce myself with my pronouns too quickly or I shake someone's hand too hard or I make too much eye contact or too little, but for once I relax a little. The jitters fade. A little.

Principal Frankel gestures to two upholstered chairs in front of her desk and makes her way around to her own seat.

"I've got your file here," she says to me. I chalk up another couple points for her actually talking directly to me. "I'm more interested in you, though."

If she has my file, she knows what happened in Montana. Dad insisted on putting a letter in there to the new school—I read it at the last one. The thought makes my throat start to tighten. "What do you want to know?"

My voice cracks, and my tone is too flat. I'm too warm. I pull my thumbs out of my sleeve's loops and push the sleeves up to my elbows. Principal Frankel's gaze falls on my arm and, after a millisecond delay, locks onto the tattoo like it just registered that those colors are actual ink in the skin of a high school student.

Dad jumps in, and I shoot him a grateful look. "The tattoo was a deal Sam and I made last year. They stayed in pre-calc and passed, and when they hit eighteen, I told them we'd get it done."

"I'm sorry," Principal Frankel says. She looks at me, trying to make eye contact. "I didn't mean to stare."

I nod, but I don't meet her eyes, looking instead at the bookcase behind her. Neurotypicals think eye contact is reassuring, but it's the opposite to me. So I focus on the shelf. There are pictures of her kids, a full portrait of a golden retriever and what looks like an Irish setter, a print of a mandala. The colors in the mandala match her shirt and her earrings. I'd put money on those being her favorite colors. Like the lower half of my sleeve, watercolors.

"To answer your question, Sam, you don't have to tell me anything you don't want to, but if there's anything you'd like me to know before we have your IEP meeting, I'm all ears." She gives me a warm smile.

I meet Dad's eyes and give him the nod. "Dad can tell you whatever."

"Did you have any specific questions?" Dad asks the principal. "I'll leave it up to Sam if they want to talk about the incident."

Neither Dad nor I like to call it "the time I almost died." We both know. We both hate it. We both have to live with it. But we don't have to delve into it every time it reminds us of itself. I think that's why he gives it a euphemism. It's his way of telling it that it is not in control.

Principal Frankel waves her hand. "I think I read all I need to about that," she says. "I'm very sorry to hear it happened, and I want to assure you that we take the safety of our students to be our foremost priority here. I am appalled the administration concluded that the attack was a prank, and I want to make clear that in my school, I will not stand for targeted violence against my students. We also have a very good counselor if you want to see her, Sam."

I look up and meet her eyes briefly because she is looking for neurotypical-friendly reassurance, and then I look away. "Thanks."

She gives me a smile and sits up straighter, like a physical subject change, and her eyes fall on something in my file.

"Oh!" exclaims Principal Frankel. "You bought the Glasgow Avenue house! I saw someone had moved in but didn't assume they had a high schooler in the mix."

"You know the neighborhood," Dad says with a wry chuckle.

"I noticed it was for sale—it was on the market for ages." She pauses, then adds, "I grew up next door."

She shakes her head a little and gives Dad a hesitant smile before asking about something else entirely.

I tune out a little while Dad talks. He goes through the boring stuff, like my grades and my experience at the Portland school. He offers to connect her to the principal there if necessary. Principal Frankel waves her hand about that, too. She points at something on my file, and Dad tells her about my being misdiagnosed as having reactive attachment disorder before he adopted me and got me assessed by someone who didn't take one look at me and decide my autism was *just unresolved trauma*. I form attachments just fine.

Adopting as a single dad by choice was a pain in the ass, I guess, but the second he saw me, he said he knew was my dad. He didn't have *too* many problems. Turns out older kids with scary disabilities are hard to give away, and since he had his own home and a good income, they figured if someone wanted me at all it might be my only shot to avoid being a ping-pong ball in foster care.

He always told me I never once scared him. He said he'd have picked me over a cherubic, neurotypical baby any day. He says I saved him the trouble of ever having to change a diaper.

20

"Girls are severely underdiagnosed with autism spectrum disorder," the principal says. She's speaking to me, not Dad.

My whole body snaps to attention with those words, and some of the hope I felt earlier squishes like a rotten berry.

"I'm not a girl. I'm an experience," I say, maybe a little louder than I should, and she goes bright red. She doesn't seem to get the Steven Universe reference, but Dad gives me a nod and a smile.

"I seem to be putting my foot in my mouth here today," Principal Frankel says softly. She runs her fingers through her dark curls. "Please excuse me. To be more precise, I meant that diagnostic criteria for autism spectrum disorder are heavily skewed toward phenotypes observed most commonly in cisgender boys. I am glad you have a parent who pushed for the correct diagnosis. Many kids don't have that."

My hands clap my fingers against my palms a few times at the words "cisgender" and "phenotypes." She's trying. I'll give her that. Most people do not know what she just said—or believe it. Including, very frequently, the people who hold the diagnostic forms.

"Mr. Quach should be here to fetch us shortly," Principal Frankel says. "He and a few of the teachers are meeting now to review your IEP, and when he gets here, we can go join them to see if we need to make any changes."

"Who's Mr. Quach?" I ask, trying to delay the impending boredom of navigating my Individualized Education Plan with a new set of teachers.

"He'll be your case manager here. He's one of our inclusion teachers for English and biology, and he also serves as the staff sponsor of the Rainbow Island, which is our school LGBTQ-plus and allies club. I believe they're having a holiday party at lunch today for their weekly gathering if you're interested in meeting them before you start school here after winter break. If you want to," Principal Frankel adds hastily. "You certainly don't have to."

"That sounds nice, Sam," says Dad, and I give him a wry look. He knows I'll go just because he thinks it's a good idea. We agreed when we moved here that a prerequisite of me going back to public school was going to one where I could be out, but even so, it's weird for me to be invited to a group of local teen queers right out of the gate. I remember the backpack and the maybe-Pride flags and the curious eyes. Will that person be there? I'm not sure I'm ready to be quite *that* out.

Then again . . . I look at Dad's face, and his eyebrows are raised, his forehead leaned a bit forward in that way he does when he's really trying to believe in something good. Yep. That's his Hopeful Face again. I'm done.

"Okay," I say to Principal Frankel. My Portland school was the first I'd gone to with a club like that, but I never worked up the courage to check it out in the few months I was there—too much anxiety.

Just then, Mr. Quach knocks at the door and pokes his head in when the principal tells him to enter. He's a tall, young Vietnamese man with black hair that is almost as long as Dad's locs used to be. He's wearing a black blazer and jeans with a dark gray T-shirt I kind of wish I could have for myself. It looks soft.

"Hey!" He actually beams when he sees me. "The fabled Sam themself! Awesome to meet you."

I stand up and shake his hand. "Yeah," I say. "Nice to meet you."

I mean it, too. This time when my throat starts to tighten I don't think it's because of my nightmares or anything that

22

happened in Airdrie. Nobody's ever used my pronouns from moment one before.

Dad gets up and claps me on the back, and I think he's having the same lumpy throat problem I'm having.

The meeting for my IEP goes about as well as can be expected from such a thing, and that's a drill I've done a thousand times by now, so I do most of my own talking instead of having Dad explain stuff. I get special goals in both math and English, probably because I got so bored in my last English class in Portland that I got a D.

The teachers here seem nice enough, but one spends half the meeting staring at my hair, and I catch Principal Frankel staring at my tattoo again, so by the time we break, I am more than ready to follow Mr. Quach to his classroom even if it means meeting a bunch of new people.

"You okay with this? Really?" Dad takes me aside as the teachers and the principal gather up their SAM SYLVESTER manila folders.

"Yeah," I say, glancing over my shoulder at them. You'd think I'd be used to that part, everyone having a dossier of me-ness. "It's like a trial run. Plus, just think. A bunch of queers in one place. It's like my natural habitat. Tumblr IRL."

I'm actually terrified, but for once, my curiosity and desire to find people *like me* is outweighing my social anxiety, so it's not a lie.

I think Dad wants to roll his eyes at me, because he always knows what I mean, but he doesn't. Instead, he just says, "Get it, kid."

Mr. Quach chatters at me as we walk down the hall. It's not quite lunch bell yet, so the halls this time are empty with just the sound of our feet and his voice.

"It's not a huge group," he says. I think he's trying to reassure me. He's got a quick walk with some bounce in his step as if his feet have their own caffeine supply. "They're good people. They don't know anything about you, so you get to choose what you say. Even if what you say is just *hi*."

"Roger that."

"We've got pronoun stickers for our meetings, too," he says. "He/him for me, by the way."

A smile tugs at my lips. "That's pretty cool. The sticker thing, I mean."

"One of our members has an older sibling who goes to a lot of conventions. I think that's where the idea came from."

"Like comic book conventions?"

"Something like that." Mr. Quach stops in the doorway of the next classroom and pulls out his keys. "They should be here pretty soon. Sky has his office aide period right now, so he was going to pick up pizza."

"I ate all the waffles in Astoria this morning. I'm fine." At his amused look, I go on, "I mean, I didn't really eat all of them. And uh, thanks."

Mr. Quach gives me a thumbs-up as he jostles the door open. His classroom is colorful. One wall has a construction paper tree with each branch made into some form of figurative speech. The students have written out examples of metaphors, personification, simile, and allusion on little leaves, all stuck to the appropriate branches, all different colors.

"Mornings are my prep and meeting time," he says. "I've got learning lab after lunch for kids who need it, and I pop into inclusion classes as well."

I'm not sure what to say, so I head toward a fluffy, dark purple loveseat in the back corner of the room. There are only about fifteen desks, and right by the two-seater sofa there's a book-shelf. I recognize a few of the high-low titles. Dad got them for me to help catch me up since I started school so late. We read every night after he adopted me, and pretty soon I was stealing his books. *Before* (that's the only way I like to mention my pre-Dad life), everybody assumed that since I didn't talk, I couldn't learn to read. I make my way back toward Mr. Quach, who has put my file into a drawer in his desk. He locks the drawer, then leans across his desk to offer me a basket of pronoun stickers. I feel like he's given me an entire bowl of red Skittles.

"*Dude.*" I don't know if I've ever called a teacher dude before, and I probably shouldn't. I take mine and look at it for a sec. I almost don't want to peel it off.

"You can take a couple if you want." It's like he's read my mind.

I take an extra and stick one to my sweater.

"Oh my god, your hair is even *more magical* up close." A breathless voice makes me turn around before I can sit down.

"Shep, this is Sam Sylvester. They're joining us next semester, and I invited them to come say hi today."

"Hey," I say with an awkward wave.

Shep snags a *she/her* sticker and flops down behind a desk. "I saw you the other day," she says. "I wasn't trying to be a peeper or anything. I think you moved in on my street."

I remember the person-with-backpack and nod, surrepti-tiously looking around for the bag itself so I can confirm what was on it. It's still slung over her shoulder, but she drops it on the floor just as I belatedly say, "Yeah, that was me."

"I mean, I know it was you. Who does your *hair*?" She smacks her sticker onto her chest. Every sentence she says has this sort of hurried wonder to its emphasis. I like the cadence.

"My dad," I say. The backpack's straps are facing me, but that *is* a bi flag I see, and the rainbow flag with the trans flag corner and the brown and black stripes.

"Dude." This time it's Mr. Quach who says it. "Give your dad my sincerest compliments."

"That is awesome," Shep says. I finally manage to look at her face. She's Latina and tallish, not quite as tall as I am, with warm brown skin. Her own dark hair is buzzed all the way to bare stubble except on top, where it's starting to get shaggy. It makes her brown eyes look huge. "You moved into the Clement house."

"Is that who lived there before?" The name has to be a coincidence. It can't be the same Clement family as the one in my book. Clement as in *Billy* Clement. The boy who died.

"Shep—"

"Relax, Mr. Quach," Shep says. "I'm not going to scare them or anything."

"Shep's developed a bit of an interest in your house," says Mr. Quach, his voice resigned. He rubs his face with one hand, almost-but-not-quite hiding a grimace. "But she sometimes overwhelms people with theories some might find morbid."

I'm still stuck on two people using my pronouns right in the space of an hour. It takes a minute for their words to sink in.

"You know the history of my house?" I ask. My skin feels all tingly, like it did when I touched the wall in my room.

Shep leans forward eagerly. Her eyes are big, and they're the darkest brown with tiny flecks of deep green and gold. I usually can't look people in the eye, but right now I can't look away. She actually does a little excited shimmy. "Yeah, a kid died there when my parents were in high school—"

26

"Shep." I can hear Mr. Quach rubbing his hand over his face again.

"—It's a huge town mystery because a bunch of people thought it was *murder*—"

"Shep!"

"I'm not scared." I try to assure Mr. Quach, but he looks up from his literal facepalm to give Shep a stare that shuts her up.

He looks to me with a sigh. "It's not that. I'm afraid your house is a bit notorious, Sam. We get a lot of hardcore true crime fans because of an old website that suggested Billy's death wasn't an accident. But as I've said to Shep before"—Shep breaks eye contact with me and shrugs, uncomfortable and abashed, while Mr. Quach shifts his weight in his chair—"Billy's death tore this town apart. He was a real kid with a real family. He was friends with everyone—he played baseball with my dad. He volunteered in the community. Billy was buddies with people who are now teachers at this school—and in a town this small, it's hard to find anyone who lived here at the time who wasn't directly affected. So please, *please* be aware that this isn't just some story. Be sensitive."

Shep opens her mouth, but after a moment, she closes it again.

Holy shit. It *is* the same Clement. Billy Clement. The kid whose story is in my *Book of Half-Lived Lives.*

He died in my house—he died in my *room.*

My research said he died in the upstairs bedroom. I didn't even—I didn't recognize the room without—

—the *shelves.* In the picture, the room had shelves.

I *need* to get into that wall. I need to see it the way it is supposed to look.

I open my mouth to say something to Shep, then immediately close it, because right at that moment, a kid—Sky, I assume—wafts through the door in a cloud of pepperoni smell, followed by a gaggle of others like he's the Pied Piper of Pizza, and I don't have a chance to ask Shep any questions because ten people call out their names to introduce themselves, and I remember approximately three of them by the time someone shoves a plate of cheesy carbs into my hands in this torrent of sensory input.

Sky sidles over with his own plate full of pizza, giving Shep's foot a nudge with a pair of silver glitter Chuck Taylors. He's got the same sort of "will burn if the sun so much as touches him" sort of pale skin as I do, and he tosses shaggy blond hair out of his face, revealing blue eyes for only a moment before one is hidden again by his side-swept bangs. A *he/him* sticker sits on his chest, and his gaze flickers to my sticker before he speaks.

"Hey, new kid," he says. "I'm Sky."

"Sam."

"Those are some killer boots," he says.

"Thanks. I like your Chucks."

Sky turns and calls over his shoulder. "Ronnie!"

A pretty Black girl with her hair in twists looks up from a thick book across the room. "What?"

"Sam here just complimented my twinkle toes," Sky says, then to me, "They were a birthday present."

Ronnie ducks her head, causing a stray twist to fall in front of her eyes. She tucks it back into the knot at the back of her head. "They weren't the rainbow ones you wanted, but I thought they were amazing."

"They're awesome," I say, surprised at finding my own voice. Ronnie gives me a shy smile and turns back to her book. She's

28

reading a cinderblock of a book about . . . Python? The coding language?

Sky waves his hand. "We worked together all summer in hell, and we're both summer babies, so while *some people* were off in Mexico—"

Shep coughs.

"—Ronnie and I were having trauma bonding time." In spite of Sky's light tone, he reaches over and gives Shep's hand a squeeze.

"I brought you both souvenirs," Shep says to them. She shrugs at me. "Mom took me to Oaxaca to bring my abuelita's body for burial, so it wasn't much of a vacation."

"I'm sorry," I say. That's the right thing to say about death, right? Shep shrugs again, but for once, I think I know what someone wants from me in a conversation because I also have a big heavy thing that hurts to dwell on.

The conversation turns to astrology, which Sky seems to find vital to understanding how my presence will shift the school dynamic, and to my surprise, everyone seems to be all about it, even if they're just humoring him.

"What are you?" He eyes me carefully as if he already knows.

"Pisces," I say, and Sky's blue eyes light up.

"Oh, thank the gods. Another water sign. Ronnie's a Leo—"

"*Barely*," Ronnie says, affronted. "I'm like twelve hours from being a Cancer like you, and you know with my rising sign—"

Shep points and says, "If you needed any evidence of the Leo in her."

Ronnie holds up a hand with a flourish. "I am what I am."

"What are you?" I ask Shep.

She beams. "Scorpio all the way."

"Yeah, you are," Sky says.

Ronnie leaves a few minutes later with a "Welcome to Astoria" to me and a "later" to Sky and Shep, and Sky turns to me, steepling his hands. Most of the others have already trickled out of the room, now that the pizza's gone. Mr. Quach sits at his desk, quietly working on an IEP on his computer. Maybe mine.

"Shep's *so excited* that you moved into that house," Sky says. He doesn't look away from my face.

"Sky—" Shep's eyes open wide.

"It's all she's talked about, the mysterious stranger—"

"*Sky*—"

"She just *had* to meet you—"

"Oh, my god, Sky, *stop*."

"I'm glad I did meet you," I say to Shep, and her cheeks get pinker.

"I was a little skeptical," says Sky as if I didn't say anything, "but at the very least, you have good taste in shoes, and I needed more water signs on Rainbow Island. Pisces, Cancer, Scorpio in one group? Plus Ronnie, because as much as I tease, she really is a Cancer at heart. And a good foil to the more fiery water sign that is Shep. Legendary."

He touches his fingertips to his heart and flutters his eyelashes with the sentiment before buffing his fingernails against his chest and shaking his head like there's nothing more to say.

I somehow feel like that's the biggest seal of approval Sky can give.

"Oh, my god," Shep mutters again, blushing enough that her collar bone is changing colors. "I swear, if you don't stop, I'll tell everyone about karaoke—"

"Relax, Sting-y. I still love you." Sky says it hastily, finally looking away from me. He takes Shep's hand and kisses it and grins. "Nearest town was an hour away, hey, Montana? How did you *live*? Did you talk to cows? Are you like, a bovine Doctor Doolittle?"

By the time I text Dad to come get me, I'm flushed and full (was I really going to say no to pizza?) and have Sky and Shep's phone numbers in my phone.

On my way out, when a few of the Rainbow Island people in the halls call after me, "See you in January!" they sound like it's a good thing.

I'm not used to this. Maybe I could learn to be.

CHAPTER **THREE**

"**W**e're gonna go make like the holidays and tree that house." Dad says it with such determination the moment my seat belt clicks into place in the car that I just stare at him.

"What?"

"There's barely anything else in the house, but there will be a very merry tree."

He pulls the car out of the school parking lot. We threw all our boxes from the Subaru into the entry of the house yesterday. When we left Portland, we only stuffed toiletries, my white noise machines, a couple rolls of egg crate pads, sleeping bags, and a few suitcases of clothes into the car. And Dad's tools, since he'll probably ask to be buried with them.

Dad's in finding-task mode again. I look at the new numbers I put in my phone after we get in the car as Dad cranks up "Superstition" by Stevie Wonder and pulls the car out onto Chinook Street, singing the bassline as soon as it starts in a series of "bow-bow-bow-bow-baw-ba-ba-bow-bow-bow" sounds.

"Dork," I say, but his silliness is a buoy, and I grab my sunglasses from the clip pinning them to the visor and go with it. He knows I'll tell him about the meeting when I want to.

We buy a tree from a local lot hawking them and decorations from the first supermarket we find and return home and order a pizza online from the nearest pizzeria—pizza twice in a day feels lush. Dad opens the door when it arrives, and I peek out from the kitchen at the other end of the hall long enough to get a glimpse of a teenage boy with brown hair and a tan who glances curiously at me before hastily taking his tip and leaving. Dad and I eat sitting on the floor in a tangle of red and gold lights, folding our slices into pizza-ritos like we always do, him tapping his feet on the floor with the beat. He's wearing *Nightmare Before Christmas* socks. The man likes his novelty socks.

For a while, I can forget why we left Montana and spent the last eight months hopping from sublet to sublet in Portland while Dad job hunted. Stevie sings us through the evening, and the tree's new outfit is lopsided by the time we're done since we decorate it and dance at the same time.

When we hit the end of the playlist and the music stops, it's ten o'clock, and that immediately makes it too quiet. Air blowing from the heating vent creates enough wind that the light strands on the tree sway a bit in the smaller branches, kind of like the tree's drunk. It casts moving patterns on the shiny hardwoods. When it's quiet, I can hear my own heartbeat too loudly, feel my own breath too keenly, remember what it was like to not have enough of it. I close my eyes and try to get back the fun, hoping Dad didn't notice my mood drop.

"It's going to be okay here," Dad says suddenly.

I look over at him, and he's tearing up. *Shit.* "Dad—"

"It's not going to be like Airdrie anymore. I won't let it."

"It's okay, Dad. You never did anything wrong." Dad always does everything *right*.

He smiles a bit, and his eyes are glassy as he looks away. He wipes his eyes with his blue flannel. It hits me with a wave of something I can't put my finger on for a moment. Before, he always smelled like the coconut deep conditioner he used on his locs and a hint of fruit from the balm he rubbed into his hands when they'd get chapped from work. It was the opposite of the woodsmoke and pine we lived in in the Bitterroot Valley in

33

Montana, and it always smelled like home. He smells somehow muted in Oregon, the same scents but quieter, like a memory. Maybe it's just that most of his hair is gone. Maybe it's that the air isn't as dry, so he doesn't use the balm as much. Maybe I'm imagining it. But it's enough to notice. Weird what one change can do. It makes me feel motion I can't control, like the colored lights shifting on the polished floors or the illusion of movement that happens when the car beside yours in the parking lot starts moving before you've budged. Like the aurora on my arm and in my dreams.

"It's getting late, and we have a busy few days ahead getting this house turned into a home," he says. "You should go to bed."

"I don't have a bed," I respond automatically.

Dad grins then, the way he always does when I say something too literal. "Go to your egg crate and sleeping bag then."

I nod and turn on my black-socked feet to head upstairs. Before I make it two steps though, I spin back around and throw my arms around him.

I don't hug people often, but right now I need Dad. After a moment of surprise, he wraps me in a bear hug.

"Love you, Sammy," he says.

"Love you too." Before I let go, I catch the slightest whiff of coconut oil, and it's like a shield I can wrap around me as I head upstairs to my empty room with secrets in its walls.

. . .

Going to bed is easy. Sleeping is harder.

This is precisely where Billy died. My dream the other night—what if it wasn't just a dream? It's too quiet in here. I'm not afraid of Billy, but nighttime has its own Sam-specific challenges.

I set up my white noise machines near my little sleeping pallet on the floor yesterday, but even before I lie down I know the

34

windows will be a problem again. I'm going to need curtains. There aren't even blinds. There's enough light from the two dormer windows that I don't even need the flashlight on my phone to see. There's no light fixture in the ceiling, though there is a light switch by the door. I assume it's tied to an outlet but don't care to find out right now.

My therapist in Missoula used to tell me not to use any screens when I'm trying to sleep. That particular therapist also told me I have to forgive to heal after the attack, so fuck her. She can go live the last year of my life and try to tell me that again. Belligerently, I stare at my phone for a long time as if I can make a text from Shep or Sky appear, sleep be damned.

Both Shep and Sky said to text them and *sounded* like they meant it.

People say things they don't mean all the time, like "how are you?" when they don't want to know the answer and "text me whenever" when they'd rather you forget they exist. I never know the difference between *I truly like you* and *ugh, get lost*. Dad always knows. The only way I know how to blend in with people is by watching what he does. Once, I told him I thought I was an alien, and he laughed until he realized I was serious. When he figured out that I meant it, he pulled me into his lap (I was eight) and told me that my brain just figures out the world differently but that I belonged here as much as anyone. I'm still not sure I believe him.

Nothing appears on the screen as I lie on my egg crate trying not to drop my phone on my face—maybe Shep and Sky are as shy as me about using new phone numbers. Dad has moved us over literal mountains to make my life better—but it's the not knowing what to expect that gets me. I want to get a message that will tell me how this new school is going to go. Something that will tell me I'm safe here. My body doesn't want to believe I'm safe. Behind my eyes are flashes of memory I can't look at too closely, and my pulse pounds in my throat dangerously close to my scar.

My phone shows the minutes pixeling by, and I give up on sleep, my skin clammy and that tight racing flutter I hate so much dominating my chest. Today I've brushed too closely against the memories of Montana, and they're sucking me in like a whirlpool.

Part of me wants to reach for my book—more of a portfolio, really. It's about the dimensions of a large laptop, black suede on the outside and acid-free paper on the inside. It's where I keep important things about *them*. The kids like Billy. Copies of book pages or photographs (or copies of photographs found on book pages), and my own chicken scratch. At last count, it was somewhere around eighty-seven stories of people who were just kids and didn't get to become adults. Lisbeth and Mary and Jacob and so many more. Matthew Shepard. Brayla Stone. Billy. When I was younger, I titled it *Sam's Book of Half-Lived Lives*, and even though I realized when I was thirteen or so that being dead by nineteen is nowhere near the halfway mark on life (and hasn't been for centuries), it stuck. Nineteen should be the real beginning of being a grown-up—out of the house and ready to rock. But for these kids, that never happened. I knew Billy lived in Astoria. And now I'm in the room where he died.

It's funny. It kind of clinched us moving here, since I lit up when Dad mentioned the town's name where he'd gotten the job offer. I definitely didn't explain why to him. I can see Billy in my mind, a blur where his face should be. I first learned about Billy from a stray forum post that led to a website someone had obviously kept up with heaps of information about him. I can picture the Move the Stars website dedicated to his story that I devoured and printed out bits from to add to my book. An old yearbook picture with floppy, blondish hair and a sideways grin. Another picture of him dressed like Jareth in *Labyrinth*—kid was obsessed with David Bowie. His favorite song? "Space Oddity." Billy at a birthday party surrounded by friends, a candid moment that caught genuine laughter, love. Billy's school pictures, pictures of the house—of this room, which gives me a jolt—things about him. More than that. I relate to him latching onto a song so alien, as alien as I often feel—I watched the film and listened to the song over and over when I first learned about Billy, as if I could tap into whatever drew him to them. Before the site vanished last year, I got a lot of stuff into my book, but whoever ran the site took it down before I could get the rest. Sometimes I forget even the internet isn't permanent.

I can see Shep's face when she was gushing about the house— someone who maybe, just maybe, could understand. I could text her.

Nope. Nope, nope, nope.

Instead, I sit up and open my laptop. We don't have internet, not yet, but I find an unsecured network strong enough to hop on. My book's not what I need right now, and the idea of initiating social contact with very nice new queer people is not something I am ready to do, not when the only friend I ever really had is living rent-free in my brain.

Logging into my second Tumblr, which I named "Letters from Andromeda," I hit the new text Post button. I get the spike of adrenaline that comes from doing something I know I shouldn't.

Nobody who I want to see it is ever going to read this, but it's all I've got right now. It's safe to let my anger out anonymously. Productive, even, according to my Portland therapist, though

I'm not sure she'd approve of the risk of putting it on Tumblr. Maybe I hope it *will* find its way to the eyes it's meant for.

I know you'll never see this, and I know I shouldn't miss you after what you did.

I stop typing for a second. This is a bad idea. When I started this Tumblr, I told myself I would not do this. But I can't help it. I can't *sleep*, and it's all *her* fault. But my Portland therapist—the better of my two in the past year—did tell me that writing to her might be cathartic, even not planning to send it directly to her. There's a chance she could see this. It's a big internet, but Tumblr is like an Escher drawing that always leads back to itself. In putting it here, I'm letting the part of me—the part that wishes *she* would take responsibility—grab the reins.

I don't care if she ever apologizes; that's not the point. This small patch of Tumblr is for me. I'm not great at figuring out exactly what I feel, but sometimes writing it out helps me get closer.

We made it to our new house yesterday. You'd like it. We're only a few blocks from the ocean—the actual, honest-to-fuck ocean. There's a palm tree growing in the yard next door.

That's vague enough that no one would be able to pinpoint it. I've got a VPN set up on my IP address anyway. She used to call me paranoid for that, but nobody can call me paranoid now. There are thousands of miles of palm tree-friendly coastline in the world, and she'd never think Oregon.

Dad took me out to get a Christmas tree today. I doubt there'll be anything under it with the move and all, and both he and I hate the consumerism of it anyway, but it's pretty. It's kind of top heavy. And lopsided, like us. And I went to my new school and sorted out all the IEP shit, which is the last thing I really wanted to do, but whatever. I met other people like me, not hiding like you thought all of us should.

I'll live.

I leave it at that and hit Post, my heartbeat warring with shallow breaths in my chest and that awful tightness crawling back up my throat. I feel it again, the zip tie around my neck and the hands tightening it and the zipper-like sound of death. It's because of her that fear lives in my neck now, that it hovers right at the gateway to everything—speech, breath, song, life, screams. All because of her. That last spiteful pair of words—if she ever does read this, she'll know it for what it is. And I think of Billy again. His death was supposedly an accident, but in some ways it's similar to my almost-death. We both found out what it's like to drown swimming in air we couldn't reach.

The memory is the final impetus, though. Whatever I feel or don't feel right now, the only thing I know is that it's *too much*.

Belatedly, I remember "I'll live" is exactly what Dad said to me when I accidentally headbutted him in my sleep this morning.

I push my laptop over to the side and hit myself in the leg twice with a closed fist. It makes me feel better for a bare instant like when Dad does a quick release on the Instant Pot and flicks the valve to send pressurized steam hissing out for a moment, but I don't know how I'll ever sleep now. The pressure immediately rebuilds.

I stare at Shep's name in my phone for several minutes, even go as far as opening a new text to stare at that. But it's the middle of the night anyway. Trust me to get the courage to do a human social thing right at the time where it would be socially inappropriate to do it.

Bed. Sleep. I can't imagine it will be easy to make relaxing happen.

I resolve to try anyway.

CHAPTER **FOUR**

Over the next few days, Dad and I get ready to tear down the walls in my new room. He doesn't have any of his big power tools besides his core kit, but we manage. With the ghosts in my dreams each night, I half-expect we'll find something hidden behind the drywall, when he lets me make the first punch through with the sledgehammer, but just seeing the shelves behind it is thrill enough. It feels important, like discovering an ancient tomb lost to time. Even more so, knowing that this was Billy's room itself for real. I try not to let Dad see my fingers shaking on the edge of the drywall when I run them along the dust-covered edge, itching to touch the shelves but not trusting myself to do it while Dad's watching.

These were his. Billy's. He touched these shelves.

When we pull the first sheet off, Dad looks at me sideways, his fingers dusted with white plaster, as if he's discovering all over again that when I say something like, "There are bookcases behind the walls," or "Anum and Bogusław are both names that mean 'blessing of god,'" I'm right. I'm always right. He never asks how I know. He accepts it, or did after the first few times. Once he threatened to put me on Jeopardy.

One of the perks of having random macabre history as my special interest is I tend to remember random (usually not macabre) facts at random moments.

All these kids I read about, they died before they turned nineteen. I'm eighteen now. I feel like I'm running out of time. On top of all that, I shouldn't be alive now. I'd be dead, because of the last person I trusted to really see me.

It's that part I'll never tell Dad, and it's that part that leaves me waiting while he and I wrestle chunk after chunk of sheetrock away from the shelves, hearing Shep's words over and over in my head—*a bunch of people thought it was murder*. I *feel* she's right, because it's Billy. I don't have the nerve to text Shep, despite her face appearing unbidden in my mind, her brown eyes shining with excitement.

I push all those thoughts away with the last remnants of drywall.

Dad picks up a stack of plasterboard to take downstairs, humming something that sounds like "Ice Ice Baby," but he hates that song, so I don't know why he's grooving to it as he goes.

I chew on my lip, wanting to bite off the hangnail that stings on the side of my thumb, but my hands are covered in plaster, and now that I'm alone, the desire to touch the shelves turns to hesitance. I don't know if I want some connection to Billy or if I fear it.

But standing there, after a long moment while I wait for Dad to come back, I reach out one hand to the shelves and place my fingertips on the dusty surface.

Nothing immediately happens, so I'm still frozen there when Dad's footsteps come up the stairs again. But he's singing a different song now. This one I recognize, and the sound of the melody in Dad's voice—a deeper bass than Bowie's tenor—immediately makes me jerk my hand back, tingles cascading from the crown of my skull down over my arms and back like the world's most effective ASMR.

He's singing "Space Oddity." Billy's favorite song.

"You look spooked, Sam," he says with a laugh. "You all right?"

I nod, trying to wipe the dust off my hand and instead just smearing it onto my opposite palm. "What took you so long?"

"Distracted by the backyard," Dad says. "There's all sorts of space out there. We could put in a garden. We could grow tomatoes!"

"Whoa," I say, holding up my chalky hands. "Tomatoes are a big responsibility."

"You're right. We should get a herd of puppies instead."

I snort, and the puff of air makes a little cloud from the dust on the shelf right in front of me. Dad switches to a Bruno Mars song, and we get back to work.

During that first night with the first wall of shelves bared to the light, I wake up twice more after having the dream again, the dream of that boy I dutifully recorded into *Sam's Book of Half-Lived Lives* dying in this room where I'm living now. I don't tell Dad about the dreams. He'll think it's just about what happened in Montana—residual trauma, not about something that happened here. He can't change this house's past or mine. But maybe I can see Billy more clearly. If I were him, I think I'd want that.

CHAPTER FIVE

Christmas creeps closer, and Dad and I get the remainder of the bookshelves open and cleaned of dust. He tells me we'll paint them if I want to, and we do that the next day because this white-white is not the color they're meant to be. We paint them a sage green that looks gorgeous next to the deep, dark brown of the wood floor. It feels familiar and right. On Christmas Eve, our furniture finally arrives, filling the house with box after box of puzzles we're going to have to put together if we want anything to sit or sleep on.

"Lots of gifts to open, eh?" Dad winks at me, and I reward him with an eye roll. He's futzing with a tall chair that'll live at the breakfast bar.

I lean against the kitchen counter with a glass of orange juice in my hand. "So many. And if we can't put them together right, we can always just build a tree house in the backyard."

"You need some faith in me."

My phone buzzes on the counter behind me, and I jump hard enough that I slosh OJ over my hand. Licking a dribble off my finger, I set the glass down and look at the lock screen.

"Sam," Dad begins, one eyebrow raised.

"It's nobody from Montana, Dad. We changed the number, remember? We're in the five-oh-three world now, not the four-oh-six."

He relaxes marginally, but he sets both pieces of the chair down on the breakfast bar. "Who is it?"

"It's Shep," I say. "A girl I met at school. She lives down the street."

"Oh! Look at you, making new friends. What's she have to say?"

He sounds unabashedly excited, but I can't help the tiny twist in my stomach or the *what if* that unhelpfully pokes me in the back of the brain.

I unlock my phone and look at the message, which hits me with a jolt. "Uh, she's at the front door."

Before Dad can say anything and before I can talk myself out of it, I scoot past him, socks skidding on the hardwoods. My heart skips along with my feet, and I drum my nails against my palms as I go. I throw open the door, and sure enough, Shep's perched on the porch, eyeing a stack of broken-down cardboard boxes we weighed down with rocks that were cluttering up the front yard's dormant flower beds. Her head's covered in a brilliant cerulean knit cap.

"Hey, Shep," I say. "Come on in."

"Looks like I have bad timing," she says, but she does come in, holding a small bundle wrapped in blue plastic wrap. "My mom made cookies, and I thought it'd be a good excuse to come over and say hi."

I shut the door behind her, nonplussed by her bluntness. Usually people don't do that. Face value. That's what both of my therapists said I need to do with people, that I can't assume they're hiding something or that they *don't* mean what they say, because they might be earnest. I decide to respond in kind. "Sorry I didn't text. I'm bad at knowing when people are just being polite or really want me to talk to them."

"That's legit," Shep says. "But for me, I really mean it. You should text me."

I hear a creak of floorboards and a cough, and Dad leans around the corner, chair leg in hand. "You planning to introduce me?"

"Uh, Dad, this is Shep. Shep, this is my dad, Junius Sylvester."

"Nice to meet you," Dad says. "You can call me Junius. Did I hear something about cookies? Are there nuts in them?"

Shep reaches out with the bundle and hands it to Dad. "No nuts. They're molasses. Mom hates nuts in cookies." Her face lights up as she then gestures in the direction of my head. "I have to give you serious props for your hair abilities. Sam told me you do their hair."

I listen to them chatter for a minute, trying to acclimate. For a moment, I think of *her*, back in Montana. I wonder what she's feeling, if she has any guilt or regret over my near-death experience. I wonder if she misses me. I wish she wasn't the only data point of friendship I have.

I punt those thoughts back into the far reaches of my brain and catch the cookie Dad tosses me.

"You should show Shep the house," says Dad. "I'll guard the cookies. Just don't go in the basement unless you want to spoil your present for tomorrow."

I'm about to gesture at Shep to follow me, but Dad's words make me turn on my heel. "Present? You said we weren't doing presents."

"Might have fibbed."

"Da—" I start, then shift words mid-vowel, "—ang it. I don't have anything for you."

"You made a friend who brought cookies. That's an amazing gift. Now scram."

Shep is looking back and forth between us with an unreadable expression on her face. She salutes Dad—actually salutes—and follows me up the stairs after a moment. Halfway up, she leans over, still climbing.

"You lucked out, dude. Your dad is awesome."

"He's pretty much the best."

"I'd say I'd trade you, but nobody'd take that deal."

"Your dad not great?" I reach the top of the stairs and swivel. She pauses on the top step.

"Eh. Mostly apathetic when he's not overflowing with disappointment. I'm pretty sure he peaked in high school when he and my mom were captain of the basketball team and head cheerleader, respectively. He and Mom were high school sweethearts, you know? *Very* on and off. Mom even married someone else in one of the longer off periods after they graduated, but he died, and Mom got back with my Dad . . . and obviously left him again. I'd take cool and good-with-hair over that drama any day." She sounds like the *mostly apathetic* bit is an understatement, but I won't press. Shep peers around me, scuffing her knuckles over her buzzed head, cap in her hand. "Actually, saying all that out loud, yeah, he is indeed not great."

"Does he live with you?" I ask.

"Nope. I go over every other weekend and halfway through the big holidays. That's your room?" She points. "Damn. It's huge."

Most of the dust has been cleaned up, but the shelves are all pretty barren. "This is it."

"Wow," she says. She shivers hard after a second.

"You cold?"

"What? No." Shep walks over to the bookshelves and runs one finger along the edge. Dad already sanded away a lot of the nicks from the hastily done drywall, but there are still little grooves and dents where the nails hit the shelves.

46

"So you said you moved here from Montana?" Shep turns away from the wall again, and I can't help but notice the way she suddenly jerks her fingers back from the shelf she was touching as if it turned hot without warning. She looks a bit like a cat with a bottlebrush tail.

She looks like how I felt when I first touched it.

"Yeah," I say, trying not to stare.

"What was Montana like?"

"Big Sky." I want to say *small minds*, but that's not fair to the decent folks of Montana.

Shep raises an eyebrow. "You don't want to talk about it."

"Maybe some other time," I say. "Let's just say that there'd be no rainbow anything at my school that wasn't actually refracting water droplets from the sun."

Shep's quiet for a moment. "I don't know what I'd do without Sky and the others. That must have been hard."

I know I just said I'd maybe talk about it some other time, but I feel words bubbling up in my mouth. It's only then I realize I kind of want to talk about it with someone other than Dad.

The quiet stretches out, and I am not ready to break it. Shep doesn't either at first. She's looking around again. She swallows suddenly.

"You okay?" What I really mean is *did I do something wrong?*

"That kid who died here," she says. "He died like . . . *here* here, didn't he?"

Now it's me who swallows, feeling again the itchy tightness of a throat that isn't mine and is at the same time. She asks like she's sure I know the answer. "Yeah."

"Does it bother you?" She paces then, suppressing another shiver. For all her excitement at the school about it, now Shep looks as if this house has burrowed into her like a worm.

47

"Yeah," I say, because anything else would be a lie.

"Did you just find out? This house has more than two bed-rooms. You could pick a different one," says Shep.

"This one's mine," I say, and she gives me a strange look that's more understanding than confusion. "I think some part of me recognized it."

A moment later, she nods. "Abuela lived with us for a while before she died. She was born in Guatemala but moved to Oaxaca when she was a kid, and even after like forty years in the States, Oaxaca was home. It's weird, though. Even though she only stayed with us for a few months, I still feel like I'll come home after school and she'll be there, shit-talking my dad in Spanish and teaching me family recipes. But like, even though it feels kind of haunted, I still love my house. Mom grew up there. Abuelita gave her the house when my abuelo died."

"You said hospice at the holiday party," I say.

"Yeah, she died in September, right after school started."

"I'm sorry."

Shep shrugs. "She had a pretty long life. I miss her, though. Used to talk to her every day when I got home from school. And if she hadn't taught me how to cook, I'd be subsisting on micro-wave dinners and pizza sticks."

I don't know what a pizza stick is, but it sounds new and different.

She sits cross-legged on my pallet of egg crate and sleeping bag. Now the dust is cleaned up, I think my real Christmas gift will be finally having a proper bed. That's probably not what Dad was hinting at in the basement, though.

"Do you always befriend the new kids at Astoria High School?" I ask.

More than anything, I want to know why she's here, why she seems to care. I press my tongue against the smooth line of my teeth, feeling a single ridge where one is just barely out of place. The room is huge but feels too small, or maybe Shep feels too big. Downstairs I can hear the knocking sound of Dad hitting something with a hammer. In the room I can hear the whisper of the HVAC and feel cold air that should be warm. For a moment it's too much, and I claw my hand and hit my fingernails against my leg three times before I can stop myself.

Shep doesn't seem to see anything amiss. She looks up at me and beckons at me to sit. I sit, nibbling at the cookie in my left hand that I almost forgot about.

"I don't usually make new friends at all," she says slowly. "I just—"

I realize I haven't breathed in, and I try to make myself take in air. "Just what?"

"It's gonna weird you out. If Sky didn't already make you think I was freakishly into you."

"If you want to have a weird-off, I'm gonna win," I say, blushing at her second sentence.

"I'll hold you to that," Shep says. She takes a deep breath. "I just—I saw you and thought I was supposed to know you. And you moved into this house, of all houses. Sometimes I just get these *feelings* about things. It sounds nuts, but I'm never wrong. My mom calls it intuition. And Sky says *that* is because I'm a water sign. Like him—and you."

Like me. I let that sink in for a second, and I find myself again looking right into Shep's eyes. I usually can't remember what color someone's eyes are, but I think I could grab a set of colored pencils and recreate Shep's from memory. They're like the peat Dad uses in landscaping highlighted with moss and gold. Warm like fire, a living brown. I break eye contact after a long, long moment, glancing at the shelves I knew hid behind sheets of hasty drywall for thirty years.

"I get it," I say finally. "Intuition, if that's what it is."

Shep is quiet for a moment, completely still like a pond without a ripple. Then her lip quirks, and she asks a question all in a rush like a fish jumping in that stillness.

"What is it you want, Sam Sylvester?"

"You mean in general?"

"I mean right now." Shep's eyes burn like stars. "More than anything, what do you want?"

It's an intimate question. I don't think anybody has ever outright asked me anything like it, not even Dad.

I chase away the sensation of suffocating.

"I want to live," I say.

Shep looks at me, and something reverberates between us like a sonic boom. "Me too."

In those two words, I think Shep actually gets it. Really gets it. Not in the *oh, obviously we both want to keep breathing* sort of way. Not even when we're sitting in this room where Billy died. Life isn't just breathing—it's that and everything else Billy lost. A moment later, she cements that thought.

"I am sure the boy who died here really was murdered."

CHAPTER SIX

Shep's words take a minute to sink in, but when they do, they make their home somewhere in my gut.

"A kid with a well-known peanut allergy dies of anaphylaxis in his own home? It's not impossible, but these days you can't so much as bring a peanut butter and jelly sandwich to school if someone has an allergy that bad," Shep says. "No way would he just be hanging out at home, grabbing a snack, and suddenly his airways swell up and suffocate him and the parents just . . . drop it?"

"You're right. Dad would raise hell to get to the bottom of it. Even if he didn't think it was murder, he would need a lot of convincing to believe it was 'just' an accidental fatal reaction to a known allergen. He'd want to know exactly how it happened. He'd need something to blame." I swallow, a reflex, as if to prove I can. I've seen Dad's hell-raising firsthand—how he reacted to my near-death being called a prank.

"Did you ever see the old website about Billy? The Move the Stars site? Whoever made it didn't think Billy's death was an accident, with the way they asked for people to send relevant information. The website was full of *life*. Even the name— I googled it, and it's a reference to a quote from Jareth in *Labyrinth*. Billy's love for Bowie, pictures of his birthday parties . . . whoever made it knew him. And like Mr. Quach said, this town loved him."

Shep's nodding, fervent. She hums a couple notes of something.

"Space Oddity"—that's what Shep's humming. Just like Dad did in this room.

I want to win that weird-off right here and now, but a memory of *her* face, her skin white and drained of blood, eyes wide with horror, blurs and refocuses in front of my eyes.

"That's just it—people get *jealous*," Shep says. "Of the popular kids, of the ones who get attention because they're actually nice. And kids are cruel. Even if they don't mean to really hurt someone, well. Impact matters more than intent."

From the bite that comes with that last sentence, I want to ask Shep if she is speaking from experience. I corral the words I want to say behind my teeth and instead just say again, "I think you're right."

"I know I'm right," Shep says. "I always am."

"He's thirty years dead now," I tell her. "But you are— absolutely right. Even if someone didn't commit a *premeditated* murder, it doesn't mean someone didn't kill him."

I know that better than most people alive.

"The whole town still says it was an accident. I mean, except for the whispers." Shep scoots closer to me, and our knees touch.

Usually I hate casual physical contact, but this is welcome. It confuses me, like biting into a food you've always hated and finding that for some reason, today it's fine.

Good, even.

I almost forget what we're talking about.

Shep's eyes sparkle, and I think I see her throat move as she swallows. "We could solve this, Sam."

"The murder?"

"Of course, the murder." Ferocity makes her words come out like the crackles of a burning fire. "That boy deserves *justice*. So does his family."

52

Shep's face is aglow with fervor when she says *family,* and I think of what she's said about her own. If she could heal this impossible thing, maybe there's hope at home for her too, is that it?

"We're not on *Cold Case,*" I say dubiously. My dad loves that show. He's got an entire shelf of DVD box sets. There's a spark of excitement flickering in me, in spite of any doubt. "I don't even know where we'd start."

"My mom knew the kid, I think. Once she gets started talking about something, she usually doesn't stop. I haven't had any luck getting her going about this yet, but maybe—" Just then, Shep's phone sings out with Estelle's voice. The ringtone is "Stronger Than You" from Steven Universe, and if I didn't already want to be her friend, that would have clinched it. *She* hated Steven Universe. Probably afraid she'd catch queer germs from it.

Shep picks up the phone. "Mom, I'm hanging out with Sam."

I can't hear her mom's answer, but Shep makes a face and hangs up.

"I've got to go. I maybe sort of said I'd only be five minutes."

The sudden departure of her warmth leaves a strange void.

She remains sitting for a moment, knees pulled up to her chest. "You said you'd win a weird-off. Do you get feelings about things too?"

"Something like that," I say quietly. *Why me?* That's what I really want to say. Is it me or is it him?

Shep waits, then realizes I'm not going to extrapolate. I want to tell her about the shelves, about knowing they were there, but not when she is about to run out the door. She hops to her feet.

"*Text* me," she says. She mashes her cerulean hat back onto her head. "If you don't, I'll never bring you cookies again."

"If I get to eat another of the ones you brought this time, it'll be a miracle."

Shep winks at me. "I'll see you later, Sam Sylvester."

She breezes down the stairs, and I hear her holler at my dad to save me a cookie before the door slams.

Solve a murder. Solve *this* murder. I remember lying on the floor of my room and feeling like something was wanted of me. Could I do it? How weird is it to solve a thirty-year-old murder?

I take a breath, and the way my lungs shake around the intake of air surprises me. I wish it was as simple as sifting through my own memory, but it's not. Whatever lives I've studied, whoever I've sought out, the connections to their existences are like broken pathways. A spiderweb with holes punched through it. Or maybe broken code. Error 404: Whole Story Not Found.

But maybe I can piece it together. I don't know if Shep's psychic or if I am or both, but either way, she sounded so confident that I half-believe we can do this.

The thought cuts through a tightness I hadn't quite registered. I feel almost giddy.

I try to slow my breathing, counting the way Dad taught me long ago. My breath sounds like waves.

Dad calls up to me a minute later from downstairs. "You didn't walk your friend to the door?"

"Is that a thing humans do?" I yell back.

"They also sometimes come to the same room to talk!"

I scramble to my feet and head downstairs, where Dad's waiting with two completed chairs and a cookie in his hand. I take the cookie and eat half of it in a bite.

"Your friend seems nice," Dad says.

"Yeah, she's cool," I say.

"Cool."

"Dad."

He puts his hands in the air. "I didn't say anything."

I put my hand on the back of one of the chairs. "If I sit in this, will it break?"

"Give me a little credit. If I wasn't good at this, we'd probably be on the streets."

I start to sit down in the chair—I'm just joking with him, since Dad could build a chair from popsicle sticks and masking tape and I'd trust it—but he stops me.

"Don't get comfy. I want to give you your present."

"Christmas is tomorrow, not today."

"I know, I know, but I don't want to wait." Dad grins and motions toward the basement door.

I have no idea what to expect, so I follow him.

When he opens the door and I reach out to flick on the light switch, the moment my fingers touch the plastic switch I get a whiff of stale cigarette smoke and pizza that has no basis in the twenty-first century. There's a *whish-whish-whish* sound too, one I immediately recognize as air hockey even though I've never played. An echo of thirty-years-dead laughter. It's all gone in a moment when I take my hand away, but I stop at the top of the stairs anyway, watching Dad descend. There were photos of the whole house from when Billy died. Someone put them on the internet. I cringe, thinking of what Mr. Quach said. I might be an asshole for going all voyeur on this dead kid's life, but . . .

This is the first time the chance to get close to one of these half-lived lives has been this . . . vivid. I make myself step down once, then again, moving one foot in front of the other with a strange sense of someone else's effervescence warring with my own shaky trepidation.

The basement was a place of excitement, friends, fun. And for a moment as I trail my hands down the old, polished banister, I feel like I'm him, or he's me. I don't know which, but he's with me right now and I feel like him. Not really, of course. I don't believe in ghosts, do I? But still. I imagine the sensation of a cotton T-shirt against a flat chest that needs no binder to conceal nonexistent bulges. And yeah, I feel the presence of extra flesh between my legs. I reach down and adjust the crotch of my jeans even though I know I'm Sam Sylvester, not that murdered boy, and I don't have balls to move around in my Underoos.

I speed my descent as if I can chase away this kid's presence. It's never been this *much* before. Usually it's little things, mundane, ultimately pointless—never anything even close to one of the lives I've studied. My hands are shaking. At the bottom of the stairs, I turn left, then right, looking for Dad. When I see him, the whisper of excitement I felt with that touch melds with my own. I suddenly have something in common with Billy—this place was a haven for him. Now it looks like Dad wants it to be that for me. Dad stands beaming in front of a large bulky shape suspended from the ceiling and wrapped in bright silver paper. There's a big-ass purple bow stuck to it.

"Oh, my god. Dad!" My hands wave at hip level for a moment of pure, fluttering excitement, and then I clap them together. I bounce excitedly, fluttering my hands again.

"Hold up; you don't even know what it is yet."

A couple years ago, I perfected the teenage eye roll just to get on his nerves, and I employ it now. It's uncomfortable, but his exasperated sigh is worth it. I smile widely at him.

"Can I open it?"

56

"Go for it."

I leap toward the present and tear into the paper with my fingers and nails, pulling it away from smooth black upholstery. The punching bag swings on its bright silver chain, and when I look up with the wrapping paper in a crinkled mess at my feet, Dad's holding a pair of boxing gloves.

"*Dad.*"

"Whenever you need it. I wanted you to have it. I don't care if it's three in the morning. I'd rather be woken up by the sound of you giving this bag a beatdown than see you with bruises."

I swallow hard. There was never any secret or pretense to this present, but him saying it chokes me up anyway. Sometimes I feel like a balloon with a thousand inputs filling me with conversation noise, smells, clanking chairs, whispers, someone talking to me, so many things until I'm full to bursting but can't pop, and the only way is to release that pressure with my fists. My leg's the most usual casualty. It's an autism thing. Dad's the only one who really sees me do it; I've learned to control myself a bit. In the Before time, before Dad, I used to bang my head on the floor. The sight of the punching bag is a strange kind of hope.

Maybe this'll help.

I give him a tight hug. "Thanks."

"Well," Dad says. His voice cracks. "We'll have you giving Stallone a run for his money in no time."

CHAPTER SEVEN

January comes too fast, and school starts up right on the heels of the new year, it seems. Shep comes over a few more times during break, but we don't talk about the murder because her mom always drags her away by calling or texting before we can.

The morning of my first day of school, I wake up to a text from Shep sent at four in the morning.

Dad's house is the shittiest place to spend the night. He leaves the TV blasting all night, and I can't sleep. He insists on giving me a lift to school. Can we pick you up to save my sanity? Plus, it's your first day. I wanna be your escort.

A small jolt goes through me at her words. She texts in full paragraphs and sentences. I like that. But her dad sounds like an autistic person's nightmare. I text her back a quick *Sure, just tell me when to be ready* and head for the shower.

My hair has a fresh fade and color job, thanks to Dad. This time he did an extra buzzed-in line like a design beneath the longer bit on top that comes to a point at the back of my head. The top is silver and lavender with a hint of rose gold this time, and I think it might be my favorite color combination yet. He likes to experiment.

I've managed to hold off most of the new school anxiety till now. My stomach feels like I swallowed an anthill, but the knowledge that Shep will be there with me soothes it a little. I feel like her text this morning leveled up our friendship.

My clothes routine is pretty set by now. Today I don my Steven Universe boxer briefs along with my favorite binder, which I embroidered myself to have silver swirls from the straps to the boob-constrictor. Black distressed jeans. Oversized silver-gray sweater with a cowl neck.

My heaviest Doc Martens.

The smell of fresh-brewed coffee greets me as I clomp down the stairs.

"Wasn't sure if that was my kid or an elephant," Dad says, right on cue. He planned his first day of work for today, too. He's in fitted black slacks and black square-toed dress shoes with a dark green shirt. He's even wearing cufflinks, a pair of crescent moons that I bought him. His hard hat is on the table, bright yellow and dented.

"Shep wanted to know if she and her dad can take me to school," I say.

Dad looks momentarily injured. "You don't want me to drive you?"

"I think Shep both needs moral support and wants to be it for me. She said she'd be my honor guard."

That satisfies him. He pours some coffee into a to-go mug for me and winces as he stirs in four tablespoons of peppermint creamer. He hands me the mug and a ten-dollar bill. "For lunch. You'll probably be starving."

My eyes go a little misty. He knows well enough that I won't be able to eat this morning—and precisely how I like my coffee, even though I know he thinks it's an offensive amount of sugar.

Ten bucks seems like a lot of money for a school lunch, but I put it in my wallet anyway. "Maybe I can get a part-time job—"

"No way, Sam," Dad says. "There's plenty of time to work when you finish high school. The rest of your life, probably, since your generation isn't likely to get to retire."

He winks, even though I know he's serious. Dad had to help pay his rent when he was a kid. He bussed tables at a restaurant as soon as he was legally old enough (probably a bit before that, to be honest). He's always said that he knows I'm not going to think life's full of freebies, but he didn't want to put the same kind of pressure on me. There's more to that, for him. I know there is. But he hasn't told me yet, and I won't press.

I'm pretty sure it's partly because he has to prove to himself he can support us both, but I believe that he means it, too. Dad likes to say that many things can be true at once.

"Thank you, Dad," I say quietly.

He knows that means *I love you*.

There's a shine to his eyes when he turns to pour his own coffee, and my phone buzzes in my pocket. I jump.

"It's Shep," I say. "She's here."

"Good luck at school, kid," Dad says. "If you need anything—"

"I know. I'll call you. Good luck at work, Mister Foreman." I salute him and clonk the heels of my Docs together.

We don't hug. I grab my new backpack and head for the door.

Shep's dad drives a vintage Cadillac. An actual, honest-to-goodness Cadillac. It's painted bright red and so shiny it looks wet. It has wings on the back and the engine sounds like I imagine a sabretooth tiger's purr would sound like if it were sitting on my head.

I open the rear door and slide in on white leather seats, feeling either supremely out of place or like I need this car for myself. I'm not sure which. Shep's dad is a lanky white man with brown hair that has a spattering of gray. I can't see his eyes, since he's wearing a pair of sunglasses and staring in the direction of my house past where Shep sits on the passenger side

60

of the front bench seat. A smiley-face air freshener hangs from the rearview mirror, and I think it's supposed to be "new car smell" scent—no matter what, it doesn't help me feel comfortable. Artificial smells like that feel like worms writhing into my brain.

This was maybe a bad idea. The anthill in my stomach turns to a swarm pouring out of their tunnels in a sea of twitching legs. I'm afraid to take a drink of my coffee in this car, so I wedge the travel mug between my knees and try to remember how long it will take to get to school.

The air in the car feels like there are taut strings between every molecule. It's so tense I can almost taste it.

Shep turns around. The skin around her eyes is tight, looking indeed like she hasn't slept, but she gives me a grin of utter relief that somewhat breaks the tension in the air. "Sam! This is my dad, Carl Wayne."

"Hi," I say. "Sam Sylvester." I leave off my pronouns, because Carl Wayne turns around right as I say my surname and gives me a once-over I can feel even through the sunglasses.

"Steph's been talking about you. Moved into the local haunted house and encouraging my kid's obsession with it, eh?" is all he says, then turns away and pulls the Cadillac into the road.

I look at Shep, jolted by the different name even before I process the rest. My phone buzzes a minute later, distracting me.

Stephanie Shepard. I hate my first name. He hates that I took Mom's name back when they split. Especially since it's her name from her first husband, not even her maiden name, which was Estrada Iglesias.

You look like a Shep to me, I write back.

She gives me another smile over her shoulder. I can't tell if this one is happiness or gratitude or something else.

The car ride passes with no conversation. None. Even I know that's weird, and from the way Shep lets out a breath when we turn onto the school's street, I think she's as relieved as I feel.

"Sky's supposed to meet us," Shep says when Carl pulls the Cadillac up in front of the school. There are students everywhere, and while no one can see me, I hit my nails against my palm. The slight pinch helps focus me. A little.

Carl snorts at the mention of Sky's name, and Shep turns a dangerous look toward her dad.

"I didn't say anything," he says, holding his hands up.

Shep rolls her eyes (*not* ironically like I did with my dad—I'd put money on it) and opens her door.

"Uh, nice to meet you, Mr. Wayne," I say as I push open my own.

"You too," he says. "Call me Carl." He takes off his sunglasses for a second and I can see that his eyes are blue. "Your first day here, eh? Hope it goes well."

His tone is almost warm, and it's so different from the rest of the drive that I stutter out, "Th-thanks. I like your car."

"Nineteen-sixty Cadillac DeVille," he says. "Nothin' not to like."

"Guess so," I say.

He nods and reaches into the glove box and pulls out something metal and shiny. I don't know if Shep sees or not, but I see Carl spin open the screw top and wedge the flask between his legs like I did with my travel mug.

Then he drives away with a roar of that Cadillac engine, and Shep stares after him.

"Oh, my god, I'm so sorry," she says. "He's such a *dick*. And that car is his baby. I'm just his . . . offspring."

I don't know if I should mention the flask, then after a second decide maybe I should. "Does he, uh . . . always drink and drive at eight in the morning?"

"Oh, my god," Shep says again. "He got out his flask? You saw him?"

I guess the answer's yes.

"Yeah," I say.

"Mom'll have a stroke if I tell her that, and if I tell her, she'll stop letting me go see him at all. He's supposed to be *sober*."

"I'm sorry." For a moment I've forgotten where we are. I scuff my foot on the sidewalk, the voices around me materializing.

"Ugh," says Shep. "I am so sorry. I haven't actually seen him drink from that thing in ages. I thought he'd at least be friendly for the drive. He's mostly been better since—since my grandma died. I even tried asking him about Billy last night because I told him I'd met the people who moved into the house, but he blew me off because the game was on and—ugh, I wanted your first day to start out on a good note."

"It is," I say, and I mean it. For all the ants in my stomach, being around Shep makes me feel strangely calm.

I don't think she believes me, but she takes off that cerulean beanie and gives me a half smile anyway. "I think I see Sky."

Sure enough, Sky heads toward us across the grass. He greets Shep with a kiss on each cheek.

"Don't let Blaise see you do that," Shep says. "She'll poison my chicken sandwich at lunch."

At my questioning look, Sky gives me a sideways glance. "Blaise is my ex," he says, pronouncing each word with the precision of a sniper. "She fell out of Shep's good graces when she told the whole school I was gay after I dumped her."

"That sucks." I don't know what else to say.

Sky rolls his eyes. "I bleed rainbows as much as either of you. I spent two years trying to convince the plebes at this school that yes, I can be the little bisexual butterfly that I am, and Blaise undid my efforts within a month."

"Barf emoji," I say. "It probably doesn't make it any better, but at my old school being any letter in the acronym was enough to get you beaten up."

Shep gives me a piercing look, and Sky purses his lips.

"Perspective is a useful thing," he says thoughtfully.

"You're still allowed to be pissed." I belatedly remember that offering your own experience is often taken as spotlight-stealing among neurotypicals.

"I'm pissed. I still might punch Blaise if I get the chance," Shep says, voice flat. "But hey, there's at least one person for you to avoid, Sam! Wouldn't be high school without that."

At that, Sky changes the subject to the web comic he's working on, and I listen as the two of them flank me and head into the school.

I'm shocked to realize that the ants in my stomach have calmed.

CHAPTER EIGHT

I have no idea what to expect in my first class. It's on my schedule simply as "Advisory" because it's Wednesday and a Purple day, and I have no idea what the hell that even means even though both Shep and Principal Frankel tried to explain it. Monday, Tuesday, and Friday I have all seven classes, but Wednesday and Thursday I have odd and even periods, respectively, plus the whole Advisory thing.

"It's like study hall or homeroom," Shep says. She's in a different class, and so is Sky.

I've never had either of those things. They show me where my classroom is, and on the way, I can feel eyes on us. I stick out, but I'm used to that. In my Docs I'm slightly over six feet tall, and because I'm an eighteen-year-old junior, I look like a senior. A big senior.

"I'll see you in English, okay?" Shep says. It's one of the two classes we have together, and I'm thankful I have that to look forward to, at least.

"Yep." I look at Sky just as he gives me a tight smile.

"So much for avoiding Blaise," he says. "She's in this Advisory class."

Shep looks back and forth between us, then groans and tugs Sky away. "English," Shep says. "You'll live."

I blink at her, and then they're gone and someone is shouldering past me to get into the room. I follow them in, thankful that the teacher is already there. When I approach the desk, she turns and looks at me. I vaguely remember her from my IEP meeting.

Mrs. Hernández, I think. She's got a picture of herself with a nice-looking woman and two kids on her desk. I can't quite imagine ever having an openly queer teacher at my old school. I almost forget what to say.

"Sam, it's good to see you again," she says. "There're no assigned seats, so you can sit wherever you want. I don't think you have anything to work on this morning yet, so you're welcome to read quietly if you want. The others might have rollover projects or homework to try and finish before class. Would you like to introduce yourself to the class, or would you be more comfortable if I did?"

Standing up in front of twenty-some teenage strangers is not something I feel like doing. "You can, if you have to."

She gives me a small, sympathetic smile just as the bell rings and a few other students scoot through the door.

To her credit, she keeps it short and sweet as I find a desk midway back on the window side of the class to my right.

"Everybody, this is Sam Sylvester. They just moved here from Portland. Please make them feel welcome."

"Are they plural?" A tall, square-shouldered guy a few rows over from me asks the question, and a couple of his nearby friends snort.

"Sam's pronouns are they/them. What are yours, Aidan?" The note of challenge in Mrs. Hernández voice is clear enough, and however much sass Aidan has stored for the day doesn't seem to be enough.

He shifts in his seat, but he looks over at me. I look back, heart pounding but face as smooth as I can make it. I'm suddenly too warm, so I roll up my sleeves, which prompts Aidan to say, "*Nice ink*" under his breath in a tone that sounds sincere to me.

Tattoo privilege: apparently a thing with high school wannabe badasses.

When the bell rings, I scoot up from my desk, wondering if Blaise came in and which student she is, if Sky was right about her being in this class with me. From what Sky's told me, I don't particularly want to meet her. But none of the girls in the class are immediately identifiable as a biphobic bully. She could be the slender white girl with blonde hair to her waist—that person keeps peering at me as I shoulder my backpack and dig out the piece of paper where I scribbled my locker combination. She could also be the tall girl with brown skin and brown eyes. She could be over by the far wall—the short redhead with freckles and big brown eyes—who seems to be trying to start a fire on Aidan's back because he's blocking her route to the door.

I have no idea. My next "class" is Tutorial, and I already know I'm supposed to go see Principal Frankel to check in.

But before I can get out of the classroom, a pretty white girl with auburn hair flounces through the door, making the line of students waiting to exit split like bowling pins. A wave of intense rose scent crests over the room with the movement of air. Aidan is gone so fast it's like he hit the light speed button at the sight of the redhead. The girl has a slip of paper in her hand, and the students who bounced back inside the door grumble. I fight the urge to hold my breath. Floral scents—the ones that come from a bottle, anyway—are one of my migraine triggers. Between this and the Cadillac's air freshener, I might be in trouble.

"Blaise," Ms. Hernández says. "The holiday break is usually not so long that students forget when school starts."

"Dentist appointment," says Blaise, flashing a blindingly white smile at the teacher and proffering the slip of paper.

I study my own slip of paper, trying to memorize 31-17-57.

It's as if thinking about Blaise summoned her.

Her eyes turn to me, still stuck behind half the class. The feeling of glass cracking beneath my feet is all too familiar. I take a breath because I have to and immediately regret it when my nostrils catch a full dose of rose perfume.

"You're new," Blaise says. Her gaze is hard, intent as she looks me over like she's trying to memorize *me*.

My voice vanishes into my throat with her staring at me. That hasn't happened for a while. Since early Portland, when everything was still fresh. I suddenly feel like I walked barefoot out onto a barely frozen-over lake.

Ms. Hernández glances up from reading the excuse Blaise handed her. "Sam just moved here from Portland."

"That explains the tattoo," Blaise says, too sweetly, and that thin sheet of ice cracks under my feet.

"Blaise," says Ms. Hernández starts, a warning tone in her voice.

Blaise's eyes widen as if she's scandalized by the very thought of being misunderstood. "It's cool! You're brave to get one so young in such a prominent place."

That sounds way more like a jibe than a compliment even to my usually literal perception, and other students glance at me as if they think so too. Ms. Hernández motions to her desk, and Blaise follows, and I finally escape the classroom's cloud of eau de migraine and my impending polar plunge and head toward the principal's office.

Outside is not much better than inside, though. I can't get that cloying, floral scent out of my nose, *and* I feel like a circus animal.

I hope I get to a point where everyone stops staring at me. I know I stand out; I always do. And I know I'm new, but I wish they'd be more discreet about it or something. Their eyes feel heavy on me while I walk. And they say we autistic people are the rude ones.

"Yo, new girl!" someone hollers from down the hall just as I reach the office.

The guy who yelled looks vaguely familiar, and because I haven't seen that many high schoolers up close to remember faces, I manage to place him: he's the kid who delivered pizza to our house and stared at me over Dad's shoulder.

I don't know what to say to him, though, and the word *girl* feels so not me that it throws me. If I blow it off, I accede to his assessment of me as *girl*. If I call him out in this crowded hallway on my first day in front of everyone, it's gonna spread like a GIF of Misha Collins kissing Jensen Ackles on Tumblr. No stopping it.

But my voice doesn't seem so far away now, and this place *has* to not be Montana.

So I make a decision I never would have made in Montana.

I hit the Tumblr fandom button.

"Yo, white boy. I'm not a girl or a boy, but I am new. What do you want?"

If I was caught off guard by his exclamation, he's flummoxed by mine. "I—uh . . ."

"I'm supposed to meet Principal Frankel in exactly two minutes. Time's a-tickin'." The words come out of my mouth, and they're even coherent despite the sensory press of everything happening. The kids in the hallway around us have stopped all semblance of pretending not to notice and are now all staring at the guy who shouted at me.

"Dylan just got schooled—" someone whispers with no small amount of glee.

"Careful, Dyl, your ass is showing!" Someone says *that* way louder than a whisper.

The guy Dylan seems to recover a bit of his bravado, and he stands up straighter and gives me a pretty okay bow. "Just . . . saw you moved into the local haunted house and figured I'd say hello!"

"Pro tip," I say with what I hope is a friendly smile. "Hello sounds exactly like *hello*."

I pull open the door to the office and hear a murmur of excitement behind me as I walk through. My heart feels like it's on a roller coaster of *oh, my god, I did that* dipping into *oh, my god, what have I done* and back. I want to puke.

The office is bustling with teachers, and Principal Frankel is talking to one of the administrative staff when she looks up and sees me. Her curly hair is pulled back from her face with a clip.

Her face lights up. "Sam! You're here! Come on back!"

I follow her back to her office and sit in the same chair I sat in last time.

"How's your first day so far?"

"It's okay," I say. "I've only had Advisory, and I still don't really know what that is."

Does she always meet with new students on the first day, or am I special? I don't voice that question.

"You'll be working more closely with Mr. Quach than with me," she says, "but I wanted you to know that if anything happens at all, you can come speak to me immediately."

Anything meaning getting misgendered or *anything* meaning getting told to pee in the wrong bathroom or *anything* meaning . . . my wind pipe starts to itch.

I clear my throat. "Thanks."

"I mean it," she says. "The notes in your file are—well. If anything even close to that shows a whiff of happening here, Sam, please. Come straight to me."

"Okay," I say. I don't know what else to tell her. My eyes fall on the picture behind her again, a young girl and someone else's shoulder. "Those your kids?"

"What?" Principal Frankel turns. A flush creeps up the sides of her throat, delicate but persistent. Her voice is carefully modulated when she speaks again. She gestures at the young girl in the picture. "No, Sam. That's me, way back in the eighties. The boy with me was my best friend, Billy."

She moves aside, and I see him clearly for the first time. I don't know how I didn't recognize him when Dad and I were here before—probably because from this seat, she's partly in the way, and I was a little overwhelmed.

But now Billy's face is clear.

The room narrows to that one single photograph. I don't have to be psychic to recognize him when I've seen his picture so many times, even if it's been mostly one clear image in a sea of blurry pixels left over from Move the Stars. I see his face in the mirror in my mind, and for a moment it feels like my face, my face, I'm Billy and that's *Margie* in front of me, and that really is Billy Clement because I've *seen* his pictures online and she's *the principal* I can't breathe and—

"Sam?" Margie —*Principal*—Frankel says my name with a tone of alarm. "Are you okay?"

I press my nails into my palms, both sets, both palms. Four sharp crescents per hand. The skin by my eyes flutters. I hear Dad's voice in my head. *Breathe in.* I do. *Breathe out.* I do.

71

"Sorry, Principal Frankel," I say. She's staring at me, ashen-faced. "I'm okay. I—Your friend was the boy who died in my house, wasn't he?"

She grew up next door. I remember her remarking on us having bought that house, that particular house, the first time we met her.

Her mouth falls open, and at the same time a curl from her forehead slides down and lands on her lip. It takes her a moment to push it away. What I said was just too blunt. Probably insensitive.

"It's a small town," she says after a beat. "And Billy's death was a tragic accident."

Something about the way she says it is robotic. The words come out without a thought, more like they were programmed than emoted.

I feel a twisting swell of pity for Principal Frankel. For once, I am certain of exactly what someone else is feeling. I was the one whose almost-death was called a tragic accident.

"I'm sorry," I say. "I shouldn't have brought it up."

"I keep that picture because I want to remember him," she says simply. "If I wasn't okay with people asking about it, I wouldn't have it on my desk."

There's something else between her words that I can't pinpoint. Instead, I just nod. "I understand that."

This conversation has gotten too weird for a student and a principal, especially for our second meeting. Principal Frankel seems to recognize it at the same time I do, because the creeping line of red on her throat immediately enflames her cheeks a bright pink like a fuse, and she stumbles her hands over some papers on her desk.

"You've got English next, correct?"

I nod at her. She goes on for a bit, telling me about my teachers and that she's given them each a packet of information about how to be sensitive to their LGBTQ students as well as preemptively going over my pronouns with them. It's a little overwhelming, and after a while I simply hear the ebb and flow of her words like waves on the beach. I know she's trying to help, and a small voice somewhere deep down says that I should be more *grateful*, like she should get a whole bushel of cookies for this.

But this is just how it should be. Ideally, teachers wouldn't even need a packet to teach them how to treat students like people. She pauses and shuffles through my file again, and a swell of yearning threatens to capsize me in my chair. I just want to *be*.

My throat makes a sound that I didn't authorize. First note of the Bowie song that was Billy's favorite. *Ground control to Major Sam.* I need to snap out of it.

I almost started singing Billy's favorite song. To his best friend, who is now my principal.

My chest feels crowded with emotions that I can't pinpoint. When I look at adult Margie Frankel, that sense of yearning comes back like a wave when I misjudged the height of the swell.

Digging my fingernails into my palm, I try to center myself here. *I'm alive. I'm alive. I'm alive. I'm alive.*

When I finally escape the office, I catch my reflection in the small window on the office door. It's not Sam Sylvester.

It's a blond boy named Billy.

He looks back at me through thirty years, and for one absurd, impossible moment that chills even me, I wonder if he can see *me*.

When I blink, he's gone.

What is *wrong* with me?

CHAPTER NINE

I catch up with Shep at the door to the English classroom after a detour to the nurse for something to ward off the Blaise-migraine, and Shep pulls me in with a hurried whisper.

"Everyone's talking about how you schooled Dylan Lackland on your gender in the hallway, and I would have killed to see that. He used to cut my shoelaces down the middle when we were in seventh grade." Shep looks around. "And Aidan Hammond is telling everyone about your tattoos. Well done, Sam Sylvester. You're already famous."

I think I'm going to hurl. My stomach sloshes with all the water I chugged to wash down the painkillers.

"It probably helps that you look like you could beat up even the football players at this school. You're like Ruby Rose or something. Sam?"

Shep seems to realize that she's freaking me out, because she takes a step backward and ushers me to a seat near the back of the crowded classroom.

"Sorry," she says as we sit down.

"I went to the same school for six years where everyone knew me and then one for a semester where no one gave a shit, so this is a lot." It feels different. I feel different.

"It's going to be fine," says Shep. "I think people are kind of in awe of you."

"Just call me Stevonnie," I say meekly. I wish I had a water bottle or something.

Shep at least gets the Steven Universe reference that *she* wouldn't have. "I mean, Stevonnie is a BAMF."

"They are at that," I say. There's still a minute and a half till the bell. Words that were absent this morning now tumble out in a rush. "I met Blaise this morning. Sort of, anyway. She knows my name and was catty about my tattoos. And I found out something. About Billy."

Shep's lips, which were drawing into an unhappy scowl at the Blaise cameo turn into a small O of surprise when I veer onto the subject of Billy. She leans across the aisle. "You found something out since this morning? How?"

"Principal Frankel has a picture behind her desk. She was best friends with him."

"Holy . . . and she just told you that? Suspicious."

The teacher—Mr. Duncan, if my memory of Principal Frankel's speech serves—comes in. He wasn't at my IEP meeting even though they gave me special goals in English to improve my understanding of figurative language and spelling. I can define a metaphor well enough, but seeing them in the wilds of literature still baffles me if it's not a basic statement like *my brain is scrambled eggs.*

He peers through the faces of students and sees me. "Ah," he says just as the bell rings, which drowns out his next word. He clears his throat when the squawking finishes. "I believe we have a new student. Sam Sylvester. From Montana, I believe?"

Every eye in class except Shep's turns toward me (Ronnie's in this class and looking at me, and her face is one-hundred-percent *glad I'm not in your shoes*), and I hear someone bleat like a sheep.

I nod, but don't stand up.

"Welcome, Sam. Is Sam short for—"

"It's just Sam," I say before he can finish. "My pronouns are they/them."

He looks startled, and the rest of the class peers at me in silence. Guess Mr. Duncan didn't read his packet. I wish I could say I was surprised. Some of the students probably witnessed my morning fracas with Dylan Lackland, but most just seem bemused.

Mr. Duncan starts the lesson by handing out a stack of books. *The Call of the Wild.* Mine is worn, an edition that looks like it came straight out from behind those sheets of drywall Dad and I pried loose. Sure enough, the edition in my hand was printed in 1980. More than two decades before I was even born. This worn, tattered book is a survivor, apparently. Like me. Shep's, by contrast, is a movie tie-in cover from the nineties.

I've read it, back in Montana.

Night came on, and the full moon rose high over the trees into the sky, lighting the land till it lay bathed in ghostly day. [. . .] Faithfulness and devotion, things born of fire and roof were his; yet he retained his wildness and wiliness.

I read that to *her* once. Next to a fireplace in her log home near the Bitterroot River.

I've got goosebumps. I really do, even beneath my sweater. The hairs stick straight up, and I stifle a shiver.

I look over at Shep, who's surreptitiously texting someone before she shoves her phone under one leg and bangs her knuckle on the desk on the hand's way up. She jumps and gives me an almost cartoonishly adorable shrug and mouths "oops" while Mr. Duncan is helping a student tape a cover back onto their book.

The shiver dissolves into warmth, tugging my lips into a grin.

The rest of my classes go by in a blur, and I scurry between them, dodging my reflection in classroom windows and doors just in case it's not my face looking back again. Mr. Quach pops in to my biology class to say hello, and part of me flinches from the knowledge that in addition to my first-day escapades, everybody's going to know I've got an IEP, too.

Shep has to go straight home after school, and Sky flits off to go to work, arm in arm with Ronnie with a "We'd *so* rather hang out with you guys" that makes me feel pleasantly wanted, so I walk home on my own. The air is breezy and brisk, but I feel warm anyway. When I get home, Dad's still at work. I kick off my Docs, drop my backpack (it's way heavier than it was when I left), and make for the basement. The punching bag from Dad hangs there, innocuous.

It's only then that I realize how much I've been holding in. I drop my phone on a papasan chair by the wall.

The bag's chain clanks when I punch it the first time. The bag itself is heavy, pendulous. It absorbs the power of my fist without a problem. I hit harder. I have gloves somewhere, and I should use them. But right now I want the pain of my knuckles hitting the bag.

In spite of the day's many oddities, all I can see is Billy's face in that pane of glass.

My therapists used to call this overidentifying. *Smack.*

I've never imagined one of their reflections. *Smack.*

It didn't feel like my imagination.

What is happening to me?

Smack-smack-smack-smack-smack-smack.

A loud *bong* sounds through the house.

I wait for a second, but it doesn't happen again. Belatedly, it hits me. The doorbell. This is the first time we've had one. I slow my breathing while the punching bag creaks on its chain, then pad back upstairs.

My knuckles are red and throbbing. Dad might not be too happy that I didn't use my gloves, but he'll forgive me. I'll need to cut my nails, though. A few of them busted through the skin on my palms when I punched the bag.

I peek out through the semicircle window at the top of the door. I don't see anyone there.

Opening the front door, a breeze hits my warm face and hands, cooling off the blood-heated skin. Nobody's on the porch. The little wooden boot house where Dad doffs his dirty work boots before coming inside is empty. Its door creaks in the breeze. I nudge it shut with my foot. I'm about to close the front door when I see it. Taped to the door itself. When I pull it off, a tiny fleck of paint comes off on the tape.

There's no address on the paper at all. Is this Shep's idea of neighborhood fun?

I head inside and shut the door, locking it behind me.

The paper's one sheet of average computer paper. When I unfold it, there's one line, printed in a crisp font directly in the middle.

Think you're so smart, don't you?

I read it three times, and each time it kicks the anthill in my stomach a little harder.

Think you're so smart, don't you?

Again, I feel the tightening in my throat. It's the beginning of January. My birthday's coming up in a couple months. Maybe someone else wouldn't read those little words and immediately assume mortal danger, but I'm not someone else.

This is it, then, the thing that'll steal the rest of my life away.

I don't know who sent it or what it's about. It's vague enough that it could be anything. From anyone. But I've only been here a few weeks—who the hell would already hate me enough to send me a note like this? Dylan didn't *seem* too bothered by my hallway clapback. This feels like a threat. Could he have done this?

I'm probably just projecting.

Someone knocks at the door, and I jump because I'm standing three feet from it still.

I look out through the window again, half-expecting to see only open air. But I don't. It's Shep. She's got a piece of white paper in her hand too.

I scrabble at the deadbolt to let her in.

Shep nearly pushes past me, brandishing the paper in her hand. "Someone left this in my mailbox," she says. "It says 'You're not as smart as you think you are.'"

I hold mine up. "I got one too, just now. Stuck to the door."

"Who *does* that?"

In spite of her words, each breath Shep takes seems to only make it as far as the top of her chest. Her shoulders are hunched up, and her hat's pulled down almost past her eyebrows.

"Do you think it's about Billy? It almost has to be, right? We've talked about it at school and other people have been around, but I didn't think anyone would care. It was ages ago. Like . . . I've asked my mom and dad a few questions even before you moved in here, and they just nattered on for a while about it being a horrible tragedy, yadda yadda. It's like they learned the same line and just regurgitate it now." Shep seems to realize she's rambling and shakes herself, but she can't seem to stop. "In school, Dad was a couple years older than Billy and Mom

79

was one year older, and it's not like they *knew* him, but Astoria was even smaller then than it is now, so of *course* they knew him—"

"Shep, it's okay." Her near-panic somehow calms me.

"It's not okay. I have to know who would do this." She shakes her note at me. "Is someone just trying to fuck with us? It's literally your first day of school. And it's so . . . it's a *note*. A note. Really? It has to be about Billy, right? What other reason would there be?"

She's silent for a moment, and I lock the door again. "Do you want some orange juice or something?"

Offer guests drinks. That's a thing humans do.

Shep lets the note dangle between her thumb and forefinger like it fell into a Port-a-Potty. "I *want* to find out what happened to Billy Clement."

The house inches closer on all sides of me, and it's as if all the talk of him has summoned the house's memories of him to the surface here. I feel his T-shirt, his jeans this time. His straight hair that he kept shaggy except in that one picture I saw on Move the Stars where he was dressed up like Bowie as Jareth and was wearing a wig. There's not really a *reason* to connect these notes with our barely begun investigation, but Shep's got a point. What else could it be?

It's you, an unhelpful voice in my mind whispers. *You're a magnet for the worst type of person.*

That note feels too similar to the thin-ice-beneath-my-feet feeling I always got with *her*. That negging way of putting someone in their place where someone adds just enough barb to otherwise-innocuous words. And now Blaise, who has demonstrated exactly that. Could Blaise have done this? That would be quite an escalation after one conversation. The instinct to keep my head down, to be silent and ghost-like as I was in Montana, nearly overwhelms me. I could dial back the hair, the combat boots, the glittery eyeliner, the obvious queer vibes I now broadcast. I could go back to the way I was, crawl back into the closets I occupied in Montana like concentric matryoshka dolls to keep anyone from seeing me. I could let Billy go.

Shep sees me, though. She's looking at me with an expression I can't identify. Urgency, maybe. Some fear. I hurriedly look away.

And in spite of all that, I feel Billy here. Maybe it's because there will be no justice for what happened to me—no real punishment, nothing but a half-hearted slap on the wrist for "the Barry boys." But maybe, just maybe, Shep and I can somehow find justice for Billy.

"Look," I say. Shep's big brown eyes draw mine, and I want to fall into them. I've only said this out loud to one other person before. Saying it now might be the most ill-advised thing I've done today, but . . . "I already knew about Billy Clement."

"What?"

I can't stop my fingernails from digging into my palm. It stings the bits of broken skin from punching the bag. To my utter shock, Shep reaches out and takes my hand. Her skin is still cold from outside, but smooth. The contact sends a jolt skittering up through my wrist. Shep's gaze falls on the little half-moon indents with their thin lines of blood, and her thumb gently moves over them as if she can smooth them away.

"What do you mean?" she asks quietly.

Am I really going to do this? I remove my hand from Shep's to lead her upstairs to my room. It's more lived-in than it was before my bed and desk got here, but the glossy black nightstand by the bed still has that too-shiny, showroom look. I cross the room to my *Book of Half-Lived Lives*. Shep watches me from the foot of my new bed where the black comforter dangles off the side where I kicked it this morning. Shep's hand moves just a bit as if it feels empty now.

She reads the cover when I bring it over. I can't look at her, though I can feel when her eyes land on me again as I open the book with fingers that quake on the familiar pages. I flip past so many others on the way to Billy, about three-quarters of the way into the book. Mary, who drowned. Hezekiah, who lied about his age and died in the Civil War fighting for the Union.

"The Move the Stars website—how well do you remember it?" I ask.

"Not *super* well, since it vanished. There were a lot of entries I never got a chance to read."

"Same," I say. I went through a lot of the archives, but even a post per month over years adds up.

"I've been kicking myself for a year for not taking screenshots. But you got it! Some of it, anyway." Her hands twitch like she's itching to reach out and grab the book. "I thought I remembered some things from it, but that's the site that got me thinking about him so much after I realized it had disappeared. Whoever made it—"

"Didn't think his death was an accident." I can feel it again, the way I felt reading his story for the first time, almost hearing Bowie's voice in the background, Billy's voice singing along. *Ground control to Sam and Shep.* I point to the page where I pasted one of the screenshots and read from it. "'Family and friends were baffled by Billy's sudden death. Due to the precautions his loved ones took to ensure his safety, they couldn't understand how he could be fine one minute and dead the next when there seemed to be nothing nearby to explain it.'"

"That's what first made me suspicious. I remember they also said the official police report says anaphylaxis and that it was accidental, but the Move the Stars blogger came to believe someone triggered it on purpose because Billy was so meticulous about being careful." Shep knows what she thinks. "That's a horrible way to die, to have air all around you and not be able to get enough."

I know what it feels like.

I haven't noticed the tears till now. They're dripping on the hardwood, and my eyeliner stings when it sneaks into my eyes. I can't tell if they're for Billy or me.

"Sam," Shep breathes. "Are you okay?"

"I—" I say. I don't want to lie to her, but I can't talk about what happened to me and why I'm crying. Pushing the feelings down could lead to a worse meltdown, but right now I need to risk it. I change the subject. My fingers tighten on my book, my gaze falling on one of the paragraphs I screenshotted, an almost whimsical detail about how his room smelled like popcorn. "You say you have feelings about things. I—one of my . . . things is a special interest for researching historical accounts of kids who died as teens. When we moved here, I had no idea we were moving into his house—I should have. I saw pictures of the whole thing, and I didn't recognize it when we got here, but now I can't think about my room without feeling him in it. I felt him. I still do."

I leave out the weirdest part, about how touching things sometimes gives me *feelings* about them. Still, for all Shep's assertion a couple weeks ago, I can tell she is freaked out. My face flushes. Shame, maybe. I feel hot and sad and angry at myself for being such an *alien*. My knuckles turn white from the force of my grasp on the book.

I turn the page to the only non-blurry picture of Billy I have in it.

Then, nearly prying my own fingers off the pages, I hand my most private possession to her. "That's him. This is his yearbook picture from the year before he died. 'Eighty-seven—'eighty-eight." I found it in the archives of the website that vanished. "Think you can get your hands on a yearbook from 'eighty-eight–'eighty-nine? Maybe we could see if there are any other pictures of him in there and identify the people he hung out with from their pictures in the yearbook. I think he was popular—he was probably photographed a lot."

"My mom's still got hers." Then as if saying the word has summoned Shep's mom into my very bedroom, she winces. "I've gotta run or she will flip."

"I'll see you tomorrow?" It's a question molded from the clay of a still-fragile new friendship—and the sudden precarity of having shown her something I don't show even to Dad. It was an impulse, and I don't always have the best impulse control. I hope I don't regret it. It's also me giving Shep an exit strategy if I won the weird-off too handily.

She gives me a crooked smile. "Of course."

For once, I can tell she means it. That tight place in my chest eases as I walk her downstairs to the door.

A sudden thought strikes me. "Do you think we could maybe find out who made that website?"

Shep's eyes widen. "I don't know. Ronnie's the Rainbow Island tech genius. We could ask her."

It sends a small thrill through me. Right. She was reading a book about Python. I manage to make eye contact long enough to give Shep a smile that I hope isn't too crooked. I probably look like Toothless the dragon trying to smile back at a human.

Shep leaves with both notes. I sit at the breakfast bar with a glass of orange juice, tapping Dad's drafting pencil against the countertop.

The sound of the Subaru in the driveway is a very welcome distraction, though knowing how upset he is about Montana, it kicks the anthill of anxiety in my gut.

What would Dad think of this?

CHAPTER TEN

I wonder what you think about me.

What do you think now? That I was some freak you happened to let into your life?

I guess I wouldn't blame you for that. Or at least I wouldn't, if what happened didn't happen.

It's four in the morning. I managed to wake myself up this time, after the dream. I didn't startle Dad for once. My therapist in Portland said it's normal for people to process traumatic feelings long after the fact, but it feels like stuff is coming up more and more often here. In this room. I think I catch a whiff of popcorn smell, but it's gone from one breath to the next.

I wish there was some sort of mystic guide who would tell me why this is happening to me. Some sort of explanation. But I guess that's the joke, right? Life and death are the two things we never get an answer for when we ask "why." And for whatever reason, I've collected a hell of a lot more of both than everyone else seems to. Or maybe pretty much everyone else has obsessions like this too and just doesn't know it or talk about it. Like herpes. They don't want to be different, so we never figure out that we're all actually the same.

Tonight I dreamed about what you did again.

Some days I wish you hadn't stopped it, so it'd be over. So I wouldn't have to keep reliving it. As if that would somehow make it my prerogative.

It takes me a three-minute battle with the squiggly red line to spell prerogative right, and it takes the punch out of my last line.

But I don't want it to be over at all.

I hit Post and immediately regret it.

I shouldn't do this to myself. She's never going to read it or care.

But it's not for her, I guess. She is inconsequential now. My therapists—the one in Missoula and then the one in Portland—have told me that bottling everything up isn't healthy. I don't think an anonymous Tumblr was their idea of a healthy processing strategy, but it's all I've got right now. I should ask Dad if we can find a new therapist. I know what's stopping me—having to go through it all again with a stranger.

My phone is charging on the bedside table. I pick it up, and there's a text from Shep from a little after midnight.

With an image.

It's Billy Clement in a different yearbook photo, which she's pointing to in the book itself. It's better quality even in this photo of a page than the low-res image I printed for my *Book of Half-Lived Lives*.

His collar is all prim and pointy. His parents must have wanted him to look nice that day.

I wouldn't really blame Shep if she's assuming I'm too much. But when I scroll up, she's written *I'll wait for you to go through the rest of the book.* That seems optimistic, if ambiguous about whether I freaked her out or not.

· · ·

Dad takes one look at me when I walk into the kitchen a few hours later and sighs. "No sleep again?"

"I tried not to wake you up."

"You succeeded. You gonna be okay at school?"

I reach out to grab the microwaved breakfast burrito he's holding out, which he relinquishes with a surprised twitch of his lip.

"Yeah, I'll be fine," I say. "Today's a Gold day."

"I don't know what that means."

"Neither do I," I tell him. Last night he helped me with my homework even though it's not due till tomorrow since I don't have any of those classes today.

The burrito is way too hot to eat, so I nibble away enough tortilla and watch the steam pipe out of the corner while Dad puts another burrito in the microwave for himself. He and I both have a penchant for these things, even if I seldom eat one at an actual breakfast hour. They're total processed crap, but they're delicious. I bounce a little from side to side.

"You okay?" Dad asks. "Happy food bounce seems cautiously optimistic at least, but it clashes with your face."

Some people think autistic people don't show emotion well, but that's horse hooey. At least to the people who love us. I can't hide an errant thought about a rainstorm without Dad thinking something's up. My heart's not on my sleeve. It's on my forehead. It's just written a little differently than the other hearts people can read. And sometimes the font is too big or too small, but people who know us well can tell when something is wrong.

(That, I think, is a metaphor like I'm supposed to be learning.)

"Sort of," I say. "Did you know a kid died in this house in the eighties?"

Dad blinks. "You seeing ghosts, Sam?"

"Figuratively speaking." I try not to think about my birthday as much as I can, try to push away the fear that I won't live to see it. But right now, looking at Dad, I wonder what he's gonna do when I'm gone. He doesn't deserve this. Tears form again in my eyes, hot and eager. I hate that.

"I didn't know that, no," Dad says. He runs his hand across his hair. "What happened?"

"Allergic reaction, I think. The bad kind that makes your throat close up. What's the word for it again—"

"Anaphylaxis. Like me with walnuts, but worse."

"Yep." I'll remember it now. Shep said it yesterday, too. Last time Dad ate something with a walnut in it, he got *really* wheezy until the Benadryl kicked in. Billy wasn't that lucky, I guess.

"How'd you find out about this?"

A pang jangles through me. These obsessions are something I've kept from him.

"It seems to be a town legend." I brave a bite of the still-steaming burrito. "There's a question of whether it was an accident or not."

Dad's face quickly becomes his Alarmed Face, which I haven't seen much recently and haven't missed. "If I had known, I wouldn't have bought this place. The Realtor seemed a little—"

"Dad, it's okay. It's just making me think a bit. Who would murder a kid? If it wasn't an accident, that is. That's the kind of stuff that happens on your shows."

I don't say *and even "accidents" can still be murder* since he and I both know that all too well.

"If living here where someone died is making you afraid—"

"I'm not afraid of the dead, Dad. They're dead." It's true. I couldn't be afraid of Billy Clement if I tried, no matter how much his story is haunting me. "The living are scarier."

He goes silent at that, and then the microwave beeps on his own burrito and it's time for us to go.

. . .

"What even *is* a pizza stick?" Sky asks as we sit down at a gray speckled table in the cafeteria.

"I don't know, but you've got one, and I was already wondering." I nod at it and feel thankful for the salad bar that exists here. One cannot survive on pizza sticks alone.

The cafeteria is a long room on the edge of the school with a slanted ceiling of terraced metal and glass and a weirdly patterned floor of green and beige tiles up against slightly darker beige and brown blocks. Rain patters sideways into the rectangular windows, dulling the sound of conversation. I like that. Usually cafeteria time is the worst part of my day, sensory-wise.

Someone plunks down beside me, too close. For a second I think it's Shep, but it's not. It's Aidan Hammond, the guy who thought I had "nice ink." I ignore the auburn head that swivels in our direction a few tables away. Blaise isn't even pretending not to stare, but she looks away when Sky fixes her with a glare that I think would vaporize me, then turns to Aidan.

I'm glad I'm far enough away that I can't smell Blaise's perfume over the other cafeteria aromas. That Dylan kid is near her, along with a few other kids whose names I don't know.

Sky looks at our table's newcomer as if he can't decide whether the muscular boy smells bad or looks hot. Aidan's attractive enough, if you swing the jock way. Square jaw. Brown hair with a little curl to it. Brown eyes I suppose someone could compare to a puppy dog if they really wanted to.

"Hi," I say, trying to be human.

"Hi," says Aidan. "What's up with your tattoo?"

Sky sighs into his pizza stick and opens his chocolate milk with one hand.

"Deal with my dad," I say. "I passed pre-calc instead of dropping it for consumer math."

"Your dad let you get it?"

"My dad's awesome," I say without hesitation.

"My dad would pound me into the pavement if I tried. How'd you get somebody to ink you? Thought they couldn't tattoo minors even with parental permission." This guy seems genuinely curious, and since Sky hasn't shooed him away yet, I guess he passes some level of approval for conversational safety.

"I'm eighteen," I say.

"Aren't you a junior?"

This question always makes me uncomfortable. Sky's watching me with his own curiosity obvious by the way he ignores the milk and pizza stick occupying each of his hands.

"Had a late start to school," I say simply.

Just then, Shep comes weaving through the tables with her tray, looking harried. We have US history together right after lunch, and this is the first I've seen her all day.

"Aidan," she says, sliding her tray over next to Sky's. "Will wonders never cease?"

"Hey, just because you made friends first doesn't mean I can't," Aidan protests. He has the bewildered look on his face of someone who's used to their friendship being currency, not a bounced check.

The cafeteria is at its peak crowd level, and the noise level rises like a tide in the bay outside. Principal Frankel walks by with a banana in her hand.

She pauses beside us. "Afternoon, Sky, Shep. Billy, good to see you making new friends."

I stare up at her, but I don't think she realizes what she just said.

Aidan looks confused. "Who's Bi—"

Shep's jaw is hanging open, her eyes glued to Principal Frankel.

"Sam's awesome!" Sky says brightly, raising his half pint of chocolate milk into the air. "New student extraordinaire. Even Aidan likes them, and he's usually more interested in balls."

That snaps Shep out of her stare when she realizes what Sky just said, and Sky looks like he wants to crawl inside his milk carton and die of embarrassment. Weirdly, Aidan doesn't. Respect.

Principal Frankel, though, goes a paler shade of white and gives a tight nod, walking away with strides so straight she looks like she turned to wood. I can't help watching her retreating figure and wondering what just happened. I do not for one minute think her reaction had anything to do with Sky saying "balls."

I don't really look like Billy. He was shorter and way blonder than my dingy, dishwater natural hair. Scrawny where I'm tall and toned. Different faces. Maybe I just brought up the memories of him. But the fact that both I and Principal Frankel have looked at my face and seen Billy is chilling. The cafeteria feels colder.

"Who the eff is Billy?" Aidan says, jolting me back to the table.

"Nobody—" Shep starts.

"Billy Clement," I say at the same time.

"That kid who died in Sam's house a bazillion years ago?" Sky says dubiously.

Aidan shakes his head in a *I don't know what the hell you're saying* way. "What kid?"

"You moved here, what, three years ago?" Shep asks, looking resigned at having to explain rather than discuss what Principal Frankel just did. "This kid who died in 'eighty-nine. Supposedly an accident, but we think it was murder, never solved."

"No way," Aidan says. He looks at me. "In your house? Oh, shit, you live in *that* house? Someone said it was haunted or something one day when we were walking into town, but I just thought they were messing with me."

"Yeah." I don't know what else to say. Aidan's looking at me as if having someone die in my house increases my coolness quotient, and it grosses me out a bit. Me, the macabre morbidity magnet.

The bell rings out just as a crack of thunder makes everyone jump.

Saved.

CHAPTER ELEVEN

In US history, Shep texts me.

Sorry I haven't gotten to talk to you much today. I wanted to say that I don't think you're weird. I realized I left kind of suddenly last time and wanted to tell you it wasn't you. Stuff's been weird, but it's parent and grades drama at home. Definitely not you!!

I stare at her text, trying to hide it in the folds of my sweater so the teacher, Ms. Gowan, can't see me. Shep's two rows away, watching. I meet her gaze with what I hope is a *you don't think I'm weird?* look and then try to shift it to relief. Relief is one of the many expressions I've had occasion to practice in the mirror to try and get close enough to make neurotypicals happy.

Shep smiles, so I must have been close enough.

Can you come to the library with me after school?

Her next text buzzes my phone, and Ms. Gowan looks around to try and see the source of the noise. The teachers here can't take our phones away, but they can find other ways to punish us. Usually by public humiliation, that old school staple.

I nod at Shep and go back to reading.

The rest of the school day passes too slowly and without much incident, even though my next two teachers make me introduce myself in front of the class. I wish there was something in my IEP that made it so they weren't allowed to do that. Once, a kid mentions Montana to me in a small group exercise out of the blue, and I can't help the gooseflesh that breaks out up and down my legs. It makes my toes tingle. My Missoula therapist said that I have a psychosomatic memory response to trauma, probably because she knew I hated the increasing overuse (and misuse) of the word *trigger*, no matter how appropriate it is for me.

I tell the kid something about cow tipping, pat the stereotype on the head, and hope he lets it lie. He does.

By the time the last bell rings, a headache pulses at the back of my skull.

The rain has passed, and Shep meets me outside the school with her backpack slung over one shoulder. It's almost the same color blue as her hat.

"You okay?" When she's concerned, she squints a bit, making a little V of creases between her eyebrows. It's kind of adorable.

"Headache," I say. "It happens sometimes when I'm overstimulated. My brain doesn't know where to concentrate, so it works too hard."

Shep frowns harder. "Quach works with you. He's a special ed teacher."

"I'm autistic."

"Oh."

Shep nods toward the crosswalk, and I follow, afraid she's going to say something dreaded like *but you don't seem autistic* or *you must be "high-functioning"* or *you should say "person with autism"* or some other horrible thing that neurotypical people say to me when they find out, all of which just mean *you're really good at pretending to be "normal," but you'll never really be normal.*

Instead, the next thing out of her mouth is, "What's it like?"

We cross the street. The rain's stopped, but there's a stiff breeze that smells of salt and somehow, pine.

"I don't know what it's like to not be autistic," I say once we're on the opposite sidewalk. "I didn't talk till I was seven. But not because I couldn't. Some people can't, I guess. For me it was just . . ."

I trail off. I'm not sure there's a "just" anything about my tendency to go non-speaking. It still happens when emotions are buzzing like a tuning fork behind my eyes, as evidenced by my first encounter with Blaise.

"You don't have to tell me," Shep says. "If it makes you uncomfortable."

"I was just thinking. About what it means to say *can't*. I guess I couldn't. Sometimes I can't make words happen. Once at my old school my gym teacher yelled at me for not dressing out. I hated having to go into the girls' locker room. My teacher started yelling at me in front of everyone and it was like I just froze. I even stopped stimming."

"Is that what it's called when you tap your nails against your hand like you do?" It's an earnest question from Shep, and she's looking at me with serious eyes.

"Yeah," I say. As much as letting Shep see my book felt like stepping out on thin air and hoping for an invisible bridge, her gentle questions feel like my feet are on solid ground. Like I can breathe and not fall or scramble. "Sometimes I just shut down. My brain still works and I hear what's happening, but if I let it in, it feels like I'll explode. I'm not good with confrontation."

I don't think I've ever talked to a friend about it before. Not *her*, not anybody but Dad and the people who diagnosed me. But I like this is the second time I've wanted to talk to Shep. It feels safe.

"What changed when you were seven?" Shep asks.

We cross onto Alameda Avenue, which I know will take us all the way to Glasgow Avenue, where Dad and I live.

"Dad adopted me," I say quietly. "If it weren't for him, I'd probably still be in the foster care system."

Shep gives me a blank look.

"Stigma," I say. "People are assholes about disabilities and diagnoses. Dad always said he would have loved me no matter what."

I remember my eighth birthday party. It was before we moved to Airdrie, when we were still living in Missoula under Mount Jumbo with its giant white L for Loyola on the side of the mountain. He had the party at Caras Park by the river, with the beautiful carousel and the playground that's built like a castle with dragons everywhere. It was just us. He tied back his locs with a bright gold ribbon, and we both wore party hats, and he pushed me on the swings until his arms must have been burning but kept going because I was laughing so hard. I still remember the feeling. Like I was flying. When I got off the swing, that's when I said thank you. The first words I ever said to him.

I don't realize that I'm talking out loud until Shep stops walking and stares at me. She has tears in her eyes, and it fills me with the hot, greasy shame of being pitied when you don't want to be.

Shep swallows and looks down the street. I see her wipe her left eye with the sleeve of her shirt. "You have the best dad. Ever."

Then I realize that it's not pity that's making her cry. It's . . . longing. Envy? I don't know what to say or do to comfort her.

"My dad—you saw him. I used to show him my schoolwork, bring him stuff my abuela taught me to cook when he had me for the weekend. He just focused on every little thing I didn't do right. If I got an A–, he asked why I missed what I did, said my mom spoils me. I don't know why I always think *this* visit will be different. I guess I got my hopes up when he was nicer after my grandma died." Shep holds her breath for a moment and then lets it out in an explosive burst. "He said a tres leches cake—Abuelita's own recipe!—I made was *soggy* and threw it away. It's supposed to be like that. It's delicious."

Her expression eludes me, nameless, when I pull my gaze up to look at her. Her eyes are big, and she keeps blinking. *You have the best dad. Ever.*

I imagine her bringing things she's proud of to Carl and him just—shitting on her instead of being a dad. She keeps trying, and he keeps hurting her.

Ugh.

"My dad can be your honorary dad," I say. It sounds absurd the moment it leaves my mouth, but Shep doesn't look like she finds it ridiculous.

"Can I—" she holds up her arm, bent at the elbow. Not really knowing what she wants, I hold out my left arm. She links hers in mine and pulls me against her side.

My stomach dips the way it used to on the swings when I'd go so high that the chains would go slack for a minute as I came down.

"Let's go find out what really happened to Billy," she says.

I wonder if Shep sees herself in Billy—or maybe *wishes* she had the life he had. I wonder if she's trying to prove she can do something no one else can. Like maybe that would open the door to her dad that nothing else ever has.

A small seed of hope sprouts. Maybe if she and I solve his murder, we can help break the goddamn curse that's perched on my shoulders since Montana. Maybe it can help me figure out how to live.

I tighten my arm in hers.

· · ·

The Astoria Library looks like a fortress. It's made of gray-white stone with what looks like actual battlements until I see that those belong to the Hotel Waldorf behind it. Technically the library is the Astor Library, according to the sign, but I have no idea if anyone calls it that.

"I know we could like, google, like you did," Shep says, only unlinking our arms when we cross over the threshold of the library. "But I don't think they had the internet yet in the eighties. Plus, I've always wanted to go through newspaper archives for a real reason in a library."

The librarian seems bemused by our request, but when Shep mentions Billy Clement, the woman takes us to a study carrel and tells us that she'll bring us the newspaper archives from that month.

When she leaves, Shep turns to me and drums her fingers on the small table. "I was hoping they'd have it on microfilm or something and we could look at it on a projector."

"I think the twenty-first century has doomed our detective dreams," I tell her. I don't think we're going to find thirty-year-old DNA in my bedroom, but we might understand the whispers in the walls. Or something here.

The librarian comes back with a binder of printed-out news articles. "We get a lot of people asking about Billy Clement, so we got the articles all in one place so it wouldn't occupy the microfilm station."

Shep looks momentarily crestfallen, but she nudges my ankle with her foot under the table at the word *microfilm* as if to say, *hope lives!*

"His parents had donated a bunch of his books to the library when they split up," the librarian goes on, then points over in the direction of the children's section's bright colors. "We used to have a picture of Billy on the wall over there because he tutored some of the elementary kids in reading after school, but some tourists stole it a couple years ago."

"That's *horrible*," Shep says, scandalized.

The librarian gives us a tight-lipped smile.

"Thanks," I say.

Shep opens the binder before the librarian is five feet away. "There's not much in here."

"Is that his obituary?" Tingles swirl down my back at the sight of it. I don't know if it's possible for your hair follicles to feel numb, but that's what it feels like, looking at that high-lighted paragraph of text and Billy's yearbook picture again.

William Sorenson Clement, known as Billy to friends and family, was born in Brooklyn, New York, on March 12, 1973, and moved to Astoria in 1979. Billy attended Astoria public schools and was deeply beloved by fellow students, school faculty, and all who met him. Billy's favorite activity was art. He played trumpet in the school band and was a three-year member of the Fishermen baseball team. He passed away on Wednesday, March 22, 1989. Billy is survived by his mother, Ruth Clement, his father, Soren Clement, his grandmother, Marta Goldberg, and several cousins. Memorial services will be held this Sunday at 2 P.M. at the Hughes-Ransom Mortuary. The family has asked anyone in the community with photos of Billy to contact Ruth Clement at (503) 555-9381.

"That's weird," says Shep. She runs her finger along the last line of the obituary. "Is it normal for people to ask for photographs of their own kid?"

100

"Maybe they wanted to see him through other people's lenses," I say slowly. "People can be different around friends than they are around family."

I know this all too well, thanks to *her* and her cousins. Lee. I make myself think her name.

"This was pre-Facebook, too. My mom's never *not* on Facebook." Shep's gaze goes distant, like she's just remembered something or is trying to. "He was on the baseball team."

"That's what it says. Why?"

Shep shrugs, then shifts her shoulders as if something's poking at her spine between them. "My mom was a cheerleader. They don't cheer at baseball games like with football, but they decorate the players' lockers and other school-spirit things. I guess it feels like she would have known him better than she says."

My migraine gives me a reminder pulse of pain. I reach up and dig my fingers into the muscle at the base of my neck, which is tight like rubber stretched to breaking. It helps a little.

We skim through the rest of the binder. There's not a lot in there. There's one newspaper article about Billy's death and a note that the police questioned several students, but it doesn't identify them, because one of them was with him. Billy's parents weren't home when he died. He was about to start baseball practice for the year the next week. Move the Stars also said someone was home with him, but it was fuzzy on the details. Though the whole thing was written in third person, like a narrative, parts of it felt closer to grief. This file is so different; it's all official stuff, public record. The website felt *personal*.

When I tell Shep so, she gives me a funny look. "We forgot to ask Ronnie about finding out who owned the domain. I'll text her."

"Whoever kept that old website didn't say who was with Billy, but maybe they didn't remember. Thirty years is a long time."

Or maybe they were with him—if that website felt *so* personal, maybe it *was*.

A wave of hopelessness hits me. How are we supposed to find out what happened in a thirty-year-old murder when everyone in charge decided it was an accident?

Shep doesn't need to be psychic to know what I'm thinking.

It's only as I flip through the folder again that I realize something major isn't here. "Did they do an autopsy? The police report just says he was in his room, but"—my breath hitches with me about to say the quiet part of my *Half-Lived Lives* obsession out loud—"usually when a kid drops dead, the parents want to know exactly what the hell killed them."

"Huh. That's a good question," Shep says. I was so distracted, I didn't notice that her phone appeared in her hand. She must have texted Ronnie. "And a good point. My mother would dangle the district attorney by the ankle over a cliff if she thought there was an explanation she wasn't getting about something that happened to me. We'll look."

She sounds so certain that I almost believe her. It'd be more effective if her phone didn't buzz immediately after, making her cringe. My heart thuds—maybe it's Ronnie answering.

No such luck.

"Ugh, it's my mom. Time for my parentally mandated study time. We should go. I told her I'd be home by five and it's already four-thirty."

I nod, and the movement sends a new spasm of pain zinging down my neck. I wince.

"Headache still bothering you?"

"Yeah. I think it might be a migraine. I'll take something when I get home." It now hurts like a motherfucker, and the familiar pit forms in my stomach thinking of the time delay between leaving the library and getting to the migraine pills in my medicine cabinet at home. My vision is going blurry around the edges. Resigning myself to a night of pain, I waggle the binder at Shep. "I want to see if we can make copies of this before we go."

Turns out, enough people have asked that they keep stapled copies in a file folder at the circulation desk.

On a whim, I stop the librarian before she turns back to her inventory. "If it was an accident, why do so many people still ask?"

"Why are you asking?" She says it pointedly, her eyes darting back and forth between me and Shep behind her glasses.

"Because I don't think it was an accident. There's no mention of an autopsy. Do you know if they did one?"

She shrugs. She's young, probably only a few years older than me and Shep. She bites her lip and seems to make a decision.

"No idea. My mom went to school with him, but she doesn't know anything that's not in that file." The librarian gives us a wry smile. "For a while, Mom was game to talk to people anyway, but these days she doesn't have much energy."

"We wouldn't expect to talk to her," I say hastily, drumming my nails against my palm a few times in quick succession. "It's just that I live in Billy's old house. It's weirding me out, and I want to know what happened."

She softens at that, and I think I catch a quick lift of her eyebrow at the news that I live in that house. "People think it wasn't an accident because Billy's allergies were really severe. Mom said everyone at school had to be careful not to bring so much as a PB&J in the building, and she said he wouldn't even go in a Dairy Queen because they had chopped peanuts for sundaes. Anyway. EpiPens weren't common then. Billy would have known to be extra careful—and the school and kids all knew too. That he was only sixteen hits people, you know? When I started working, folks asked to see this file a lot, and I talked to my mom about it. She was a senior at the high school when he died. She said things were really tense at school for the rest of the year. Fights and stuff. Kids accusing their friends. Billy was popular, but my mom says he wasn't popular in the way where people were afraid of him. He was popular because people genuinely liked him. They thought he was interesting and talented. Kind. My mom says that even the jerks in her class didn't mess with him. Small towns, you know? Something bad happens, there's as many ideas of what to blame as people who live there."

Oh, I know. I know exactly how small towns react to shocking events.

"What's your name?" Shep asks the librarian.

"Kate," the librarian says. A dad with three young kids comes around the corner with stacks of books, and Kate hands me two packets of articles, clearly about to shoo us away.

"I'm Shep, and this is Sam," says Shep. "Thanks for the help."

"Good luck," Kate tells us. Me, I think, since she's looking right at me. "I hope I never find out somebody died in my house."

CHAPTER **TWELVE**

I half-expect another note taped to my door when I get home, but there's nothing. Dad's not home yet. Boot house is unoccupied.

Passing over the threshold fills me with a strange sense of relief. I drop my backpack on the floor just inside, absently heading for the bathroom. We keep migraine meds stashed in every bathroom and the car, since both Dad and I get them. Too much sensory input for me is always a trigger. But today it feels almost like something's pounding at my head like it's a door, trying to get in.

When I close the medicine cabinet, the smell of popcorn reaches my nose. I freeze, one hand still on the door. I sniff again, and the smell grows stronger.

I know we don't have any popcorn in the house because last night Dad was bemoaning the fact that he couldn't make any, and he kept saying he'd had a hankering for days. Maybe the neighbors are making some, but it feels like the smell is haunting me. First in the middle of the night and now today. I snag two pills from the bottle and down them with water from one of the paper cups Dad keeps in the bathrooms. He calls it his evil carbon footprint habit, and he gets so puffed up with defensiveness about it that I stopped poking him about it last year.

The popcorn smell fades as quickly as it came. I hear someone laughing outside the front door, footsteps on the sidewalk. A dim crinkle of plastic. Someone out for a walk with a snack, apparently. Even so, the coincidence weirds me out.

Now that I'm home, whatever defenses I had against this damn headache have deserted me to kick up their feet and play Among Us. The light in the hallway feels like it's behind my eyes. That's the crappiest part of a migraine for me. I don't have the right curtains for my room yet. I'm tempted to shut myself into a closet until Dad gets home and can hang a blanket over my windows or something.

My stomach does a nauseated turn. I swallow the sudden surge of saliva that fills my mouth. Much as the idea sounds awful, maybe eating something will help.

I put one hand on the wall and head toward the kitchen, closing my eyes against the light.

The moment I close my eyes, everything changes. There's just the red-black inside of my eyelids and the migraine's sensation of brightness beaming forward from behind.

I try to distract myself by imagining the pale green walls turning to heavy dark wood paneling at the bottom with dark blue above a strip of molding.

More than that, I imagine voices. Laughter coming from the kitchen instead of outside. Every molecule in my body yearns toward that sound with a burst of warmth. I imagine a world where Billy got to live.

I open my eyes, and the migraine is not gone.

I close them again, and no distraction will help.

My stomach heaves, and I vomit right onto the hardwood floor.

Dad chooses that exact moment to walk in. I didn't even hear him pull up.

"God, Sammy! Are you okay?"

"Migraine," I manage to get out. The air turns acrid with the smell of my own bile. I haven't eaten anything since lunch, and my stomach still churns. "Didn't see that coming."

"Shit," Dad says. He drops his hard hat with a clunk, and I hear the jingle of keys as he hangs them on a hook by the door. "That's a first."

"Yep."

I fumble my way back into the bathroom, aiming to grab some toilet paper and mop up my puke, but Dad stops me. Probably for the best. Toilet paper would just make it worse.

"I've got this, Sam," he says. "Sit down and hug the porcelain god if you need to, but let me handle the cleanup."

Dad is a saint. I lean against the cool ceramic of the toilet. My brain buzzes with blank pain until Dad's gentle voice intrudes several minutes later.

"I ordered us both some blackout curtains for our rooms," he says. "I know that doesn't help much now."

I want to close my eyes, but I'm afraid to. I can still smell my barf and now some Lysol. Less urgently, the pine from our tree in the living room. The scents activate the fault lines in my brain. Smells are bad enough for my senses when I don't have a migraine. I groan, pushing against the toilet.

Dad knows this part. "Smells?"

I don't have to answer for him to know he's right.

"I'll make you some soup later," he says.

I head upstairs and want to cry at the amount of light in my bedroom. I can't escape it. It's sneaking through the window and somehow, something inside my head shines floodlights out my eyes. Sometimes when this happens, I feel like if I look at someone, I'll blind them. Like my body is soaking up every particle of light, every photon around me, concentrating it in that bony bowl I call a skull.

I lie facedown on my queen bed. My sheets are black, partially for just such occasions. My phone buzzes, but I can't look at it. It's got to be Shep. Even though Sky and I keep saying we'll text each other, neither of us has won that game of chicken yet.

With my face wedged between two pillows, I can stare at the black fabric of my sheets instead of closing my eyes. Eventually I'll have to close them again. Not yet. The black is a relief.

Right before I finally lose consciousness, I feel a gentle, cool hand on my forehead. And then I'm out. My dreams don't wake me, though that doesn't mean they're not invasive.

After what feels like days of reliving another person's death, the colored lights in that misty world lull my mind to stillness.

. . .

I've never been hungover, but Dad tells me that the day after a bad migraine is kind of like that. It's pouring rain Friday, so he drives me to school while I lean my head on the cold window, watching droplets merge for the short drive.

I remember the hand on my forehead just as we reach the school.

"Did you come up to check on me last night?" I ask.

"Nope," Dad says. "Didn't want to bother you if you managed to conk out."

I give him a smile that feels lopsided. Maybe I had already conked out.

I don't know what else would explain it.

The school is drab and damp, with students shaking off umbrellas in the entry. It smells like wet fabric and sweat. I didn't get my homework done last night, and I have all my classes today. Shit.

Two steps inside the door, that kid Dylan stops me.

"Dude," he says. "I'm so sorry that happened to you."

"What?" At first I think he means the migraine. I texted Shep about it this morning to apologize for not answering her slew of messages last night. The migraine hangover shrouds me still, but somewhere in that quagmire is the burst of warmth that someone likes me enough to send me a slew of texts.

"What those kids did to you in Montana. That's just . . . it's wrong. Everybody here thinks you're cool. We've got your back."

My blood seems to stop short in my veins, freezing me to the floor where I stand.

Every voice in the hallway burrows directly into my brain. The piercing squeaks of sodden shoes on the laminated floor. Wet cotton smell.

Somewhere distant, part of my brain tries to tell me that Dylan's trying to be nice. Somewhere those words *we've got your back* make a home with the slew of texts from Shep. But somewhere isn't now, because he shouldn't even know about this. No one should know about this.

My vision turns fuzzy around the edges. Someone's keys jingle. Lockers opening and clanking shut. Zippers.

The zipper noise is down the hall, but I hear it right next to my ears.

I hear it again, the zip tie's *zhhhhhuuuuuuuuuuup* as it cinches tight around my neck.

I'm in a tunnel of white, lights the colors of my hair flickering through silver mist.

It's coming. It's my time, it's my time, it's my time, it's my time.

It's always my time. Always mine.

Pain blossoms in my right leg, sharp and bright like a flower made of shards of glass.

My fist hits my quad repeatedly, and everyone is looking at me with hot stares that threaten to flash boil every drop of rain still clinging to my hair and sweater. My punching bag is blocks away, hanging silent at home. My leg beats like my heart is in it.

"Shit," Dylan says, ten thousand miles away. "Shit, Sam, I'm sorry."

A hand clamps down on my shoulder. A gentle voice parts the waves of sounds and smells and heat.

"This way, Sam."

CHAPTER THIRTEEN

I can't see through the mist yet. It's too bright behind my eyes, from the echoes of the migraine or something else.

My feet move somehow, letting whoever it is lead me.

Mr. Quach.

"It's going to be okay, Sam," he says. "You're safe."

He takes me to a small, cozy office that I've never seen before. There's a murmur of voices outside the door while I sit down on a worn burgundy armchair. When he comes in, he has my backpack. I don't even remember dropping it.

"Would you like me to call your dad?" Mr. Quach pulls a chair to sit in front of me, but not too close.

My mouth opens, but no sound comes out. It's so loud in my head that I wonder that merely parting my lips doesn't rend the air with thunder. I see Dad's Alarmed Face again in my mind and do not want it to be real, here, in this room with me.

It doesn't have to be. Not yet.

Instead, there's only silence in the office.

Time passes. The bell rings. Mr. Quach makes a quiet phone call. I don't hear what he says. I tune him out as soon as it's clear he's not asking for Junius Sylvester.

I want to ask him to get Shep, but my words are gone again, retreated inward like my voice has imploded into a black hole where nothing will escape my lips. Go figure. The first time I trust someone enough to talk about the incident and talking is off the table.

The thought of all of Astoria High School knowing about the worst day of my life makes me want to walk straight into the bay and never come out. Be a fish forever, maybe. A smaller, more surreal part of me takes a grim look at the calendar on the desk where March is clearly visible. Nineteen is fast-approaching. Eighteen seems like it's sadistically letting me know it won't let me out alive.

If I can't make words about my own mess, though, maybe I can talk about something else.

"You don't want Shep trying to find out about Billy Clement," I blurt out. "Why?"

Mr. Quach looks up from some papers he's grading. For some reason, I think he knows I need a distraction.

He sighs. "My dad went here at the time," he says, which jolts me because that means his dad is the same age as Shep's parents. He must not be that much older than us—he looks young, but I have no idea. Mr. Quach goes on. "So did several faculty members. Things were intense after Billy died. A lot of fights, tempers and emotions running high. My dad got caught in the middle of it, and he *hates* that people come here like tourists looking for conspiracy theories. He and Billy played baseball together. I don't think Shep's in the conspiracy tourist category, to be clear—I think she needed something to latch on to after . . . anyway. I still don't want to encourage it. Grief is a funny thing, Sam. Like a wound that never heals over. Even after thirty years, getting poked in that spot still hurts."

When I manage to make a moment's eye contact, he gives me a look without blinking, his brown eyes earnest, and I remember we're in this room because someone poked me in my wound.

I don't know what to say after that, so I just nod, and he goes back to his grading.

A light knock sounds at the door an hour or a lifetime later. This is the first time I've gotten lost like this in a while. It's a type of catatonia, I was told. Mr. Quach doesn't seem freaked out by my silence, which is nice. I've had teachers keep pelting me with questions like machine-gun fire, as if the constant barrage will make me more likely to answer instead of less.

Mr. Quach gets up and opens the door after a moment, his mouth drooping apologetically. "I'm really sorry. Mrs. Phillips needs her office for second period."

I nod, though I suddenly feel like none of my bones fit together.

Mr. Quach holds the door for both of us as we exit. For the first time today, I actually see him. He's dressed up in slacks and a gray shirt, his hair braided down the center of his back.

A woman squeezes past us, looking at me like I might break if she speaks to me. Mrs. Phillips, I assume. I wait outside while he murmurs something to her and closes the door. I think she's the school counselor.

Mr. Quach confirms that a moment later. "If you need someone to talk to—"

"I know the drill," I tell him, finding my words at last. "You wanted to say something?"

"Mrs. Phillips talked to the principal," he says. "She says she doesn't know how people found out what was in your file, and she said that Principal Frankel will need to see you—you or your dad or both—to discuss this, but it doesn't have to be right this second, okay?"

I see Principal Frankel's face in my head again the moment she realized she'd called me Billy. I shake my head. "It's fine. She doesn't need to do anything."

"It's not fine," says Mr. Quach. "It's okay for it *not* to be fine for you. And Sam, it's not fine for the school, either."

"It's not fine, then," I tell him. Which is true. It's really not.

He opens his mouth, then closes it again. When he tries once more, his voice is very gentle. "The principal really will need to speak with you about this, Sam. Student personal information getting disseminated is a big deal, and we'll have to account for it. It doesn't have to be right now, like I said, but . . ."

I swallow. Rules, I guess. Can I make a rule where no one is allowed to perceive me but Dad and Shep? Probably not.

"Can I walk you to your next class in case we miss the bell?" Mr. Quach's voice is even gentler.

"Don't you have meetings to go to?"

"Not today," he says. "I can catch up on my prep stuff later."

I nod, uncomfortable. We walk to my locker in silence, since my chemistry book is still in it. The halls are crowded, and everyone's pretending not to be looking at me. Badly pretending.

"I don't have my homework done," I blurt out. "I got a bad migraine last night."

"Sam, it's your first week, and you're already facing a lot of stress." Mr. Quach's lips flatten out like he wishes he could say some choice words about the situation but won't, no matter if he's the cool teacher or not. "I'm sure Ms. Halethorpe will understand."

Students scurry into classrooms, draining out of the hall like the last bit of bathwater.

The bell rings, making a few stragglers quicken their pace. My locker is painted purple, which I liked at first. I spin the lock on my combination: 31-17-57.

There's a note dangling from the coat hook. Attached with a zip tie.

I jerk backward and run right into Mr. Quach.

"Whoa, Sam." He moves me aside and peers into the locker. I think I hear him say *goddamn* under his breath.

If the halls weren't totally empty aside from the two of us, I would not still be standing right now. But without the press of bodies, the noise, the sound of zippers jolting me back to that moment, I can look at this thing. Strange how it's not the sight of it that pulls the trigger, but the sound. Or maybe not strange. I didn't see what landed around my neck, only heard it. I found out what they'd used later.

He takes the zip-tied note from the locker like it might explode and gingerly unfolds it.

"What does it say?" My voice is robotic, mechanical.

"Perhaps now isn't the time—"

"Mr. Quach, please." I force myself to make eye contact with him.

He holds out the paper, looking every inch like he's doing it against his better judgment. He probably is.

I take it from him, avoiding the plastic of the zip tie. My throat burns, and the healed mark just beneath my hairline flares to life, remembering the feel of it, reconciling this hard plastic with the sensation.

Don't you just love attention.

It's printed on the same type of boring printer paper as the first note. My fingers remember it. It's normal printer paper, the kind that comes in reams of five hundred sheets and is used in just about every office in America. Same font, but since it's Times New Roman, that's not saying anything either. In my head I hear Lee's voice talking about how trans people just want attention when some news story or another about pronouns came across her feed. Logically, she—Lee—could not have done this. But I can almost feel her next to me.

"We need to call your dad now," Mr. Quach says. "And Sam, I'm a mandated reporter by state law. All teachers are. If I see anything that suggests a student is in danger, I have to report it. I think we'll need to call the police."

I nod numbly.

CHAPTER FOURTEEN

I know even before Dad gets to the school that that's it for school today. Principal Frankel gathers me, Mr. Quach, and Dad into her office as soon as he arrives, and I want to throw up again at the look on his face.

His eyes are red and puffy, and I know Dad cried in the car on the way over. I do something I haven't done in ages. I reach out and take his hand when he sits in the chair next to me. He squeezes it as if he needs to prove to himself that I'm really here.

Principal Frankel gives him a rundown of the morning, from word somehow getting out to the students to the note in my locker. Dad recoils when Mr. Quach hands him the note and he sees the zip tie.

"You don't know how the contents of my kid's personal file got disseminated to the entire school?"

Principal Frankel's face droops, like the muscles holding her neutral expression decided they needed a break. There are smudges around her eyes like she rubbed them without remembering she was wearing makeup. Her curls are pulled into a tight ponytail.

"Please believe me when I say that I am doing everything in my power to find out how this happened, Junius," she says. "I fully understand how frightening and disturbing this is. Sam, I assure you that you are welcome here, and that the faculty and staff are going to be vigilant on your behalf."

I know the principal has already read the note by now. She gestures at it like she doesn't want to touch it. I don't blame her.

"Do you know what this note means?" She asks the question softly. I feel like a deer she's trying not to spook.

"Shep and I each got another note the other day saying we're not as smart as we think we are," I say. "We thought it's because we've been trying to find out what happened to Billy Clement. Someone must have heard us talking about him or something. But I don't know now. Maybe they're connected. Maybe not."

"Sam, why didn't you tell me?" Dad doesn't drop my hand, but I feel the shock go through his arm.

"He died thirty years ago," I say. My voice sounds brittle to my own ears. I tighten my right hand against my leg where a bruise or three has already formed.

"This is the boy who died in our house," Dad says. "You've been . . . researching him?"

"Yeah."

"And it was an accident, according to the police."

"Yes." This time it's Principal Frankel's voice that sounds brittle, like iron half-rusted through. "It was ruled an accident."

Her word choice sounds very careful.

"Why would someone use that as an excuse to harass my kid?" Dad squeezes my hand, looking back and forth between Mr. Quach and the principal.

"It's likely a student thinking they're clever or pulling a prank," Mr. Quach says.

"A 'prank' that targets specific students is *not* acceptable," Principal Frankel says with force at the same time Dad says, "I left all my tolerance for pranks in Montana" every inch as vehemently.

I've only heard that tone in his voice once before, and at this moment I hope I never hear it again. He and Principal Frankel look at each other as if grateful to be understood.

"I apologize, Junius," Mr. Quach says. "That was an insensitive choice of words."

"Stop," I burst out, the word taking an exhausting amount of effort to push past the almost physical-feeling barrier in my brain. A little bit of spit flies from my lip with the burst of air and lands on the corner of the principal's desk. I hit my nails against my knee three times quick, pulling my hand back. Behind Principal Frankel, Billy's smile is bright and alive. I feel all three adults' eyes on me. "Sorry."

The silence that follows is almost worse.

"What do you need from us, Sam?" It's Mr. Quach who breaks the silence. "How can we best support you?"

It's such a—a shrink-y question that I almost laugh. What do I need? I need to not croak before March. I mean, *at all* would be preferable. I wonder if any of the kids I've read about have ever felt this way, if they ever saw it coming like a train when you're tied to the damn tracks.

"I just want to go home. And I want to come back on Monday and act like this didn't happen."

"Sam—"

"Dad." I turn to look at him, my gaze somewhere around his chin. I catch a whiff of coconut and fruit, and unlike the million other smells that have battered me today, this one gives me some bit of steadiness. "It's probably someone just being an asshole."

"What if it's not?"

I don't have to see his eyes to know how much fear is in them. "The Barrys and Lee didn't—"

"Do not tell me that they didn't mean to do what they did."

I jump at the finality in Dad's voice.

"Can we agree that it is reasonable to believe the two notes my child has received, delivered in this manner—" Dad nods at

119

the zip tie on Principal Frankel's desk with revulsion "—could be considered death threats?"

Principal Frankel and Mr. Quach exchange a long look.

When the principal speaks, it's slowly and with no small amount of trepidation. "I think that is reasonable, yes."

"The police should be here soon," Mr. Quach says.

I wish I could sink into my chair and disappear.

The rest of the day passes in a surreal blur. The cops show up within twenty minutes. I'm eighteen, and while I do have an IEP, Dad said no to the guardianship process when a bunch of sharky lawyers tried to get him to hire them to make it so he could make all my decisions indefinitely. The cops question me alone.

I've been through it before. I answer as best I can. I can't tell if they take it seriously or not. One of them, a stocky white guy with a buzz cut, rolls his eyes at the mention of Billy Clement. I ignore the gesture and tell them what they ask until they let me go.

Principal Frankel pulls Shep out of class, too. She asks if Shep still has the other notes. Shep has them in her bag and gives them to the cops as they call her mom. The look on Shep's face says her mom's going to have shit bricks before the day's over. I only see her mom from a distance because she arrives just as I'm running to the bathroom, and my first impression of Shep's mother is that she is a sleek, polished missile ready to do serious damage. Shep shoots me a tight-lipped smile over her shoulder. I duck into the bathroom before her mom can see me.

After another century of adults buzzing around, I'm spent. I pass the time staring at a cheerful poster on the wall warning against plagiarism. At three when the final bell rings, one of my new teachers knocks on the office door. I'm not always good with recognizing faces, and I don't recognize hers. Or at least I can't pair it with her name. Sometimes my life feels like one horrible game of Memory.

"Ms. Stock," Principal Frankel begins. "Can I help you?"

Ms. Stock is a short white woman in a pristine green pant suit. Her shiny dark hair falls straight to her shoulders. She stands a little too upright, holding her hands stiffly and, from the way she purses her lips before she speaks, I think she's having a very bad day.

"I believe I know how the information in Sam's file got out," she says. "It's entirely my error. During my prep period, I was familiarizing myself with Sam's IEP to better help h—uh, them with meeting their math goals. I got an urgent call from my daughter's daycare ten minutes before lunch, and I left the file out on my desk because there's barely service in my room. The file was disturbed when I returned, but I assumed I had bumped it on my way out in my haste. I should have locked my classroom. Sam, I am horribly sorry. Mr. Sylvester, I take full responsibility for this."

Dad was sitting near the edge of the room when Ms. Stock came in, but he stands up at her words. His sigh seems to originate in his toes. He reaches out a hand to Ms. Stock, and she takes it.

"A momentary lapse in judgment is quite different than someone maliciously spreading my kid's personal information around or sending them threats," he says. "Particularly when dealing with a matter with your own child. You're not accountable for someone taking information they had no right to look at."

Something shifts in the air, and I don't know what it is, but the adults all seem to relax a little.

Shep texts me when Dad finally drives us home.

What a day, dude. I hope you're okay. Mom's about to molt she's so pissed, or I'd invite myself over.

I text back, *Dad's super upset. Wouldn't be a good day anyway.*

I've never seen Mom like this, Shep says. *She keeps clacking her fingernails, and she's waiting to talk to Dad. I think she's scared. She looks like she's either going to cry or go Hulk smash on the granite countertops, and I wasn't even the one who got the brunt of this. You are. Like, what the fuck.*

Maybe she's just freaked because she knew Billy? But maybe the notes aren't even about him. They're pretty . . . vague. My reply is likely not helpful.

I just have a feeling they are, Shep says after a moment.

There's a long moment of ellipses appearing and disappearing while Shep types.

Thirty years, Sam. It's been thirty years. Whenever I've asked about him, she always brushed me off. I can feel the confusion in Shep's texts.

I got nothing, I tell her. This has been the longest Friday ever.

"I don't know if this school is going to work," Dad says, making me jump. "For this to be happening during the first week is not a good sign."

"I'll be okay," I say, hating that it could be a lie. I can't let him see me upset. Not now. "I'm sure it's just some high school jackass who thinks they're funny."

"I should have looked into the history of the house before buying it."

"Dad." It starts to rain, little sprays of mist that sound like a giant squirt bottle aimed at the windshield. "It's not like we moved into the Amityville house or anything. It's a convenient excuse to be a jerk, that's all."

"You don't have to be brave with me," Dad says.

"I'm *not*." I pause, watching the wipers squeak across the glass. I make sure the lump in my throat is gone before the next bit. "Can we just give it till my birthday? Like a trial period."

Dad pulls into the driveway and puts the car in park. "If you're getting threats, I don't want you in that school for another day, let alone two months."

"Two months isn't that long," I murmur. Long enough to piece together Billy's story, maybe. Not long enough for anything else. I see Shep's warm brown eyes in my mind.

"You really feel that hopeful about school here." It's not a question.

"They use my pronouns." My voice cracks. "A kid came up to me today to tell me how sorry he was about what happened. He said—he said they have my back."

Dad turns to stare at me. "What kid?"

"I dunno. His name's Dylan and he's kind of like a doofus but seemed like he meant it, before I got all . . ." I touch my leg where the bruise is already tender. "And Shep and Sky and Mr. Quach, I know they mean it. Principal Frankel too, probably."

The sound of another big Dad sigh fills the car. "Okay," he says. "Till your birthday. But if anybody leaves another note on our door, in your locker, on your Tumblr or TikTok, anywhere—you tell me. Immediately."

Hope balloons in my chest. It's irrational and impossible, but part of me feels like if I can just find out the truth about Billy, maybe I could stay. Maybe this life could be real, better. The way we hoped when we got here. I think of Dad dancing and trimming the tree in our still-empty house and how much I want this to be home. More Christmases rockin' around the Christmas tree to Stevies Wonder and Nicks. If I even had a TikTok, it would be one hundred percent videos of Dad's sick dance moves, for sure.

I peek at him until he looks back. "I promise."

CHAPTER FIFTEEN

The blank Tumblr post glows balefully at me. It's like it knows everything inside of me that wants to come out. The white text box and blinking cursor ooze resentment. Anger.

My fingers hit the keys with crisp taps.

Coming here was supposed to mean getting away from you.

This was a place where no one knew what you'd done but me and Dad and those who have to. A place where everyone could know me, *but where I wasn't defined by what you did.*

That's all ruined now. I don't know whose fault it is.

I started to tell someone myself, but I got interrupted. I have to believe that . . .

I stop typing. My fingers are shaking too much.

I hit Post, even though the thought isn't finished. I don't quite know what I have to believe. That I can talk to Shep? That I'm safe with Shep? That I'm safe here?

The last thought makes me laugh. As if I can be safe anywhere.

My laptop goes on the window seat behind my bed. I pull *Sam's Book of Half-Lived Lives* out from beside it. I snuggle down into the covers, tugging them up to my chin. The pages of this book are worn on the edges, and it doesn't close neatly because it's so full of pasted-in things, but that just makes it more mine. I open to a page at random and grimace. Lisbeth. She's one that gutted me for weeks when I learned about her. I have her entire journal on my Kindle and copied a few passages into this book. But it's not her I need to see right now. I flip to

Billy's page. Almost as soon as I do, a shiver washes over me, and any sleepiness is carried away on the tide.

This time, the popcorn smell is unmissable.

The buzzed part of my head feels like a startled porcupine. I sit up, shrugging off the covers and picking up my phone to text Shep, but something stops me.

When I see my face reflected in the screen of my phone, it's just me. Just Sam.

But the smell doesn't go away. I close my eyes and put the phone back down.

The air in my room feels like it felt in the principal's office today. Heavy and tense, like the electricity in the air before a lightning storm. I see blue and green waves behind my closed eyes like Margie Frankel's framed mandala, feel the snap of friction.

My stomach growls, and the smell of popcorn is so strong, I shove back the covers and get up, going to the door to open it. I make it to the top of the stairs, sniffing like some kind of blood-hound, but the smell fades as soon as I leave my bedroom.

So does the tension.

When I go back into my room, though—Billy's room—it's still there.

It feels . . . insistent.

My fingers are shaking. "What do you want?"

I don't expect an answer, and I don't get one. After a while, the sense fades with the popcorn smell, and I crawl back under the covers.

I read till my eyelids grow heavy, over and over, everything I have about Billy, then push the book under the other pillow on the bed.

When I close my eyes, sleep sneaks up faster than I expect.

There's a strange comfort in the silver-white mist and the undulating pastel of the aurora that lights it from all sides and none. No place on Earth is more mine than this.

Is this where I'll go when I die?

The thought passes, its words almost visible to me like the Caterpillar's hookah smoke in Wonderland.

Billy stands next to a girl, places a hand on her shoulder like he gets it, he understands. Like there's something he wants *me* to understand. Their hands are dirty, like they've been working in the field or the garden. There's a trowel beside him. Billy looks right at me. For the barest moment, his hand tightens on the girl's shoulder. She's a young girl with curly hair whose face I cannot quite make out.

I sit straight up in bed. It's four in the morning, and I can still smell dirt and mulch and popcorn. My heart sounds like an approaching train in my chest, and I breathe in deep.

There have been plenty of times I thought I was crazy.

Somehow even more than the smell of cigarette smoke in our basement, more than Billy Clement's face in reflective glass— the look on Billy's face roots me in myself.

I've never had this before, this clarity. My researched kids were lightning strikes, whispers in the mist. There and not, all at once.

It's like living in this room where one of them died is bringing *me* back to life.

Their lives.

Billy is *present*, and some part of me still weaves fury from the injustice of his truncated life.

My phone buzzes. I reach for it, expecting Shep, but it's Sky. The first time he's texted me. I blink away the remaining sleepy eeriness as best I can.

Yo, I know you're asleep, but Shep and I have been talking, and she said I should loop you in, because she really would rather be talking to you *about Billy, but I was conveniently awake. :P*

There's a pause while I digest that, and a message from Shep pops up. Group message.

I'm not going to dignify that *with an answer, Sky. It's not a secret that I'm interested in this shit,* she says. Another ellipsis and then, *Like everybody knows. Sky said something and I think he's right.*

Idk if I'm right. (Sky)

You're RIGHT. (Shep)

My thumbs hover over the keyboard on my iPhone, and after a moment of hesitation, I switch to the Messages app on my MacBook.

I'm awake. Couldn't sleep. What did you think, Sky?

Pause. Long pause. It's like Sky or Shep keeps writing and then stopping and starting again, though I can't see the ellipsis in the group chat to know if I'm right.

It wouldn't make sense for those notes to be from whoever killed Billy. Like wtf, really. Some forty-something is floating around threatening high school kids? Or someone even older? I guess it's possible, but combined with whoever told the school about your personal trauma, it seems too petty, Sky says.

I take that in.

Could be someone who knows what happened, I say.

HA. That's what I said! (Shep)

I mean, I guess (Sky)

Could it have been Dylan? People said he was talking to you right before everything (Shep)

128

He was the first person to come right up to me. But I don't get the sense that he's that . . . forward-thinking. I really don't. Even if he was bothered by me calling him out in the hallway, I can't see him being enough of a manipulative mastermind to act this convincingly. If it was him, bravo.

Another long pause.

ANYWAY basically I think somebody's pissed off that you're all tattooed and popular one week into school. This is the most excitement Astoria High has seen all year. (Sky)

Sky's probably right. Somebody probably just wants a piece of that sweet Sam Sylvester fame. (Shep)

Lord almighty (Sky)

It's almost five in the morning now. We make plans for both of them to come over in the afternoon, even though I think Shep's mom might chain her to the doorjamb when she tries to leave the house.

It's a long while before I drift back to sleep, but what finally relaxes me enough to close my eyes is a sensation I didn't make. It's coming from someone (or someones) long dead, and I can't quite name it. It feels like *hopecomfortjubilancesafety*. It's a little like the way I felt when I met Dad for the first time. Maybe it is me. Maybe it's Shep and Sky.

It's like a lullaby.

I let it rock me back to sleep.

CHAPTER SIXTEEN

Dad is so excited at the prospect of Shep and Sky coming over that he magically transforms into Betty Crocker, fully in over-compensate mode. He busts out his bunny-patterned apron when I roll downstairs at noon with my hair sticking up in twelve different directions, and I stumble into my coffee while he raids the cupboards for ingredients. He makes rainbow cakes with fruit fillings. He also starts on a pan of chicken enchiladas, which makes the competing smells a little less appealing. Vanilla–green chili isn't my favorite combo.

While he works, I talk to him about Billy Clement, just the basics. I let him think my sources are the news articles and obituaries I've only just read (on top of the big Astoria paper, there were also a bunch from Billy's friends in the high school paper, and I still haven't been able to find anything about an autopsy). Dad listens, and when the sun slices through the clouds and beams into the kitchen, he pulls back the blinds to the sliding glass doors that lead onto a little back porch.

"Nice little yard," he says. "Come springtime, I'll put you to work pulling weeds so we can garden it up right. I was out there a little earlier turning over some topsoil to see about putting in a flower bed and found something."

I've been fine all morning (well, afternoon), but this stops my heart for a moment. I remember Billy in my dream, which had faded from my memory but now returns with sudden force. I look outside as if just that will answer my questions.

Dad gives me a wry look. "Gardening that appealing, eh?"

"I'm happy to weed it," I say without thinking, still staring past Dad into the yard. "You found something buried back there?"

"I was going to wait till your friends get here to show you. Thought it'd be a bonding experience." Then he grimaces. "I hope it's not somebody's pet."

Ew. I hope not too. But it could be something of Billy's. What would he bury, though?

"Do you like Bowie?" I ask Dad suddenly, thinking of Billy dressed up like him.

"I was always more of a Freddie Mercury fan, but their collaboration of 'Under Pressure' is pretty awesome."

"Freddie is a god," I agree. "But I haven't heard that one."

Dad feigns faintness. "Excuse me? A child of mine hasn't heard 'Under Pressure'? Impossible. You'll recognize the bassline, since Vanilla Ice lifted it pretty much intact for 'Ice Ice Baby.'"

I wince. "Eesh." But after a beat, my foggy, half-asleep brain remembers him singing that bassline when we opened up the shelves.

"To the Spotify!" Dad reaches for his phone, not noticing the way I rub my arms as if I can erase the sudden flurry of goosebumps that have appeared.

"Can you play it for me in a minute? I kind of want to poke around the yard." *Billy wants me to go out there*. The thought invades me. It makes me want to laugh because it's absurd. Last night feels like that time I had pneumonia and was lost in the fever. Smells in my room and swirls of color, strange dreams and group texts at four in the morning. Delirious.

And yet. When Dad nods and makes a shooing motion with his hand, I grab a pair of his flip-flops and nudge the security bar up so I can unlock the sliding door.

I haven't been out here, but Dad has. His gardening tools are stacked up on the side of the porch, which is covered. I can see a patch by the fence where he was digging about. He'd mulched it already for the oncoming spring. The sound of waves reaches me, and next door, the palm fronds sway in the breeze, sparkling from the remaining raindrops.

Before I close the door, I call in to Dad, "We need some patio furniture. It's nice out here."

"Already on the to-do list," he says, talking through the oven mitt on his hand like it's a puppet.

I slide the glass door shut.

The sight of the overturned earth drains the moisture from my mouth as I get closer. Shep and Sky are supposed to be here soon. They said they'd be here by two or two-thirty, but I can't go back in yet. They could still be passed out. Belatedly, I recognize Dad's overly busy energy as anxiety. I don't think he wants to cast suspicion on my new friends, but he's definitely being very . . . extra.

I don't know how to make him feel better.

I pick up Dad's faithful trowel, then put it back down. It looks just like Billy's in the dream.

The rational part of my mind says that of course it does. It's Dad's. I've seen it heaps of times. It's probably the platonic ideal of a trowel for my subconscious brain.

But, at the same time, something whispers that there's some other reason.

There are a few short steps that go down to the yard from the porch.

No trees yet. Whoever owned this place last was a landscaping minimalist. Maybe they just rented it out. There's only the weed-stricken mulch bed at the back near the privacy fence, weeds all scraggly and lank on a piece of Visqueen.

Now that I'm here, I don't know what to do. What did I think was going to happen, that just seeing this spot where Dad dug something up that is hopefully not a decayed cat would magically tell me who killed Billy?

The weirdest thing is that I think whatever it is *isn't* a cat or a ferret or anything dead. I just . . . feel it. Intuition's a weird thing. That's what Shep called it, right? Really it's just a guess or a hope, I suppose.

The image of the girl in my dream pops into my mind. Margarie Frankel? I think it must have been, even if I couldn't see her face.

Maybe I can hold on to Billy's memory long enough to really find out what happened to him. Maybe I can sketch him out into my mind so he's as real as I am.

"Breathe, Sammy," I say out loud. My hands shake, and the air feels colder around me. Not because Billy's a ghost. He's not. But this—

A knock sounds at the sliding glass door. Dad. It must be.

A presence behind me makes me turn. I'm only expecting Dad, but he's staring down at me flanked by both Shep and Sky.

"Well, hell," he says. "You're gonna blow the surprise."

"Dad dug something up in the yard," I say, then, remembering how polite humans do, add a belated, "Hi, guys."

"Holy sh—crap." Shep shoots a guilty look at Dad. Sky just stares.

Dad sighs, then goes over to the side of the porch, where there's a dirt-covered rectangle that was out of sight when I came out. It's a metal box, like those money boxes we used to use at school fundraisers.

I'm aware that my mouth is hanging open a little like a surprised bird, but it's not surprise that pulls my lips back from my teeth in a wide grin. There's a surge of ineffable joy and pain that causes tears to drip from my eyes onto the knees of my jeans. This has to be about Billy. It has to be.

"You should go to the beach with my uncle, Mr. Sy—I mean Junius," Sky says breezily after a long moment. "He'd probably pay you a cut of anything you find. I think you're more effective than a metal detector."

It breaks the tension, and laughs tumble out of our mouths.

Dad motions for me to take the box, but I can't. Not yet. He meets my eyes with a question in his gaze.

It's one I can't answer. Not yet.

And oddly, when I take the box from him, he seems reluctant to let it go.

My fingers vibrate on the old metal.

CHAPTER SEVENTEEN

We all seem to know the box has to do with Billy Clement, but none of us say it out loud. Instead, I clean it off in the basement's laundry sink as carefully as I can with a damp rag, drying away stray drips with Sky and Shep watching and cracking jokes about sending Dad after the Holy Grail or the Holy Hand Grenade or something.

It's a strange feeling, holding the box. It's as if space and time have split open and I'm in two places at once. The box is old and new, rusted and pristine. My fingers are mine—long fingers and square nails—and they're not. They're shorter and nail-bitten. Whoever kept that website wrote that he used to bite his nails. Not for the first time, I wonder if it was his mom or dad memorializing him there, still hoping for answers. In my research, I discovered that they split after Billy's death. In all the stories I've found, that's one common thread. Mr. Quach said his death tore the town apart. His own dad knew Billy.

Upstairs, cumin and chili chicken have won the war against vanilla cake. Down here in the basement, I smell popcorn.

"It's like a message straight from the eighties," Shep mutters. "I can almost smell the Jiffy Pop."

My head snaps to her, and she starts.

I can't help but nod.

"You're both full of shit," Sky says. "All I smell is basement. And rust."

"Don't tell Dad that. He'll be horribly offended," I say.

"Are you going to open it or just stand here with it dripping on the floor?" Shep waggles her fingers at me.

"It might not even have anything to do with Billy," says Sky.

"It has to," Shep and I both say at the same time. A flush warms my cheeks, and I see it mirrored in hers.

I'm not used to being on the same wavelength as anyone else, even Dad, really. I'm tuned to give off and receive a different frequency than most people. Dad just knows how to change his channel to pick mine up. (*That* one is his metaphor, not mine.)

Sky puts his hands up as if to say we've both careened off the logic train track.

We head back upstairs, me in the lead. I can feel Shep behind me like the glow of a campfire. I have the urge to stop, turn around, and kiss her.

The feeling is so new that it almost tips me off balance to fall down the stairs.

I get to the top, skipping two steps to make sure I don't plunge backward.

"If we're eating this late, does it make it tea time?" Dad affects an English accent, placing the pan of enchiladas on the table. It's set for four. That might be the most he's ever gotten to cook for since he got me.

"I think the enchiladas are a little untraditional," says Sky. "But they look bangin'."

"You kids with your slang." Dad grins.

"Is there anything you don't do?" Shep pulls up the chair next to mine and sits.

When I sit down too, I can feel her warmth. I don't know what to do with the box, so I keep it in my hands.

"Knit." Dad answers Shep's question and plunks down next to Sky. He looks at me. "My enchiladas are gonna get cold, aren't they?"

"We can open it quickly," I say. I scoot back from the table so I don't get rust on my plate. The catch on the box still works, somehow. When it falls off in my hand, that answers the somehow.

"It could be rusted shut," Sky says.

The top comes off easily.

Shep leans closer to me. At first all I see in the box is plastic.

"Smart," says Dad. He peers over the table. "In this climate especially."

Smart indeed. Whatever's in here is buried in layers of ziplock bags. Moisture has seeped through the first couple of bags, but the third one is dry. So's the fourth and fifth.

By the time I get past the damp plastic bags, images start to take shape. There's a rectangular plastic thing and what looks like an envelope.

I pry open the zipper on the fifth bag, pulling out the contents. MESSAGE TO THE FUTURE!

The envelope bears giant all caps. By now Sky and Dad have gotten up to see better.

My head jerks up to look at Shep. "Maybe you are psychic."

"Oh, how precious," Sky says.

I open the envelope. The first thing out is a picture of Billy and a girl with dark curls who I'd bet money on being Margarie Frankel. On the back, sure enough. Tidy cursive says, *Billy and Margie, 1987*. Again I see him in my dream, that brief flash of him with his hand clamped down on her shoulder. Now they're both staring up at me. It had to be her.

"Two years before he died," Shep breathes.

I meet Dad's eyes, and he gives me a look I can't decipher. After a moment, he nods at the bag. "Give me that cassette."

I pull out the rectangular plastic thing. It's David Bowie's *Fame and Fashion*.

"Nineteen eighty-four," I say without thinking. "First song is 'Space Oddity.' Billy's favorite."

Dad gives me that look again, and I hand him the cassette. The track list and date aren't on the front. I'm just that much of an obsessive freak. My face starts to turn red again. I can feel it.

"Wow." Sky chews on one long finger, teeth worrying at a hangnail. "My mom would kill for that. When Bowie died, she bawled for a week."

"So that's a cassette tape. That really plays music?" Shep looks at it dubiously.

"Oh, honey," says Dad. "Child."

For a second I think he's going to pat Shep on the head, and for a weirder second, I think she wouldn't be pissed. She grins at Dad.

There's another cassette in there. When I pull it out, I can't help but grin at Dad too. "Looks like Billy and Margie knew the pantheon."

This one's Queen's *Hot Space*. I flip it over, already guessing what I'll see on the back. Sure enough, "Under Pressure" is the last song on this one.

"Bless these kids. What taste." Dad wipes away a fake tear.

There's a letter in the envelope that I'm afraid to unfold.

"Can I?" Shep looks at me, eyes eager.

"Go for it."

She takes the paper and unfolds it. Her fingers tremble on the letter.

"Dear future dwellers," she reads. "While we don't think it's really that likely that anybody will forget the magic that is David Bowie or Queen, we want to record for the world that we, William Sorensen Clement and Margarie Sarah Frankel, recognized their rock."

Shep pauses.

"The handwriting changes," she says, then continues reading. "I used to hate my dad's music. He'd tell me it was *history in the making* or something, and I'd roll my eyes. But then one day he put on *A Night at the Opera,* and I heard 'Bohemian Rhapsody' for the first time. That was it. I was done. Everything about it was rad. I listened to that album so much that Dad had to replace the LP. He gave me this cassette of *Hot Space* for Chanukah because I was jealous of Billy's copy."

"That must be Margie," Sky says, dropping his hand to his lap. "I mean, Principal Frankel. Wow."

"The writing changes back." Shep runs her fingers across it. "I always thought I was an alien. Every time I looked up at the sky, I wished I could be up there. I watched the *Challenger* explode and my first thought was, *At least they got to die doing the one thing they had to do.* I wish they'd gotten to go to space. I always thought I wasn't meant for here, you know? When I found Bowie, I realized I wasn't the only one."

"Sam," Dad says.

I'm still in my chair holding the photo of Billy and Margie, and Sky is staring at me. So is Shep.

"What? Why are you all looking at me?"

"You were reading along with Shep word for word," Dad says softly.

My breath leaves me.

The letter's upside down to my view, not that it affects my ability to read it, but I didn't even realize what I was doing. Shep grabs my hand and squeezes it, then doesn't let go.

"Maybe we should eat," I say. I don't know what else to do. My face is hotter than the enchiladas, which are still steaming.

"Yeah, let's eat," Dad says.

Sky gathers up the items and stacks them carefully on the breakfast bar. Dad sets the empty box on the ziplock bags so the rust doesn't stain anything and grabs his Bluetooth speaker. He puts the Bowie album on Spotify, but despite the excitement, I can barely taste my enchiladas.

. . .

Sky and Shep stay till about six, and when they leave with furtive *TEXT US* looks, Dad shuts the door behind them and turns to face me.

"I think we need to talk," he says.

"That is never a good sentence." I honestly don't know if he's going to talk to me about Shep holding my hand or about the box.

Dad beckons me into the living room, where I've spent almost no time so far living in this house. Sitting on the big poufy sofa (it's eggplant purple, and Dad insists I should call it *aubergine*), I wait, hating the anticipation.

He sits at the other end, one leg up on the cushion. His socks don't match. One has penguins and the other has little poo emojis. I think he saves the poop ones for weekends on purpose.

"I don't even know where to start," he says after a beat.

"I'm not dating Shep," I blurt out. *Yet*, a little voice in my head points out. I don't know if there's a *yet* when I've probably got an expiration date fast approaching. But I want there to be, I think. And just because someone tried to kill me two years ago doesn't mean I'll end up like all the kids I've studied so carefully. It doesn't. Right?

Dad raises both eyebrows. His forehead wrinkles with perfect symmetry. Nobody's skin does that, but Dad's does. "Sammy."

"What? I'm not."

"You know I'm Team Sam and will ship you with whoever you want to date." The word *ship* sounds weird in his mouth. When he closes his eyes for a moment, I realize he didn't want to talk about me holding hands with Shep. "You seemed pretty . . . tranced out by that letter. What's going on with you?"

This is it. The question he's never asked me.

"It's not every day you find a time capsule from a dead person."

"That's not an answer."

"You won't like the answer," I say to him bluntly. My therapist in Portland used to tell me to listen to my body. Right now it feels like someone's filled my veins with liquified aluminum. My mouth tastes tinny. I don't know what emotion this is.

"Try me."

I sit silently at the end of the sofa. The sun's long since set, and the sky is darkening outside the window.

"Okay," Dad says. "I'll start with my own empirical experience of Sam Sylvester. When you were twelve, I came into the living room in Missoula to find you flipping through a library book about cancer. The kind of book a doctor might read."

I don't remember that, not that precise experience of researching cancer, though it might have been after Dad told me how his mom died. Others, sure. I looked up anything I thought could kill me, everything from falling durian fruits to meningitis to spontaneous human combustion. I don't even remember what first sparked my need to know. Slowly I push my gaze upward

141

until I'm looking Dad in the eyes. I can't hold his gaze for long, and I drop it back down to the back of the sofa where he's leaning one arm.

"When you were ten, we were at MacKenzie River Pizza one night for dinner and you started going on about someone called Màiri MacKenzie who you said came to Missoula from Scotland, and then you spent the rest of dinner telling me about the intricacies of the Highland Clearances." Dad snorts at that. "I could list a dozen other things, Sam. But you figured out there were bookshelves behind the walls in this place just by tapping on a wall, and then you seem to know just about everything about the kid who died in this house—"

"In my room." I seldom interrupt anybody, but I need him to know this.

"In your room." Dad goes still. "Sammy. Billy Clement died in your bedroom?"

Whatever liquid metal was in my veins seems to have turned brittle. Am I really going to try and tell Dad about Shep and me trying to solve a murder? How can I possibly tell Dad about this?

The answer is that I can't.

So I try what Shep did. "Sometimes I just . . . know things."

I don't know if that's any less weird than me confessing that I've spent most of my life learning about other people's deaths.

"I *know* that, Sammy. But what I saw today was something else."

"I don't know how my brain works." That much is true.

I could maybe tell him the truth. But people get weird about death, and if I tell Dad about my book, it'll be too much. It was bad enough before I almost died. Now he'll think I'm obsessing about death.

Dad looks far from satisfied. The corner of his mouth droops like he's thinking hard but not coming up with anything useful—at least nothing that he wants to share right now.

The thing he doesn't do, though, is tell me he doesn't believe me. Maybe he doesn't know if he believes me or not. Maybe he wants to believe.

This face, this Dad face—I have no name for it.

Finally, he nods. "Okay. Just tell me one thing, and then I'm going to get another piece of cake."

"What?"

"Are you okay in that bedroom?"

I look Dad in the eye and tell another full truth. "It's my room, Dad. And I'm not afraid of the dead."

CHAPTER EIGHTEEN

I'm not afraid of death because the living are much scarier, even the ones who aren't trying to kill you.

Walking into school Monday is made worse by the fact that dreading it kept me up all night. Like my first day, Sky and Shep flank me as I walk into the building. I'm not sure what's worse: being stared at or having people hurriedly look away when they see me coming. Shep is quiet, looking around as if she is still half-asleep.

"So much for my cool-kid status," I mutter to Sky.

"Principal Frankel made an announcement on Friday," he says. "After you left, during seventh period. She didn't mention you exactly, but she said that the contents of a student's personal file had been shared inappropriately."

"Oh."

"If it helps, Ronnie said she'll track down the owner of that website you two were talking about. Shep told me," Sky adds. He leans to his left to bump his shoulder into Shep's, and that gets her attention because her eyes light up. He gives her a long-suffering smile and ruffles her hair, to which she responds by rolling her eyes and elbowing him in the arm before he heads off down the hall.

I'm still not used to the school's schedule. Shep and I have English first because it's a Purple day, and I remember too late that I was supposed to read the first section of *Call of the Wild*. Ronnie is in this class, too, though she's plunked in the front row and so glued to a book that she doesn't see us come in. I wonder what Ronnie will find out. Maybe she'd have an idea about how we could find out if there was an autopsy, though that's probably less website-y and more bureaucracy.

There's an unease in the classroom that feels like strands of spun glass that could shatter into jagged points at any moment. I can't help but feel like it's my presence spinning those swirls.

I settle in next to Shep and pull my book out of my backpack. I'm not a very fast reader. I could open it and try to get through some more, but no doubt Mr. Duncan will notice.

He gets through the morning announcements, and because Purple days are short class period days, plunges right into the book.

"Can someone give me a first impression about this section, 'Into the Primitive'?" Mr. Duncan is a tall man with pale skin and limbs that look like the pulled saltwater taffy down at the beach. He leans against his desk when he talks, long fingers curled around the lip of the desk.

"Yeah, Shep's Buck's *mom*," a white guy in a green Under Armour shirt calls out. A wave of giggles goes through the room and someone woofs. Brent, I think.

Shep slumps in her chair, spots of pink forming on her cheeks. It's like someone's yanked her out of a dead sleep to find a nightmare in real life—she looks exhausted, angry, and I think I should ask about what's been up at home, because that look isn't just about this jackass of a bully. I'm not good at remembering to ask questions. I hope she doesn't think I don't care.

Since I can't do anything about that right now, I meet the guy's eyes, and he looks back. I don't blink. I hate every second that passes, but for once it's someone else who breaks eye contact. The rest of the class is silent.

"Inappropriate, Brent," Mr. Duncan says belatedly.

My hand goes up, seemingly of its own accord. I don't have many superpowers, but aside from supersensitive senses, I am good at connecting things other people don't.

"Sam?" Mr. Duncan's eyes transition from narrow slits to wide surprise. "Did you have a first impression about the book?"

It's about safety. That much, I got. Why I'm about to say it out loud, I don't know. Then I look at Shep, and I do know. She has retreated into herself, as if her chair might agree to swallow her if she sinks low enough. I can use my connection superpowers to distract the class from their asinine bullying.

"It's about safety," I say, staring at a point on the white board beyond Mr. Duncan's shoulder. "The illusion of it. Buck had a privileged life in Santa Clara. He was proud of that life, even though he didn't do anything to earn it. The opening of the book is about how quickly that can change, and Buck discovers that he was only ever safe because of a structure that depended on others enforcing it. When the people around him stopped creating that structure, he wasn't safe anymore."

I hear a sharp intake of breath somewhere in the room, but I can't tell who it comes from.

Mr. Duncan stands up straight. "Very astute, Sam," he says. "That's an excellent description of these opening pages. It's a powerful thought, that safety is always an illusion. Do you have anything to add?"

This time I want to speak. My voice sounds too loud in the quiet classroom, and even though people aren't watching me, I can almost feel them listening. "Safety is a social contract," I say. "We have these unspoken agreements not to hurt each other, which is why we're able to live in cities and huge groups. *Some* people break those contracts and agreements." I can't help my glance in Brent's direction, and from the shuffle of movement I hear around me, it didn't go unnoticed. "But even though we know that, most of us just try to live as if it won't happen or can't happen to us. Either out of optimism or denial."

"Excellent," says Mr. Duncan. "Now—"

"Buck gets doomed to be an outsider," I say, thinking of Billy dying in his own bedroom, unsafe in his safest place. Everyone else reeling from the profound discomfort of such knowledge. Margie Frankel growing up next door, having spent who knows how much time in that room. That room is now mine. And I'm the outsider here. "The same way people are in our world when they experience something horrible. When you see how fragile the illusion of safety really is, other people don't always believe you. It makes them uncomfortable to confront even the possibility of danger."

Now everyone *is* looking at me. I know exactly where I am and how those words apply to what just happened to me.

"Daaayum," Brent mutters from across the room. "Getting real in here."

The glass threads in the room shatter, and suddenly I'm the new kid again and I've just talked over the teacher. I can't make myself small enough in my desk. My neck feels hot. I think my distraction worked a little too well. My neck's probably covered in splotches. Shep's looking at me, but I can't turn to look back.

The discussion goes on a little longer, with a few others chiming in, but eventually Mr. Duncan asks us to quietly journal until the end of class.

My fingers don't want to hold my pen over the paper. Each time I try to press the tip of it down, something stops me. It's not that I don't know what to say. I'm afraid of whatever words might come out.

I haven't reread all of the first section of *Call of the Wild*.

I don't know where my story ends and Billy's begins, but I'm starting to see why I can't push his mystery away.

. . .

Chemistry passes without incident, thank everything.

There's a brief break afterward, and before I can wave to Shep, somebody approaches me. Aidan again.

"Hi," I say warily.

"Hey," says Aidan. "How's it going?"

I really hate small talk. "Fine," I say. My mental script kicks in. I'm a beat too late, letting an awkward pause take shape before I get out a "You?"

"All good," he says. "People being okay to you?"

"I guess." Students are mostly scurrying around, trying to pee or get a drink before Advisory. "Do people not like Shep?"

I don't know what makes me ask it, but the sound of somebody *woof-woofing* like a dog won't leave my brain.

"She's a little weird, but I think she's cool," Aidan says, sounding perplexed, like he's never given two seconds thought to Shep before now. He's about an inch taller than I am and wearing an AHS hoodie, and he shifts his shoulders and pulls the sleeves down over his palms.

"I'm a little weird," I say too loudly.

A couple people turn and look. A locker bangs down the hall.

Aidan shifts his feet. "I dunno, Sam. Everybody here is a little scared of you, but in a good way."

"I don't want people to be scared of me. I'm just a person."

"You've got tattoos and punk hair and you're built like you came from Themyscira," Aidan says as if this should all be obvious. It is. Obviously. "Anyway, I just came over to say that I

148

think what that person did was shitty. Your business is your business, and nobody should be spreading your personal business around. If I hear anyone talking about it, I'll tell them to shut up."

"Uh, thanks."

"Don't worry about it. It's the right thing to do."

With that, Aidan gives me a nod and starts to walk away. It's only then I see that his shoes are worn almost all the way through the soles. His jeans are similarly tattered, though the average eye would probably see their distress as fashion, not a sign of a lack of fortune. I swallow around the sudden dryness in my throat, not sure if I'm more confused or touched.

The only person I've ever inspired protectiveness in is Dad. And now Shep, but she's quickly become a close friend. It's weird coming from a relative stranger. Two, really, if I count Dylan.

I make my way to Advisory or Tutorial or whatever it's called today, a small pang in my chest for missing the chance to see Shep.

A tiny redhead blocks my path into the classroom. Blaise. Even though there's an open hall behind me, she and her cloud of rose perfume are standing between me and where I'm supposed to be in approximately seventy seconds. She's two for two in making our brief encounters uncomfortable. She behaves like everyone else is simply in her orbit and she's the gravitational power in the solar system.

"Hey," she says.

"Hi," I say. "Can I get into the room?"

"Sam Sylvester." She says this thoughtfully, though I can barely hear her over the smell of that perfume.

The smell is floral and piercing.

"No shit." The words fall out of my mouth, too loud, and I suppress a guilty flinch, but Mrs. Hernández is talking to someone inside and doesn't notice.

"Wow, rude."

"You're blocking the door," I point out. "And apparently the entire school knows about the worst day of my life, so if you're stopping me to ask me about it, the definition of rude is less me and more you."

Blaise gives me that dazzling white smile and moves to the side with a flourish. "No doubt Sky's told you all about me."

"Barely mentioned you," I say, which is technically true. It was just a very efficient mention.

I don't know what makes me do it, but Blaise seems determined to hit every button I have.

I walk past her, confident in the space I take up. She doesn't flinch back, and my shoulder passes within an inch of her chest.

I pick out a desk near the window and sit, feeling like my joints have all turned to metal.

The bell rings a second later, and Mrs. Hernández waves an impatient hand at us to do attendance.

Blaise watches me for the whole ten minutes we're there today.

I've never been so excited to flee to a math class in my life.

CHAPTER NINETEEN

"I had another run-in with Blaise," I hurriedly whisper to Shep as we hurry to Mr. Quach's room for the weekly Rainbow Island lunch meeting. My shaky fingers still smell like sawdust from woodshop, and that scent is strangely comforting, if bittersweet. Reminds me of Dad working in his own shop back in Montana. It used to be his haven.

"Oh, god," says Shep. She rubs her eyes. "What did she do?"

"Blocked my way into Advisory." I tap my nails into my palm. "Then called me rude. Which I was, but she started it."

Sky is already in the room with a gaggle of others I vaguely recognize. Shep tells him what happened while I pull desks together for us to sit at.

"Sounds like classic Blaise," Sky says. He slaps pronoun stickers on each of our shoulders, mouth pinched on one side. "I take full credit for letting her pull the wool over my eyes when I dated her."

"She used to come to the Rainbow Island meetings," Shep says.

"Who?" a short kid with buzzed hair asks. They look young, like freshman young. They're also wearing a *they/them* sticker. They look at me with something like awe, and I give them a wobbly smile.

"Blaise," Shep says, the B in the name sounding like a small explosion.

"She's never talked to me," the kid says.

"Count your lucky stars, my dear," Sky tells them. "Stay off her radar if you can."

Mr. Quach comes in with a trayful of salad. Two more students follow on his heels and shut the door. One of them is Ronnie. She gives me a nod, and her friend's—girlfriend's?—face takes on a curious light, though they're in quiet conversation with each other. They each take *she/her* stickers out of the basket on Mr. Quach's desk and sit on the sofa in the back of the room, holding hands. Girlfriend.

"Most of you have met Sam already," Mr. Quach says when everyone's settled. "I probably don't have to say it, but if you've heard anything about Sam's personal past, don't bring it up in here. This is a neutral zone. We don't out people."

Everyone chitchats while they eat. I find out that the freshman's name is Aerie, which I can't help but love. They ask me about my hair and if they can touch it. I don't think I'd say yes to that if it was anybody else asking, but Aerie is kind of adorable and looks like a smaller, shyer version of me. Though I don't think anyone's ever called me adorable.

No sooner does Aerie put a tentative hand to my wavy curtain of aurora-colored hair than the door opens, and Blaise breezes in, smelling of freshly applied rose perfume. Way too much of it. Ronnie looks like she is halfway to getting up, but she sits right back down at the sight of Blaise. In my peripheral vision, Shep's face looks as though she's just made eye contact with Medusa.

"Sorry I'm late," Blaise says, smiling brightly around the room. Her lip gives a twitch when she sees Aerie's fingers in my hair, and the freshman drops their hand as if my hair set it on fire.

Agonized, I look to Shep, who now looks half a step away from throwing her desk at Blaise.

Sky's Adam's apple bobs, and his mouth falls open a little bit. I half expect venom to drip over his lips.

"Oh, *hell no*," Ronnie's apparent girlfriend says. Ronnie looks as if her girlfriend took the words right out of her mouth.

"What? I'm an ally," Blaise says and pulls a desk over near Mr. Quach with a screech of metal on laminate.

"Yeah, bi-erasure and spreading rumors really helps the cause," the girl says. "Super classy way to deal with getting dumped."

"Easy, Jax," Mr. Quach says. He squints like the light in the room has turned too bright. I don't blame him. I want to shrink down in my chair and melt into the floor.

"I'm just here to listen and support," says Blaise, sounding wounded. She lets a lock of perfect red hair fall down in front of her face, peering out from behind it.

"Yeah, listen so you can gain ammunition," somebody mutters.

The rest of lunch goes downhill from there. When the bell finally rings, Blaise waggles her fingers at me. "See you in Spanish, Sam!"

I can't answer that. How in Satan's knickers does she know my schedule? I don't remember seeing her last week in Spanish.

Blaise blows Sky a kiss and practically waltzes out of the room. That perfume is going to linger here. Ugh.

"Mr. Q, can't you make sure she doesn't come to these things?" Shep asks, anger dripping from every consonant. She flexes her hands as if fighting against the urge to make them into fists. "Neutral zone, my ass. Nobody's ever going to feel like they can talk again if she shows up."

There's a murmur of agreement.

"I can't kick her out," Mr. Quach says with a grimace. "I'm sorry, Shep."

Shep kicks the desk. Its foot squawks on the floor, somehow louder than the sound Blaise's desk made. Aerie jumps.

"Shep," Mr. Quach begins, but Shep waves him off and throws the door open. It slams behind her, and everyone jumps.

I want to go after her. The impulse surprises me. I don't know if she wants me to go after her, so I look at Sky.

He sighs. "Blaise was Shep's best friend before I broke up with her," he says. "I mean, besides me. I think she felt more devastated than I did, but after her grandmother died, she got even angrier."

That makes my heart want to fold in on itself.

"I get it," I say.

Dad yanked me out of school pretty fast after what happened in Montana, but he couldn't just tell me to stop going immediately and forever before we figured out our next move. After a couple of weeks of excused absences, I had to go back to class, see the Barry boys and *her*—Lee—every day.

"Yeah, I think you do," Sky says. He looks at me for an uncomfortably long moment. "Seeing Shep so betrayed was almost as bad as being betrayed myself."

I note the word *almost* and swallow. "I don't want to betray anybody."

"Most people don't," says Sky. The serious tone evaporates from his voice. "And then you get people like Blaise, who get their kicks from it."

He seems to consider something for a moment, and I stand there, unsure of what to do with this much more serious version of Sky.

"That's when Shep got obsessed with Billy, too. After everything with Blaise and after her grandma died," he says all in a rush under his breath, eyes darting to Mr. Quach. "Billy had everything—heaps of friends, a loving family, a rockin' Jareth cosplay game—and then he died. I think it just got under her skin in a way it hadn't before when her life fell apart. And Abuelita was kind of her oasis. Without her grandmother, her grades dropped, and the tension between her and her parents just got . . ."

Everybody else in the room is talking quietly, and Sky's voice barely reaches me, fading as he trails off.

"Harder to ignore," I finish for him. I think of the longing in Shep's eyes when she told me how awesome my dad is. "That makes sense. It really does."

"You better get to class," says Mr. Quach. He runs his fingers through his long hair, looking like he's tempted to pull half of it out. I don't blame him. I've got another headache coming on, and I can't tell if it's from Blaise bathing in perfume or the constant presence of Billy's story invading my brain space in English.

I feel so much closer to Billy than I ever have to any of the others I've researched. What's changed in me? Why can't I just let it go?

Then I realize: he's the one I feel most wanted to *live*.

Aerie gives me a shy half-smile on their way out the door, grounding me back in the present. I smile back.

I can't quite keep up with my emotions today. Sure, this school has its typical bullies, it seems, but there's a place here for Aerie, and there's a place here for me.

Everything in me aches to keep it.

I want to live too.

"Hey," Ronnie says as Sky and I leave the room, tucking one of her twists back into the band holding them off her face as Jax squeezes her free hand and jets off alone down the hall. "I was going to tell you before Blaise ruined everything, but I looked up the domain name you gave me, and it doesn't look like it's changed hands, but whoever owns it bought it through a private service, so the WHOIS identification just comes up as that instead of someone's name. Anything beyond that is kind of above my pay grade."

Sky gives her a slight bow. "You're a legend. Thanks for trying."

She shrugs and gives me a small smile. "Sorry it was a dead end."

"Thanks," I say, and Ronnie heads in the opposite direction Jax went with a half wave.

I part with Sky and war with myself all the way to Spanish.

For three whole minutes, I feel like I really do have a place here, but the first thing I hear as I cross the threshold into Spanish is Blaise's voice raised to say a loud, "¡Feliz cumpleaños!"

The *happy birthday* is directed to a beaming brunette in a sparkling tiara. Someone just turned the page on another year alive. The painkillers have only just chased away the early tension in my neck, and now I'm going to have to steep for a full class period in Blaise's cloud and the reminder that most people see birthdays as a celebration.

It's enough to remind me that if things had gone just a hair differently for me in Montana, the only place for me would be a grave.

. . .

The rest of the day goes by in a blur. I get a note from the office saying Principal Frankel wants to see me, but when I get there just in time to miss gym (a personal life goal is to avoid locker rooms), she's not there. I sit and wait for twenty minutes, and while I'm there, I text Shep.

You okay?

She doesn't text back. I wait for the ellipsis to appear until the admins tell me Principal Frankel had an urgent matter to attend to, and they send me back to gym.

It's too late for me to dress out, so I sit awkwardly on the bleachers while the teacher, Mr. Unterwagner, tries to get me to tell him about what physical education was like in Montana. He's built like a brick wall and sounds about like one too. He's wearing shorts and an Astoria High sweatshirt with a fisherman on it, the school mascot—I guess this school had to have at least one thing less cool than Airdrie, where we were the Mountain Lions. He smells like cigarette smoke has seeped into his clothes, which is such a jarring and unusual smell these days that it overtakes even the smell of sweating high schoolers with variable reliance on antiperspirants.

"What kind of warm-ups did you do?" Mr. U asks.

"Mostly we did a lot of burpees," I tell him, which is true, and it sucked.

"Sounds like boot camp," he says, then spends the rest of class alternately blowing his whistle to get people to switch stations and telling me about his time in the Marines.

I head out of the gymnasium as fast as I can, checking my phone. I haven't been this antsy about a text message since Montana.

The walk home is slow, and I'm surprised to see the Subaru in the driveway when I get there.

"Dad?" I shut and lock the door, checking my phone again.

He pokes his head around the corner from the kitchen. "Oh, good, you're home. Shep's in your room."

157

"Shep's here?"

He nods, glancing up at the ceiling. He lowers his voice. "I gave her some OJ and a piece of cake. The kid looks like she had a hard day."

"How long has she been here? How long have you been here?"

"Job ended early since we finished getting the framing in. I got home about a half hour ago. Shep was on the porch when I got here."

She must have skipped seventh period. Maybe sixth too.

"Thanks, Dad."

"Go see if she's okay."

I drop my backpack by the door and head upstairs, taking them two at a time.

"Shep?" My door's cracked open. A wave of dizziness washes over me, and I push the door the rest of the way open.

Shep's lying flat on her back on my bed, not moving. My heart does a stutter-stop, and then she moves, and I heave a breath way too forceful to be called a sigh.

"I'm sorry," Shep says, her face upside down to me. "I couldn't go home. I didn't know what to do."

She makes a motion with one arm and jumps as if she's encountered something unexpected. She has—it's my *Book of Half-Lived Lives*, still where I left it under the pillow.

"Why couldn't you go home?" I take off my Docs and set them by the door to the bedroom, then pad over to the bed and sit near my pillow.

"Mom's still freaking out about that note, and I'm afraid she's going to tell me I can't hang out with you."

"Would she do that?" My skin goes cold at the thought.

"I don't know."

158

"I texted you earlier," I tell her.

"My phone's dead," she says. "Didn't want to rummage in your room for a charger."

Now that I'm closer, I can see that Shep's eyes are puffy and red.

"Is that all that's wrong?" The question almost asks itself.

Shep's eyes get a teensy bit redder and gain a sheen of tears.

"You don't have to say," I say hastily. I don't want to force a confidence.

She scrambles to a sitting position and faces me, cross-legged. "No, it's fine. It's just my parents. And Abuelita. And my grades have sucked since she died, which always helps parent problems. And it's Blaise. And Brent. Brent used to bark at me every time he saw me in middle school. Because my last name is Shepard, get it? Like a dog. He's super clever. He hadn't done it for like . . . a year. Then this morning. Ugh."

"I'm sorry," I say. I pause, tracing the sewn seam on my comforter with my thumbnail.

"It's not your fault. I feel bad even bringing it up when you've been going through so much. I'm sorry I haven't said anything—I didn't know what to say and didn't want to, like, make it worse." Shep sniffs, her sinuses sounding the way mine do when I've been crying. "Blaise always used to tell me I never say the right thing when bad shit happens."

The acute pang that hits me with that simple sentence is far too familiar. "It's okay," I say, twitching at my own uncertainty about what to say here. "Sky said you and Blaise used to be close."

"Yeah, we grew up together," Shep says. "She was my best friend since we were in preschool, and she used to be fun. Funny in ways that *weren't* at other people's expense. Sky dumped her because she started getting mean when we got to sophomore year. Like . . . she'd make some crack about my haircut and use a transphobic slur and then laugh it off because *she's an ally* and she didn't *really mean it*. She expected me to just be cool with what she did to Sky. She'd say it was a joke. I thought maybe Sky breaking up with her would be sort of a wake-up call, you know, like she'd go back to making really bad puns instead of mean-girl snide bullshit if she realized she was losing friends?"

"But she didn't."

"N-ope." Shep draws out the *n* and enunciates the *p* with a pop of her lips. "You saw her today. That was nothing."

I don't know what to say, and the silence doesn't feel awkward. Just quiet.

"You're a Pisces, like Billy. Your birthday's in . . . March?" Shep says suddenly.

The word *birthday* hits me like an ice bucket challenge to the face. It takes me a few heartbeats to recover. "Yeah, March fifteenth."

"You don't want to do anything to celebrate it, do you?" Her inflection rises at the end, but I get the sense that she doesn't really mean it as a question. Her brown eyes are big and bright from crying, and I can see she knows the answer.

"I don't want to plan anything, no," I say. "I just want to see the damn sunrise."

It surprises me that the words even come out of my mouth. Now the silence is awkward.

"I get it," I tell her, just like I told Sky. "About Blaise. It's— it's tied up with what happened in Montana."

"You don't have to talk about it if you don't want to," Shep says carefully.

"Thank you," I tell her. I want to ask her what's really going on with her parents, but I don't dare. Instead, I ask, "You really didn't hear?"

She shakes her head hard. "A couple of people assumed you'd told me and tried to ask me questions, and I told them to go to hell."

I've never had a friendship like this. I remember—I force myself to think her name—Lee always pressing, pushing—she needed to know all my secrets all the time. The freedom not to say is beyond liberating. Just to be given the choice. With Shep, it tells me it's safe to say. Plus, she's going to understand.

I can hear Dad downstairs in the kitchen, probably getting ready to heat up some dinner.

I meet Shep's eyes. It takes effort. It feels like I'm lifting barbells with my eye sockets to bring them up to level with hers, but when I see them and their warmth, I can't look away. She leans forward, cross-legged on my bed, forehead tilted toward me, little V crease back between her eyebrows. Her lips are parted, her hands moving on her knees as if they're processing her thoughts for her like gears.

Shep will find out eventually. Someone outside this room will tell her, whether she seeks it out or not. This one person maybe I can tell on my own terms.

I close my eyes, breaking our eye contact. I pull in a deep breath and open them again.

. . .

"I've known her—known Lee since sixth grade," I say. "We lived in the same subdivision. Dad had me in private school for a few years because I was a couple of years behind after he adopted me. He taught me to read in the evenings, and when we moved to Airdrie, Lee was our closest neighbor. We did every-thing together. She was the first person I could really talk to besides Dad. We'd climb trees and explore the woods. We always talked about camping out, but we were always too scared to do that alone. There were mountain lions in the Sapphire Range sometimes.

"When I figured out I was queer, Lee was the first person I told. She disappeared for a few days. Not a text, email, Snap, nothing. When she called me, I even answered the phone, I was so desperate to talk to her. It was just before winter break. She said she'd had time to think and that even though she didn't agree with my lifestyle—" I have to pause because Shep makes a derisive sound like a steel plate breaking in half, and the mattress ripples with her accompanying sudden movement of disgust. "I know. But she was my best friend. I heard how people at school talked and made fun of the one kid who was out. I was terrified if I lost Lee, I'd have no one.

"Everything was kind of fine for a few months. I came out to Dad. He found me a therapist in Missoula who he wanted me to talk to, to help me process stuff. Not to fix me. Just to talk. Lee talked to me less and less, though." My chest feels like a trash compactor, like my ribs are going to collapse in on them-selves and smash my heart and lungs between them. "Then she invited me to a party that March. For my birthday, she said."

"A birthday party." Shep's voice is flat, but there is com-pressed emotion under it, barely held down.

"Yeah." I take a deep breath through my nose. "We used to have parties in the woods. People would bring tents, we'd build a campfire, and we'd hang out there. I rarely drank since I was almost always driving, but a lot of people did. That night I got to the usual place and no one was there. I was even late. I thought I'd mixed the date up."

"You drove?"

"Yeah, I got my license when I was fifteen. Montana's funny like that." I don't want to talk about it at all. I don't want to even admit that it happened. But I want to tell Shep about that night before anyone else does. More than that. I want to tell someone of my own volition. It's a paradox.

It's the thought that someone else will eventually tell her that makes me start talking again. It'd take one overheard sentence: *You hear that new kid came here because someone tried to kill them?*

I try to swallow, but my throat's all sticky and dry.

I remember my breathing, like Dad taught me.

"I parked the car and wandered around the campsite. There was some wood stacked like someone planned to start a fire, and a couple big jugs of water like someone planned to do the right thing and put it out afterward, since Montana has a tendency to go up like a lit match in a pool of kerosene." Now that I'm talking, the words keep coming. "I didn't see or hear anybody. But something snapped around my neck and I heard a sound like a zipper."

"The zip tie," Shep says. Her mouth hangs half open in horror, then shakes her head. "The cops or Principal Frankel told Mom someone put one in your locker, and she told me. I didn't want to upset you by bringing up something painful."

My neck burns with the memory, that sharp line of plastic cutting into my throat, cutting off my air. "I didn't know it was a zip tie. Only felt something hard and sharp and heard the sound and then I heard the boys laugh."

163

You'll stay away from our cousin now, fucking freak.

I don't say that out loud. Shep doesn't need to hear that. But I hear it, in my head. Over and over.

"They thought I was . . . I don't know. I don't know what they thought. That I'd come on to Lee or something and she'd freaked out. She was there, babbling at them. I couldn't hear anything. I couldn't breathe."

My voice sounds like I'm in a cave. My words echo around in my room, off the still-empty shelves.

"You know what makes me the most pissed off?" I hear myself say it. "I'm so much more than this bullshit. I'm more than their asinine fears and stereotypes or whatever the hell they think about people like us, Shep. You know we used to play a game in gym called *smear the queer*? Like . . . in *school*. With teachers beatifically watching. No fucking wonder they thought they could do what they did."

"How are you still here?" Shep whispers. She reaches out and takes my hand.

"Lee saved me," I say, a sharp laugh following that sentence. Shep's hand is warm in mine, solid and real. Alive. "She freaked out because I passed out, and she cut the zip tie with a pocketknife."

With my free hand, I move my hair away from where it hangs down below my left ear, where the scar is. It's not big, but it's always there.

"She knew I was autistic, and she'd seen me go into not-speaking mode before, but that time I physically couldn't have made words. I could barely move. I tried to crawl toward her, tried to make my voice work. Then they all took off and left me on the mountain."

I skip the blur that happened directly after she gave me that scar. Lee sobbing and screaming at her cousins that they'd killed me. The boys telling her to loosen up, that I'd be fine, and besides, they were trying to protect her.

I didn't tell you so you'd hurt her!

That sentence. Lee yelling. She never did get my pronouns right.

I pull myself back to the present, to Shep, feeling her skin against my palm.

"We left when it became obvious that the police and the school were useless. The principal was those boys' uncle, for Christ's sake. Lee's uncle, too. They were football stars, because of course they were. Not that it meant anything in a one-stoplight town. I was out of school for two weeks before I had to go back, and then as fast as he could, Dad moved us to Portland for a few months while he figured out where next. We ditched our phone numbers, and Dad took out restraining orders on what felt like half the town, and now we're here."

"To get away. But now the whole school knows." Shep almost whispers it.

I look up and Dad's standing in the doorway, his face so broken that I wish I could fix everything for him. I didn't even hear his footsteps. Dinner must be ready. After a moment, he turns and silently moves away.

Shep doesn't even notice. She holds my hand tight, tighter, so tight I think she's trying to pull out whatever memories I have and devour them so I don't have to carry them anymore.

"We came here so what happened wouldn't have to define me," I say. "Because I'm so much more than that. I don't think Dad believes that's still possible, but I do."

I mean it. If this thing that haunts me, this idea that I've only got two more months to live, I want them to be months where Montana is hundreds of miles away and I'm here. Alive and defiant and surrounded by people who I know won't betray me. Like Dad. Like Shep. Like Sky and hell, Mr. Quach. Maybe even Aerie and Ronnie.

"It's already different here, Shep," I say, and now I'm the one squeezing her hand. "Don't you see?"

Suddenly she's only inches away. "I do," she says. "Sam, I want to kiss you."

My hand is in the short length of her hair, and her hair is so soft under my fingers.

"Please—" I get out, and then she does and our lips touch. I can taste her tears and the mint of her lip balm and she tastes like hope and newness and life.

Her arms are around me. She is warm and sparks with energy and want.

I always thought I'd feel like I was falling, but this is so much better.

I suddenly feel every space between every atom that makes me up, and it feels like possibility. Life, here, electric between us. In this moment, Shep and I can do *anything*. Maybe even live.

I'm anchored here, to her, and in this moment a tsunami could break upon our shore and we would be unmoved.

CHAPTER **TWENTY**

There's a straight-haired woman downstairs when we finally disentangle ourselves and venture out toward the smells of—from the spices meeting my nose—jerk chicken and rice. Shep freezes when she sees the woman, and I run into Shep's heels.

I don't know what I expect—I haven't met Shep's mom (I got a glimpse of her once), and my only data points are her telling Shep to come home. It clicks that this must be why Dad came upstairs in the first place. I don't know how neither I nor Shep heard anybody knock at the front door.

"Shep," the woman says. "Junius was just telling me that you and Sam have become really good friends."

Shep's mom gets points for using Shep's name. I venture a look at her face. My first impression of her as a sleek, flawless missile seems accurate. Her skin is so smooth and brown she looks like she could be in a makeup commercial, but I don't think she's wearing any makeup at all. She has brown eyes like Shep, but darker. She looks like one of those people who is completely contained at all times—not a hair out of place. This woman is zeroed in on whatever exists in her crosshairs. I can see why Shep doesn't want her mother's anger aimed at her.

"I invited Esme to stay for dinner," says Dad. "Since Shep's been spending so much time with you, I thought it'd be nice."

I nod, not sure what to do. I think I should introduce myself, but I can't make my hand move.

Dad to the rescue, as usual. "Esme, this is my Sam," he says.

"My pronouns are they/them," I say, on cue.

Esme Shepard takes my hand with a firm grip and shakes it after a brief hesitation. "It's a pleasure to meet you, Sam. Shep's talked a lot about you. You're welcome to call me Esme."

Shep pokes her mom in the shoulder, and Esme jumps like a startled cat, her previous glass-smooth calm shattered.

"Did I develop electric superpowers when I wasn't looking?" Shep teases, and Esme visibly puts herself back together.

"You promised to stop sneaking up on me."

"Hey, that was not sneaking!" Shep grins sidelong at me.

I like the smile that lights on Esme's face when she looks at her daughter, and it makes her seem less intimidating and more . . . mom-ish.

I have no doubt Esme and my dad have been talking about the notes we got. When I go to get the orange juice for me and Shep, I notice that Dad's added Esme's cell number to the list of important numbers he keeps on the fridge door.

Shep's mentioned that her mom's sort of perpetually single, like my Dad. I guess one husband dead and the other Carl could factor into that. Some of what Shep's said has made me think Esme has tried, but they all bail after two or three dates. I guess Esme's maybe decided dating's not worth the risk anymore.

I think on Dad's part, he's just never been interested in marriage. I asked him once, and he said he had all he needed just being my dad. Said he never felt the need for romance. Once I sent him a link to some info about asexual aromanticism, and he read it and shrugged and then after a long pause said, "Yep, sounds like me. Who'd have thunk? There's a name for it! Your generation thinks of everything."

The thought of romance makes me look over at Shep just as she sits down next to her mom, across the table from me. She meets my eyes, and the eye contact feels physical. I swallow, hearing my own voice again say *Please* just before she kissed me.

Dad picks up the tongs and puts a drumstick and wing on Esme's plate while she spoons some rice next to it. There's a bowl of fried plantains, too, and I am so tempted to just take the whole thing and eat it myself.

Instead I get two and offer some to Shep.

Her foot finds mine under the table, our socks a fuzzy little barrier between us.

"Have you lived in Astoria your whole life?" Dad asks.

Esme nods. "My parents moved here in the seventies, just before I was born. I haven't been in this house in a long time," Esme says, looking around. "It's changed a lot."

I want to ask her about it and about Billy, but that would be too much for me. Besides, my social script says asking near-strangers about dead people at the dinner table is probably not neurotypical-friendly.

But then Shep mouths *ask about Billy* to me.

"If you've been in this house, you probably knew Billy," I venture, with Shep's permission to break the social script.

For a moment, I'm sure I just derailed the entire dinner. Esme and Dad both stop with their hands hovering over serving utensils, and Shep looks down at her plate, baring her teeth and mouthing *sorry*. The pause stretches out long enough that I hear my own heartbeat.

"We were friends," Esme says slowly, breaking the silence. "Everybody loved Billy. What happened was a tragic accident."

It's almost verbatim what Principal Frankel said to me. It sounds so mechanical and . . . wrong.

Shep steps on my foot. She thinks it's wrong too.

"I don't like that someone seems to be using my daughter's fascination with Billy Clement as a way to bully our kids," Esme says a moment later, her tone so forceful that she sounds ready to fire upon the enemy. Then to Dad, "I wish they'd let his memory rest."

"Amen to that," Dad says. He drops a thigh and the other drumstick onto my plate.

I don't know that I even want to eat.

"I just want to understand what happened to him," Shep presses. "He deserves that. Principal Frankel was his best friend, but we can't really go ask her for answers."

"She wouldn't tell you, anyway," Esme says, making unblinking eye contact with Shep. "She and Billy had been fighting. She was silent for months after it happened. I think she went over to make up with him and that's how she found him dead."

A wave of emotion crests, filling me with bubbles of feelings I can't name. I can't process that information, that Principal Frankel is who found Billy. "They were fighting?"

That night in my room when I was writing on Tumblr at four in the morning, I felt heavy tension and smelled that persistent scent of popcorn, impossibly twisted together. And I saw Billy's hand on Margie's shoulder in dreams, how hard he gripped her shoulder. Is this what all of that meant? That Margie found him—or is it more than that?

"They hadn't been talking for a while, if I remember," says Esme. "There were rumors that she was in love with him. You know how kids are."

Dad clears his throat. Esme looks at Shep, whose foot twitches and then goes still against mine.

"I just don't want to see people giving you trouble for something that should have been resolved thirty years ago." Esme's face seems suddenly hollow. Old grief, maybe. Her calm is back an instant later.

"Billy deserves justice," Shep says, her voice like gravel. She takes a swig of orange juice. "His story is important."

"Honey, we know what his story was." Esme gives Shep an exasperated look, her fork hovering over her rice.

"But you said he was so allergic to peanuts kids couldn't even bring peanut butter sandwiches to school," Shep says insistently, and I bet she's thinking of the librarian saying the same thing. "He wouldn't be that careless if he could literally *die*."

"Companies weren't as good with listing allergens then as they are now. He probably just ate something cross-contaminated, honey." Esme's utensils stop moving in her hands. "Things are more regulated now because of exactly this sort of accident."

"Tons of people don't think it was an accident," Shep presses. "They don't believe he'd just drop dead in his own bedroom where he was *safe*—"

"It was an accident." Esme's sharp voice is punctuated with her knife slipping out of her hand, where it hits her plate with a sharp report that makes me jump. "A tragic accident."

She seems to realize that she's repeated herself. She picks up her knife with a small smile and waggles it, shaking her head as if to say *aren't I the butterfingers?*

Shep's face goes through several waves of expressions in quick succession. She starts to open her mouth, then closes it. I can't identify emotions very well on most people, but Shep is so still that I wonder if Esme's tone shocked her.

"I think we can change the subject," Dad's saying smoothly. "Perhaps by extolling the virtues of this Caribbean feast."

It works. Esme's gaze falls to her plate for an abashed beat, but then she cracks a smile. Shep takes up the torch and stuffs a huge bite of rice in her mouth.

"I don't know how you do it, Junius," Shep says after somehow swallowing the whole mouthful. "You're like a domestic demigod."

A smile splits my face, and I turn it at Dad. "See? You're awesome."

"The meal is delicious," Esme says. "Thank you for inviting me to share it."

"One less meal I have to cook," Shep mutters, a devilish grin aimed at her mom.

"I'm not a great cook," Esme confesses to Dad.

"You can thank my mother for my kitchen skills, rest her. I was an only child, and she was determined I'd be able to fend for myself. She'd teach me and Daddy at once. Your cookies were a revelation, though, Esme." Dad kisses his fingertips. "I only let Sam have two of them."

"Oh!" Esme looks down again, then chuckles. "I can do the occasional baking. I make a great walnut coffee cake."

"Alas, I'd have to pass on that. Walnuts are my kryptonite, in the literal make-Clark-keel-over sort of way," Dad says. "But coffee cake in general? I am here for that."

They begin chattering about pies and cakes, and I move my foot so the length of it touches Shep's. She smiles at me, but when our eyes meet, I know that smile isn't happiness that our parents are getting on. More that when we look at each other, we can forget they're even in the room with us.

But when I look up from Shep, I'm jolted back at the look on Esme's face. Dad has gotten up to fetch something from the fridge, and Esme's eyes are fixed on the ceiling. If she could see through walls, she'd be staring right at my bedroom. Right toward the place Billy died.

All these people who knew Billy are so insistent that his death was an accident even if they, incongruously, don't seem to actually believe it. *I* can't help but believe it's only because they want it to be true.

Shep and I both know it was wasn't just a "tragic accident." We just have to prove it.

That feeling of possibility is still there, warring with the sudden drop in my stomach. All the emotions of the day are in a jumble sprawled out through my entire body all of a sudden, and I hit my fingernails against my palm several times.

Dad comes back with more plantains, which he deposits on the table with a wink at me—he knows me too well—and he and Esme start chattering again.

Shep is watching her mother, chewing on her bottom lip. When I reach out and take her hand, she gives me a pointed look, and I don't think it's about holding her hand in front of her mom because she gives my hand a squeeze.

We can do this. We can.

. . .

Shep and Esme go home at half past seven, leaving me to face Dad on two fronts.

"So," he says. I turn off the water where I was getting a glass to drink. "You really like Shep."

"Yeah," I say. "I might have uh . . . kissed her. Or she kissed me. I dunno. We kissed."

Dad starts laughing without making much sound, his shoulders shaking as he chuckles and lowers his chin to his chest.

"What's so funny?"

"I appreciate your forthrightness," he says. "But you're not dating her, eh?"

"We've never gone on a date." I don't get what he's asking, and he just chuckles again.

"It looks like emotions run pretty high around the Clement kid," Dad says then, and all evidence of his laughter is gone. "I don't really feel comfortable with you and Shep looking into it more."

"Everyone says it was an *accident*." I hate even pushing the sentence out of my mouth since it feels like repeating a lie. Dad's words douse me with cold water though, especially after feeling like Shep and I can really do this.

Dad comes up to the kitchen sink and puts one hand on my shoulder, looking me in the eye. "That may be so, but I know you don't believe that, and let's just say that after a decade or so of Sam Sylvester, I think your instincts are right. And if they are, in this case, if somebody killed that boy, they've gotten away with it for thirty years. That makes them dangerous."

"Do you think they'd stay here? If they got away with it, they could leave and be sure they'd never be caught." I don't know if it's because of Dad telling me to back off or that he's right, but my stomach feels ready to slosh my meal right back up.

"It's possible," Dad says. "But I want you safe. That's the part that is true no matter what else is."

"I know."

"Do you?" Dad pushes my hair away from my neck, where I know he can see the scar. "I've had some bad days, and I've had some bad nights. But the worst of all by far was the night I saw the car pull up and you got out and fell onto the driveway. If Lee hadn't grown a conscience—"

"I think she just didn't want to be a murderer."

We're actually talking about it. We never talk about it.

"It would have been hours before I missed you, Sam," Dad says, dropping his hand to his side. He swallows. "Even though I knew where you were going, by the time I could have gotten someone to drive me out there—"

"Stop, please," I breathe. I can't think about the *what if*s of that night because I know what's coming. I know he could have a day that beats that one for worst of his life, and my stomach knots in on itself. "Daddy, I'm here now. I'm okay."

The acid in my stomach turns to rage. For Billy, I think. For me, maybe, or all of them at once, every page in my book. I don't know. It burns hot like the glass Dad took me to see at a glassblower's once. I feel the ripples of it expand from my center, and I don't trust myself to hold it in.

"I'm going to bed," I say, half a gasp.

The sadness in Dad's face drains away until he just looks tired. "Okay, Sammy."

He doesn't argue even though it's not even eight o'clock. My *Book of Half-Lived Lives* is sitting on the window seat, but I can't look at it. Not right now.

I close the door to my room and flip the lock. I never lock it, but I can't face Dad again right now. He deserves so much better, so much more than—

Than you? It's Billy's voice, or how I imagine he'd sound, speaking like he can hear me instead of speaking like a memory.

I'm hearing voices now? That's always a good sign.

And it doesn't stop.

Billy's shoulders shake, like he's crying, like he lost everything, because he did. The way I almost did.

Let me tell you what you deserve. You deserve love and friendship and kindness. You are all those things and more. Every moment I get with you is more than enough, but it never stops me from hoping for the next one. You're—

I don't know who's talking to who now. I can't listen. I open my eyes and banish the words away.

CHAPTER TWENTY-ONE

I get a note in Advisory on Tuesday telling me to come by the office during seventh period. Besides thanking the scheduling gods for getting to miss gym again, my stomach churns at the idea of sitting down with Principal Frankel. Through all of this—my dreams of Billy, the time capsule we dug up, what Esme shared—I've seen and heard more of Margie Frankel than probably any of the students at Astoria High.

Most of the day passes without incident. Shep and I steal glances in English and US history, and Sky teases us both relentlessly at lunch, looking so happy I think he might explode into glitter and butterflies, though a couple of times I see the look fade as if he's the one unsure of his footing.

Are Shep and I together? I don't know how this works. My social script doesn't extend to dating rules. But Sky seems to think so, or is at least happy to cheer us toward the possibility.

Blaise is absent, which makes me more uneasy than relieved. Though my nose is thankful.

When seventh period rolls around, I head to Frankel's office. This time she's there, at her desk.

"Come on in, Sam," she says. "I promise I'll keep this short."

She's got a microwave on a cabinet against the wall, and she gets up, rummaging in a drawer below the microwave. My phone buzzes.

You better let us know what she says! It's Shep, in the group text with Sky.

The microwave buttons beep as I type back, *Obviously.*

I shove the phone into my pocket and pull my sleeves down over my wrists.

Principal Frankel sits down in her chair again. There's a blue-green book open on her desk, filled with writing that doesn't look like English. She closes it and tucks it into a drawer, tidying up a small line of pens beside her desk calendar.

"I just need a snack," she says, then adds with a smile, "Popcorn hits the salt craving, though I'm under strict orders never to let it burn again."

I nod at her, trying to return her smile with one of my own. "What'd you want to see me about?"

"I wanted to see how you're doing this week. I know last week was very stressful, on top of it being your first week here."

She seems to choose her words with extra care today.

"I'm okay," I tell her. "So far people have been weirdly supportive."

"I've had a decent number of students ask how they can help," she says. "I'm very proud to hear that students are stepping up. How are your classes?"

"They're fine." I don't really know what I'm supposed to be saying. That acid anger in my stomach from last night is still there, lurking. For the first time in my life, I think I'd rather be in gym class.

The microwave whirrs, and the scent of popcorn fills the office. Real popcorn, this time. I press my nails into my palm once, twice, three times. Rage sends out tendrils, searching through me. I don't hear the principal's next question.

"What?" I hear my own voice like it's under water.

"I asked if any of your classes are too difficult right now."

"They're fine," I say. My eyes fall upon the picture of Margie and Billy, still behind her desk after all these years.

"I truly hope you'll be able to settle in here, Billy," Principal Frankel says.

I jerk in my chair. "You keep calling me Billy," I say.

When I try to practice my breathing, my lungs quake as I inhale.

"I'm sorry, Sam," Principal Frankel says, her eyes full of alarm. She scoots back in her chair.

The popcorn smell invades my lungs and seeps into my bones.

"Do I remind you of him or something?" My question is a desperate one. How can she be looking at me and seeing him?

"You both went through something, and with you living—" She stops, closes her eyes. "Sam, please forgive me. What happened to Billy was a tragic accident."

"Stop saying that! It wasn't an accident!" I can't help myself. I can't get away from that horrible popcorn smell. It's like it's fucking following me. Here she is, thirty years later, popping popcorn in her office and calling me Billy. "We both went through something—you were his best friend! I know what best friends can do sometimes."

I get up, my feet almost twisting to give out and plant my face on the floor. I keep my balance, grabbing the back of the chair, but I can only see that curly-haired silhouette from my dreams right in front of me.

"Were you there that day?" I blurt out.

The look on her face is almost proof enough. Her eyes go wide, the whites as bright as eggshells.

"It *was* you with him at his house that day," I say. Suddenly I'm certain, after what Esme said about Margarie going to the house the day he died and finding him—she was there *when he died*, not just after. I feel my throat constrict with itchy thickness, lips numb, tongue tingling. I almost died like he did, cut off from air. "You lived right next door. But you were fighting, weren't you?"

"Sam," Principal Frankel says, with a voice full of warning.

I grab my backpack and yank open the door to her office, thankful the admins and some students are outside.

The microwave pings.

"Your popcorn is ready, Principal Frankel," I say. "Unless I've done something wrong, please leave me alone."

. . .

My heart is still racing when Shep and Sky meet me outside the school after the last bell. Clouds scud above us, not quite threatening rain but making sure we know there's the chance of it.

Shep kisses me lightly, and Sky hesitates a moment, then something shifts into place on his face, and he gives us a wide, approving grin. Somebody whistles, but it sounds good-natured, the way a kid might whistle for any straight couple. Every day lately, my life feels like it has wonder and horror braided together.

We walk toward my house, and I wait until we're clear of most of the students before telling them.

"I think it might have been Principal Frankel," I say. A small flock of sophomores walks on the opposite side of Alameda Avenue, so I pitch my voice low so they can't overhear.

"Holy shit," Sky says. "You seriously think—she was his best friend, dude."

Both Shep and I turn to look at him just as he runs his fingers through his hair.

He lets it fall down onto his face. I told Shep to tell him, so he knows enough about what happened to me by now to be able to add it to his own experience with Blaise. "Shit."

"Why do you think that, Sam?" Shep looks at me, her fingers laced in mine.

"I'm not sure. But I keep smelling popcorn at home, and then Principal Frankel made popcorn in her office today while we were talking, and she pretty much confirmed what your mom said last night, that she was there with him that day. Not just that she found him, but that she was there when it *happened*. I know it's pretty . . . sparse. But your mom said they'd been fighting. And Frankel called me Billy again. There's *something* weird there."

I know Shep will get that, but I don't know if Sky will understand. He looks dubious once again, but after eyeing the sophomores across the street for a moment, he turns back and sighs.

"You two are the bloodhounds. I'll just make a web comic about this when you're done solving cold cases. Maybe I'll Tuckerize you as robots. Justicebots."

"She's the *principal*," Shep says, ignoring Sky. "How on Earth would we ever be able to prove she did it?"

"I don't know. But Dad found that time capsule, right? Maybe there's something else Billy hid somewhere." I'm reaching. It's not likely.

"You think he knew she was going to try and off him?" Sky stops walking, eyebrows knitted and skeptical. "No way would he have had the time."

"Everyone keeps saying the same thing about it." I squeeze Shep's hand and try to form my thoughts. "That it was a tragic accident. Those exact words."

"It's creepy," says Sky. "But it doesn't really mean anything."

"Maybe not."

We round the corner onto my street, and my house looms ahead of us, the mouth-like door waiting. No Subaru today. Dad said he'd be home late.

"Just leaving doors open now?" Sky gets to the top of the stairs first, and I have to drop Shep's hand and lean around him to see what he's talking about.

The door. It is cracked open, like someone left it ajar. It makes the house look almost cartoonishly surprised. Dad would *never* leave the door that way. He grew up in DC. He always triple-checked locks.

"Someone was in here," Shep says, correctly interpreting my horrified silence.

"Dad's going to flip." My head feels like it just got filled with helium. He's going to take me out of school. Sell the house immediately.

"I think somebody broke in and left this open on purpose." Shep peers through the door. "They wanted you to know they were here. They tracked in mud. Anyone who wanted to break in and *not* raise an alarm wouldn't just leave doors open and footprints on the floor."

And Dad just wouldn't do that. That's why his work boots are kept in their little boot house by the door. It's empty right now.

"I thought the door was just trying to learn to whistle," Sky says dryly.

"I mean—" Shep glares up at him. "Ugh, Sky."

When I push the door farther open, a piece of paper flutters on the floor inside.

Shep looks at me, and she doesn't have to explain why she gets up, turns, and lopes off up the street toward her own house. Sky stares after her, but he seems to get it after a beat.

"Okay, *if* this is Principal Frankel, then she is one fucked-up lady," Sky says. "Also fast, since you just came from her office and you said she was about to settle in with a snack to morosely ponder probably having killed her best friend."

"She could have done it any time during the day," I say absently, taking the paper. "We live like two seconds from the school."

"Exactly," says Sky. "*Anyone* could have done it."

Up the street, Shep's coming back. She holds up her arms as if to say, *nothing here.* I get a surge of relief from that. Knowing nobody invaded her space, especially after her mom's visit last night. I'm stalling looking at the paper in my hand. I open it gingerly.

It's a flier from a window washer. I show it to Sky, who snorts.

"False alarm!" I call out. "Just a flier."

"My house is fine," Shep confirms when she gets back. "Alarm on, locks locked. But someone definitely came in here. What are you going to tell your dad?"

"I'm not going to tell him," I say. The thought of lying to Dad causes me physical pain, like someone's welding my ribs together. I don't want to lie to him, but if I tell him when he already has told me to stop looking into Billy's death . . .

"He'd yank you out of school fast," Sky says.

I nod. "Faster than a buttered pig can go down a slide in July, as he'd say."

"So I'm guessing you don't want to call the police." Sky looks neither surprised nor judgmental.

"Only if it's clearly a burglary," I say.

I steel myself, almost hoping the TV or our laptops will be missing or something. We're insured for that sort of thing.

Pushing open the door, I *feel* the wrongness that comes along with someone having been in your space. Like my locker, but worse. This is my home. The ferocity of my sudden anger surprises me. To hide it, I go in, watching Sky nudge the door shut behind him.

"I'll try not to touch anything they might have touched."

"Somebody ask Siri if lifting fingerprints with tape really works," I say, half-joking.

I hear the tone on Sky's phone, then he asks the question and skims the answers. After a moment, he shows me the article. There's a damn wikiHow on it. I read the list of necessary items quickly.

Shep looks like she wants to run.

We go into the living room, and I look around. Nothing seems out of place or missing. The television—a brand-new, sixty-inch flatscreen that Dad called his "splurge of the decade"—is still right where we left it. I pull out my phone and text Dad to ask when he'll be home.

He doesn't read the message or answer right away, which either means he's already driving or he's in the middle of work stuff.

We make a quick circuit of the main floor, but nothing seems amiss.

"Upstairs?" Shep asks.

I'm moving almost before she gets the word out. If this has something to do with Billy, my room is where the evidence will be.

I think the others know this too, because terse silence is all I hear when I get to the threshold and stop short. Something's missing. It is immediately evident, a hole in my room, in my

184

space, in my sanctuary. It's cold in here, like the very air has turned hostile.

My *Book of Half-Lived Lives* is gone from its perch on the window seat.

"Sam?" Shep asks softly.

"My book," I manage to get out.

I can't see her behind me, but the echoing dearth of response feels bigger than all of us, all of me.

Getting into my locker is one thing, but my room? I feel like the anthill has exploded in my stomach, out of my stomach, like the ants are crawling over my skin, all of them at the same time, and it would take a blast of water the strength of a fire hydrant to get them off me. It's like what I said about *Call of the Wild*. My room. Billy's room.

Both of my hands are going, fingernails hitting my palms over and over and over.

As I stare helplessly, I realize it's not just the book that's not where it should be. Books that were arranged against one side of a half-full shelf are pushed against the wrong side. My lamp is in a slightly different place.

Without a word, I spin and run downstairs.

I go to the kitchen and grab Dad's drafting pencil and a box cutter we still have lying around from the move. I also snag a ziplock bag from the cupboard. I could try the books, but I don't think that's a great idea. Instead, I hurry back upstairs to Shep and Sky, who are both looking at me like I might bite them.

"No idea if whoever did that would be careless enough to leave prints, but I want to see just in case. Grab that packing tape," I say to Shep. I look at Sky, cringing about what I'm about to say. "In the bathroom, there's a makeup bag. Grab the soft-est, poufiest brush you see and bring it in here."

"Are you seriously going to try and fingerprint something?" Shep steps closer to me when Sky disappears around the corner.

"I really doubt that any court would admit it," I say, "but even something circumstantial could help."

I think I just want to do something right now. If I can find out what happened to Billy my own way, maybe I can be the bridge to justice for him.

Nobody got punished for what they did to me. Maybe I can make sure someone gets punished for what they did to Billy. And if I'm lying to Dad in the process, this can be my tiny way of acknowledging that this is maybe a very bad decision. I can leave breadcrumbs for him.

Sky returns with my favorite brush. I can wash it after this, but I hate the thought of what I'm about to do. I grab a page from a notebook and use a box cutter to make a small pool of graphite dust from the drafting pencil.

"There should be a ream of printer paper in the spare bed-room down the hall," I say, listening to the small *snick snick snick* of the razor on the pencil lead. "Can somebody get it?"

Sky turns on his heel to go after it.

"How did you even think to do this?" Shep asks. I can't tell if she's impressed or put off.

"Dad loves procedurals." I have a small pile of dust now. Probably enough for the base of my lamp. "Says they're a fantasy where the authorities always do the right thing and where the victims get justice."

I think about Lisa McVey in Florida who survived to help catch a serial killer who abducted her by putting her own fingerprints all over his bathroom, among other things. She was seventeen, and she *lived*.

"Try not to sneeze," Shep says. "You'll ruin your hard work."

My phone buzzes. It's Dad.

Sixish, kid. Gotta finish up with one of the buyers.

I text him back an eyeroll emoji and set my phone on the bed, carefully folding the edges of the paper so I don't spill my dust. Knowing we have a little time sets me at ease, if only a bit.

Sky comes in with a sheet of paper. "Okay, Dirk Gently. Show us your stuff."

"Can somebody video this?" The thought hits me all of a sudden that I'll have to wipe down the lamp when we're done.

"Got it," Sky says. He pulls out his phone and opens the camera app.

"If Billy's murderer kills me, at least there'll be a record of where these prints came from," I say in as light a tone as I can.

Shep moves around and perches on the window seat to watch, and after a moment, Sky follows.

The lamp is brand-new and is still glossy, the enamel coating shiny enough on the base that I can see prints on it. There's no way by looking at them to know if they're mine or Dad's or the home invader's, but they all seem to be concentrated in the middle, except one set that's choked up toward the edge, like someone used it to nudge the lamp just a tad.

It's that one I go for. Whoever did this maybe didn't expect I'd even notice right away—or at all.

"Sam." It takes a minute for Shep's voice to register, and she says my name again, more insistently. "Sam!"

"What?"

She leans over from where she sits and pulls something from behind the bedside table.

Not just something. My book. I almost drop the precious powder and freeze.

"Is that the book you thought was gone?" Sky asks, frowning.

"No way it fell down there alone," I say. The window seat isn't *far* from the bedside table, but last time I checked, books don't bounce or roll. "I left it sitting on the window seat."

Even if we did call the police now, they'd laugh at us. Just finding the door open with a bit of mud is probably not probable cause or whatever they need to decide someone's done a crime.

"Your dad wouldn't like, move anything in here?" Sky glances at Shep, who is shaking her head before I can answer as if she's already certain.

"Nope," I tell him. "Dad doesn't move my stuff. He doesn't even come in here without asking. He is very big on me having space that is just mine, safe."

I point to the bookshelf. Both of them follow my finger, but they look back at me, uncomprehending. I guess they wouldn't know how my books were arranged.

"Somebody moved those books," I explain. "They were on the other side."

"This is getting creepier," Sky says, just as Shep goes, "Fuck that."

I think what she means is an aggressive *nope-nope-nope*, and I am right there with her.

"Hopefully they were careless," I say. Everything in here is *plausibly* undisturbed.

People sometimes leave doors open or don't shut them tightly enough. This close to the ocean, there's always a ready wind to blow them open again. But I know my room, and I know my space. Maybe moving the lamp was an accident. Maybe the books were too. Or maybe whoever did this is messing with me—gaslighting me. If we did call the police, what would they say? Nothing was stolen. All we have is my gut feeling that someone moved my things and some dirt on the floor.

"May I?" Shep asks, waggling the book.

I nod without thinking because it's Shep—and then I realize Sky could very well look on in curiosity. It's the closest thing I have to a journal, and it makes me think of Principal Frankel's book.

Panic almost makes me drop the powder again, but Sky is concentrating on me, not my *Half-Lived Lives*.

"You gonna hold that all day?" he asks. "I've hit Record and Stop four times already."

I totally forgot I asked him to video this.

"I'm ready now. Go ahead," I say. "Sorry."

I sprinkle a bit of the powder over the prints on the lamp and take the brush from Sky's outstretched hand, cupping mine over the rest of the powder so my breath doesn't disturb it. I try to dab as lightly as I can, and I get the urge to giggle when one of the prints comes up fully formed. A couple of the others are smudged, and I hold my breath, going to each of them.

Shep hands me the packing tape. I'm pretty sure if she was put off earlier, she's impressed now. I keep my hands steady, lowering the tape over the handle.

"Just watch," I say, trying to break the tension. "They're all my prints."

Sky spreads out the paper in front of me, and I lay down three separate prints with the tape. Just like someone nudged the lamp with their three middle fingers.

I put it into the ziplock bag. I hesitate, my instinct wanting to wipe away the remnants of dust on the lamp. I don't want to destroy any evidence. I scoot away.

A *bing* reaches my ears.

"Boom. On YouTube." Sky makes a flourish with his free hand.

"No—" I breathe.

"I'm kidding, I'm kidding. That sound was just me sending it to both of you." Sky gives me a crooked smile. "If you croak, I'll turn this over to the cops with that baggie."

"Thanks," I say, and I mean it. Something of my emotion must come through in that one syllable, because Sky shifts his feet.

"Just try not to die, and I'll call it even."

If only it were that easy.

CHAPTER TWENTY-TWO

You know, I thought I couldn't get any angrier at you.

You always made me believe that I was a freak.

I wish you could see how wrong you are. It's not me that's the problem. I understand that now. It was never me. It was you.

Here? Everyone knows about me. They even use my right pronouns. And they know what you did and they find it abhorrent because it was. Here I'm not a freak. I might be an Amazon of a new kid and have tattoos and trauma, but I'm just me. I'm more welcome here than I ever was there.

You always used to use that "love the sinner, hate the sin" bullshit like it was an epiphany or some kind of transcendent truth.

It's not truth. It's fear. You have to add a caveat of hate to what's supposed to be a message of love.

I don't forgive you.

I'm not the only one here. I also wasn't the only one there. There are more people like me in your precious town.

Tell your cousins to be careful who they hate. It's probably someone they love.

. . .

I hit Post and feel powerful. The therapist I had briefly in Portland told me that *anger* can be powerful, and right now I feel it. It burns through me like fuel. I liked her.

Most of the time I ignore my activity on this Tumblr. I see a couple of blips here and there, but I don't follow anyone and didn't think anyone followed me. At two in the morning, it feels like a good idea to check.

My heart bounces like a rubber ball when I see the stats.

I've gotten about five new followers a day for the past three days, which in Tumblr-world isn't that many, but . . .

The anger burns away to leave blood-heated cheeks and shallow breaths. I don't know why anybody would be following this particular blog. It's not like I post interesting GIFs or Destiel fanfic or anything that usually lights a fire under Tumblr's ass. The blog's got a few over thirty followers, though. Some notes. Some reblogs.

I exit out of the app.

In the soft glow of my laptop's light, my room feels surreal, as if I'm walking through that glowing liminal space in my dreams where all my past selves can reach out and touch me.

One thing I didn't tell Shep is that Lee always listened to me about my obsessions. I told Lee all that stuff when I was too young to know better, and she went with it because she was too young to be skeptical about the appropriateness of my questionable morbidity. I wanted to share these things with her that at first, things I found powerful, sacred, like I was a memory keeper for people otherwise forgotten. Before I understood my very identity could be a death sentence. Before I realized Billy's memory still haunts this town, far from forgotten.

It's so different here. Shep is so different.

The thought of Shep makes me close my laptop and lie in the dark, timing my breathing to the small pulsing light on my computer's charger. We kissed.

Again, I feel her lips on mine, my fingers in her hair. I never thought anyone would touch me like that, with such . . . *want.*

Her touch was like air. I didn't realize how much I felt like I was underwater my whole life until that touch. When she touched me, I filled my lungs and expected water, and I got sweet, clean oxygen instead.

In the midst of all that, the worst part is that maybe I should never have let it happen. I can't shake the feeling that my escape in Montana was some Final Destination shit, like something's still waiting to get me before I hit nineteen, just like all the other kids I've spent my short life learning about. After the threats, the zip tie, the break-in—it all feels like a warning. Or an omen.

Dad's downstairs sleeping somewhere, unaware that I don't feel like I escaped anything.

Shep's at home, hopefully sleeping herself. She has no idea either about this specter haunting me.

Kissing Shep—every touch and glance and hitched breath—sets her up for grief if something happens to me.

It'll be my fault.

I hear Sky say again that seeing Shep betrayed was almost worse than feeling it himself. If I die and abandon her, how much worse is that?

Can you live with it?

I don't know whose voice that is, and I don't know the answer.

But another voice, one so quiet and ethereal that it doesn't even form words—that voice whispers something else.

Every ounce of love is always an act of desperate hope.

· · ·

Dad seems fine when I go off to school Wednesday—if worry is eating away at him, I can't see the tooth marks.

Wednesday. Gold day again, which means I see Blaise the moment I walk into Advisory.

She gives me a bright smile. Her red hair comes down to her shoulder blades like a copper cascade. The sun's out, shining through the windows, and it makes that curtain of hair sparkle. I think Blaise knows it, too.

I sit down and try to ignore her.

This is the shortest "class" of the day, but it goes by so slowly that it feels like the longest. After attendance, I dig *Call of the Wild* out of my backpack and try to read. The words feel too familiar, like I've read them a thousand times before. In spite of that, I want to keep reading. They're dynamic, magnetic.

I'm so engrossed in the book that I don't even hear the bell ring.

I fumble to get my stuff, and I'm last out the door. Blaise is long gone, but the moment I step into the hall, I nearly run into Mr. Quach.

"Mr. Quach, hi," I say.

"Hey, Sam. What's up?"

"On my way to English." I peer at him. He looks tired. His face is puffy as if he hasn't slept well. "Are you okay?"

"What? Yeah. Sorry. I had a personal emergency this weekend, and I'm running a little ragged. My dad was in a car accident."

He blinks like he has just realized he confided in a student. For a moment, he could be one of us, one of the seniors just going to his next class.

"I'm so sorry," I say. He looks antsy, too. "Can we do anything to help?"

The words are out of my mouth before I know what's happening. Mr. Quach's head draws back in surprise, his mouth tightening as if he's trying not to cry.

"Thank you, Sam," he says, straightening. "I don't think so, though. He's stable. Please don't worry about me."

He nods at me and walks away, and stare after him, catching sight of Shep down the hall, headed to English. My stomach does a roll at the sight of her. Her hair is freshly buzzed, longer on top and faded at her neck this time, and she's wearing dark red lipstick. In her jeans and plain white V-neck T-shirt, she looks like she could be a fifties bad boy. All she needs is a leather jacket. She's so gorgeous that my chest almost implodes. I want to get her attention, but I also just want to freeze the image of her in my mind forever. She hasn't seen me yet.

Dylan and one of his friends wave at me as I pass them, and I wave back, not sure what to do when Dylan falls in with me.

"What class do you have next?" He asks the question so innocently.

"English," I say. "We're reading *Call of the Wild*."

"Weird book," he says. "It shouldn't be boring because it's about dog fights and shit, but I fall asleep every time I try to open it."

"I like it," I say. "Try reading it out loud. Listen to the way the words flow. It's beautiful."

I don't know what makes me say that, either.

"Uh, thanks for the tip," says Dylan. He opens his mouth as if he wants to say something else, but then he shuts it again. He doesn't speak the rest of the way down the hall.

We reach the door to English, and I give Dylan an awkward salute and duck inside.

The seats next to Shep are both taken, so I sit in front of her instead.

"Don't you look at your phone?" She leans forward over her desk and smiles at me.

"It's on do not disturb," I say, pulling it out of my pocket.

There's a message from Shep that just says *You look hot.*

"Blush emoji," I say out loud. Then, before I lose my nerve, I say, "So do you."

"Did you hear Frankel's not here today?" Shep says (her smile is unrelated to the principal—I'm certain). "I don't think she's missed a day in three years."

"Whoa. Something must be in Gatorade or retrograde or whatever it's called." I can't think of anything else to say, but a wild—and reckless—idea forms in my head as I process what Shep has just said. "She's gone all day?"

"Yeah, Sky's an office aide and went in there during Tutorial to get something, and Miss Edith told him that Frankel is out sick."

I meet Shep's eyes. "She's gone all day," I say again.

The bell rings, and Shep tilts her head sideways. "Text it to me," she says.

I don't trust texts. If I die and it's not of immediately apparent natural causes, someone could get access to my phone. Dad watches too many procedurals. It's seeped into my brain.

Instead, I open up a notebook and write. Paper can be destroyed—or left somewhere Dad could find it before any investigator. My handwriting looks like chicken scratch, but I hope Shep'll be able to read it.

Does Sky have a key to the office? There might be something there—I saw something weird on her desk when I met with her last.

In my mind's eye, that book's handwritten pages are clear and nonsensical, like writing in dreams is supposed to look. It wasn't English, which isn't really that weird—plenty of people know other languages. But it didn't look like any language I could recognize. I'm no linguist, but I can tell Spanish from Russian and German from Hebrew and Arabic from Greek.

I am pretty sure I will have no way of reading it, but maybe if I touch it, I'll feel something like with the shelves in my house, with the banister. Maybe whatever is making me see Billy's face will show me something we need.

Mr. Duncan is talking to a student at the front of class, so I turn around and hand Shep the paper without trying to hide it.

When I turn back around, I can feel Shep's eyes on my back. Her knuckles brush my shoulder blade, just a bare touch, but comforting. I lean back in my chair, just a little. Just enough to tell her it's okay to keep her hand there.

She's a southpaw anyway; she can write with the other one.

Mr. Duncan clears his throat at the front of class. We've got a ninety-minute period on Gold days. He passes worksheets to the first person in every row.

"Take one, pass 'em back," he says.

When it gets to me, I turn to hand Shep her worksheet, and she hands me back my lined paper. Her fingers brush mine. I swallow.

The worksheet is about what constitutes sources. All I can see is Shep's (much neater) handwriting below my own.

Sky eats lunch in there sometimes and is good friends with the janitors. There are some files in Frankel's office that Sky has to get to every week or so. He could borrow a key if he needed to. We can catch him at break.

"Can someone define a primary source for me? Shep?"

Shep jumps and her desk wobbles against the back of my chair. "A primary source is someone who directly witnessed, recorded, or depicted an event," she says.

Mr. Duncan moves on, asking someone else a follow-up.

Do you think he could get me in there? I scribble it on the sheet. When Mr. Duncan heads back to the front of the class, I hand the paper to Shep.

"Good," says Mr. Duncan. He goes on, writing something on the board as he talks.

Shep hands me the paper back. *Might have to be when the admins go to lunch. Changing of the guard or something. You wouldn't have much time.*

I don't need much time, I write back.

CHAPTER TWENTY-THREE

Sky is almost too eager to help. Within the ten minutes of morning break, he has a plan. Sitting through math class almost does me in, and not only because Ms. Stock's description of calculus makes me feel like I'm trying to prove Einstein's theory of relativity with nothing but a pair of Popsicle sticks and a bouncy ball.

I stuff my calculus textbook into my backpack three minutes before the bell rings and hurry out into the hall toward the office.

"Hey, Sam!" someone calls from down the hall. Dylan again. Crap.

"I gotta run!" I call, hurrying toward the office.

Sky's there waiting. "Shep's in the cafeteria," he says. "We better be quick."

He leads me into the office, where a couple of admins are putting their coats on and chattering about grabbing panang curry from the restaurant down the street.

"Edith will be back in about ten minutes, Sky," one of them says. He gives me a polite smile. "Did you need something?"

"I'm, uh . . . with him."

Sky nods. "Sam may need an aide period next year, and I thought I'd see if they wanted to shadow me today," he says breezily. He waves his hand about in the air. "The illustrious world of office aide-ing."

"I think there are some copies to make and some filing," the admin says. "I won't tell Sam that your job's boring if you don't."

"Thank you, thank you." Sky bows.

The admin chuckles and leaves with the woman from the front desk.

"They trust you to hold down the fort when they're at lunch?" I ask.

"Only for the ten or fifteen minutes it takes Edith to get her lunch from the cafeteria. But Shep's supposed to stall her." Sky takes from his pocket a key ring that is so jammed with keys it looks like it should belong to a dragon.

"It's gonna take you fifteen minutes just to find the right one," I mutter.

"Nah," says Sky, picking out a midsize brass key after running his thumb over the flat, round end. "My buddy Jackson taught me a trick."

"Psychometry?"

"He scratched the surface of this one," Sky says wryly.

"I like my theory better."

"Yeah, well, you're going to need whatever psychic mojo you have if you're going to find anything in this office." Sky opens the door. "I'm shutting you in. Watch your phone. Shep'll text when Edith leaves the cafeteria. She'll tell you she's full."

"Thank you."

"Thank her if you don't get caught," Sky says. He winks.

I pull out my phone and turn off the Do Not Disturb feature so it'll buzz if someone texts.

Into Frankel's office on three. One. Two. Three.

I step over the threshold.

Sky shuts the door behind me. The sound feels final. I can't turn back now. I go straight to the picture in the frame, the one of her and Billy. There she is, looking almost the same as she did in the time capsule picture. Curly brown hair, toothy grin with a few teeth out of alignment. Her teeth are almost all straight now. I wonder if she got Invisalign.

The office still smells like popcorn. That smell doesn't go away.

I pull my sweater sleeves down over my hands and pick up the picture frame. The back comes off easily, but the photograph isn't written on. No date or anything, just a Kodak watermark from a bygone era. I don't feel anything when I touch it except for the smoothness of the paper.

I replace the photo as precisely as I can. The dog in the other frame grins out of the image, tongue lolling. Dad's always said I could get a dog, but I'm afraid I'd get into one of my self-harm spurts and hurt it without meaning to. It's not something I've ever told him. I kind of think he's the one who actually wants a dog.

There are a lot of drawers in the counter behind Principal Frankel's desk. When I open the first few, they're full of student files, dating back a few years. I imagine most things are on computers these days, but as Dad says, education and healthcare are the last to change systems.

None of them seem to go as far back as the nineties, let alone the eighties.

I sit down in her chair, more out of frustration than anything.

I pull open the lower drawer on the left. There's nothing in it but the blue-green leather journal, one of those really nice ones with a tree of life etched in the front cover. The pages are worn. My fingers tingle as I pick it up, seeking out the edges like they should feel familiar or something.

This is a purposeful invasion of her privacy. I imagine that home invader doing this to me and nearly put the journal back and walk away, silent phone notwithstanding.

But I remember seeing the whites of her eyes when she called me Billy for the second time, the way she keeps repeating that what happened to Billy was "a tragic accident," just like everybody else in this town does. Sitting here, I feel rage at the injustice of his unsolved murder boiling beneath my skin as if a few layers of dermis and epidermis are all that's keeping it contained.

I remember what Mr. Quach said about old grief coming to the surface all over again. Maybe it's just that. But maybe it's more. If the Barry boys had killed me, who knows whether my death would have gone down in history as a prank gone wrong. Another tragic case of a "joke" taken too far, only accidental in the sense that they intended to commit assault, not murder.

If there's something in here that talks about what Frankel did, if she did anything, I have to know.

I flip open to the first page.

And blink.

At first, I think it's Swedish or something. Not that I know Swedish. What I couldn't recognize upside down from several feet away isn't any more comprehensible up close and right side up.

Yg jag hin . . .

The words start to bleed together though, the way Latin used to be written without punctuation or line breaks, only the flow to tell you where to stop and start. It doesn't look like any language I've ever seen before. It doesn't have any diacritical marks I'd recognize, though the alphabet is Roman.

I hold it up to a small mirror that hangs over the microwave, just in case it's that simple, despite knowing it's futile. It's not just mirrored. Still makes no sense.

I flip through the pages. They're all like that, written in this weird language or code.

I grab my phone. No message from Shep.

Opening the camera app, I start photographing the pages.

My toe taps on the floor while I do it, impatiently counting through increments of time not found on any clock.

Writing a journal in code like this isn't something most people would do. It screams paranoia, at the very least. Whatever's in here, Margie Frankel wrote painstakingly over long amounts of time. It's something she never wanted anyone to read. But that doesn't mean she had anything to do with Billy's death.

She hasn't missed a day in three years.

Either she doesn't usually bring this home with her or just forgot.

I can almost feel the buzz in the cafeteria shifting from the bustle of students and staff getting their food to everyone sitting down and eating. I don't have much time.

My thumb is poised over the camera button. I fall into a rhythm, catching each set of double-facing pages. *Flip. Snap. Flip. Snap.*

Frankel has gotten almost two-thirds of the way through this book. There's so much in here, and I wish I could take it with me.

Ten pages left.

My phone buzzes, and I drop it. Fumbling to pick it up, I hit the notification. It's Shep, to the group chat.

I'm so fuuuuuuull.

Shit. I hurriedly poke at the touch screen, getting it back to the camera app.

Flip. Snap. Flip. Snap. Flip. Snap.

Seven pages left. New ink. Fresh writing.

But in flipping the pages, I realize something that wasn't noticeable when I picked the book up. Its back cover is a little thicker than the front. My fingers feel it, and I flip to the end. There's a pocket there, and I can see a few layers of something tucked into it. I hurriedly pull it out, and my heart drops into my gut.

The first thing I see is a picture of Billy. He's grinning up at me from a photograph, dressed like Jareth from *Labyrinth*, and there's Margie next to him as Sarah in a flowing white dress. Their Halloween costumes.

I take a picture of it, then flip to the next, taking pictures as I go through the small stack.

I hear a rap at the door. It has to be Sky.

I ignore it. I'm so close to being finished. I don't even look closely at what I'm photographing.

Flip. Snap. Flip. Snap. Flip. Snap. Flip. Snap. Flip. Snap.

Another knock, louder. Sky opens the door. "Dude, I peeked out and she's at the end of the hall. Get the fuck out."

Flip. Snap.

I hurriedly stack the pictures and slide them back into the cover, throwing the journal back into the drawer and slamming the drawer shut. I don't care if the chair's in the wrong place—that can be blamed on a janitor. I run out into the office, and Sky shuts the door, shoving the bundle of keys into his backpack just as a woman—Edith, presumably—walks into the office with a tray of pizza sticks, salad, and two cartons of chocolate milk.

"Sky!" She looks around. "Where's Jake and Caroline?"

"Panang curry run," Sky says. "I'm giving my friend Sam a tour of the wonderful world of office aide life."

"Oh," Edith says. She walks behind the desk and takes a seat near a phone. "Students really aren't supposed to be in here alone."

"Jake said you'd be back any minute," Sky says innocently. "They had to pick up their carry-out. You know how cranky Mr. Thongchai gets when the orders pile up."

"That man is in the wrong business," Edith agrees. "We could use him here to get teachers to show up to IEP meetings. We're running four behind this month."

She seems to recognize me when she says that, and her pale face goes red.

"It's okay," I say. "IEP meetings are boring. They make me be there, though."

Edith clears her throat and opens her milk, busying herself with her lunch.

"Think you saw everything you need to make a decision?" Sky asks. He looks at me intently.

"I hope so," I say quietly. Then, even softer, "You any good at code breaking?"

"What do I look like, an Enigma machine?" At my blank look, he raises an eyebrow. "Bunch of Poles created a machine that broke Nazi codes."

"That's badass," I say.

"Yeah, and unfortunately, badass is not me."

"We'll see about that. You staying here?"

"I've got a few things I should do. The boring stuff." Sky grins. "But you two better let me know—"

"We will."

I nod to Edith, who is still about the color of a tomato.

I think I've found something. Whether I can make any sense of it is something else.

. . .

I barely have time to see Shep between periods, let alone tell her what I found. But at "some kind of journal in code," whispered to her in the hall, her eyes light up. Then we have to scoot, and I have to face both Spanish class and Blaise, whose mere presence seems to fill up all available space in any given room.

She comes up to me when I sit down. I wish breathing were optional. Her perfume is needles in my sinuses.

"Hello," she says.

I resist the urge to say *what do you want* and instead just say, "Hi."

"I think we got off on the wrong foot."

"Feet," I say.

"Let's start over. I'm Blaise, and you are?"

I stop myself from saying Billy's name, heart banging up against my uvula. "Sam."

What is *wrong* with me?

Blaise looks around, then takes the desk next to mine. I fight the impulse to groan.

"I know what Sky's probably told you about me," she says.

"That you told the entire school he was gay because he broke up with you instead of realizing that he could maybe still be bi and just not want to date *you*?"

"Honey," Blaise says, which makes me hate her just a little more. "He is gay."

She is looking at me the way Lee used to when she wanted something. What does Blaise want from me? I don't know, but I'm not going to let her control this conversation.

"Ever hear of Freddie Mercury?" I ask.

"What?"

"Freddie Mercury. Lead singer in Queen. 'Bohemian Rhapsody,' 'We Will Rock You,' 'We Are the Champions,' et cetera. That guy. Ring a bell?"

Blaise looks at me sideways. "What's your point?"

"Freddie Mercury was in love with his best friend Mary. Called her the love of his life on more than one occasion. She was the first person he ever came out to," I say.

"Again, I say, what is your point?" Blaise taps her wrist, even though she's not wearing a watch. Bell's about to ring.

"Freddie told her he was bi. He trusted her more than anybody else on this earth. They lived together for years and years, sometimes romantically and sexually, sometimes not, but he always loved her and she always loved him."

"So what?" Blaise is trying to look bored. Her face is flat, blank. But I see the spark of curiosity in the way she keeps looking at me even though I'm not making eye contact with her.

"Mary told him he was gay. That became the narrative. Even if Freddie *wasn't* bi like he said he was, no one gets to presume they know what's in someone else's heart." Mr. Trejo clapping to get our attention punctuates my last line like applause, and I turn away from Blaise, facing forward to end the conversation.

I can still see her in my peripheral vision. Blaise tenses at my words, her mouth a little open.

"Fascinating how you've known him for two seconds and think you know him better than I do," she says sweetly.

I can't even respond to that, because it's time for Spanish class.

With the immediate annoyance of Blaise quieted for the moment, I can think about what just happened.

I've spent most of my life with these past people as no more than dreams, or puzzles to explore, or stories. Now they seem ready to fall out of my mouth when I open it. I was this close to saying I was Billy. The urge to pull out my phone and look at the pictures I took in Frankel's office is almost overpowering, but I can't do that because Mr. Trejo is looking right at me.

I remember someone telling me once about self-fulfilling prophecy. My whole life I've been digging up stories of people who died young. Is the fact that I almost did too somehow my fault? Did I really even escape?

CHAPTER TWENTY-FOUR

Neither Sky nor Shep can come over when we get out of school—Sky's working, and Shep has a doctor's appointment. I hurry home myself and upload all the images from the journal onto my laptop. I delete them from my phone after sending a couple to the group chat.

The last images I took are a little blurry due to the low light and my frenzy to get the journal back in the drawer.

Looking at the pages, I feel like I should understand them. It's been thirty years since Billy's death—maybe it's too much of an assumption on my part that he is connected with this whole journal, but the pictures in the back make me think this anyway.

The group chat starts buzzing while I make a snack in the kitchen, mind still on the laptop upstairs.

Any luck? (Shep)

Nope. It could be Swedish for all I know. (Me)

Do you think it's Swedish? (Shep)

I can almost see Sky's eye roll in his text. *It's not Swedish, guys. My gran is Swedish. I know enough to know it's not that.*

So it's either a language we're not familiar with, or it's a code. To Google! (Shep)

The microwave *bing*s. I gingerly pull my pepperoni pocket out and tuck it into its little crisper sleeve. I take it upstairs. My phone vibrates again when I turn the corner on the landing toward my room. I set it on my bedside table and perch on the side of my bed, looking through the images again. My phone buzzes and lights up.

It's not the group chat this time, though. It's an unknown number.

Hey

That's all it says, in a green bubble, which means whoever it is doesn't seem to have an iPhone. There are approximately five people on the planet who have express consent to contact me on this phone number, and while sure, it could be a wrong number, I don't think it is.

I take a screenshot of it and send it to the group chat with Shep and Sky. *Do either of you recognize this number?*

It's an Oregon number. That much I can tell by the area code. I have a moment of balmy relief knowing it's not a Montana number. There's a pause before the ellipsis appears, then after a moment Shep says no and Sky follows.

I open the new text message and type *Who is this?*

I sit there and stare at it for two full minutes before going back to the buzzing group chat, unnerved.

I've missed a few messages from Shep and Sky.

I feel like writing in code is a pretty juvenile thing to do (Shep)
Obviously she doesn't want anybody reading her journal (Sky)
No shit. But nobody wants people reading their private journals, dude. Writing it in code is . . . excessive (Shep)
Not if she's got something to hide. (Sky)

My heart speeds up reading that last line from Sky. There's an ellipsis of someone typing, but I write *She's definitely hiding something* just as Shep writes *This is freaky.*

I don't want to text them all the pictures I took, and just as I'm about to look through the last ones, the sound of tires on pavement makes me get up and peek out my window. Dad hung the blackout curtains a few nights ago, and I've got them pulled all the way back to reveal the window seat. I still want to put pillows there. The Subaru pulls to a stop in the driveway. A moment later, Dad gets out. It's still light out. For a moment, I just watch him. He grabs his black lunch box and his briefcase in one hand, hard hat in the other. He nudges the door to the Subaru closed with his hip.

He doesn't turn to come inside, though.

As I watch, he stands next to the car, holding his things without moving. I can't tell if he's looking at something up the street or just spacing out. It's an eerie feeling, seeing him just standing there. Like ants marching one by one up my spine.

I'm about to knock on the window to wave at him, anything to break whatever spell has him standing there, but he turns and walks up the path to the front porch.

BRB, I text to the group chat.

My pepperoni pocket is almost cool enough to eat. I take it back downstairs with me and meet Dad in the foyer. He almost trips on my backpack strap.

"Sorry," I say, grabbing it and pulling it out of the way.

"You never used to leave your backpack in the line of fire," Dad says. He looks tired. There are lines at the corners of his eyes.

"I know. Sorry." The ants-on-the-spine sensation grows stronger.

I put the strap over my shoulder and take a nibble of my pepperoni pocket.

Dad goes to his room first, puts his briefcase away. I meet him in the kitchen where he methodically opens and empties his lunch box. Tupperware containers get rinsed and put in the dishwasher. Empty baggies go in the recycling bin. The wrapper from his granola bar goes in the trash.

"Are you okay, Dad?" I ask him. My pepperoni pocket tastes kind of like cardboard.

"Just a long day at work. I also heard from the police, and they haven't been able to get any leads on the zip tie incident at the school."

I chew slowly, stalling. It takes two tries to swallow my bite of swiftly toughening dough and marinara. "Okay."

He keeps the hot water on a trickle and continues rinsing the few dishes in the sink. "Are *you* okay?"

"Dad," I start. Shit. I hate lying to him. I should have known he'd know something was wrong.

"Sam, I don't know about this place."

"Dad—"

"I know I said we'd give it until your birthday at least, but I've been thinking about it nonstop, and I just don't know—"

"Dad—" Something grows in me, fluttering and frantic.

I don't recognize the look on his face, but whatever it is, I don't like it.

"I was hoping it'd be safe here. Portland was a good place to catch our breath and assess our options. I thought Astoria would be small enough not to overwhelm us like the big city. Maybe we should have stayed in Portland, though. There are good things about cities, even if they are loud and crowded and expensive." He sounds like he *wants* to believe his own words more than actually believes them. He lets out a long breath through his nose. "After what we went through in Montana, this was finally supposed to be our new start. My job's good, and the school seemed so promising—"

"Dad, I'm never going to be safe!" The words explode out of my mouth, and he stops with his morning coffee mug halfway to the dishwasher.

"Sammy—"

"Not here, not Portland, not anywhere." I interrupt him again. "No matter where I go, I'll always be queer. I'll always be someone who fucks with people's ideas of gender and what I should or shouldn't be. Even if people look at me and think I'm a butch woman or a glitter-wearing gay dude, I'm never going to be safe. Half the country doesn't want me to be able to *pee* if I have to. I'm never going to fit in, because I don't know how to person like other people do. I'll never be safe. Anywhere. I know you get that, Dad."

For a moment the idea of being taken for a glitter-wearing gay dude in passing almost seems like a fantasy, a dream of growing up enough to wander the streets of Seattle or LA or New York and *be* misgendered if only I get to live to do it. I want to tell him that he could lock me in a padded room on an island in the middle of the South Pacific and I wouldn't be safe. Something could find a way to kill me. A lightning strike or heart failure. Who knows? You name it and it's probably happened to someone.

The thought fills me with desperation. I can't keep following this line of discussion, or he will bundle me off to that island and try to protect me. Because that is what Dad does. He protects me.

This time he can't. Just like I know that him being forced to interact with the police as a Black man is its own major trauma. He's done it in Montana and he's done it here. For me. But he can't protect me from life, just like I can't protect him from everything that makes him unsafe.

And neither of us can protect me from this. Not from whatever capricious trickster of the universe slapped my soul with a zip-tie reminder of mortality. If I even have a soul. I don't know how this works.

To my utter surprise, Dad sets down the mug on the top rack of the dishwasher, slides it back in, and closes the door. He heaves a sigh.

"I know," he says.

Suddenly I'm the tired one. My back aches where the binder compresses my chest and ribcage, that familiar pain I almost never even notice anymore.

Of course Dad knows. I meet his eyes, those perfect dark brown eyes that saw me when no one else did.

"I ever tell you about how I got to Montana?" He says it so quickly it's like he's trying to convince himself not to change his mind.

I shake my head.

"I grew up in DC," he says. "Southeast. Anacostia. There are only two high schools left open south of the river in DC. Both are all-Black. I went to Anacostia Senior High. I was an only kid. My mom and dad did the best they could, but Momma got sick when I was a freshman. We couldn't get her treatment, because Dad worked at a shop that didn't give benefits. She'd get bad, we'd take her to the emergency room, they'd stabilize her, and we'd go home."

He's never told me any of this before, not about his school or about the struggles with hospitals. Only that they died. He talked about Gran and Gramps sometimes when I was younger, these hazy memories where I could almost hear Gran's Jamaican accent and smell the garage grease on Gramps's calloused hands. Right now, I feel like I'm seven years old again, seeing Dad for the first time.

"I got angry," he says. "I started yelling at teachers, fighting with other students."

That gives me a jolt. Dad, fighting? *Dad? On purpose?* I remember his tooth and the bridge that covers the hole in his gums during the day and suddenly wonder what the story behind it is.

"Teachers got together and brought Dad in, and they diagnosed me with emotional disturbance." His lip quirks when he says it, like it still bothers him. It probably does. *Emotional disturbance.* It sounds like reactive attachment disorder in my head. He goes on. "I wasn't the only one. Bunch of young Black boys in a rough neighborhood in a city where the race and class lines are one and the same. The teachers called us the chair throwers. I remember hearing one of the older teachers warning this young white newbie about us when she heard that teacher was teaching special ed. That young teacher was my case manager. She only lasted a year. She was from Montana."

"She only *lasted* a year?" I say. "What happened to her?"

"I never found out, just that she quit." Dad shrugs. "I never knew much about other states at that point, though, and she made me curious about Montana. I'd never been outside the District. Mom died, and I dropped out of school. Dad got sick after that, too. Cancer. They both smoked a pack a day."

"What did you do?" The thought of Dad left all alone is almost too much to bear.

"I didn't have any family left. But I got a bug up my ass about Montana. I remember my teacher used to talk about the mountains. She didn't care much for most of it out there, but she really loved those mountains. I sold Dad's car and as much of my parents' stuff as I could and took off in Mom's Honda. Drove all the way out to Missoula." Dad chuckles. "Went from being in a place where every damn person looked like me to one where nobody did. I went a full two months before I saw another Black

215

person in the Bitterroot Valley. I got a job at an oil change place for a while, then one of the guys, this old redneck with a beard to his chest, told me about Job Corps. Vocational training. I never knew there was anything like that. I got in, they trained me to be a carpenter and an electrician, and the rest is history."

Dad gives me a big smile. I manage a feeble one back.

"I never thought I was good at anything before then," Dad says quietly. He always speaks so quietly. "I got frustrated sometimes, with the math I had to learn and stuff. I wasn't a great reader, either, and I had to get better. But people there were used to working with angry kids who got stuck somewhere. They helped me find a counselor, too."

"And that's why you weren't intimidated by me?" I ask.

"I was stuck most of my teen years with that diagnosis. People heard 'emotional disturbance' and thought I was dangerous. Which, you know, is great for a young Black man's image." Dad says it lightly, but I hear the weight in his words. I'm not usually great at detecting sarcasm, but this is Dad. He goes on. "I met you at that group home, and they told me you had reactive attachment disorder. I saw the hungry way you looked around and the frustration I knew all too well, like you were shouting and everyone pretended they couldn't hear you. I figured if I had a reason to be angry when I was a kid, maybe you had a reason not to get attached to people, or at least not to show it."

That last sentence makes its home in my gut. It's too close to what I was thinking before he started talking. It's more than he usually talks, and as always, I don't know what I can say to make it better.

As if he's reading my mind—or my forehead again—he shakes his head at me.

216

"I think every parent tries to fix whatever was broken in their childhood for their own children. But that's *our* job, Sammy." He dries his hands on the dish towel and comes over, putting his hands out on either side of my head, waiting for my nod of permission before he plants a kiss on my forehead. "I can see you trying to make it work here, and I want to honor that. What I want you to know is that everything I've done—the moves, the restraining orders, the meetings, all of it—it's my job. But it's not like my day job where I can tweak the wiring or measure a couple two-by-fours and everything works perfectly. There's nothing scarier for a parent than knowing we can move heaven and Earth and still our kid gets hurt."

I still can't talk, so I just throw my arms around him. For a long moment I just smell the coconut and fruit that is so familiar, mixed with sawdust and construction-site smells. I can hear his heart beating. I wonder how I got so lucky. When I finally pull back, he gives me a sad little smile.

"I've got a headache coming on," he says. "I'm going to go lie down."

I nod at him, mourning my own silence. I want to tell him about the home invader, about the weird text, but something stops me. This is something I have to do. Myself. My job. I chuck the last third of my pepperoni pocket in the trash and head back upstairs.

My phone's got a heap of messages from Sky and Shep, and one more from the mysterious number.

I forget to breathe when I see what it says in response to me asking whose number it is.

Look out your window at midnight if you want to know. Tell anyone and you'll regret it.

CHAPTER **TWENTY-FIVE**

It's only ten when Dad goes off to bed for good with his migraine, and I sit up in my room with the lights off, trying not to freak out. With my blackout shades drawn, my room is like a cave.

I don't tell Shep or Sky about the message, and they're so busy trying to work out the code and do their homework that they forget I asked about the mystery number in the first place.

I try googling the number, but nothing comes up. Could be new, could be a burner phone, could be any number of reasons. None of them lessen the creepy factor. I google my own number, but nothing ties it to me. I've only had it a few months. I try searching for my number with my name as well, but nothing.

At 11:40, I open the dormer windows on both sides. There's no screens, just four panes of glass on each. I don't know who I expect to see. Who would even be texting me? The nearest streetlight is half a block away. It's cold outside, so I wrap myself in a fuzzy black blanket from my bed, covering my hair like a cloak. I feel like a moody Sith sitting there on that window seat, but at least the blanket will keep me somewhat hidden from anyone on the street. I tuck my phone into a fold of the blanket and wait.

Midnight arrives. I wish I had a flashlight, something that would help me identify whoever this creep is. It is a creep; that's for damn sure. The only people I've given my phone number to are Shep and Sky—but whoever texted me got it from some-where. My student file, maybe.

The cold breeze almost feels good. Alive.

I don't see the first rock. I hear it.

It strikes the wood just to the right of the window, and the sound of the sharp *thunk* makes me jump, my blanketed body sliding against the smooth paint of the window seat.

I can't see anyone outside.

The second one hits window frame and bounces down the shingles over the foyer, landing in a bush in the front lawn.

This isn't someone tossing pebbles to get my attention, but whoever it is has kind of shitty aim.

My hand flashes out of my blanket. As the third rock strikes hot and hard against my palm, I hear a thirty-year-old echo of a baseball slapping a glove. How did I *do* that? I can barely see.

"Fuck," I whisper to myself. The rock in my hand is jagged on the edges. In the dim light, I can see a dark welt where it hit, and when I touch it with my finger, my finger comes away wet.

Something surges through me, and I drop the stone just in time to catch a fourth one with the same hand. I suck in a hissing breath through my teeth. My palm burns. I fumble for my phone and hit the flashlight app.

It's not strong enough. I shine it out of the window and see movement across the street behind a tree, out of the small golden circle of light from the distant street lamp.

I can't tell who it is or even much about them. Average weight. Height of a high schooler or adult. Either. My phone buzzes, and I almost drop it out the window.

It's from the mystery number.

Watch yourself.

. . .

I never thought I'd use stimming to hide something. Usually I'm trying to hide that I'm stimming.

When I come down the next morning after a night of waking up every two hours, I take my juice with my left hand so Dad doesn't see me covering the purple-red welts on my right palm with my fingers, lightly grazing my skin with my nails. I've never had bruises on my palm before. They make a large V, partly scabbed over where the skin broke in a couple places. I kept the rocks on my bedside table all night, but now they're in my backpack. One has a small smear of blood on it.

I hustle out the door, dreading Advisory and having to start my day with Blaise.

I text Shep on the way to school. *Library again today?*

Sure. Why?

I want to show you the rest of what I found yesterday, but I don't want to do it at home. Or school. She'll know what it's about. I copied one of the pages into a notebook last night when I was trying to get my brain to shut up enough to sleep. I still really don't want the photos on my phone, but I brought my laptop, which is password protected.

Shep meets me in front of the school. "Sky's got a dentist appointment, so he won't be here till lunchtime," she says, reaching out with her left hand to hold my right one. She stops, taking it in both of her hands to look at the angry red V. "Dude, what happened to your hand?"

I look around, making sure no one's too close to hearing distance. "That person who texted me showed up at my house at midnight and chucked rocks at my window. I caught a couple of them."

"Jesus, Sam." Shep looks horrified. This time she looks around us, then plants a furtive kiss on my palm. Little tingles shoot out to my fingers. "Were you on the roof or something?"

"I had the windows open so I could see without a glare. Turns out that probably saved me and Dad the trouble of getting new glass." I wince, flexing my hand. Not to mention that Dad would break the sound barrier getting us out of Astoria if someone chucked a rock through my bedroom window.

"You caught the rocks?"

"More's the pity."

She goes quiet at that, and I go with her to her locker to grab a notebook. The school is quiet today, subdued. Someone laughs too loudly, and I'm not the only one in the hall who jumps.

"What's up with people today?" Shep mutters.

"I don't know," I say. My hand feels hot.

"I got you something," she blurts out.

"What? Why?" My face gets hot like my hand. "I mean, thank you?"

"I haven't shown you what it is yet," she says with a nervous laugh. "It's okay if you hate it or don't want to use it, but . . ."

She digs around in the outside pocket of her backpack and produces a small purple cube covered in buttons and bobbles of varying textures. I take it from her hesitant hand. Something in me feels very soft all the sudden. Soft and warm.

"You got me a stim cube?" On closer inspection, it's galaxy patterned. The purple changes in hue and is dotted with pinpricks of white. Stars.

"It's okay if you don't think you'll use it. I should have asked. I'm sorry!"

She looks so flustered, and I belatedly understand that she is afraid she's offended me.

"I've never had one before," I say, wondering why not. I like the way it feels in my hand. The rubber buttons feel nice, and one side has a smooth ball bearing inset next to three parallel plastic wheels with gear-like edges that turn. The texture of the wheels next to the smooth ball is *good*. "I like it so far."

That earns me a smile. "It's just small. I just saw it online when I was shopping and thought of you for the galaxy pattern and thought it'd be perfect."

"It is," I tell her, still feeling that warm softness. I can't remember the last time someone not Dad got me a gift at all, let alone one so thoughtful. On impulse, I lean forward and kiss her lightly. She kisses me back, and we both dart a glance around to make sure we're not about to get yelled at for public displays of affection.

Shep's next sentence comes out all at once in a rush. "I kind of wanted to ask you if you want to be, uh . . . date friends. Like together. Like a couple. Only if you want to!"

Her voice actually squeaks on the last bit, and I am nodding almost before I am able to process what she's said. "I—yes, very yes!"

The smile that lights up her face threatens to overwhelm the fluorescents above us.

"Oh-my-god," she says just as quickly, and a breath gusts out of her. "Wow, that was terrifying."

"You didn't think I'd say yes?" I ask, suddenly unsure of my footing.

"I didn't want to assume!"

We are both quiet—but grinning—the rest of the way to my classroom.

Shep leaves me at Advisory. "I've got to make up a test at lunch," she says. "See you in history?"

That comment hits me in a weird way. I can't make my vocal cords give her an answer, so I just nod, watching her—my girlfriend!—walk away down the hall.

I shuffle into my chair in Advisory. No Blaise yet, but she scoots through the door just before the bell right as I flex my hand. She sees the welts. I know she does.

For the second day in a row, one of the office aides does the morning announcements. Is Principal Frankel out again? I don't think too long about it, because the memory of Shep's kiss is still fresh, and it hits me that I kissed my girlfriend in the hallway of my high school without fear of other students, just nervousness about teachers fussing about PDA—which, in my experience, they apply heartily to straight couples. It's such a normal *positive* high school feeling, one of the few I think I've actually had. To just get to *be*.

I fiddle with the cube Shep gave me through my first class, and it's nice. More than nice. It gives me an outlet when I need one, which is often. It's so easy to just roll that little ball around with the pad of my thumb or press the gearwheels into the edge of my thumb, and when I discover the ball-bearing is also a button, I feel a surge of excitement that makes my hands dance before I can stop them.

Woodshop is calming when I get there, too. I can put on headphones and work on my project without having to worry about anyone else or what they're doing, just a soothing rhythm of sanding, which doesn't require pressure on my wounded palm.

Lunch is after that, though, and I can't face the cafeteria. Instead, I go to Mr. Quach's room and ask him if I can eat there. He frowns when he notices my hand, but he lets me stay and eat and read.

"Are you doing okay, Sam?" he asks me as I gather my things to leave.

"Yeah," I say. I don't think he believes me, but he doesn't push it. "Is your dad okay?"

His face softens. "Yes, thank you. He's out of ICU. I got to talk to him last night."

"Is he around here?" I ask.

"Yep, lived here all my life," says Mr. Quach. Then, wryly, "His picture's in the trophy case by the office. He was a starting pitcher once upon a time. They won state when he was a senior here."

"I bet he's proud of you," I say without thinking before realizing maybe that is not a student thing to say to a teacher.

Then again, I imagine most teachers have heard worse. Mr. Quach just gives me a smile and holds the door for me.

By the time I get to US history, my head feels full of weird buzzing.

I can't concentrate on what Ms. Gowan is saying about the Civil War, and I can't even concentrate on the sight of Shep out of the corner of my eye, though I catch her looking at my hand, where I'm fiddling with the cube, and I think I see her smile.

After class, Shep goes with me to my locker to grab my odd-number period stuff for tomorrow.

"Still up for the library?" She's looking around like she expects someone to jump out at us.

"I think so," I tell her. My voice sounds far away. "I feel weird."

"Everybody is off today," Shep says. "Frankel's out, Blaise didn't bother me, Sky didn't come in after his dentist appointment, and I'm pretty sure I made a massive fail of that makeup test for chemistry."

I putter with my combination, trying to get it to work. On the third try, I drop the lock. "I don't think this is my lock."

It's the same color purple, but the dial sticks instead of spinning easily. It's one of those things you notice when you have to use something every day.

Shep picks it up and looks at it. "It looks the same to me."

I run my hand through my hair without thinking. The bruises throb. "It worked fine two hours ago. I think I'm slipping into another dimension or something."

Spinning the dial again, I go through the numbers. I tug on the lock. Nothing.

"I didn't forget my combination between woodshop and now," I say to Shep. "You try."

I tell her the numbers, and she puts them in. She jerks on the lock when she gets to the third one. Nothing for her either.

"Damn," she says. "Want me to get a janitor and a lock cutter?"

I almost laugh, but at the same time, my eyes feel hot and watery. I am not going to cry in the hallway at school. Absolutely not.

"Yeah," I say, letting my forehead fall against the metal door of my locker. "Please."

The halls have mostly cleared out by the time she gets back with the janitor. The older woman is in coveralls and has her blonde hair pulled back in a stubby ponytail.

"Gotta be better at remembering your combo," she says.

"I didn't forget it. It's just not working." Pain prickles at my temples.

The janitor shrugs, then wedges the bolt cutter between the lock's U bends and grunts as she pulls the bars together. "Second purple lock today. I always just had the boring black ones."

Shep and I look at each other and almost speak over one another.

"Second purple—" She stops, deferring to me.

"This is your second purple lock of the day?" I ask.

"Not mine, but I saw the other one in the bin in the closet," she says. "Bob cut that one, I think."

"Could I look at it?" I ask. I think I already know the answer.

The janitor looks at me sideways, but she gestures to me to follow.

"I'll wait here," Shep says, which I interpret as *I won't peek in your locker without you.*

The janitors have an office off the cafeteria that butts up against the woodshop. She leads me in and points me to a plastic bin of cut locks.

"You save them?"

"We take them to the scrap metal yard every semester." She shrugs.

Sure enough, there's another purple lock right on top of the pile. I pick it up and spin the dial. I wouldn't even have to put in the numbers to know that it's mine from the way the wheel turns alone. It pops open.

"I don't want to be rude when you just opened my locker," I say, "but is there any kind of check for whose locker you're opening?"

She raises an eyebrow at me. "How do you mean?"

I waggle the purple lock. "This one just opened to my combination. It was on my locker three hours ago, but someone replaced it with the one you just cut off."

"Well, hell."

"Somebody's been messing with me," I tell her. "Can you ask Bob—that's the other guy's name, right?—not to cut off any locks from locker three-sixty-seven unless it's me asking?"

The woman grabs a legal pad and jots it down. "What's your name?"

"Sam Sylvester," I tell her. "Thanks."

"If someone's messing with you, you should tell Principal Frankel."

"I think she already knows."

I leave before she can ask any more questions. I take my old lock with me.

Shep's leaning against my locker when I get back. "Somebody replaced the lock, didn't they?"

"Yep," I say.

She moves out of the way and puts a light hand on my shoulder. "Sam," she says softly. "You don't have to open it. I can open it for you, or we can get Mr. Quach—"

"I don't want him involved in this. I'll open it on three." I put my hand on the locker latch and count under my breath. Mr. Quach has his dad to worry about.

The locker opens easily. I don't know what I expect. Another zip tie and a note, maybe. A dead animal? That'd smell too bad.

Instead there's nothing. At all. My locker is completely empty except one thing. A rock.

"Fuck," I say. "My textbooks were all in there, except history and my *Call of the Wild*."

"I think you should tell your dad," Shep says. "This is escalating."

"I can't tell Dad," I say. "He'll pull me out of school so fast, he'd break through space-time and will be like I never existed."

"Sam—"

"Shep, somebody really doesn't want me looking into Billy Clement's death." I pull in a deep breath and let it out through my nose. "Which means either someone's a sadistic fuck who just wants to see me squirm when they don't know me from Adam or somebody knows what happened to Billy and they don't want anyone else to figure it out."

"Shit," says Shep.

"Lee used to drag me to church with her sometimes," I say. "I mostly hated it because I was a stealth queer in a zone where they'd talk about the dangers of *the homosexuals* but one of the ass-backward things they said makes some sense in this context."

"What?"

"That if somebody's fighting us, they think we're somehow dangerous."

Shep's quiet for a moment. The hall around us is empty.

"If it's too much, I won't blame you for backing away," I tell her. I can't ignore Billy, and I can't ignore this.

She steps closer to me, taking my injured hand in hers and kissing me on the cheek.

"I'm not going to leave you to do this alone," she says. There's a strange light in her eyes, and for a moment I feel like somehow, impossibly, she's making eye contact with Billy, not me.

CHAPTER TWENTY-SIX

The library is an eerie kind of quiet when Shep and I get there. We pick a study carrel as far from any other patrons as we can—and in a corner, so no one can see my laptop—and together, Shep and I look through the images I got from Principal Frankel's journal.

Shep stares at the picture of Billy and Margie dressed up for Halloween. "Look how happy they look."

"I know," I say. It comes with a pang in my chest. I rub one hand on my sternum through my shirt and binder, but it doesn't ease the tightness that has nothing to do with constriction.

The next pictures are similarly mundane—Margie on her bike with her hands off the handlebars, Billy and a kid with black hair (back to the camera) playing air hockey in what is now my basement, a picture of Margie and Billy and who I presume is the black-haired boy at the beach. The third kid is Asian, and he's proudly holding up a massive conch while Margie gives him bunny ears, a sly grin on her face. Billy himself looks like he's trying to keep from doubling over with laughter.

"God," Shep says. She sniffs, and I look over to see that she's got tears dripping down her face. "They're just like us."

I swallow the additional pang that comes with that. I've . . . never had an us like that. I think she must mean herself and Sky, or maybe how it used to be with Blaise. None of us have taken pictures of each other yet, but maybe we will someday.

"Principal Frankel couldn't have killed him," I murmur. "I think she just misses him."

"It's like she's stuck," Shep says. "At the school, in this town—she never left."

We find nothing helpful online for breaking the code in the journal, and after a while, we leave the library and walk home. Shep leaves me on my doorstep with a promise that she'll keep looking into it when she gets home.

I don't know what I'm going to do about the missing textbooks. I need them for class, and they're expensive to replace. Plus, they're checked out to me, so it's not like the school won't notice they're missing at some point.

Dropping my too-light backpack inside the door, I move to the sofa in the living room and flop down. My head hurts, and my stomach doesn't feel much better.

I put a throw pillow over my head and let it pad my eyes into darkness.

I don't mean to fall asleep, but after a few minutes, the anxious wakefulness of last night catches up to me and I step into the misty tunnel. My breath crashes in my lungs like shallow waves on rocks.

I can see them, through the light and mist. Like I've never seen them before. Faces from photographs I found, from paintings. Some of them appear in my mind's eye like they were painted in meticulous oils, others in sepia tones. All of them were real.

It feels like only a second later when I hear someone saying my name loudly. Dad.

"Sammy, wake up!"

No mist. No undulating pastel lights. Just Dad's face inches from mine, the whites of his eyes showing all around the irises. I get a whiff of coconut and passionfruit instead of dust or rain, and my head wants to split down the seams of my skull.

I meet Dad's eyes but can't speak, unable to remember what I was dreaming about but certain there were dreams. The sun has set, but outside the window it's still light out.

"Your hand," Dad says. "You were thrashing about bad. Daymare?"

He keeps his tone casual, but I know he's freaked. He holds out his left hand and grabs mine to hoist me to my feet. The world spins, and I almost lurch over.

"Yeah," I say. "Daymare."

My scar throbs, and my throat is its own choker.

My heart beats heavy and loud in my chest, and for now it's a reminder that I am alive. I am completely alive, and I want to stay that way. I want to stay that way.

"What is it this time, Sam?" Dad asks. "You sounded pretty scared."

I drop my gaze to the floor. "I don't remember."

I wish I could tell him everything. Lay it all bare. Dad always wants to help.

But I'm hearing literal voices. Imagining things. Smelling things, maybe, for fuck's sake. I know Dad doesn't think there should be a stigma around mental health, but there still is. If he thinks I need it, I could spend my last remaining weeks in Astoria in inpatient psychiatric care. And then he'll bustle us far away from here—if the mystery texter doesn't get me first.

I can't risk it. I can't.

Dad looks at me for a long moment, then he turns and heads toward the kitchen. "Can you move your backpack, please? I'm going to start dinner."

"What?"

"It's right in front of the door again."

He disappears around the corner, and I turn to look. I remember dropping it, but . . .

I look at my hand again, at the welts where I caught those rocks. I don't know how I did it—catching flying objects in the dark. It was like a reflex, like muscle memory. Billy was the baseball player, not me. I close my eyes, shutting out the room around me.

My own personal parade of the dead; I've summoned every one of them.

. . .

The rest of January passes in a strange sort of routine. I have nightmares each night, filled with faces and stories of lives half-lived. When I wake up, I can recall them as if I just finished researching them that moment.

How many times has this played out across the ages?

School becomes the easiest part of the day, except I have to go to the vice principal and tell him how someone stole my textbooks. He gets me replacements and tells me they'll review the camera footage to try and see who's responsible for getting the lock cut.

I carry them all in my backpack and stop checking my locker at all. By February, my lats are getting pretty strong, and my suspicion that the cameras won't solve the mystery of the locker break-in is even stronger.

Blaise mostly backs off. I don't know if my inspirational Freddie Mercury story did the trick or if she just got bored and decided I wasn't a threat to her. Because I'm obviously not. If anything, Shep is the one who wants to punch out all Blaise's teeth every time she waltzes through the door of Mr. Quach's room. After a couple Rainbow Island meetings where Mr. Quach is the only human who talks, Blaise stops showing up.

Dylan still talks to me in the halls sometimes, and Aidan has decided to semi-permanently join the lunch table with me and Sky and Shep, and he's even been added to the group chat, though we haven't told him about everything with Billy. He doesn't say anything about me and Shep holding hands. I can't tell why he wants to sit with us, but he laughs and jokes and apparently has started reading Sky's web comic.

Principal Frankel shows back up after a week of absences and when I see her in the hall, she doesn't look at me.

None of us make any progress on decoding the journal.

To cheer us up, Sky suggests we all go to the Valentine's Day formal. Even Aidan, who for some reason lights up at the idea when Sky brings it up at lunch. He doesn't know why the rest of us need cheering up, but he nods so eagerly that I don't think Sky has the heart to exclude him.

The real surprise comes the week before the dance, just as I'm leaving woodshop.

Dylan stops me in the hall just by the office. "Hey," he says. "Hey, Sam."

His feet keep moving, scuffing the floor a bit. He's looking at my feet in their Docs.

"Hey," I say. "What's up?"

"I, uh . . ." he trails off, waiting for a loud group of sophomores to wander past. "What are you making in shop?"

"Sculpture thing," I say. "Trying, anyway. My dad's the real carpenter in the family."

"Your dad seems pretty rad."

"Did you just say rad?"

Dylan grins down at his feet and shifts his shoulders. "Yeah, guess I did. My dad still says it."

I give him a tight-lipped smile, now thoroughly confused. "I've gotta get to lunch or all the good pizza sticks will be gone."

"Wait—" Dylan reaches out and grabs my arm.

I freeze, and after a second, he drops it. I can still feel the imprint of his fingers, and my hair follicles all decide now's a good time to mambo.

"I was wondering" —Dylan mutters it almost too low for me to hear— "if you'd maybe want to go to the dance with me."

I can't help it. I blink. "What?"

"Will you go to the Valentine's Dance with me? I can get us a limo, and I clean up nice in a tux. Least that's what everybody said when I was a groomsman at my cousin's wedding in Napa Valley last year—"

Oh, no. I take a shaky breath, suddenly feeling like I won't be able to eat a pizza stick after all. "I'm—uh . . . I'm really sorry, Dylan. I'm going with Sky and Shep and Aidan, and . . ."

"I know that, but I thought you might want like . . . a date."

"Shep is my date," I say haltingly, staring over Dylan's shoulder at the trophy case behind him without really seeing it. "We're kind of dating."

"Oh," Dylan says. Then looks at me wide-eyed. "Oh!"

"Um. Yeah?"

"So you don't like guys then." He looks like this makes him feel better. Because of course it does. Lines-for-eyes emoji.

"Actually, I just don't feel attracted to anybody most of the time." I don't know what makes me say it. "I'm on the ace spectrum."

"That's like, an autistic thing, right?"

"Uh, no. I am autistic but uh . . . different spectrum. Ace like *asexual*."

"Is that why your pronouns are *they/them*?"

Oh, god, how did I get in this conversation? My face is on fire. A basketball player shimmies down the hall, and I'm tempted to kick the basketball he's carrying into the sprinkler system just to cool off my cheeks. But with my luck I'd just smash the trophy case and be literally walking on broken glass.

"Sexuality and gender are different things," I say, instantly regretting it, eyes still locked on a football trophy for some championship or another. "And my autism isn't the cause of either? Look. Basically, I don't care what anybody's gender identity is on the rare times I feel attracted to someone. Hypothetically, guy or girl or both or neither. I just—"

"This shit is complicated," says Dylan, still looking like I've blown his mind when I sneak a glance at him.

"Only because we're trained to see it as black and white," I mutter. "But, uh . . . the point is, I'm flattered you asked me to the dance, but I'm already going with my girlfriend and some friends. Are—uh . . . we cool?"

Dylan's frowning. Not at me, I don't think, just sort of an in-general frown. "Wait, if you're not a girl, does that make me gay?"

"Oh, god." This time I say it out loud. "I don't think I'm the person to tell you about your sexuality, dude. Mr. Quach or one of the counselors would probably be a better sounding board."

Mr. Quach. Staring at the trophy case, I remember what he said about his dad being in a picture somewhere in there, which is very unhelpful in this current moment.

My skin feels like it's been turned into aluminum foil and someone's put a tuning fork up against it. It could vibrate off me at any moment. Being autistic—I forget people just assume it makes me . . . I don't know. More sensitive, less gender-y. That it causes my queerness instead of just being part of me, and my queerness is just . . . mine.

My only kiss before Shep was a guy at school I'd known since my first year there. We were at a party and the only two sober people there and he asked if he could and I said yes because I was curious and—after what Lee did, he was one of the first to go full rage against me in the halls. For making him think he kissed a "freak."

For making him consider that maybe his attractions weren't as binary as he thought.

I'm backing away from Dylan before I know what I'm doing without tearing my eyes from the trophies.

"Hey, Sam," he says. "What's wrong?"

I can't make words happen. Why is it him *again*? He's the one who set me off the first time and—

My hand balls into a fist. It still twinges even though the bruises from the rocks faded.

"Whoa, whoa, whoa," says Dylan. He closes the distance between us and takes my hand in his before I can slam my fist into my leg. I shake off his hand, and he puts both of his up in surrender. "You're okay. I'm sorry. I shouldn't have pried. I just . . . I like you. I didn't know you and Shep were a thing, and you've got me thinking about things I never really thought about before. Things I never thought about even *thinking about* before."

I still can't make words, but I manage to look him in the eye for a split second. His eyes are big and green and . . . earnest.

"I know what happened at your old school." He rushes on. "You don't have to say anything. But . . . I dunno. My mom was in Afghanistan for a while. Sometimes me or Dad'll say something, and she'll get that same look. Like suddenly she's not there anymore. I'm sorry. I think your old school sucked. I've heard about some of the shit that goes on at this one, but I hope it's at least been better."

"Thank you." My voice comes out all gravely and distant, and this is all too much to process right now whether he's earnest or not.

"We're cool, Sam. Friends?" He gives me this hopeful look that I can't shatter, or I couldn't even if I wanted to.

"Friends," I echo. "Yeah."

He leaves me staring at the trophy case. I dig in my pocket for my cube, and it immediately helps. I depress the ball-bearing button several times in quick succession, which is satisfying. To calm myself, I move closer to the trophy case. Seeing a baseball trophy, I start looking for a picture of state champions that would be old enough to have Mr. Quach's dad in it. How old is Mr. Quach, even? I'm a terrible guesser of ages. He could be twenty-five or forty, though I think he's far closer to our age than forty.

But there are only a couple team photos in there, and only one is from a state championship. Guess the Fishermen don't win that often.

Squinting through the glass, I can barely make out the names on the roster at the bottom of the photo, but there is an S. Quach listed in the front row. Front and center, actually. Of course. Pitchers are important.

No Billy. It's only then I register the date of the championship: 1989. This was taken after he died.

Mr. Quach's dad was a senior that year. My face is almost pressed up against the glass to find his face.

When I do, I almost drop my cube.

Mr. Quach's dad is the boy in Principal Frankel's pictures. He was one of Billy's *friends*.

CHAPTER **TWENTY-SEVEN**

I found something.

I stare at Shep's text for a solid five minutes before I can respond. Dad's not home yet, and even though it's staying marginally lighter later now, the sunset was an hour ago and my room is full of a dim sunlight. It's two days before this dance now, and I don't know whether Shep's text means she found something for the dance or something about Billy.

I don't think I should ask Mr. Quach to ask his dad—his dad who is in the *hospital*—about who killed Billy. What would I even ask? "Hi, Mr. Quach the Elder, can you think of anyone who might have wanted your friend dead?" That probably wouldn't go over well. I can almost hear Dad's patient explanation the time I asked him to tell me the rules of funerals after we watched some episode of a show where the humor was based in someone breaking them (I didn't understand what was funny), and I feel like those rules are probably applicable here too even though Mr. Quach is okay.

I text her back. *Me too, actually. What did you find?*

She didn't send it to the group text. Must be about the dance, then.

I'll be right over. That okay?

Yep, I text back.

I turn on my lamp before I go downstairs to wait for her knock, which seems to happen in an otherworldly quick fashion.

Seeing Shep always gives me a little thrill, like the electric currents of our bodies touch noses and spark each time.

"Hey," she says. She steps inside, carrying her backpack.

Mine's in front of the door again. I pick it up, pushing away the unease that comes with knowing this house has taken over my own habits.

I sling it over my shoulder and take Shep's face in my hands, kissing her on each cheek before letting our lips meet. She sighs into me, one hand on my chest. I'm still wearing my binder, and the sense of being touched is always somehow heightened with the constriction, even though there's an extra layer of clothing between us.

"Dad'll be home soon," I murmur into Shep's hair. It's growing out a bit on top. She's gotten the bottom faded into the longer bits again, by which I mean she came over and had Dad do it. (He was delighted.)

Dad's been cool about us dating, but I think he's not quite sure what boundaries to set. Cis dudes always seem to be confused about what sex is if it doesn't involve a penis. Not that Shep and I have had sex. Yet.

"Then I'll be good," Shep says wickedly. "Besides. Wait'll you see what I found."

We tromp upstairs to my room. I've started adding some things to my shelves. My first woodshop project was a carved wooden box. That's on one shelf, still empty. Sky keeps giving me books, and those are lining out my shelves faster than I can read them. On one of the center shelves is that time capsule Dad dug up. I open it every couple of days, hoping it'll give me some sort of clue. So far, diddly squat.

Shep drops her backpack on the bed and unzips it. Even though I expect it, the sound still makes my spine straighten.

"Sorry," she says, noticing. "I keep forgetting."

"It's okay," I say. "It's not as bad anymore."

It's true.

"First, I should tell you how I found this. Because I think you'll find it reiterates my psychic powers."

I grin at her. "I was never in any doubt of those. Where was it?"

"In the attic of my house. Which up till today, I didn't even know we still had." Shep's smile stretches out wide and smug. "Mom is working till eight tonight, so I was alone and I was digging around in her, like, *wing* of the house for accessories to wear for the dance."

If whatever Shep found is for the dance, it's either thirty years out of fashion or the coolest retro outfit ever. Then again, someone could Photoshop Esme Shepard onto the cover of *Vogue* and she wouldn't look out of place, so she probably has plenty of current things Shep could raid for dance purposes.

"Your mom must really like her space."

"You have no idea. She practically gave her wardrobe its own suite when she remodeled a few years ago." Shep rolls her eyes. "Anyway. I'm not supposed to go in her room, but I was pissed off and did that instead of my mandated study hour. I went into her closet to try and find something flashy—she has a whole vanity for purses and scarves and statement necklaces. *So many,* Sam, and I had this ridiculous moment of thinking maybe she'd be more chill if I like, came with a Gucci logo on my forehead or something, and I looked up at the ceiling out of pure angst"— Shep pauses to make a dramatic face—"And that's when I saw the hatch door."

"Whoa. You didn't know it was there?"

"I guess I did, but the ceiling in the old hallway was textured when Abuela gave her the house ages ago. She had a trestle . . . not trestle. Tray. A tray ceiling put in when I was a kid. I remember her talking to the builders about a crawl space, but then she never mentioned it again, so I guess I thought it was boarded up. *But* when she did the remodel of that section of the house, they must have taken off the tray tiles that were covering the hatch. Which is now in her closet."

"Holy shit, Shep."

"Yeah. And the hatch was all clean and functional. I pulled it down and unfolded the ladder and climbed right up. There's even strip lighting up there, Sam. She must have had someone install it as part of the remodel. Though it's covered in dust."

"She never told you?" Now it's my turn to have my spider senses tingling. Do all the adults in this town hide their secrets? This doesn't seem like somewhere Esme Shepard would have stashed an old prom dress.

"Nope. We've got a half-finished basement. I always thought that was where all our storage went. Hell, I'd never looked up in Mom's closet before. I think I'd been in there once before today."

"Your mom is weird."

"She really is." Shep pulls open the flaps on her backpack and pulls out a thick book with a worn cover. "She has almost nothing from her own childhood in the basement—I thought that was all there was. Apparently just those few boxes of knick-knacks like the yearbook and one little trunk upstairs with pictures of her husband who died and . . . this."

"What is that?" I already know, but I have to ask.

"It's her journal. From high school. Nineteen eighty-six to nineteen ninety." Shep reaches out and hands me the book. "Score one for Shep, eh?"

Holy shit. Not about the dance after all.

It takes me a minute to gather myself. "You think she knew something."

"Yeah, I do." Shep bites her lip for a moment before going on. "Remember what the librarian told us? Kate? She said there were fights at school. People accusing each other. She said everyone knew Billy had a life-threatening allergy and that it wouldn't have been hard at all for someone to exploit it to hurt him."

"I still don't know why anybody would want to hurt him."

"I don't know why anybody would ever want to hurt you, but someone did," Shep says so quietly, her words like a breeze.

I swallow. "Okay. Are you okay with this? Reading your mom's journal?"

"Why not?" Shep quirks an eyebrow blandly. "She used to read mine. That's how she found out I was queer."

"Jesus." What the fuck. "I'm not saying two wrongs make a right, but . . ."

"But." Shep looks down for a second and shrugs. "She's gotten a lot better. Less paranoid. We like each other these days. But she used to be pretty over the top."

"Yeah." I pause, one hand on the journal with my fingers brushing Shep's. "You're sure about this?"

"If she wrote down anything in here that gives us a clue of what happened to Billy, it's worth it. And more than that, Sam. It's evidence."

That seals it. "Okay," I breathe. "Let's do it."

. . .

Dad comes home about an hour later when we're still reading through Shep's mom's entries from freshman and sophomore year. No mention of Billy yet, but we did find a picture of her in her cheerleading or pep squad uniform or whatever—complete with *super* eighties permed hair, a Fishermen mascot (in an uncanny-valley costume worthy of Gritty-level meme status), and a pile of bake sale sweets, in a herd of other girls. Dad calls up the stairs.

"Sam? I saw your light on. Have you eaten?"

"Nope!" I yell back. "Shep's here."

"Pizza okay?"

"Pepperoni!" Shep calls out her answer.

"Pineapple and roasted red pepper!" I grin at Shep as I holler down to Dad. "Double pineapple!"

"You're a weirdo!" he yells up the stairs.

Shep flips a page and stops. "Whoa. First mention of my dad." She reads from the journal. "*Carl is such a jerk. Yesterday he pantsed this freshman in the hall. She started crying and ran to the bathroom, and he actually followed her and stood out-side the door until the bell rang. She was late for class. Everybody knew what had happened by lunch. Kim thinks I should go out with him, because he keeps asking me. I guess he's hot, but geez. What'd that kid do to him?*"

Shep's mouth finishes the last sentence and forms a straight line across her chin.

"Ugh," I say. "I'm sorry."

"Spoiler alert, she eventually goes out with him." Shep aims both thumbs at her own chest. "Porque yo existo."

Spanish class is working, because I understand that.

"You said they were high school sweethearts, right?"

"Reluctant ones, apparently." Shep looks a little like she'd like to retroactively punch her dad in the face. "Ugh. I never really asked her what made her think he was worth going back to over and over."

"You think she'd tell you?"

"Big nope."

"I'm glad the two of you have such an open and trusting relationship," I say lightly.

"It's the best," says Shep. "The actual best."

Her gaze goes to the bedroom door, where the sound of Dad on the phone with the pizza place drifts up the stairs.

I look over at my shelves where the time capsule sits. "What do you say we take a break and see if Dad's got something that'll play those cassettes?"

"You in a Bowie mood?"

"If we're trying to find out what happened to Billy, might as well be in his headspace."

"Amplify the detective powers," Shep says. "Connect with the dead. I like it."

I give her a wan smile.

No sooner than we get downstairs with the tapes, though, our plan goes off course.

"I haven't had a boom box since the aughts," Dad says. "Before I even had a Sam. Can't you just Spotify it again?"

"Not the same!" Shep and I say at the same time.

Shep looks like she wants to despair, but I shake my head at her. I feel a new urgency to listen to the tapes, maybe triggered by the mere fact that right now, we can't. I think Shep feels it too.

"Might be able to find one at a thrift store. Goodwill maybe," Dad says. Then he snorts. "Or an antique shop."

"Or like . . . Amazon?" Shep looks bewildered. "The internet is a thing."

"Where's the fun in hunting, then?" Dad opens his wallet and pulls out a couple of twenties. "I'm going to go take a shower. I feel like I've got sawdust in my armpits. If the pizza beats me back to the kitchen, give the driver both of those. Should be about a ten-dollar tip."

Shep lets out a low whistle. "Generous."

"Making up for all the people who conveniently forget those folks work for tips," Dad says. "Thankless jobs deserve thanks. And a government that sets a livable minimum wage, but until that day comes . . ."

"Fair," says Shep.

Dad heads toward his bathroom, and a moment later, I hear the water turn on.

"Right," Shep says. "I know there's a lot of romance in poking around dusty stores looking for some lost relic of a former age, but I ain't got time for that."

"Internet?"

"Internet." Shep flips open the browser on her phone and searches *cassette tape player.* "There. Look. Thirty bucks for one that plays and records."

She hits the one-click option.

"Whoa, you don't have to buy that—"

"Chill, Sam. I want to. I never spend my baby-sitting money anyway. Mom's always telling me I'm allowed to go shopping now and then." She shrugs. "Mostly I don't want anything."

"When will it arrive?"

"I get free two-day shipping, so . . . Saturday."

"Day after the dance."

"The day after the dance." Shep puts her phone down on the counter next to Dad's money and sidles up to me. "I'm at my Dad's starting Saturday, but I might be able to sneak away."

She puts both her hands on my waist, and I put mine up on her shoulders. She looks up at me. Her eyelashes are so long, even without makeup. I've never felt this before, this desire for touch. As a kid, even when people I liked touched me, I'd turn to

245

stone and freeze up until they stopped, even if it was just a pat on the back. But with Shep, her touch feels like a lifeline.

"What are you wearing?"

I look down, because I've forgotten. "Uh, jeans and an AC/DC shirt?"

Shep guffaws. "I can see that. I meant to the dance."

"Oh. Uh . . . it's a surprise."

"Can you at least give me a color scheme?"

Right. People like to coordinate with their dates. That's a thing.

"Black and silver," I say. Then I give her a wry smile. "Like I really wear anything else."

"That makes it easy," Shep says. "I should have asked you sooner."

"Things have been quiet. Makes sense to just enjoy it a bit." I turn my hand palm up on Shep's shoulder, eyes on where the rock left a small scar.

"Yeah." Shep doesn't need to look to know what I'm staring at. Instead, she pulls me closer. "You okay with stirring the pot again?"

Valentine's Day was Tuesday, which means the dance is on Friday. I've been trying not to think about it, but I've got fewer than four weeks to be here in Astoria. Four weeks left of Dad's trial period. I let myself get caught up in a comforting routine. In the feeling of someone wanting me the way I want them. In living.

"Yeah," I say. "For Billy."

"You look sad all of a sudden."

Sam Sylvester, heart on their forehead. "Just thinking about Billy."

I think Shep realizes it's not the whole truth, but she doesn't call me on it. Instead, she kisses me, her lips finding mine and her hands tight around my waist. I pull her close. My hand is conveniently at her neck. I run my fingers down her throat where her skin is smooth. So smooth. She trembles at my touch.

Somebody bangs on the door.

We jump apart like someone turned on opposite polar magnets in our chests. After a moment, we look at each other and chuckle feebly.

"Pizza," I say. I put my hand on Shep's waist to get to the twenties on the counter. "Be right back."

The water in the bathroom turns off. "That the pizza?" Dad yells.

"Probably!" I scoot in my socks to the door. I can smell the pizza through the door. "Make that a yes!"

Opening the door, there's Dylan on the other side of it, holding a warming bag.

For a long moment we stare at each other. "Uh," I say. "Hi, Dylan."

"Uh," he says. "I'm—"

I don't know what he means to say, but he fumbles with the Velcro on the bag, the porch light casting shadows on his face. There's a small yelp from the direction of the kitchen, barely audible. I turn to look but don't see anything.

"I'm just working, I promise." Dylan blurts it out, handing me a receipt for the pizza amount. $30.79. I hand him the two twenties.

"Keep the change," I say. "And it's okay—I know. You've delivered our pizza before."

I half expect Dylan to laugh at that, but instead he just looks at me, no expression for a long moment until he apparently remembers. "Yeah, people are weird about delivering to this house so I always take it. My boss's sister says it's haunted, and a bunch of the other drivers are chickenshit."

"People are weird about this house in general." I say that because I don't know what else to say. Small towns, big stories.

That seems to upset him more. He shakes his head, his hand quivering as he stuffs the twenties into his pocket. He hands me the pizza boxes.

"Enjoy the pizza," is all he says. He looks over my shoulder then, so I follow his gaze, and we both jump at the sight of Shep, who I didn't even hear come down the hall from the kitchen. "Hey, Shep. Uh. Bye. See you at school tomorrow."

He's down the stairs and back in his little Honda so quickly I don't even know what to make of it.

"What was that sound a minute ago?" I ask. "You okay?"

"I—uh. Thought I saw something in the sliding glass door. Probably nothing." Shep gives a small, nervous laugh, then shakes herself and asks, "Was that Dylan? He knows where you live?"

I told her he asked me to the dance, and about the awkward conversation that followed.

"Yep, second time he's delivered our pizza. I forgot he worked there when we ordered."

"I didn't," says Shep. "But he's usually working counter, not delivery." She stares after his retreating tail lights.

"Did you hear what he said about everyone else being chickenshit?" I ask wryly.

From her head shake, I guess she was still in the kitchen.

"Maybe we did move into the Amityville house." I close the door just as I hear Dad open the bathroom door and turn to see him emerge in a pair of sweatpants and a plain white T-shirt.

"You two look like you just saw a ghost."

"Just a kid from school," I tell him. "I think we were all surprised to see each other."

"Yeah," says Shep.

But she's quiet as we head to the dining room to eat and keeps looking at the ceiling like she's hoping to see into the past. It's as if she's the one who saw a ghost.

Or maybe she thinks Dylan's behind the notes.

CHAPTER TWENTY-EIGHT

In almost three months, I've never been to Shep's house.

When I arrive Friday night with my garment bag of official dance clothes, I knock on the door. From every teen movie I've ever seen, getting ready at your date's house with your date is, like, the opposite of what you do, but Shep and I are . . . well. Me and Shep.

Footsteps on the other side of the door feel like a bunch of moths in my belly.

I'm not expecting to see Carl Wayne as the person opening the door, especially not in a maintenance uniform as if he's just gotten off work. He's taller than I expected, but I've only ever seen him in his car. A little over my height, he's got the wiry build of someone who used to be athletic but who has burned through everything but sinew.

"Uh," I say. "Hi, Mr. Wayne."

He grunts. "Well, come in, come in. I've got to go get your ride situated for Ste—I mean Shep."

Esme's in the wide entryway and glaring up at Carl. Some of that good old divorced-parent tension seeps through the air. I have no doubt that his self-correction is due to Esme's hard stare. Like the other times I saw her, she's in full makeup, but she's barefoot, showing perfect, pedicured toenails. She's holding a glass of white wine in one hand, and one of her fingernails looks like part of it got gnawed off, which is strange considering the rest of her is so immaculate. She tucks a glossy lock of deep brown hair behind her ear with a free hand.

"Hi, Sam," Esme says as Carl leaves and closes the door behind me. "Sorry about Carl. He's—"

I don't hear the rest of what she says, only the memory of her journal entry, *such a jerk*.

"Sam!" The stairs in their house are right in the middle, like it's a mansion instead of just a largish middle-class home. Shep's in a towel with wet hair, and she positively beams at me.

I've never seen her not-in-clothes. I can't help but blush.

"Shep, will you please put clothes on before your date goes upstairs?" Esme raises a pointed eyebrow.

"Sure," says Shep. Then when Esme shakes her head and turns away, Shep grins and winks at me. "Come up in ninety seconds, Sam."

"Roger that."

I take off the slip-ons I wore over, the weight of boots in my garment bag pulling against the crook of my arm.

Their house has a floor plan so open that I feel exposed. The kitchen is in the back of the house, but on the left instead of the right like ours. The house looks kind of like ours if all the walls got knocked down. Living room directly to my left (it looks unused, like a showpiece), dining room at the back of the house with a tray ceiling and inset lighting. Esme's back in the kitchen, pouring more white wine into a sizable glass. She sees me, and I try to smile.

"I'm celebrating not having to go anywhere tonight myself," she says lightly, but when she lifts the glass to her lips, she doesn't sip. She slugs it back.

I figure it's been long enough. I escape up the stairs.

The hallway that makes a T with the staircase is longer on the right than the left. To the left is Esme's remodeled wing of the house, it seems. To the right, a door is cracked open, light spilling out.

"Shep?" I ask hesitantly.

"Come in!"

I push the door open. Shep is in a blue bathrobe with constellations all over it. At least, at first glance I think they're constellations. When she steps forward, I see the Pythagorean theorem. Not constellations. Math equations. The surprising sight delights me, but then Shep kisses me and I forget about what she's wearing.

Her lips taste of sweet mint, and she smells like soft pine and sage.

She pulls back, breathless, after a moment. "If Mom comes up and finds us making out, she'll never let this happen again."

I almost teeter on my feet. I can't quite make words, but not in the bad way. I nod instead.

Shep's room is like Shep herself. The ceiling is the same cerulean as the winter beanie she wears, with tiny pinprick LEDs lighting it like stars. The main light in the room is a globe lamp off-center in one corner, and the blue paint of the ceiling darkens downward to the silhouettes of trees. I love it so much that I wish I could step through one of the walls and live there forever. The LEDs even make constellations. No Pythagoras here, but I do see Cassiopeia and Orion.

"Wow," I say. "Your room is . . ."

"It's my safe zone," Shep says. She smiles at me shyly. "I'm glad I finally get to show it to you."

"I might never leave," I tell her. I can't keep my eyes off it. It reminds me almost of the blue-greens in my tattoo and the aurora borealis, the night sky speaking to her the way it speaks to me. The trees on her walls even look sort of like the tree silhouettes on my arm. There are no framed decorations on the walls or anything, but there doesn't need to be. She's got a silver corner desk on the edge of the room with her closet, and on top of that is an array of multicolored bottles.

I'm still holding my garment bag. Shep's bed is in the middle of the room, under Cassiopeia. I set the bag on the bed, which is covered in a moss-green comforter and matching pillowcases.

"I can't wait to see what you brought to wear," Shep says. "You can change in here or in the bathroom just on the left." She points out the door.

I make a decision and unzip the bag. Shrugging out of my sweater, I lay it across the foot of the bed.

When I tug at the bottom hem of my T-shirt, I'm aware of Shep's gaze. I don't think I've ever let anyone see me in my binder before. It feels strange to pull the T-shirt up over my head. I feel almost more naked than I would if my boobs were bared to her instead of bound tight to my ribs.

The button on my jeans fights me just a bit. I shimmy out of them, leaving a pool of black denim on the floor.

I unzip the garment bag slowly, but over that sound, I hear quiet footsteps behind me.

"Sam," Shep says. "May I touch you?"

I stop with the garment bag's flap half-hanging. I turn to my left, meeting Shep's eyes. "Yes."

Her fingers are light, curious. She starts with one hand on my left arm, trailing it down the sleeve tattoo to my wrist. Tracing the Pisces fish and its twin's impaling sword, her other hand goes to the side of my neck. The pad of her thumb brushes against the small ridge of the scar where Lee cut the zip tie away.

My skin pebbles into gooseflesh as if it's all trying to get closer to Shep's touches at once.

Her robe droops over one shoulder, showing only golden brown skin beneath it.

"May I?" I whisper. She nods.

I lay one hand across that expanse of perfect skin, feeling the slight swell at the heel of my palm.

Footsteps sound on the stairs.

"Shit," Shep hisses. She grins sheepishly and bounces backward, tightening her robe.

I can't help the dopey smile that spreads across my face. My skin sings. The footsteps reach the top of the stairs, and a door opens and closes at the other end of the hall. I reach for my garment bag.

The contents are something Dad got me before we left Montana. The plan had been that I'd wear it to prom before everything went to shit.

The first thing I pull out is my pants. They're soft and black, made of cotton lining and a faux suede outer layer that feels like kisses on my fingertips. Along the outsides of the legs is silver embroidery in vines and swirls. They lace up the front and button with a silver embroidered button over my hip bone. Behind me, I can hear Shep rustling in her closet. I pull on my shirt. It still fits perfectly, the sleeves just long enough that I know the embroidered cuffs will show when I get the coat on. The buttons are tiny silver moons, and from top button to bottom, they go through all the phases. They won't show when all's said and done, but I love them. Every last one of them.

I pull out a strip of black linen and tie it carefully at my throat until it bunches just the way it should. I'll probably be the only kid at Astoria High's Valentine's formal in a cravat.

The coat goes on next. The embroidery on the light black wool is quiet, thin lines from the box collar down my arms to circle my wrists and vines that flow out from the bottom button to the tails that almost reach my knees. My boots are last, soft black leather that lace up the sides and are topped with a set of three silver buttons.

"Holy—" Shep's voice makes me turn. "Sam, you look like Alexander Hamilton mated with Jareth in *Labyrinth*."

"I don't think anyone's ever given me a more gorgeous compliment." The mention of Bowie's character gives me a lightning jolt. It seems to wake the story of Billy from my mind with a silvery glow I can feel in every inch of the embroidery that decorates my body. I guess this outfit does look like Jareth. I got it before I knew Billy'd worn that costume.

It takes me a minute to see Shep. Really see her. While I was dressing myself, she did her hair, tousling it so the grown-out bit on top falls over her forehead in dark brown waves. Her eye makeup is smoky, with flecks of gold in her eyeliner bringing out the gold in her eyes. She's wearing a red-orange, like the height of autumn leaves, dip-dyed pant romper with gold sandals. She looks like a walking ember. When she looks at me, I'm half-certain I feel her smolder.

"Wow," is all I can say.

We both swallow at the same time, just as the door down the hall opens.

"You two ready?" Esme calls. "Carl's about done with the car."

"We'll be right down!" Shep yells. Then she says with a sly smile, "I can't believe Dad's letting us take the Cadillac. Sky's gonna freak when we pick him and Aidan up."

I've never had this, the full dance experience.

"Do you need anything else?" Shep asks me. She steps closer, the soft thumps of her flat sandals on carpet barely audible.

Then she's in the circle of my warmth and our heat combines. I can't think of anything I need but her. Then something seems to strike her. "Dad's car has a tape player. I think it works. I mean, if you don't want to wait till tomorrow."

"I'll text Dad to bring them," I say. He's supposed to meet us here for pictures. That part we're doing traditionally.

I send him a quick text, and he responds with a *10-4*. I show it to Shep.

"He's such a dork," I say fondly.

"Your dad's the best," says Shep. She glances guiltily out the door. "Though I guess Carl gets some points for the car thing tonight."

"Shep!" Carl himself bellows his daughter's name. "You two hustle down here! Your parents need pictures!"

"We better head down," I say, but Shep grabs my arm and kisses me once, hard.

Then she grins. "What? One for the road."

I can't help but grin back.

We tromp down the stairs, and Esme lets out a low whistle when she sees us. "Definition of formal has changed since our day, eh, Carl?"

Carl looks us over, and for once I don't see any of his trademark gruffness. His eyes look oddly shiny.

"You kids got some style," he says finally. "That's some suit you got there, Sam."

"Thanks," I say. "Think we'll do the car justice?"

"I'll be damned if you don't," he says, then he looks away, avoiding Esme's eyes.

A knock at the door, and Shep slides on the rug to get it. "Junius!"

Dad comes through the door in dark jeans and a blue shirt tucked in. He's got both tapes in his hand. "Shep, you are a vision," he says. "And Sam—I am damn glad you get a chance to wear this."

Seeing Carl, Dad holds out his hand. Carl shakes it like the gruff, machismo detectives in Dad's procedurals shake hands with people they want to intimidate, and while they exchange introductions, I can't help but notice how Carl eyes the cassettes in Dad's other hand. Dad holds them out to me a moment later, and with the movement of air comes the slightest whiff of popcorn instead of coconut.

"You all are kicking it retro style tonight," Dad says. It might be the dadliest thing he's ever said. I take the tapes and shake my head.

At first, I think Esme's startled gasp is just Shep's sandals sliding on the carpet again, but a second later Esme takes a full step backward.

"What—where did you get those?"

Shep gives her mom a strange look, then she looks at me as if to ask permission. Dad's giving me the same look.

"I found these in a time capsule in my backyard," I say after a beat. "Thought we could give Bowie's 'Space Oddity' a listen on the way to the dance."

"Those were buried? In your backyard?" Esme stares.

Carl's face changes, all expression draining away. Flat.

Esme takes three steps to close the distance between us and takes both tapes from me.

Shep leans forward. "Mom?"

Esme swallows once. Then she seems to realize she's snatched a couple of old cassettes out of her daughter's date's hand. She offers them back to me, blinking rapidly.

"I'm sorry, Sam," she says. "That was rude of me."

Dad's eyes say he has questions. Lots of them. I avoid his gaze.

The air in the foyer feels like someone's hooked it up to an electric charge. I'm surprised our hair isn't all standing on end.

"We should take some pictures before the kids go," Dad says, dispelling some of it.

Carl nods firmly and puts his hand on Esme's shoulder. She jumps, then looks at him and says, "Yes. Of course. We need pictures."

Shep and I pose while the parents bustle around us with their phones, shooting picture after picture, but I know my smile is forced. When the final flash goes off, I want to rip my cravat off my throat. I can't breathe. All I can see is a curly-haired silhouette in front of me, but when the brightness fades, it's just Esme, her hair straight and shiny.

When Carl finally hands Shep his keys, I'm ready to bolt.

Shep is silent when we get in the car.

"What the hell was that?" I ask her when she starts the engine. On the porch, I can see all three of our parents waiting for us to drive away.

"I have no fucking clue," Shep says. "I've never seen Mom that rattled. Can I see the tapes?"

I hand them to her, Bowie on top. She holds them for a long moment, turning them over in her hands.

The tape deck is a small slot in the dash by the radio. I take the Bowie tape from her and open the case. It's such a strange little piece of plastic.

I insert it into the slot. Shep presses the On button on the radio. The dash lights up with a red glow.

Rolling down the window of the car, I turn the volume dial up. Guitar chords fill the car, and I can feel them drifting out the open window.

Just as Bowie's voice spills out the opening lines of "Space Oddity," I happen to look right at Esme as Shep puts the car in gear and pulls away from the curb.

Haloed by the porch light, Esme's face stretches out in a look I know all too well. She sways on her feet. Her eyes are miles away . . . or years.

Just as Shep turns the corner onto another street, I see Esme's hand clench Carl's arm.

I know that cornered look in her eyes. That's one emotion I can always recognize.

Fear.

CHAPTER TWENTY-NINE

I can't speak on the drive to Sky's house.

It wasn't just the tapes that hit Esme's freak-out switch. The song itself.

Billy's favorite. The one a now-defunct website insisted he was listening to when he died. I need to look in my book again and see if that bit is in there, if my memory is correct. I haven't been able to touch it since someone was in my room and moved it.

My heart beats out a *rat-a-tat-tat* in my chest along with the drum line of "Space Oddity."

I've never been so certain of anything as I am right now. That dream I had, the curly-haired silhouette of someone with Billy when he died. I just assumed it was Margie because her hair was—and still is—curly. But Esme's hair was permed in the eighties. Every inch as curly as Margie's.

Two things that are so true I can feel them from my aurora pompadour to my fucking fantastic boots.

Esme Shepard was in the room with Billy Clement when he died. And she doesn't want Shep to know.

That reaction to the tapes was out of proportion. There's something else going on here, and my stomach is sloshing with acid.

"Are you okay?" Shep asks the question so softly that it's hardly audible over the roar of the Cadillac's engine. She looks amazing against the white leather and chrome, even in the dim light of the car.

"I don't know," I say. How do I tell Shep this? How do I keep it from her?

You're already keeping a secret that will destroy her.

Billy's was thirty years ago. Even now I can picture it again, the blurred golden light of his room—my room—with this very song playing while he suffocated to death.

"Shep, your mom didn't always have straight hair, right?" I ask. I think of Margie's curls, how sure I was that she was who I saw in that dream.

Shep looks sideways at me, hitting the blinker to make a right turn onto Sky's street. I've never seen his house.

"Permed to *death*. You saw the picture. Her yearbook picture is unreal. I mean, she grew up in the seventies and eighties, for god's sake. She doesn't even use heat on it now—said the chemicals left it practically deep-fried."

I let my breath out and sit there, lungs deflated. It wasn't Principal Frankel in the room with Billy when he died. It was Esme.

"Your mom was married before she got back with your dad?" This question leaps from my lips, unbidden. "You said they were high school sweethearts, but your mom married someone else for a few years before they got together and had you. That guy died, right?"

"Sam, are you okay?" Shep pulls the car to a halt and pulls the emergency break, shifting into neutral.

"Is this Sky's house?"

"No, but you're scaring me."

It's true. Both her hands are at ten and two on the steering wheel, clasped tightly against the white tooled leather. And I'm sitting here wondering if her mom killed Billy Clement.

"They just seemed wigged by the tapes," I say, as lightly as I can manage. I'm a shit liar, but for once my voice sounds half-way convincing, at least to someone who wants to believe me.

"Yeah, my dad's the classic rock fan," Shep says. "Mom's always been more into current pop than I was. Plus, the whole town has like . . . post-trauma about Billy and they were prob-ably freaked out that you dug up Billy's actual old tapes. Like Mr. Quach said, thirty-year-old grief is still grief."

It sounds plausible, so plausible I relax a little.

"Sorry I scared you," I say. Nothing fits here. Not Frankel's coded journal, not Esme Shepard and Carl Wayne's reactions to this music, nothing.

"It's okay," Shep says. "I just get a little weird about my parents. They split because my dad was drinking so much and even though he didn't get violent to me or anything, I spent about a month in foster care because the school called CPS when I was thirteen. I guess a counselor or somebody saw him screaming at Mom after they dropped me off one morning. Mom kicked him out, got a restraining order, and then got me back."

"Holy shit. But you see him sometimes now."

"Yeah, after he did the whole twelve-step thing for years. They don't have official joint custody. It's kind of my choice. Especially since Abuelita died." Shep's staring straight ahead over the top of the steering wheel. "Family, and all that. Blood is thicker than water or whatever. Sometimes I just want my dad. Even if . . ."

She trails off. Even if what? If he sucks? If he's mean?

I can't tell her what I'm wondering about her mom.

"Hey," I say, reaching out to touch her bare shoulder. The car is warm, but she has goosebumps. Shep looks at me. "I'm sorry

I brought it up. Moratorium on heavy stuff for the night, starting now. Let's get the boys and get to the dance."

The car is filled only with music for a long moment.

"It's okay, really. It's just that I haven't actually dated anyone before." Shep's words come out all in a rush. "Never mind being gay and everything, but my parents' relationship is so fucked that I am afraid it's genetic or something."

"I never have either," I say, almost in a whisper. I don't know what nature I might have inherited, but god, I hope the nurture side counts for something. "All I know is that you are kind and warm and you *care*. Life feels possible when you're around. I don't know what you want us to be, but—"

"Sam," Shep says, her mouth falling open. For once it's her who seems at a complete loss for words.

"You're not your dad or your mom. Not even a little bit." I hope this is the right thing to say.

Shep leans over and kisses me softly. "We can be—we can be whatever feels right. I just want to keep being with you."

That warmth nearly chases away my fear.

"Me too," I tell her. It's painfully true.

I smile at her as she puts the car back in gear, but there's a pit of gravel in my stomach as she looks back to the road, checks her mirrors, and pulls us back out into the street.

I think I'm going to have to figure this out alone.

. . .

Sky is resplendent in a suit the same color blue as his name. His blond hair is textured in perfect tufty waves, and he's wearing black eyeliner rimmed in periwinkle blue that makes his eyes look like the hearts of glaciers.

"Damn, boy," Shep says when she sees him. "The whole school's gonna fall at your feet."

"Wait till you see Aidan," Sky says.

I would have put Aidan in the "classic tux" column. He's the basketball guy, the football guy, the every-sport-under-the-sun guy. But when he comes out onto Sky's front porch, giving a shy laugh in the direction of Sky's mom who must have just said something to him, both Shep and I take a half step back.

His hair's been cut into an undercut, the top teased and combed backward not too unlike my own, but dark brown. His suit is forest green, and at first I think it's solid. When he steps under the porch light, though, I can see a light plaid design. The jacket has a tuxedo cut, and at his left lapel, he's got a gold brooch in the shape of a rose. His vest underneath has four gold buttons, and he's got an actual polished pocket watch with fob tucked into the vest pocket. His shirt is ivory with a box collar and no tie, and his slim-cut trouser legs give way to a gorgeous pair of polished, square-toed leather shoes that I kind of want to steal right off his feet.

"Hey, guys," Aidan says.

Shep lets out a low whistle. "You two are—"

"Fire emoji," I supply.

"Fire emoji," Shep agrees.

"Look who's talking," Aidan says, his face turning ruddy in the light as he blushes. "I don't know if the school is ready for us."

"Sister, my field of fucks is barren," Sky says. His fingernails are painted with silver glitter and he's even got acrylic nails filed to tapered points. He clicks them together. "Ready or not, this little butterfly is ready to shake his booty."

Even after a few weeks of hanging out with us, Aidan still looks a little bewildered when Sky says stuff like that, like he's fighting against some ingrained impulse to turn his masculinity gauge up to eleven. But I swear, when that little look fades, I catch something else on Aidan's face. Relief, maybe. Comfort. Sky's mom and dad bustle out of the house just then and subject us to another round of pictures, but these ones are smoother. Sky's dad makes a remark that we look like a crack team of spies set to infiltrate a high school dance, and someone starts laughing nervously, which turns into real laughter, and before I know it, our poses are genuinely playful, finger guns in one and Aidan checking his fob watch in another. Thinking the camera is on Aidan and Sky, I look at Shep, and like the fire emoji we were joking about moments ago, heat engulfs me, and I lean toward her, and she leans toward me, and in the instant before our lips touch, I see a flash go off. I kiss her anyway, and Sky's mom flutters over with her iPhone to show us the picture, half-squealing with delight.

It's a gorgeous photo, both our eyes open and small smiles pulling at our lips. We look like ash and flame, the silver embroidery on my suit and my silver eyeliner lit up like the glimmers of gold on Shep's cheeks and eyelids.

"You have to send that to me," Shep tells Sky's mom, eyes wide. "I think I need to blow it up and frame it."

I can't speak past the sudden lump in my throat, but I nod vigorously. Then we're moving, Sky herding us toward the Cadillac while Shep answers his mom's questions about the car.

Sky insists on riding shotgun, so I sit in the back with Aidan.

"You really look awesome," I tell him. "Dapper as fuck."

Aidan blushes again. "Thanks. I pulled extra shifts at Lou's for a month to pay for it. Had to hide cash so my mom wouldn't take it to pay ren—I mean." He looks so mortified that he just admitted to his parents taking his money for rent that I instantly wish I could rewind time.

Lou's is a brewpub down by the boardwalk. "Do you wait tables?"

"Too young to serve booze," Aidan says, shaking his head, letting out a breath that sounds like relief. "But old enough to clean it up, I guess. I'm a busser."

Bowie starts back up on the radio, loudly. Sky turns around, meeting my eyes for a split second as his hand falls from the radio dial. The music seems to soothe Aidan enough to get past the awkward moment.

"You look like Bowie," Aidan says to Sky, leaning forward as Shep pulls the car out. "He wore a suit like that."

"Never could anyone pay me a better compliment than that," says Sky. It's so similar to what I told Shep earlier that my heart gives a happy little flutter. Sky flashes sparkly nails at the radio. "Is this the tape our resident parental treasure hunter dug up in the backyard?"

"Yeah," I say, glancing sideways at Aidan. We haven't told him.

"Somebody dug up this tape?" Aidan leans back against the bench seat.

"Yeah. My dad." I don't know how much to tell him, and the question reminds me again of the absolute shock on Esme and Carl's faces when they saw these tapes.

"Whoa," says Aidan. "Just like . . . in your backyard?"

"Yep. He was trying to put in a flower bed." We haven't really discussed Billy Clement with him, but since everybody at school knows I live in the Clement house, he can probably put it together. He confirms it a minute later.

"Was this tape Billy Clement's?" Aidan's voice is so earnest and curious.

I meet Shep's eyes in the rearview mirror. I know she and I called a moratorium on serious talks for the night, but Sky and Aidan don't know that.

"Yeah," Sky says, twisting in the front seat to turn and grin at Aidan. "He and his bestie, Principal Frankel, left a *time capsule*."

"Whaaaaaaat." Aidan leans forward again. "Frankel? No way."

Something seems to click with Aidan.

"Dude." He turns to me. "She called you Billy that day at lunch."

"She's got a picture of him in her office," Sky says. "That frame behind her desk."

"I've never been in there," says Aidan. "I mean, maybe once."

Shep pulls the car up at the school and parks in an empty corner of the lot, carefully setting the emergency brake again and turning off the engine. "Okay. We are not going to talk about a dead kid the whole night. We" —she points at Sky and me and indicates herself with her other hand— "are going to dial back the Billy drama for tonight, my dears. And you two" — she points at me and Aidan— "are going to dial *up* the dance drama with me, and we are all going to walk into that spritzed up gymnasium with its streamers and sparkles and be the glitteriest bitches in it. Do you hear me?"

"Got it," says Sky.

"Got it," I say.

"Hey, guys?" Aidan opens his door. "I'm all in on that, but I just wanted to say thanks for letting me hang out with you."

I get out of the car just as Sky does, and he peers at Aidan over the shiny red roof of the Cadillac. "Dude, you are literally one of the most popular guys at school. Pretty sure you could hang out with anyone you wanted."

"I've known you since you moved here," Shep says. "Everybody wants to hang out with you."

Aidan looks flustered for a moment, and he looks at me, as if for help. Suddenly I get it.

"There's a difference between wanting to hang out with somebody because they're popular and wanting to hang out with somebody because you like them and want to be their friend," I say, meeting Aidan's eyes.

He visibly relaxes, letting out a breath and nodding at me. "That."

"Heart emoji," I murmur, and Aidan grins.

Shep and Sky both look abashed. I still barely know Aidan, but I remember the way he told me that his dad would beat his ass if he got tattoos, and that seems like a thing the average ripped high school sports hero wouldn't say. That and the whole-hiding-money-from-his-parents-to-pay-for-a-suit thing. He got ready at Sky's house. I wonder if he did that so his parents wouldn't see the suit at all. Damn.

"I'm glad you're here with us," I tell him. And it's true.

We walk two by two toward the school, Sky and Shep at the front, still looking a little embarrassed. I'm next to Aidan, giving him what I hope is a reassuring smile as we stride through the door.

The gym is supposed to look magical, I think. Shep was right about the streamers and sparkles. The music is blasting, but like most high school dances I've been to (a relatively small sample size, but still), nobody has quite gotten comfortable enough to actually dance yet.

Principal Frankel is here. She's in a simple black dress and ankle boots at the side of the gym with a teacher I don't recognize, talking. When we walk in, heads actually turn.

"Hammond!" Someone bellows. It's that guy who woofed at Shep in English class, and I steel myself for some fuckery. Brent. But he doesn't even look at Sky or Shep. He goes straight to Aidan. "Look at you, dude. What kind of tux is that?"

"Comfortable," Aidan says easily. "No tie."

Even from where I'm standing, I can smell booze on Brent's breath. I hope he's not driving.

He blinks at Aidan, then laughs.

"We're all over there," Brent says, slinging an arm around Aidan's shoulders and gesturing to a crowd of people I can now recognize as basketball players (from both the boys' and girls' teams) and cheerleaders (also a mix of genders, which was a pleasant surprise for me when I first found out). I don't see a lot of familiar faces, since most of them are seniors, but Dylan's over there. He keeps looking over his shoulder at us, then nervously looking away.

"I actually came with these guys," Aidan says, making me forget Dylan.

Brent seems to see us for the first time, staring first at Sky with a lingering glance at his eyeliner. Sky gives Brent an extreme *I-am-not-impressed* look, which Shep echoes a moment later.

"Huh," says Brent. "You gay now or something?"

"Nah," Aidan says. "You realize you can be friends with people and be different than them, right?"

"Whoa, whoa, whoa," Brent says, putting his hands in the air. For a second, I think he's serious. Then to my utter surprise, he grins. "No shit, Sherlock. You know I got your back either way though, bro."

Shep's mouth drops open, and Brent seems to remember making fun of her in class. I can't help staring at him.

"Uh. Sorry about . . . the barking and shit. Dick move. My bad." With that he turns to go, but he looks over his shoulder once. "If you guys want to join us, you're welcome."

"What the actual fuck just happened?" Sky breathes when Brent moves away. "Did he just *apologize* to you?"

Aidan looks just as confused. "Barking?"

"He called me a dog because Shep is one in *Call of the Wild*," Shep tells him. "Then woofed at me in class. Bunch of people used to all the time just because my name's Shepard, but he started it."

Aidan opens his mouth, then closes it. Then he opens it again. "What a douche. I'm sorry."

"Hey, I just witnessed a miracle," Shep says good-naturedly. "Brent's been an ass to me since middle school. I think we can thank your social currency for this one, Aidan."

"Speaking of asses," Sky mutters. "Blaise alert. Three o'clock."

Sure enough, there she is. Blaise is in a group of people near Brent and his crowd. She's not looking this way, but from the small pulse in Sky's jaw, her mere presence is enough to deflate him. She's in a dress that, at first glance, looks like a damn wedding dress. I think it's white until the light hits it, and I can see that it's silver. It sets off her red hair as she laughs with a friend.

"Okay, there is not enough dance drama happening," Shep says. "Of the good variety. Forget Brent and Blaise. I'll be right back."

She heads toward the makeshift stage at the end of the gym where a DJ is set up.

"What is she doing?" I ask.

"Looks like she's putting in a request. If it's anything people are supposed to line dance to, I'm going to step on her feet." Sky drums his fingernails against his thumb.

Shep bends her head, and the DJ takes her headphones off one ear to listen, looking around at the crowd while Shep talks. After a moment, the DJ chuckles and gives Shep a low five, nodding at her.

Shep walks back to us, looking satisfied.

"What did you ask for?" Sky asks.

"Just you wait." Shep winks and holds her hand out to me. The music changes to a staccato guitar.

I look around for a bare instant, tears I can't help prickling my eyes. It strikes me where I am. A school formal. With my girlfriend. Her hand is outstretched, waiting for me.

I place mine in hers.

She's in my arms, and we spin in a single circle and then she pulls me close. Her warmth melds with mine, melds with the music.

No one catcalls us. I don't see any eyes on us but Aidan's and Sky's. Sky meets my gaze once, brings his hand to his heart.

And then I forget everyone else.

CHAPTER THIRTY

Two hours of dancing. Aidan, Sky, and I have to ditch our jackets an hour in, but I can't remember a night where I've had more fun. It's not my first dance, nor my first enjoyable one.

This dance is different.

The music is loud, but my friends don't expect me to have a conversation over it, so we just dance, and I am allowed to just *feel* the music instead of trying to engage with people through it—heaven.

Even better? No one stares at me and Shep when we slow dance. No one says anything cruel. Aidan and Sky both dance with a few girls, but I notice Sky *only* dances with girls, even though once a cute sophomore guy asks him. He declines with a flourishing bow, begging a rest break. Twice I see Blaise's eyes on him, but she looks away as soon as she realizes I see her staring. Shep gets asked to dance by people of multiple genders, and somewhat to my surprise, so do I. I dance with Aerie at one point, who is in a full-length blue dress and Chuck Taylors, and Dylan even asks me, though the whole time we dance, he seems nervous and keeps stepping on my foot.

"Hey, Sam?" Before he goes back to Brent and the others, he taps me on the shoulder.

"Yeah?"

"You look awesome. Thanks for dancing with me." He looks as though he's at war with himself but can't figure out why.

"Thanks," I say, and he turns and leaves so quickly it could be called a scurry. Kind of a weird dude.

The night starts to wind down around eleven, and in a quiet lull, I find myself alone. Shep has run to the bathroom, Aidan's chatting with Brent, and Sky is at the drinks table with Ronnie and her girlfriend Jax.

It's in the quiet that I can't forget.

Principal Frankel stands across the gym from me, and I don't know what makes me want to get up from my perch on the bleachers and walk to her, but I do. I wish I could just pinpoint it, seek out Billy's memories. I wish I could watch his last day like a film in my mind, figure out this thing I'm missing.

Frankel sees me looking at her, and her lips form a stony, pained smile that looks like a frustrated artist drew it on with a Sharpie.

Tell her.

The impulse is so strong it almost drags me off my feet.

Instead, I snake through the crowd, my steps falling into pattern with the beat of the current dubstep song the DJ is spinning, and I meet up with Sky at the drinks table.

"Middle one's spiked," Sky says helpfully. "Do with that information what you will."

"I'll pass, thanks."

Sky looks like he's already had a few glasses from the middle bowl. I catch him scowling in Blaise's general direction.

"What's up?" I ask.

Shep turns away from her conversation with Ronnie and gives me a bright smile. "He wanted to dance with that sophomore, but the presence of Blaise has made him afraid to show that he likes boys anymore."

Aidan chooses that exact moment to appear from behind me, and he frowns, but doesn't say anything.

Sky raises his plastic cup and taps one pinky nail against it. "Fuck Blaise," he says in a perfect imitation of a posh Londoner accent.

"I'll drink to that," Shep says. She grabs a cup and gestures at the dipper in the middle bowl, looking to me with a question in her eyes. I shake my head. She fills it from the left bowl instead, getting one for herself from the same un-boozed bowl.

"At least Ronnie and Jax'll drink with me," Sky says with a pout. They each sip from their cups quietly.

"I'm driving, asshole," says Shep.

"I'm solidarity sober," I say, though really I just don't like drinking after Montana.

Aidan grabs a cup and fills it from the middle bowl. "I've got you, man," he says, and he clinks—clunks, rather—cups with Sky.

Just then, the DJ grabs the microphone. "Listen up, Fisherfolk! We've got one last slow jam tonight before our grand finale, so you better find that person you want to dance with and do it."

I hold my hand out to Shep, but just as she takes it, out of the corner of my eye I see Aidan make a sweeping bow. He holds his hand out to Sky.

"You have nothing to prove," Aidan says to Sky. "To anybody. You are who you say you are."

"You're straight, dude," Sky says, but I see the way his chin tightens and the way he starts blinking quickly.

"So?" Aidan says. "I can share a dance with my friend if I want. If you do, of course."

Both Ronnie and Jax look away, and they're blinking too. Jax mouths, *something in my eye* and Ronnie mouths back, *bullshit*.

The four of us head out onto the dance floor, and as Blaise sees Aidan and Sky, her face lights with triumph, though it's marred by something else I can't quite place.

Aidan raises his hand over Sky's shoulder with his middle finger straight up.

Her grin vanishes completely, and she stalks away.

Shep's and my grins almost break our faces. The slow dance goes by too quickly. Shep is fully against my body, her warmth and mine mingling. She looks up at me, eyes sparkling.

"What?" The last chords fade, and there's a pause.

"Last dance, Astoria High! Let's throw it back!" The DJ hits a button, then throws a finger gun in Shep's direction.

Shep grins wider.

When the bass line of the next and final song begins with a now-familiar *dng-dng-dng-duh-duh-lng-gng,* I release Shep from my arms in time to see her beam.

Freddie Mercury's voice singing do-wop beats joins in, and a moment later, Bowie belts out the first line.

Shep grabs my hands, swings me out into the middle of the floor, belting out lyrics.

Sky and Aidan both screech along with the song, and a laugh bubbles up in my chest.

The DJ clicks something on her laptop, and the projector aims at the white wall, projecting the music video with the lyrics. I never would have thought so many high schoolers would be into this song, but I see Dylan grinning and singing along, and Aidan shakes his shoulders in time with the beat, and it seems to be contagious. The bellow of voices pounds through the gym.

Shep spins me again, her face glimmering with perspiration. Sky and Aidan are head banging with Jax and Ronnie and all four laughing themselves silly when Sky suddenly attempts to nae-nae, and on the next spin Shep releases me, and I meet eyes with Principal Frankel. The laughter evaporates from my chest like a droplet of water in the Sahara.

The lights flicker across her ashen face, wetness shining on her cheeks. She stares at me for an endless moment and then turns and almost runs from the gymnasium.

. . .

I find her in the hallway, leaning against a row of lockers, shoulders shaking.

"Principal Frankel?" She doesn't answer me. Something twists in my chest. Something not me. "Margie."

Her head jerks around. "Why did you call me that?"

The stillness in the hallway is frozen time.

There is no good answer. I decide to pretend it didn't happen. "Are you upset about something?"

"You are a student. That is not a question I need to answer from you."

She's right. It's already weird and not okay. Billy loved her, but I'm Sam Sylvester, not Billy Clement, no matter how much his story haunts me. I'd rather be back in that gym with my own friends and my girlfriend. But I'm here, facing off with someone I now feel certain did not kill anyone. I can see her younger, standing behind Mr. Quach's dad, holding up bunny ears with a goofy grin, Billy beside her.

Tell her. That impulse is back, insistent.

"I found something buried in my backyard," I say in a rush.

276

For the first time since I walked up to her, Principal Frankel turns to look at me. Her eyes search my face, as if she doesn't quite believe me. Her head tilts to the side, and I can hear how quickly she's breathing.

"There's no way you could—"

"Anyone putting in a flower bed there in the past thirty years could have found it," I say to her.

She shuts her mouth. Her throat moves as she swallows. She makes a vague motion back toward the gym.

"You've listened to the tapes, haven't you? They're just old music. You shouldn't go digging into the past," she says.

"Are you going to do something to try and stop me too?"

"Too? What? Of course not." She snaps into principal mode so quickly that I'm even more certain it wasn't her sending me those notes. "Sam, did someone—"

"Someone really doesn't want me trying to find out what happened to Billy." I don't have a lot of time. Not when we're not supposed to be talking about this tonight. "Why do you keep calling me Billy?"

Principal Frankel bites the inside of her cheek. She hesitates.

"I don't care if the answer is weird," I say.

"I don't know why," she says finally. Then she gestures at my forearm, where only a hint of my ink sleeve shows under the cloth cuff. "You don't really look like him. That first day though, your tattoo? Both Billy and I are Pisces. We joked about being soulmate fish. Seeing one fish stabbed—"

"I'm a Pisces too," I tell her. I can feel the tattoo now. I got the sword for myself, after Lee's cousins almost killed me. For the knife that set me free and broke my life all at once. I want to pull up my sleeve and look at the ink, but I resist. "Were you with him that day?"

277

"Yes," Principal Frankel says. Her face flashes, in a lightning strike of a moment, she's younger. Wild-haired and frightened. "But no. I was in the bathroom. I am lactose intolerant and didn't figure it out until about a year later, and he and I had just eaten a bunch of ice cream. I came out and found him."

She could be lying, but I don't think she is.

"Was there anything you noticed about the room that was different?"

Shep's going to wonder what I'm doing.

"There was a spirit box of popcorn balls. One of the things the cheerleaders did for the baseball team's start of season. I figured he'd just grabbed it from the pantry while I was in the bathroom. I was in there for a long time. He was blasting music so I wouldn't feel embarrassed." Principal Frankel looks startled that she even answered. "I would have never hurt Billy. Ever. I loved him."

Popcorn. At my look, she seems to think I am thinking something else and rushes on.

"He was . . . he was—" Her face lights with such anguish that I almost reach out a hand to touch her shoulder. I stop with my hand frozen in the air.

"I believe you," I say.

"I've tried to find out what really happened for thirty years," she says, almost in a whisper. "I put my memories and tidbits I could find on a website that I even kept up till . . ."

She trails off. The Move the Stars website. Which Ronnie said was registered to conceal the owner's identity. It was Principal Frankel's. Then Frankel gives me a wan smile.

"Well, until I got the principal position and got some violent pushback about it anonymously. No idea who figured out it was mine, but it wasn't a secret that Billy and I were close. I doubt you'll have any more luck where I've failed." She seems to shake herself back to principal mode. "Sam, if anyone tries *anything*, you come and *tell me*."

"I will," I say. My head feels light, like someone filled it with helium. Lies again. If I can't tell Dad, how could I tell her?

"I'm not kidding," Principal Frankel says, hesitating like she isn't sure she wants to say more. "Back when Billy died, because I was there, some people got very inappropriate and cruel. They sent me hate mail and harassed me for over a year, bullied me about my stomach problems, someone stole my journal and photocopied parts of it—well. I know what it's like to feel as if you have a target on your back. I even write things in a cipher now when I don't want others reading it. If anything at all happens—"

I just stare at her. "That's awful. I'll—I mean, thank you."

I am about to turn and start to walk away, but she stops me.

"Sam." Thank god it's the right name when she says it.

"Yeah?" I stop, more peeking back than looking.

"You know I was out sick last month," she says, still hesitant but with an expression that is becoming dangerously similar to Dad's Alarmed Face, as if she's trying to parse something. "I think someone filled my non-dairy creamer with half-and-half. Do you have any allergies, Sam?"

The fear in her eyes is so sharp and bright, it wants to pierce my skull.

"None that I know of," I say.

She relaxes visibly. "Someone put a note with a smiley face on my creamer. At first, I thought it was just one of the admins being silly. But I also know that the harassment I got about my website was no joke. Someone was scared of what I knew about Billy's death. There were threats then, and it would be

279

imprudent to ignore the possibility that some individual would intentionally escalate threats to actions, despite my taking the website down."

She takes a breath, calmer now. Back to principal mode.

"How sick were you?" My skin feels cold where my sweat is drying. I need to go back into the gym. I need to get my jacket and meet back up with Shep and the others.

"I spent the night in the hospital," she says. "Mostly because of dehydration."

"Still," I say.

"Still."

Now I really do head back, each step feeling unstable on the smooth, glossy surface of the high school's floor. Shep and the others are waiting for me just inside, with everyone else milling about. Shep has my jacket slung over one arm, and she hands it to me.

"You're covered in goosebumps," she says, rubbing her hands up and down my arms. It feels good, that touch. But it can't warm me right now.

What if someone we know killed Billy Clement? Esme was at the school the day those notes were found. What if she's the one who wrote them? She could have gotten into the office mini-fridge. Or one of the administrative assistants.

"The whole school's going to be speculating about you now, Aidan," Sky says, shattering my dark thoughts with his own for now. "Somebody already came over and asked me if we were dating."

"Who cares?" Aidan says. "I mean, I told you that you have nothing to prove. I don't owe anybody an explanation either. Plenty of other friends danced together tonight. They can think what they want. I know who you are, and I know who I am. If somebody thinks I'm gay, I'm not gonna run around flailing and yelling *no homo*."

Shep snorts, waving goodbye to Jax and Ronnie.

Sky frowns as we head out into the chilly night. He's swaying a bit. I didn't realize he drank that much. The parking lot between us and the car feels too large all of the sudden.

"It really bothers you what Blaise did, doesn't it?" Aidan asks him.

"No shit," says Sky.

"It bothers you that people think you're gay?"

"It bothers me that no matter what I do, people assume my sexuality on my proximity to other people!" Sky yells it loud enough that a group of freshman stops in their tracks. Sky doesn't seem to care. "They think I'm straight if I date a girl, gay if I so much as look at a guy. I'm not somewhere in the middle or some half-gay, half-straight Frankenqueer. You can fucking still like pizza even if you're currently eating a goddamn ice-cream cone."

"I know that," Aidan says.

"I know *you* do, but the rest of—*UGH*." Sky rubs his hand on his face.

"That's why I just go with queer and tell them all to fuck off," Shep says.

"Yeah, it's easy for you. You're a girl, so you liking all genders fits in with straight dudes' objectification of you. Hashtag not all straight dudes," he spits at Aidan.

"Whoa, dude," Aidan says.

"No, he's right," Shep tells him.

She's looking at the guys, so she doesn't see the car as we approach it. There's a white scrawl across the front hood of that shiny, fire-engine red Cadillac.

"Shep—" I try to interrupt, but she's talking.

"You're confident in yourself, Aidan. That's great that you don't feel threatened. But you're a star sports guy. You have social currency to spare at this school. Hell, your presence alone probably made one of our oldest bullies do a one-eighty and apologize. You really *don't* have to prove anything to anybody, but Sky has to argue with people who think they know who he is better than he does." She looks tired, her shoulders slumping in.

I can't read what's written on the car. "Shep."

"What?"

The others all look at the Cadillac.

"Shiiiiiit," says Aidan.

"Oh, my god." Shep reaches the car in four strides. "Oh, my god. Oh, my god. Oh-my-god. Dad is going to kill me. He'll *kill* me."

The scrawl says, *I SEE YOU.*

There's a smiley face under it.

CHAPTER THIRTY-ONE

"**O**h, my god," Shep says again. "Oh. My. God."

"Shit, dude," says Sky. He steps up to the hood of the Cadillac and pokes the giant block *I* with his index finger. He yanks it back as if it startled him. "It's still tacky, whatever it was."

Aidan does the same and sniffs his finger. "It's not paint," he says, sniffing again dubiously.

I can't stop reading the message. I am absolutely certain this message was meant for me.

"Is anyone going to react to the content of this message or nah?" Aidan looks around at Shep and Sky, then at me. "Sam?"

I shrug. I don't know what else to do.

"Like okay, the car, but this is some stalker shit," Aidan says. "Anybody?"

Shep slumps against the front fender. "We weren't going to talk about this tonight."

"Yeah, I think that's out the window," Sky says, rubbing the white residue off his index finger with the pad of his thumb.

"We should call the police," says Aidan.

"Yes, let's. I'll volunteer for my first ever minor-under-the-influence charge," Sky says. "You can go second."

Aidan looks sheepish.

"Is there a DIY car wash anywhere in town?" I ask.

Shep almost laughs. "Oh, god, Dad would *die*."

"Better than him killing you?" I mean it as a joke, but her smile fades. Wrong thing to say, Sylvester. Bad timing.

"They usually have those vending machines with chamois cloths in them. Wouldn't scratch the car," Aidan says thoughtfully. "I've got a little cash. We could get tokens."

After what Aidan said in the car earlier about money, Sky's head snaps up at the offer. He nods slowly.

It's enough to decide it. We all climb in the car—this time I take shotgun. I want to take Shep's hand, but something stops me. If I find out what really happened to Billy and it turns out it's her mother's fault, that Esme also tried to poison Principal Frankel, what is that going to do to Shep? To us?

Would she hurt Shep?

The ride to the car wash takes too long.

Aidan gets us tokens and chamois cloths while Sky and Shep and I stand around, none of us speaking.

The clink of the tokens going into the machine startles me. Aidan holds the water gun. "Anybody particularly want to do the honors?"

"I should," Shep says. She puts the keys in a pocket of her romper that I didn't know even existed. She takes the sprayer from Aidan. "Stand back if you don't want a shower."

The first spray of the power washer cuts a swathe right through the letters.

"What the—" Sky moves around my shoulder to get a better look.

"It's coming right off," Shep says, her voice almost sagging with relief. "I might live to see spring."

Her words slice through me. They're accompanied by my own bit of relief. She'll be okay, even if I won't. Those words on the car felt like a promise.

In the end, we don't even need the chamois. The water is enough to get rid of the words.

"Maybe the vandal has a deep respect for classic cars," Aidan says.

"I don't even care." Shep replaces the water sprayer in its metal holster with a clank.

"What do you think it meant?" I don't really know that Aidan expects an answer. "Does this have something to do with Sam's file getting leaked to the school?"

"Yes—" Shep says at the same time I say, "No."

We frown at each other.

"Maybe," I compromise. "I think it's more to do with Billy Clement."

Shep's eyes flash like polished stone. "Oh, these fuckers can bring it," she says. "We're *going* to find out what happened to him."

"Principal Frankel was at the dance tonight. Looking kind of freaked at times," Sky says. He looks at me. He must have realized I ran off to talk to her.

"Wait. You guys think Frankel offed a *kid*?" Aidan shakes his head. "No way."

"It would have been while she was a teenager," Sky offers, as if that helps.

Seeming to agree with my own thoughts, Aidan makes a face. "That's creepier."

"I don't think she did it," I say quietly.

Shep brushes her hands together to dry them off. "Feel kind of bad we broke into her office."

"You guys broke into her office? Jesus. I fell in with quite the crowd of rebels." It sounds like Aidan's trying to make a joke. His expression is a strange combination of hurt and confusion, though.

No one says anything.

The silence stretches on, punctuated only by the water dripping from the nozzle and the car.

"I get it," Aidan says after a long minute. "You don't want to tell me what's going on."

This time the hurt bleeds through his voice.

"Aidan," I start, but he cuts me off.

"No, it's okay. You don't have to. You barely know me."

"I just moved here, dude. I barely know anybody."

Now hurt crosses Shep's face, and I wish I could take it back.

Sky looks like his drunk brain is processing something his sober brain missed. "If Billy really was murdered, you have a literal murderer writing stalker-y threats on your car."

"Yeah," says Aidan. "Exactly."

"Like . . . if it is Principal Frankel, she knows where you live. She knows everything in your file, for dog's sake," Sky says.

"I don't think there's anything in it she could really use against me that someone hasn't already," I say. Again I hear her say, *Are you allergic to anything, Sam?*

Suddenly I doubt my instincts. What if that wasn't concern and she was fishing for ammunition?

It takes a minute for me to realize someone's talking to me. Shep.

"Billy deserves justice," Shep says. "Isn't that right, Sam?"

Her ferocity hurts my heart. He does deserve justice, but he's been dead for thirty years. He's not going to come back to life.

Part of me wants to believe that finding out what happened to Billy will save me. I lived through one near-death experience already, and I've spent the last year feeling like I'm on borrowed time. Maybe if I can find justice for Billy, I can also find peace for myself. Maybe I can stop waiting to die and actually live.

How can I keep pursuing this if it turns into something that could hurt Shep even more than my death would?

She's watching me so intently, trusting me to agree with her.

My heart cracks a little more with each word when I give her what she wants to hear. "Yes. Billy deserves justice."

The car ride home is almost silent. We drop off Aidan and Sky first, and then Shep drives me back to my place.

I pop the tapes out, tucking them into the pocket of my jacket.

"Are you okay?" Shep asks. "You've been quiet all night."

"I'm okay," I say. I hate the lie. I don't know what I'm even doing, trying to have friendships and relationships right now. Billy's story is a walking bomb, about to explode and rip through everyone I love with shrapnel. I settle for a vague truth, Shep's brown eyes watching me and clearly not believing that I really am okay. "I'm scared."

"If you don't want to keep looking—"

"I do," I say. "But what if what we find out is too big?"

"Bigger than a murderer living happily in Astoria for thirty years without getting punished?"

"Yeah."

"Then we'll deal," she says. "I have to know."

"But why? Why does it matter to you so much?" I reach out to her, take her hand. A year ago, this kind of casual touch would have been unthinkable for me. Now it's as easy as breathing, because it's *her*, because it's Shep.

"I don't know," she says finally. "It's just one of my *things*. I have to know this. I have to solve it. For Billy and for me. Even before you moved in there, I just felt like I needed to know. And then you did and it was like . . . like you were what I'd been waiting for. He had everything, you know? Loving parents, awesome friends, and he wasn't a *Brent*, he was a good kid, a good person. And when he died, everyone fell apart. His friends, his parents—they all just split. I need to know."

Her eyes are trained on the now-spotless hood of the car, this car that she's taken such good care of tonight, showing her dad's baby the kind of love he won't show her. If I need to know I'm allowed to live, maybe Shep needs to believe hurts can heal.

I close my eyes and bring her hand to my lips. I kiss the back of it gently, like an exhausted prince. "Then we will."

For an odd moment I wonder at the things that fell into place for Dad to buy this house. It sits back from the sidewalk with its brief little lawn, its front porch like knees pulled up to its chest, that red ring of a mouth that *tried*. All this time I've wondered if it was fate reaching out to me. Maybe I'm not the only one it was reaching out to.

I see why it'd reach out for Shep.

"You look miles away," Shep says.

"I'm right here." I put every ounce of conviction into the words, and her chest rises with a happy breath.

Shep leans across the bench seat and kisses my lips. There's no hunger like earlier, just a small cocoon of safety.

For now.

I get out of the car and watch her drive the short half block home. I go inside before the taillights turn off.

Dad's waiting just inside the door. "Hey there, Sammy! Did you have a good time?"

"Yeah, it was fun." I give him a smile and will him to believe it. "I'm pretty tired though."

Dad deflates a little. I think it's cute that he wants to sit and gush about the dance.

"I'll tell you all about it tomorrow," I promise. Now that I'm inside and it's quiet and I'm home, my brain seems to unbuckle its too-tight belt and flop. I held up pretty well with all the music and the loudness, but now . . . "I think I need to go de-sensitize."

"Fair enough, kid. As long as you had fun and you're okay."

I salute him. "I'm good."

He smiles, then, looking at me fondly. "You look like you had fun."

I smile back, a real smile. "I did."

He gives a sniff, and at first I think he's going to tell me I stink.

"Do you smell popcorn?" Dad asks, bewildered. "Do dances have popcorn now?"

My back straightens like someone's plucked the top of my spine. I don't smell anything but myself. "Probably just the bizarre chemistry of teenage sweat glands."

Dad frowns, and after a beat, he shrugs, saying "Good night" as he shuffles off to the kitchen.

Upstairs, I shut my door behind me and lock it. I'm covered in dried sweat, and I want to shower the sticky away, but I can't.

Instead, I take off my boots, freeing my calves. My pants cling to my legs. I peel them off, too, changing into a pair of non-brief boxers and a tank top. My binder sticks to my boobs and my ribcage, and I strip it away, tugging it out the sleeve of the tank. I stare at my discarded outfit, slung over the back of my desk chair. I love this suit. I want the chance to wear it again.

It's just been me and Shep who have smelled popcorn until now. Not even Sky has smelled it. Sitting in my room on the edge of my bed, it hits me that the people who have spent the most time in this room are the ones who do. Part of me wants to invite Sky over for a day to see if he notices anything—when he and Shep came over, we didn't come upstairs, and the day of the break-in, we all had other things on our minds.

I swallow. "Billy?"

Nothing happens.

My eyes sting. I press the heels of my hands against them, which makes it worse because my tears make my eyeliner and mascara run, and that stings more.

I grab my laptop and open Tumblr. I need to blame someone for this entire mess—my premonitions about my own death, my trauma, Shep's dad's car, lying to Dad and Shep—and Lee's good enough. Especially because she'll never even see this stupid blog.

You did this, you know? All these people who are going to be hurt when this murderer gets me—Shep, Sky, Aidan, Ronnie and Jax, maybe.

Dad.

I pause and then delete the names, except for their first initials. And Dad, since most people have at least one of those.

I should be grateful, maybe. I never would have met them if it wasn't for you and your cousins. I never would have known what it was like to get to go to a dance like tonight, to dance with my girlfriend and friends and not have to fucking hide.

But in a month, they're all going to hurt. I'll either be dead or Dad'll move us to another planet. I hear Elon Musk wants to colonize Mars.

I wish you had just finished the job when you had the chance.

It's a horrible thought, and I'm so angry that I hit Post before I can delete it.

The worst part is it's not even true. I don't want that. I don't wish it. I don't wish for this to be over or for my life to end. Anything *but* that. I don't want to die. I want to fucking live, but so far I never got to live. I don't know how many times I've read about people who didn't even get the second chance I did, but I know I never really get to live anyway. There's being a warm body that feels one wrong move away from death and there's being *alive*. I never get beyond basic fucking survival. Existence feels like silent drowning, wondering which breath will be my last while everyone else is swimming around me, lungs full of air they take for granted. That tiny hope I felt in the car shrivels and burns to dust.

I can't tell if this is me or Billy. If he's going to pull me with him into the grave.

My eyes burn now too, and I can taste the salt of my tears with the chemical tang of makeup. I hear Dad's footsteps on the stairs, getting about halfway up. I turn off the light.

I sit there in the dark until I'm sure he's gone to bed.

Tiptoeing out of the room, I make my way down the stairs to the hall, around the corner to the basement stairs, down those too. I shut the door behind me to muffle sound.

It's dark down here, but with the light of my phone I can see well enough to find my punching bag. I put my phone on a small table and totter in the dark back to my bag.

That picture of Billy and Mr. Quach's dad playing air hockey here. Right here.

My right fist hits it, hard. Then the left. Then the right. Then the left. Then right. Then left. Right, right, right, right.

Left.

Right.

Left.

Right.

Each thump is satisfying, each jolt of pain reminds me that I'm still here now.

My sweat mingles with tears and drips to the concrete floor. The chain of the bag rattles a bit against the beam where Dad secured it. The sound of my fists hitting the bag punctuate the rattles until a whisper of something else barely catches my ear, and I jump as something creates a small breeze past my face a split second before something pokes me in the shoulder and bounces off.

I let the bag swing, unable to see what fell from the rafter.

Shuffling back over to the table again, my heart rate is elevated not just from the exertion. My fingers shake when I pick up my phone. I press the screen to turn on the flashlight.

There's a square of paper on the floor, glaring white in the brightness from the phone.

I smell popcorn. Just a whiff, here and gone again from one sniff to the next.

Walking over, I pick up the paper. Not a paper—a card.

The front of it is the solar system, but it has a bunch of red hearts on it. It's caked in dust so thick, I have to brush it off to read the print, and the dust sticks to my sweaty fingers.

"Say, Valentine," it says on the front. I open it to read "You're out of this world!"

I almost drop it when I see the name signed under that printed line. There's only one other thing written here—"Will you go to the Sadie Hawkins dance with me?"

The person who signed it is Esme.

I look up above my head with the light. I don't know why this was up on that beam or how it's sat there for what, thirty-three years? I told Dad I wasn't afraid of the dead, but this is freak-out worthy.

I take the card and my phone and only manage not to sprint up the stairs because I don't want to wake Dad.

In the bright light of the upstairs bathroom, the card looks ancient. It's not very big—probably because it's a valentine, not like . . . a Hallmark card—and for the life of me I wouldn't know how it got up there on that rafter. Or how it got down, but I choose to believe me pummeling the bag jostled it just enough.

Esme asked Billy to the Sadic Hawkins dance. I think that's the kind where the tradition of boys asking girls got flipped— learned that in a book.

I don't know what to do with this information, and I can't tell Shep.

Did Billy say yes? Did he say no and piss her off? There's no way for me to know.

I clean up the card and my hands as best I can, washing my arms up to the elbows to get the dust off.

Hours pass before I finally manage to sleep.

CHAPTER THIRTY-TWO

Faces surround me in my tunnel of mist. I'm the eye of this cyclone.

They all look to me.

Their expressions are blank, but their eyes are alight with fire.

Billy is front and center. I see the Scottish boy somewhere in the crowd, his hair dark and rain-wet, his face in black and white. A girl in the heavy drowning dress whose name I never even found. Pale faces. Dark ones. Faces I have looked for through the depths of history.

They all want something, and I don't know what.

I fall to my knees in their midst and sink farther still, pulling my hands in a circle around my legs with the weight of their gazes heavy, constricting.

The lights in the sky move and murmur the way the strands of my hair do in the breeze, lavender to green, green to rose, rose to silver.

I don't know if a murderer awaits me in Astoria, but my mind is full of the dead, and I think they know I'll join them.

. . .

I wake up the next morning still coated in sweat. Lines of it have dried into white creases on my black sheets, and I get up, disgusted. I don't look at the card where I left it on the window seat.

I strip the sheets from my bed, balling them up into a clump. I resemble them more than I'd like. Throwing on a pair of sweatpants and a white T-shirt I stole from Dad, I haul them downstairs, back to the basement. I can hear Dad in the kitchen, but I'm not ready to see him yet. He probably heard my little punching bag extravaganza last night, and I don't want to see that worried look on his face. Not yet. I deliberately avoid looking at that rafter.

I have to tell him.

Even if he tries to take me away for this, I have to tell him. About the notes, the rocks, Carl's car, the card, everything. I've gotten this far by myself. I owe him that much, to trust him now. It's strange. I used to look to him to fix everything. I know he can't fix this. There's power in knowing that it's my choice.

The washer smells fresh and clean. I dump my sheets in, along with a small pile of socks and underwear and T-shirts. I watch as the water rushes in, pouring out bright blue liquid to mix with it.

I sneak back upstairs, even though the smell of coffee almost overpowers my desire to avoid getting asked if I'm okay. Even now that the decision is made, I want to flinch from it.

My phone says it's almost noon. No texts from Shep or Sky or anybody. My heart sinks a little at that. Maybe they're all sleeping in, too.

I make myself a deal, like the whole "car doors open on three" thing.

I need to shower. That's my timer. When I get out, I'll come downstairs. I'll tell him everything.

I crank the water up to nearly scalding, even though hot water like that is shit on colored hair like mine. I let the water run over me, washing away the sweat from my body. Scrubbing my face with a washcloth seems to exfoliate some of my helplessness along with the remnants of glitter eyeliner and tears.

When I emerge, I feel almost like a human again. Ready to face Dad.

Shep left her mom's journal here, maybe to avoid the off chance that Esme would find it in Shep's room. Esme won't poke through my room, that's for sure. *Unless she already did.* I slam dunk that thought back into the recesses of my brain. Maybe I can figure this out without Shep. Spare her some . . . something.

That tension in the room is back, heavy. First, I need to tell Dad everything.

I head back downstairs to get coffee. I don't hear Dad anymore, though the smell of coffee is still strong.

"Dad?" I exit the hall, peering around the corner over the breakfast bar. "Dad?"

He's not there, only a half-full coffee pot.

"Dad!" I holler. Maybe he's in his room. I turn around, confused.

No answer.

I pad back down the hall to peek out the front door's window. The Subaru is in the driveway, just where it was when I got home last night.

Back to the kitchen. "Dad!"

I round the end of the breakfast bar and I see him. On the floor. One hand stretched out, the other at his neck.

"Dad!" I hit the floor so hard that my knees jolt with pain.

I don't know what to do. What am I supposed to do?

See if he's breathing.

That. That's the right thing. I lean down, putting my cheek in front of his face. I hear it before I feel it, a soft wheeze. He's not conscious, but he's breathing. Or trying to.

911.

I stumble to my feet, lurching for the breakfast bar where the stupid landline I thought we didn't need sits. I grab the phone from its cradle and stare at it.

I don't know how to even dial it.

There's a green button. I push it. I hear a tone. Does that mean I can dial? I hit 9-1-1, my chest tight and with breath that fills only the top of it, fills it like it might burst. I can see my iPhone upstairs on my stripped bed where I left it after my shower. I should get it, but Dad—

The phone rings once. It worked. It worked.

"Nine-one-one, what is your emergency?" The voice is too calm.

"It's my dad! He's on the floor and I found him and—"

"What's your address?"

I manage to get the words out over my tongue that wants to choke me.

"Is your dad breathing?"

"Barely." The word comes out with a sob and I fall back to my knees. "He's wheezing."

"Is he conscious?"

"No."

"Okay. What's your name?"

"Sam."

"Sam, I need you to stay with me, okay? An ambulance is coming. How long has your dad been unconscious?"

"I don't know. I was in the shower." Stupid, stupid, stupid Sam. My right hand is holding the phone, but my left hand balls into a fist and slams into my leg once, twice, again.

"What's that sound, Sam?"

"I—" I can't make the words. Shame courses through me. "Tell me what to do!"

His skin is ashy. I put my hand on his chest so I won't keep hitting myself. I feel his heartbeat, a faint flutter under my palm. He's alive.

"You're sure your dad is breathing?"

"He's breathing. I can feel his pulse, too."

"Okay, Sam. How is he positioned?"

"He's on his back."

"Okay. I want you to put me on speaker, can you do that?"

"I've never used this phone before." I look at it. There's a speaker button on the keypad. I hit it. "I did it, I think."

"Good, Sam. Good job." The voice comes out loudly, telling me I succeeded. I put the phone on the floor. The dispatcher goes on. "Is there any chance of a spinal injury?"

"I don't think so. He's just . . . he's just on the floor."

"Good. I need you to carefully roll your dad onto his side, okay? Keep his neck straight as best you can. Check his breathing again as soon as you do."

"Okay." He's warm, but his body is deadweight. I pull him toward me. His head lolls on his neck, and I sob again. With both hands, I straighten his neck out, my wrist in front of his nose. I feel only the faintest breath. My whole chest seems to jerk as if I can breathe for him. "I did."

"Is he still breathing?"

"Yes."

"Okay. Bend his top leg so that his knee and hip are both at right angles, got it?"

"Yeah." I move his left leg into that position. "Now what do I do?"

"Sam, do you have a blanket of some kind? You said he's on the floor—is he on carpet?"

"No. I mean, I can get a blanket, but he's on tile."

"Go get the blanket. Cover his core, but don't put it over his face." The instructions are specific, and I'm grateful for them.

I jump up, kicking the phone away from me accidentally. I run to the living room and grab the throw from the back of the sofa. It's thick and fluffy.

I run back to the kitchen, terrified he's stopped breathing in the fifteen seconds I was gone. All I see is Dad on the floor, and tears drip from my chin. I throw the blanket over him and grab the phone back from where it skittered.

"Sam, are you there?"

"I'm here." My voice cracks.

"Check your dad's breathing for me again."

I put my face down by his, dripping tears on his cheek. But I hear a wheeze again and feel the slight warmth of his breath. "He's breathing and I got the blanket on him."

"Okay, Sam, good job. You're doing a great job. The ambulance should be there any minute."

"Thank—thank you." A sob breaks the sentence in half.

"Of course. You're okay, Sam." The sound of a siren blooms in the distance. "Is that the ambulance?"

"I think so."

"I'll stay on the line until they are inside, okay? Check your dad's breathing once more, then go open the door for them. You can just open it and leave it open, okay, Sam?"

The dispatcher keeps saying my name, and it helps ground me. "Okay. What's your name?"

"Corey," the dispatcher says.

I check Dad's breathing again. "He's still breathing. I'm going to open the door."

I don't wait for an answer. I rush for the door and fling open the dead bolt, yanking it open just as the ambulance comes speeding up the street, the siren piercing the air. I don't care that the door hits the closet door behind it and makes a dent. I run back to Dad.

Two EMTs hurry through the door less than a minute later.

"Where are you?" one calls out.

"Back here in the kitchen!"

They appear over the breakfast bar. I skitter out of their way, clutching the phone to my chest.

"This is your dad?" one of them asks. His shirt has my name embroidered on it. His name. His name is Sam too. He's got brown skin and a slight accent.

I can't speak. I nod as hard as I can.

"What's his name?" Paramedic Sam looks at my tear-streaked face and softens his voice while his partner, a white guy whose name I can't see, checks Dad's vitals.

"Junius Sylvester," I manage to get out.

"What's your name?"

"Sam," I say. "My pronouns are they/them." My face contracts, and my eyes twitch, and I can't stop it. I ball my fist and strike my leg again.

"Hey, hey, hey there. It's okay. We're going to take care of your dad."

I can't talk. The voice of Corey on the phone makes me jump, but I can't make words from the sounds.

"Sam?" says Paramedic Sam.

I can't answer. Words won't come out.

"We're here with them," Paramedic Sam says. "Sam. We have the same name. It'd really help us if you could talk to us. I know this is scary."

He looks at me, but I can't meet his eyes. I can only look at Dad.

Dad's going to die and it's going to be my fault. I punch my leg again, again, again. I should have told him sooner. I should have—

Paramedic Sam takes the phone from me gently. "Hey, dispatch? Sam reminds me of my son. I'm going to hang up. We'll take care of their dad."

The other paramedic starts arranging Dad on a stretcher.

"Anaphylaxis," he says. I don't see what he does next, except suddenly there's a plastic EpiPen in his hand, and a sharp spring noise tells me he's just poked Dad with it.

Even after his last reaction, we didn't think he'd need an EpiPen.

Paramedic Sam turns to me.

"It's hard to talk when you're this scared," he says, and I actually feel like he gets it. He pulls a pad and pen from a pocket and hands it to me. "Can you write down any allergies or anything that could help us find out what happened?"

I take it and nod, hating myself and my brain. There's a plate in the sink, empty except for a few crumbs. A half-drunk mug of coffee on the counter. Nothing else I can see, except—

There's a note on blue paper at the end of the breakfast bar.

I can read it from here. It's in Sharpie.

Junius,

I promised you coffee cake (nut-free, of course!), so here it is! We'll have to trade recipes if you like it.

Esme Shepard

Every electron zooming through the matter that makes up Sam Sylvester stops mid-orbit.

"Walnuts," I say, stumbling over a paramedic bag to reach the note. "Walnuts. Fridge."

Paramedic Sam opens the fridge, where I can see a coffee cake with a big slice taken out of it.

CHAPTER THIRTY-THREE

The paramedics don't trust me to drive the Subaru. Dad's still unconscious when they load him in the back of the ambulance, but even I can hear his breathing is getting better. I run upstairs to grab my phone—and Esme's journal when my eyes fall on it—and then climb in the back of the ambulance. As the doors slam shut and the driver backs out of the driveway, flipping the siren on again, I look down and realize I forgot shoes.

Paramedic Sam is with me in the back with Dad. In the front I can hear the other paramedic radioing ahead to the hospital.

"Can I hold his hand?" My voice comes out hoarse.

"Of course," Paramedic Sam says. "The EpiPen is helping. His blood pressure is improving, and his breathing is much better already. We'll get him into the hospital, and they'll take excellent care of him, okay?"

"Thank you." Tears spill over again, and I clutch Dad's hand in mine. Usually how different we are brings me comfort—his dark skin against my paleness, his callouses against my smooth palms—but right now I'm so scared that I'll lose him that I can barely look at the line between our hands. Dad always used to cup his hand against mine when I was younger and say we were like the yin-yang symbol. Perfect harmony.

"How old are you, Sam?" Paramedic Sam looks over at me.

"Eighteen," I say.

"You in high school?"

"Junior." I add a belated, "I'm *a* junior" in case he thinks I just said I was an eighteen-year-old kid in middle school.

"My son's about to go into high school," he says. "He's a bit old for his grade too."

"I'm autistic," I say.

"So's my son." Paramedic Sam gives me a tight but genuine smile. "His name's Manuel."

"That's a nice name."

There's a pause, and I listen to Dad's breathing. It's the most beautiful sound I've ever heard in my life.

"You did really well, Sam," Paramedic Sam says. "You kept your dad safe till we could get there to help him. He's going to be okay because you found him when you did."

"He's going to be okay?"

"I can't see the future, but I think he's going to be just fine."

I squeeze Dad's hand tighter.

When we get to the hospital, Paramedic Sam and his partner help me out of the ambulance while nurses hurry toward us.

"Can I tell them you're autistic?" he asks me, and I appreciate it. I nod.

He goes to one of the nurses and murmurs to her. They usher me inside and I watch as Paramedic Sam vanishes. He nods at me as if to tell me it's going to be okay.

The hospital smells weird and is too bright, too loud. The fluorescents hum against my skin. Someone starts asking me questions, carefully. I answer as best I can, and after they finish bustling about with their ten thousand tests, they finally leave me in a curtained-off corner of the ER.

I don't know why I brought Esme's journal. Maybe because of the note. Probably because of the note.

If she did this to Dad—the thought makes my vertebrae want to disassemble themselves into a pile—and also to Billy, this journal is maybe the most valuable thing I possess.

If she did it. Why would she do it? Why would she do this to Dad? You hear of people getting violent when they don't get their way, but could she have killed Billy because he turned her down for the dance?

But the coffee cake. The assurance that it was safe for him when clearly it wasn't. None of this makes sense.

I need to look at that coffee cake, but I can't. Dad would have known if he bit into a walnut, and he finished the whole piece. Maybe she ground them up?

The thought makes me sick. My knuckles ache from the punching bag last night. My knees throb from hitting the floor. My left quad hurts where I punched it. But none of that comes close to the sheer fury and pain that burns through me when I look up from my chair at Dad. I wish I had the fidget cube Shep gave me. I wish I had Shep.

Dad's skin looks better, more alive. That's good. But he still hasn't woken up.

I look at my phone. Still nothing from Shep. The little green icon with no red notification bubble makes me feel worse. Is that normal after a date? Maybe I should text her. Maybe this is what she felt when she didn't know how to talk to me about Montana and the school finding out. Worse—how can I text her from the hospital where my dad is recovering from anaphylactic shock when it's her mother's fault? Maybe she's just taking a nap or something. Too many maybes.

I crack open the journal, paging to about the point where Esme first mentioned Carl.

I read through most of 1988, hoping for some kind of indication. Esme doesn't even mention Billy. There's a big gap from September 1988 until November 1988, then Esme starts back up again.

Almost all the entries are day-to-day frustrations, venting about homework or teachers or teammates or family. It looks like she had a lonely home life. Dad in the Navy, almost never home. Mom working weird hours as a nurse. She mentions going on a few dates. None with Carl. December 1988, she finally mentions a crush on someone, but she doesn't even say who.

High school sweethearts, according to Shep.

It's not till it picks back up that I see a word that finally sticks out at me.

Cheerleader.

Esme was a cheerleader. Shep told me that. I even saw the fucking picture of her and I didn't put it together.

Some luck, finally, she writes in February of 1989, *if you can call it that. Janet is off the squad because she slipped a disc in her back, and I'm finally on. Just in time for basketball play-offs . . . if we make them. And baseball starts practice next month, which is going to make the pep rally awkward now since somebody didn't even answer when I asked him to the dance.*

I read it again. "Somebody" is underlined hard. I think she means Billy.

The sound of the curtain sliding back makes me snap the journal shut.

The doctor who comes in looks me over as if trying to parse me. "Afternoon. I'm Doctor Chester. This is your father?"

I always feel a little belligerent when white people ask me that question. When Paramedic Sam asked, it felt like a mere confirmation. When this doctor asks, it feels like he thinks I ended up in the wrong room.

"Yeah, that's my dad. Junius Sylvester. I'm Sam. Is he going to be okay?"

"I've just been looking over his tests. Is he aware that he has such a severe allergy?"

"Walnuts aren't in many things," I say. "Last time he accidentally ate one, he just took a Benadryl and was fine. We're careful, but he didn't think he had to be paranoid."

"So there's no chance he could have ingested a large amount without knowing."

I shake my head. "A neighbor brought a coffee cake over this morning, but she specifically said there were no nuts in it."

LIAR.

"She knew about his allergy?"

"Yeah, he told her when she came to dinner one night. Her daughter's my girlfriend."

"What's the neighbor's name?"

"Esme Shepard," I tell him. "She lives on our street."

He makes a note.

"Is my dad going to be okay?" The words are coming easier now. It's Dad. He saved me. I have to . . . something.

"Since he never stopped breathing and we didn't have to resuscitate him, he's in pretty good shape. It's best he rests now. Can your mom come—"

"I don't have a mom," I say. "It's just me and Dad."

"How old are you?"

"Eighteen."

It's the second time today I've had to say that out loud.

Dr. Chester seems to think for a moment. "We're going to move your dad into a hospital room shortly. After that, I'd suggest you go home, get some rest. We'll call you if there's any changes or if he wakes up."

If he wakes up.

I stare at the doctor a little too long. He shifts his feet uncomfortably, looking down at mine, which are still bare.

"Do you have someone you can call? Did you need someone to call you a cab?"

"I can call someone," I say. My words echo in the room.

Dr. Chester nods, then pulls the curtain back again to leave. "We'll take good care of your dad," he says. "Leave your number with the nurses, and we'll call you as soon as there's any news."

I do as I'm told when the nurse comes in. She shows me out to the waiting room and gives me the room number where they're going to bring Dad. He's supposed to be here to tell me what humans do. Am I supposed to insist on staying with him? I can't do anything if I stay here.

I sit down in a flat-cushioned gray chair. The floor is gritty on the soles of my feet.

My phone sits on my lap, screen dark.

I can call someone, but who? Shep? She hasn't texted me since last night, and that upsets me even though I know I could have texted her too. If her mom gave my dad walnuts, though—no way. No way can I call her. Sky? Sky doesn't know about my special interests, about how deep into this I really am, but he'd tell Shep immediately if he thought I was going to try and confront Esme.

I could call Aidan.

Or rather, text. I pull open my contacts and find his name at the top of the list. I open a text message. He and I have never texted directly, only in the group chat.

Hey

It's stupid. Not enough. I can't just say *hey* when I'm sitting in a fucking hospital.

I need help

That's worse, but it's already gone, marked with "Delivered" underneath. Fuck.

My dad's in the hospital, I make my thumbs type. *I came in the ambulance and can't get home. Can you come get me?*

I stare at the messages, feeling worse and worse with each passing second.

"Delivered" changes to "Read."

An ellipsis appears.

Holy shit of course

Relief suffuses me. Another ellipsis.

U at Columbia?

"Is this Columbia?" I ask out loud, hoping someone hears me and answers.

"Yeah," someone says. "Why don't you know that?"

"Came in an ambulance," I say. "Thanks." My reply has a bite to it, and I ignore the person's startled "sorry" as I type a *yes* to Aidan.

There in 15, he says back after a pause.

Don't tell Sky or Shep, I text back.

The message shows "Read" for a full minute before the ellipsis appears and instantly becomes *k.*

I distract myself while I wait by reading Esme's journal. I read through the rest of February, into March. Billy died March 22, a week after my birthday and ten days after his own. There's no mention of him. Nothing. But she was literally in the room when he suffocated to death, and Margie Frankel was in the bathroom. That has to be how it happened. It has to be.

There's nothing in here that indicates she was plotting a murder.

I hear Esme again, the same words as Margie's. *Billy's death was a tragic accident.*

What if it was?

What if Shep and I are just wrong?

A woman comes through the sliding doors, holding a kid in her arms, blood running down the child's face. The sight shocks me back to where I am and why.

I'm in an emergency room. My dad almost died.

Even *if* what happened to Billy was a "tragic accident," what happened to my dad was a plan.

My phone buzzes. Aidan.

Im outside

I gather my stuff and go.

CHAPTER THIRTY-FOUR

Aidan's driving a gold Toyota sedan that looks nowhere near new. I get in on the passenger side. The inside is a little tattered, but spotless.

"Thank you," I say.

"Sam," he says, putting the car in park. "Are you okay? Is your dad okay? Why can't I tell Shep or Sky?"

"I'm fine. Dad's going to be fine. And—" Agonized, I look at Aidan, sucking in a deep breath. His face has concern and fear etched into his forehead. "If I tell you this, you're going to think I'm crazy, and I can't tell Shep because it involves her mom."

"Try me."

"I'm not kidding, dude. You're going to think I'm nuts." I stumble on the last word because of what just happened to Dad and bite my tongue out of shock, tasting blood.

"I live with an ex-cop who throws a temper tantrum if you move his remote. He could put a toddler to shame." He cracks a smile that doesn't reach his eyes.

"This is beyond shitty parents. Well, kind of." My turn for a mirthless smile. "Think like . . . obsessive weirdo weird, for my part of this."

He blinks. "Okay."

"I'll tell you on the way to my house." My heart thuds. I'm really going to tell him.

He puts the car in drive and pulls out of the pickup area.

And I try to talk. To his credit, Aidan listens. Even though he's watching the road, I see his eyes get wider and wider and wider. He says *holy shit* a few times, but he doesn't otherwise interrupt, and he doesn't wig out about my special interest in dead people or try to compare it to collecting baseball cards.

I tell him about the notes, the card, the weird popcorn smell, show him the scar on my palm from the rocks someone threw. I tell him about the people whose stories I've tried to keep alive.

And I tell him about how Esme knew my dad was allergic to walnuts and even wrote a note assuring him the cake would be free of nuts.

By the time I get to that part, my knuckles are white in spite of their swelling as I grip my still-aching knees.

"I see why you can't tell the others," he says.

"Shep knows about most of it," I say.

"She said Billy deserves justice."

"I know. But if it's her *mom*?" I want to ask what Aidan thinks, but I don't dare.

"I saw the car last night," he says as we pull up in my driveway behind the Subaru. He puts the car in park and pulls the emergency brake. "I don't know what's going on here, but I do know that someone really wants to fuck with you."

"I don't think that message was for Shep," I say. "I talked to Principal Frankel last night at the dance. She told me some stuff. Someone could have seen us talking, maybe. Overheard."

"Anyone at the dance could have seen you with her."

"Ninety-nine percent of the people at the dance weren't alive when Billy died," I say wryly.

"Could have been Frankel herself."

"I know. But she wasn't the one who tried to kill my dad."

Aidan lets out a breath with a loud *whoosh*. "Yeah. Touché."

We get out of the car. I pat my pockets, for a moment panicking that I locked myself out. Keys jingle, though, and I let us in.

The house welcomes us through that red mouth around the door, and I can almost feel the walls themselves droop in grief. This house has seen so much pain.

"I need you to do something for me," I say to Aidan.

"I'll do whatever I can."

I tell him about the fingerprints I pulled from the lamp, the notes (other than Esme's, which Paramedic Sam said to leave and not touch), Esme's journal. Even though I haven't found anything in it. I take pictures of the coffee cake in the fridge. Some people might go straight to the cops, but seeing as Aidan's dad was one and seems to be an abusive jackass, I trust he'll . . . I don't know. Tell the right person. Maybe even know who that is.

"Sky has a video of me getting the prints off the lamp," I say. "I don't know if anything would be admissible in court this way, but maybe it'd spark an investigation."

"Jesus. Okay."

"Monday if I'm not at school, give everything to Mr. Quach. You know who he is, right?"

"Special ed teacher. Vietnamese guy, looks too young to be a teacher? Long hair and way too much fashion sense?"

"Yep. All teachers are mandated reporters, so if you can't find him, choose someone else you trust. You tell him something like this, especially about the vandalism and threats, and he is required by law to go to the authorities." I lean against the breakfast bar. I want to puke.

"Sam—"

"One last thing. Can you text Shep and find out if she's at her dad's today? She said she would be, but I need to know. I don't want her there if I confront her mom."

"Sam!"

312

"Please."

"I'll do it. That's not what I was going to say." Aidan puts his hand on my shoulder. I don't shrug it off. It doesn't feel invasive, just . . . scared. "Whatever you're about to do, just be careful, okay?"

I want to tell someone this one last thing, that it doesn't matter how careful I am. I will end up dead or get killed sometime between now and March 15 with or without carefulness. It's absurd and impossible and I believe it anyway. The scar on my neck always felt more like a warning than an escape. I can almost feel Billy here, waiting for me to join him.

But I don't tell Aidan that. He shouldn't have to carry it.

It's only for me to bear.

CHAPTER THIRTY-FIVE

Aidan leaves not long after, a small box of stuff in his arms. "I'll hide it in the freezer in my room."

"You have a freezer in your room?"

"Mini fridge," he says. "It's where I keep my caffeine supply."

"Mountain Dew?"

"Bottled Frappucinos."

"You're kind of a walking surprise," I tell him.

"I get that a lot." Aidan gives me a crooked smile. "Thanks for trusting me, Sam. I'm really glad to be your friend."

It hits me right then how lonely he must be. My own smile goes crooked, and in a surprise even to me, I give him a quick hug to hide my nerves. One more person I'm bound to hurt.

I watch his car pull out and then go upstairs.

If I go to Esme's, I sure as hell won't eat anything she puts in front of me. I don't have any allergies that I know of, and if I don't know, she sure as hell wouldn't know. But it's a short skip from feeding someone something that'll put them in anaphylactic shock to lacing something with cyanide.

My house feels like a shell full of ghosts. Am I one of them?

I can almost see the pages of my book.

I remember more of the half-lived lives, farther and more distant. Not just in time but everything. Their memories are fuzzy and tired, the farther back I look. The hall of my house becomes the misty tunnel, and its lights curl above my head. I've been searching for all of them for as long as I can remember.

And yet even the nameless ones I've never heard of seem to send something forward to strengthen me. They do not understand me, because they're dead, and they don't know me. But I know them, as much as anyone could. No one can look forward while we live.

I climb the stairs to my room.

I am not dead yet.

. . .

My bed is still stripped. The sight shakes me for a moment until I remember the morning, a million-year morning, when I put them in the washer. They've been in there all day.

I crack open my laptop. Check my phone. The hospital hasn't called, and I somehow know they won't. Not for a while. They told me to wait, so I'm waiting. Or maybe I'm just stalling.

Nothing from Aidan yet.

In one corner of my desk, *Sam's Book of Half-Lived Lives* sits, untouched since the home invasion. I open it to Billy's section, my hands shaking. I want to tell his truth here. Someone should tell his truth.

But his section is gone. I flip back and forth, first slowly and then frantically, staring at the ragged edges of paper that are gone. I should have noticed this sooner. Shep's gift is on my bedside table and I leap up to grab it, wiggling the plastic switch on one side back and forth with an audible *click-click-click-click*.

My heart thumps as if it's pumping Jell-O instead of blood. I can't do this. I can't sit here waiting for the hospital to call now, and I can't go face off with a murderer. I slap the book shut with my free hand, turning the cube to dig the triad of gears into the flesh of my palm.

Whoever broke into the house stole Billy's pages.

We were holding the thing they stole and didn't even notice.

For a long moment I just stand there with my cube in my hand, wishing I could text Shep and tell her everything.

The world recedes as I process what I have to do.

Finally, I get my laptop and open a blank document.

I hate this. Somewhere inside me I feel like I'm supposed to have more time. Not just after March 15, when Dad will inevitably yank us out of this place even if I live to see tomorrow, but now. Somewhere inside me knows that when I walk out my door, that's it.

I won't be coming back.

Leaving a note will make it look like I chose to die if I do. I didn't. I'm not choosing to die.

Walking out the door is me choosing to do the right thing. To end this for everyone it's touched. For Billy, for Shep and Sky and Aidan. For Margie Frankel, who has spent most of her life carrying something far too heavy. Her journal written in code, because living for three decades with that kind of burden would make anyone fucking paranoid. Thirty years in the isolation of grief. Frozen. I wonder if Mr. Quach's dad feels frozen too.

Right now, I'm frozen. I don't want to go over there if there's any chance Shep's there. She shouldn't have to find out about Dad like that.

My desktop notification goes off. It's an email. From Shep. With attachments.

I almost don't open it.

She's written only, *From last night x* in the body of the email, and the attachments are pictures.

I see the first one, and it's plenty. It's the one Sky's mom took of us about to kiss. Everything about it glows.

I close it again. Carefully, I open my system preferences and turn off my password protection on the laptop. Go back to the notes app.

A note—and it looks like I'm recklessly running into danger. But Dad knows me. He knows me. I have to trust that he'll remember all the times he's trusted me and trust this too. Hell. I can tell him that.

Dad,

I hope you never read this. But if you do, please trust me. I didn't choose to die, however it looks, but I saw it coming. There was no way to step out of the way of this oncoming train wreck. Billy Clement deserves justice, and I don't think anyone else can find it for him. I have to do this.

You're in the hospital right now because Esme Shepard gave you a cake with walnut in it somehow. I think she killed Billy. I think when I confront her, she might try to kill me. Somebody has as much evidence as I could gather. They'll know what to do with it if anything happens to me.

I hope you'll understand, Daddy. You're the best and most important thing that's ever happened to me. You raised me and protected me. You fought for me and today, you almost died for me. You saved me every day.

I'm eighteen years old, and I need to fight for myself now.

I love you.

Sammy

I close my laptop before I can make myself delete it.

My phone buzzes. Aidan.

Shep's at her dad's. BE CAREFUL. If I don't hear from you in two hours, I'm telling Coach Unterwagner. I can't just wait until Monday.

He's right. Of course, he is. Coach Unterwagner is the PE teacher, the ex-Marine. If Aidan trusts him, he can't be that bad. I text back because I know Aidan needs me to. *Thank you. I'll be careful. I'll talk to you in two hours, I hope. House key will be on the driver's side front tire of the Subaru if you need it.*

Outside, the clouds draw back to let the afternoon sun push through.

I put on fresh clothes. Boxer briefs and black jeans, a clean binder. T-shirt. Long black sweater. If I'm doing this, I'm going to at least look like me. The only armor I have. The hospital hasn't called, so I call them.

"I'm calling to check the status of Junius Sylvester," I say, then give his room number. "He's my dad."

"One moment please." There's a pause, a click, and the phone rings again.

I repeat myself to the person who answers, and she says, "Oh! Honey. Your dad's stable, but he still hasn't woken up. We'll call you if that changes, but you can plan on coming by first thing in the morning if you want."

"Thank you." I hang up before I throw up. Any hope I had of getting to talk to Dad one more time shrivels and dies. I'd give anything to have him ask if I was okay, to have him look at me with that worried crease. At least this way I don't have to lie to him ever again. At least this way, hearing his voice won't make me lose my nerve to force a confrontation.

I tuck my phone and wallet in my pocket and check my keys. Locking up the house behind me, I slip the house key off and reach under the front wheel well of the Subaru, placing it on top of the driver's side front tire where I told Aidan it would be.

It feels beyond strange, walking up the street to Shep's house and knowing she's not there.

My boots sound too loud on the steps leading to the porch. The light is on, even though the sun's still up. I have to count to ten twice to get myself to knock.

There's no answer at first, so I try the doorbell. It takes ten "on three" counts to press the button.

This time, I hear footsteps.

There's a pause at the door and a shuffling sound a moment later, as if the person on the other side is trying to decide whether they can get away with not opening it.

It cracks open.

Esme's hair is pulled back in a messy bun, and she greets me with a bewildered expression. She has dark circles under her eyes, and for the first time, I see lines around them as well as the remnants of makeup that she didn't wash off. "Sam, it's good to see you. I'm afraid Shep's not here. She's at her dad's this weekend."

"I came to see you, actually."

She looks even more confused, but she steps aside and beckons me in. "Is everything okay?"

I can't tell her about Dad. Not yet. "I came to ask you about Billy Clement," I say. It takes every ounce of effort to meet her eyes, so much like Shep's.

Esme looks as if she's half an inch from kicking me out, but her eyes dart behind me and she shuts the door. Locks it.

The sound feels final.

"If you're that determined, I guess I can't say no, can I?" Her voice raises in pitch, ending in a sharp little laugh. "Come on in. Can I offer you anything?"

"Stomach's a bit upset today," I say, and then follow that truth with a lie. "But I'm fine."

"Those two things are quite an oxymoron," she says. She leads me into the kitchen anyway and gets a glass of water from the tap on the fridge. Condensation immediately forms on the glass, just like the perspiration threatening to form on my forehead.

"I don't know how much I can really tell you about Billy," Esme says, sipping her water. There's a Bundt pan in the sink. The very one that coffee cake probably came from. She hasn't mentioned the cake at all. I don't know if that's normal or not. Maybe she expects me to bring it up? Thank her for it?

My phone buzzes in my pocket. I ignore it. If it was the hospital, it'd be a call, not a text.

"Maybe begin with why you were in his room when he died."

Esme visibly starts, her water glass slipping from her hand. It crashes to the floor with a splash of water and glass. I'm right. *I'm fucking right.*

I don't know if I really believed I was right until now. She collects herself after a moment, the silence loud. Behind her on the counter is a tidy row of baking supplies in glass containers. There's a spice rack beside them that looks like a Food Channel chef tried to be a twenty-first-century apothecary, all clear vials of brown liquids and multicolored spices and herbs.

I am sweating now. I feel it mostly on my back and in my armpits, and I can smell myself. Not the stink of sweat, but the tinny adrenaline smell of my own fear.

"How do you know I was in Billy's room when he died?" Esme's words come out a little too evenly.

I saw you. I remember. I was there. YOU KILLED ME. I have to close my eyes to push the words away so they don't come out of my mouth. Billy's dead. I feel like I'm screaming at Lee and Esme at once.

Now that I'm here, facing her down, the rage I feel is nothing like the anger I've felt before now. I mistook nervousness from

Principal Frankel as proof of her guilt, but now, incandescent fury inside me as I face his killer, I recognize it for what it was.

Margarie Frankel didn't seem guilty because she killed Billy.

Margie steeped in guilt for thirty years because she couldn't *save* him.

"You weren't the only Astoria High student at his house that day," is all I say. It comes out as a half stammer.

My phone buzzes again.

I should reach for it. Tell Aidan to just go straight to the cops right now.

I move my hand toward my pocket.

"Don't." It's all Esme says, but it's enough. She's got a knife block within reach, and I, stupid fatalistic Sam Sylvester, didn't think to bring a weapon. "Put your hands on the counter and don't move."

There's no other choice if I really want these answers. I obey.

"So you know," she says.

"I know."

But that's the thing. There's knowing intellectually and there's *knowing*.

Esme reaches in her own back pocket and pulls out her phone. I can't see the screen or who she texts, but the sight makes me slump. I hope she didn't just text Shep.

"I watched him die," she says with absolutely no emotion. Or maybe too much. Her eyes are far away, and I know she's in my room thirty years ago on an afternoon just like this one with the golden hour sun shining through my dormer windows.

"Yes." My hands are slick against the countertop.

She picks at a broken nail, not looking at me.

"At first I thought he was just messing around. He was always doing that, faking overdramatic reactions to little things. Big goofball. But then he started wheezing and gasping and clawing at his throat and mouthing *help*."

I can't speak. Her words make the room spin around me.

But there's something in her eyes I didn't expect. Something that goes against what she's saying. Her cheeks are wet.

My mouth won't make sounds happen for the second time today. The sight of her crying stokes my fury to the level of a supernova, and this time it's not my autism holding me back, but the terror that if I open my mouth, that fury will explode out of me and engulf the entire Milky Way.

Minutes tick by. Sweat trickles down my back.

"In thirty years, no one has figured it out. I guess I should be impressed. I don't know how you did it, Sam." She sounds almost conversational, like we're Hannibal Lecter and Will Graham discussing a murder scene.

"I can't let this get out," she says. "I have a daughter. Shep doesn't know any of this, and I've spent her whole life making sure she doesn't find out. She's not going to find out from you. They'd take her from me, and she's not going to live with that man. Getting away from Carl has been the other purpose of my life, and while I have not been as successful, at least I am *free*."

I find my tongue. "You murdered a kid thirty years ago—"

Esme balks, derailed. Her eyes open wider. "What? Murder? Sam, it was—"

"A tragic fucking accident, I know your story by heart, Esme Shepard."

Her face goes slack. "Sam, it *was*."

"You just said you stood in front of him" —ME— "and watched him die."

WATCHED ME DIE.

WATCHED ME DIE.

WATCHED ME DIE.

I don't know if my brain is screaming it at Esme or at Lee now. I hear Lee's voice again. *I didn't tell you so you'd hurt her!*

I yank my hands off the counter and press them to my temples, trying to drown out my own fury.

"Sam, no, not that way. I didn't kill him. I stopped by his house to give him his spirit box for baseball season's opening practice, and he bit into a popcorn ball and"—Esme scrunches her eyes shut, but tears drip down her cheeks. I hear their tiny splashes as they hit the floor—"And he died, and I watched him die, and I'll never forget how I couldn't *move*. Until I ran."

"Then what about my dad?" I point at the still-dirty Bundt pan in the sink. "I almost watched my dad die this morning because you put walnuts in that fucking cake!"

This time the only sound is the clattering of glass when she jerks in surprise and kicks one of the shards at her feet. For so long I've felt like I walk on cracking glass. Some part of me is relieved to see someone else's feet among the shattered shards.

Esme has one hand raised halfway to her face. Her eyes are wide and she's no longer staring at me but through me, shaking her head as if the entire world just shifted beneath her feet.

"Oh, my god." Esme sounds so much like Shep when she says it, panic in every syllable, that I feel her terror reaching for me like the hand of someone drowning. She turns to her left, fumbling in the spice rack, from which she pulls a clear, nearly empty bottle of something brown. "Sam, no."

"Want me to call the hospital? He's in the hospital. You tried to kill my dad!"

Any remaining blood in Esme's face drains away. I can't tell what is going on in her head, but she looks like she has turned to ash. There is a strange sound from outside, like white noise.

323

She looks at her phone as if it has just bitten her. Who did she text?

Then she skids across the broken glass toward me in her bare feet. I jump back.

"Oh, my god, Sam. Oh, honey, no. Sam, you need to go. You need to go right now. You need to run."

She runs at me, and I dodge her, my brain not processing what she's saying. She is frantic. Not running at me—grabbing a bowl that jingles with keys.

"Take my car. Drive out of Astoria and call the police." She has the keys now, and she flings them at me so fast I barely catch them. "Go!"

"What are you talking about?" I yell.

"Ca—" she says, and then a *pop* rends the air behind me, and Esme collapses onto the kitchen floor.

A wave of stale booze reaches me a split-second too late for me to register it.

I see Carl step around the corner a moment before the butt of his pistol slams into my head.

CHAPTER THIRTY-SIX

It's a testament to how much light I usually find in my sleep that the total darkness of unconsciousness is a surprise.

What's even more of a shock is that I wake from it.

My eyes open, slowly, painfully.

At first, I just see gray, then red. A fire extinguisher, a small one like you might put in an emergency kit, not like the big ones at the school. It's covered in dust, so I'm not sure it's even functional.

"You had to go fuck it up, didn't you?" Carl Wayne paces in front of me, slowly taking form as my eyes struggle to focus. His movement is jerky, like he's agitated, which I guess he is.

My shoulders are tight. I'm on my side on a hard concrete floor, and my wrists are bound behind me. Every inch of me aches.

"You did it," I gasp out. My mouth tastes like tin. I spit onto the floor and it comes out red. "You tried to kill my dad."

Carl looks momentarily surprised. He stops pacing. "Huh. Only tried?"

"I saved him."

Surprise turns to annoyance. Carl's not exactly swaying on his feet, but his eyes blink in a way I recognize as drunk. "I must be getting rusty. Maybe I didn't put enough walnut extract in that cake. I knew Esme was trying to butter him up. She's *mine*."

My head is pounding. Why didn't he just kill me?

Esme. Is she dead? A low moan escapes me. Carl is pacing, the gun in his hand.

"Where's Esme?" I manage to get out.

He gestures up above his head with the gun. It's only then I see a smiley face sticker on the butt of the magazine. Like on his car air freshener, on the hood of his stupid fucking car.

"She's sleeping," he says dismissively. "She warned me, so I didn't want her to have to see this part."

Sleeping. Not dead. What did he do to her? That pop was pretty loud, but it was only once, and this is Astoria. Gun violence isn't exactly common here. I hope she's not upstairs bleeding.

Carl got here *fast*. But this town is small. Maybe he doesn't know what to do with me. Someone could easily see him if he tried to haul my body outside. So he hauled my body into the basement. And since he has to be the one who killed Billy—and knowing what he tried to do to Dad—maybe actually being face to face with a victim has him flustered.

"You were here this morning," I say.

"Came to pick up my daughter, who you do *not* have my consent to date."

"She can fucking choose for herself, you chauvinist murdering asshole. You don't own Shep or Esme."

Carl laughs at that but doesn't say anything else. He gestures with the gun again, but I don't think it's for my benefit—he looks like he's having some sort of conversation, but not with me. Did he come get Shep when he was already drunk? Jesus. If I just sit here in silence, he's going to figure out what to do with me. He might shoot me for talking, but he might not.

"How did you poison my dad?" I ask, not sure if he will even answer.

"Esme had to run upstairs to get *Steph* this morning," he says. "But she told me she was making her world-famous coffee cake for your dad." His tone turns mocking. "Without the walnuts. She said she was leaving them out because he was allergic, but I couldn't bear for him not to get the full effect of that cake. Esme's a great baker. Always keeps the good stuff on hand. Wasn't hard to dump in some walnut extract."

The bottle she was staring at. I don't know how many recipes call for walnut extract, but the vial she held in horror was almost empty.

"And Billy?" Now that I'm here, I can see it coming, like the end of the train tracks. Last stop for Sam Sylvester. But I have to know. I have to know.

"Oh, she definitely gave him those popcorn balls. Did you know she asked him to the Sadie Hawkins dance a few weeks before? He said he wasn't sure, and she was insufferable about it. Wouldn't shut up about how much she liked him, how much she wanted him to say yes when I was *right there* and she could have asked me. She should have asked me."

I almost don't believe what I'm hearing. Carl killed Billy Clement because Esme asked him to a *dance*?

"How did you do it?" I whisper the question against the pounding in my head.

"Kid couldn't handle peanuts. The cheerleaders were making the popcorn balls to go in the spirit boxes for all the baseball players. They were all labeled with player names and jersey numbers in the home-ec kitchen. Didn't take much to dribble some peanut oil on Billy's. They weren't even wrapped. Popcorn smell covered any peanut smell."

I can almost feel Billy with me, like time is a spiral that has come back around, and I can reach out and touch him.

"She thought she killed him," I say against the floor. The concrete has almost warmed to my cheek.

"She certainly did. I comforted her, helped her through it. Told her I'd protect her, and I did. And then she went off and dumped me to marry that worthless Shepard when she was eighteen, but I got her back."

"You kill him too?"

"No need to do much." Carl taps his head with his fingers.

Oh, my god. It's not an answer, but it is. Esme's first husband was murdered.

I swallow the tide of bile that wants to rise up in my throat. It burns going back down.

A thought strikes me. "You wrote on your own car. That's why it washed off so easily."

That goddamn smiley face.

"You got into my locker *twice*."

"Only the second time," he says. "Don't know who managed the first."

Carl laughs again. "Under different circumstances, you might be good enough for Steph. She ever tell you I used to work at the school? Maintenance. Mechanical stuff, mostly. Problem was, when they let me go, I misplaced my keys."

"What about the notes? The zip tie? The principal's *creamer*?"

Carl's smirk at the last word is enough of a confirmation, but then he shakes his head. "I don't know who left the notes. Guess I'm not the only one you pissed off."

The thought of some *other* phantom out there trying to scare me is almost too much. I can't bring myself to ask the last question, the one all this has been leading to. The one that starts with me tied up on a basement floor and ends with me joining the tunnel of aurora lights in my head. The one that makes him tell me what he's going to do to me.

Something shifts in the air, and Carl stands up straighter, almost visibly shaking off the alcohol haze. The odor of booze and sweat stirs the air.

"This is messier than I'd like, kid," he says. He holds up the gun, and I flinch away. This is it.

Then he sets it down on a folding table.

"What are you doing?"

"Rubber bullets were okay for Esme," he says. "I'd like her to wake up, see if she'll see sense. But you—"

I could promise him I won't tell. I could beg him to let me live, say that my dad's life is all I need and I'll leave Shep alone and never speak to her again.

But he knows—and I know—that can't happen.

He starts pacing, moving his shoulders like a boxer before a fight. The stink of alcohol permeates the air more with every breath he takes, and lying the way I am is hurting my wrists.

My wrists. I reach through my mind, trying to identify a fleeting string of memory, something from one of Dad's procedurals. I can't close my eyes, but I try to remember.

This time it's not a voice, but a feeling, a movement. Bad knots helped a victim escape his captors, if only temporarily. Temporarily is a good start. My wrists aren't well tied, just some crappy rope wound around both at once instead of actually securing them. Dad's the one who pointed out what makes a bad tie to me, even showed me when I didn't believe him. Which means Carl intends this to be over soon or truly didn't know what he was going to do. Or doesn't know what he's doing at all. At this point, I don't care.

Carl's footsteps stop, and he turns to look at me, his decision written in the slope of his shoulders and the way he cranes his neck first one way and then the other.

I move my hands and feel the ropes give a little more. In my mind, triumph is like a pealing bell.

When Carl takes the first step toward me, the misty tunnel in my head lights up in technicolor.

I think of what Dad would say.

You can do it.

Twist like this, Sammy.

Don't be afraid.

Don't be afraid.

Don't be afraid.

Carl looms over me. If I were standing, we'd be eye to eye, but I'm cheek-to-ground and he may as well be a mountain.

He kneels, his knees by my shoulders, hip-width apart, stabilizing himself against the concrete.

He doesn't say anything.

I realize what he's going to do only an instant before he does it.

Carl Wayne grabs me by the throat.

. . .

It's happening again.

Carl's fingers tighten, and my legs thrash reflexively against the concrete.

Sammy, FIGHT.

Twist your wrists.

Don't be afraid! Don't be afraid! Don't be afraid!

It's still Dad's voice I hear, Dad's face.

And now they surround me as I huddle in a ball in my mind, feeling the weight of their stares through dusty years of history. I don't know what they want. I remember hearing once that it'd be peaceful on the other side of these violent hands. *No, Sam. You have to fight.*

I didn't think of them last time, with that zip tie around my throat. There was nothing but fear. That night broke every illusion of safety I had.

Everything is different now. Shep. Aidan. Sky. Margie Frankel. Mr. Quach. I don't even know his dad's first name, but I think he'd want me to fight. Esme would want me to fight.

They'd all want me to fight.

You have to fight.

You have to fight.

I can't breathe. My vision blurs, blue-black and fuzzy round the edges. My eyes burn and water, and I feel like I become Billy.

How can I fight this when I know what's going to happen? This is my life's one inevitability. Not one of them lived to see their nineteenth birthday. They may have died years before it or mere minutes, but none of them made it. Carl's stronger than a zip tie. He's so much stronger than me.

It's your life, Sam. Fight for it.

Fight, Sammy.

Then, in the endless moment between my last breaths, I realize something.

All of those people I sought out who died before they turned nineteen—that year, *I picked it.* I picked it because once upon a littler Sam, it seemed at once too young and so far off it was safe. I made it unsafe. Me.

The voices coalesce like the multilayered notes in a choir. Shep's. Dad's.

Billy's. The rustle of pages in my book, my half-lived lives. Voices I never heard, young and urgent.

Fight.

I can't breathe, but I can flail my arms. I can twist my wrists. Skin breaks with a flash of heat, but the ropes give more.

Like that. I imagine joy, blinding like the sun.

I keep twisting, tugging, pain blurring into a throbbing pulse that just sounds like my heart.

My wrists twist and twist . . . and spring free.

He put himself right where you need him. That urge to punch—use him, not you. This voice is mine. One hundred percent pure Sam Sylvester.

I can still see Carl's silhouette where he kneels in front of my chest.

With every ounce of strength left in my body, I slam my fist into his groin as hard as I can as if he's my thigh that I've used as a punching bag so many times. My short nails cut through the skin of my own palm. I barely feel it.

Carl's fingers fly from my throat. Dimly, I hear him cry out in agony.

I gasp a breath, rolling onto my side. Something hard digs into my leg. My lungs are pure flame and dust and ash, a deadwood forest of Montana's Bitterroots. A firestorm.

My chest convulses, trying to bring my dying cells back to life. My throat is a throbbing bruise.

There's something digging into my leg.

Carl didn't take my phone.

I pull it out while he writhes on the floor. Somehow my fingers find the emergency call button.

For the second time that day, a voice says, "Nine-one-one, what is your emergency?"

"Help me," I rasp. My throat is so swollen I can barely talk. I try to get the address out. Carl's moving toward me. I try to scramble away. "He's trying to kill me."

Time blends together.

He's going for the gun.

Rubber bullet at close range when I already have a concussion—I pull myself upright.

I hear something upstairs, far too early to be the police or paramedics or anybody.

There's the fire extinguisher in the corner of the basement.

Carl lunges for the gun. I grab the extinguisher. I've used one once before but right now I don't care about precision. I jerk the pin out and aim it and spray him full in the face with carbon dioxide powder. He's already got the gun in his hands. It goes off in a flash of sparks, and something hits me in the leg, but I don't go down. The extinguisher only had that one blast in it, but it was enough to rob him of sight.

He can't see me, but I can see him.

I bring the fire extinguisher down on his head as hard as I can.

Upstairs I hear a raised voice, increasing in panic.

Shep.

It's Shep.

I will myself to make noise. "Shep! Help!"

The sound is pitiful, and at first I think she doesn't hear me over her own cries of fright. She must have found her mom.

Then she appears on the stairs, her face a map of horror.

It's the last thing I see before I fall.

CHAPTER THIRTY-SEVEN

The tunnel is silver and full of light, and this time, I am surrounded by faces of love.

They spiral around me, faces that look like love, all of them.

I'm not afraid anymore.

There is no reason to be afraid.

It happens to everyone. It's just happened to them a lot earlier than it happens to most.

It almost happened to me twice.

I want to thank them, but they're all too long gone to hear me, except the ones who are alive now.

And there, in that tunnel of light and color, I see the one thing I've missed all this time.

In the end, sometimes you have a choice. We can't always choose whether or not we die, but we get to choose whether to be afraid to live. You get to choose.

Just like I am about to.

This is where I know. I can stay here with these people I love. I can be the next in this long line of humans stretching back and back and back to the quiet slumberers in the depths of the mist who barely turn in my direction. I can stay here with Billy. Or I can break the pattern I made in my own mind.

They're here with me because I found their stories, and this is the lesson I needed to learn from them.

There's still someone out there who wanted to hurt me.

I don't know if Dad will make it.

Shep.

I've never thought much about what happens after school.

Nothing is certain.

There will always be people like Lee, the cowards who fear what they don't understand. And the Barry boys, who do irreparable damage in their fear. People like Esme who believe too fully in their own mistakes even when they didn't do anything wrong. People like Blaise, who are made of spite. And people like Carl, who kill because it's the only way they have control.

But there are people like Dad.

People like Shep and Sky and Aidan.

Like Mr. Quach and Margie Frankel.

They don't want me to end.

I don't want me to end either.

This time I don't ball up and hide in the center of the spiral. This time I stand tall and proud while they come closer, folding in on me like the petals of a flower reversing its bloom to become a bud once more.

. . .

I open my eyes.

The light hurts at first. There is no mist.

The first thing I see is Dad.

"Oh, my baby. Oh, my Sammy." Then he's clutching my hand so tight I think he might take it off, and he's alive, and I can see him, and he isn't going to ask if I'm okay because *obviously* I am in a hospital bed, but I've never been so happy.

He's in regular clothes, jeans and a tattered old hoodie, and the sight is a shock.

"What day is it?" I croak.

He starts laughing, and he's crying, and I can't help but start to laugh too.

"March first, baby. It's March first. And I'm gonna celebrate your birthday all damn month."

I've been out for over ten days.

"Shep? Is Esme? Dad, oh, my god." Talking hurts, and maybe I shouldn't be able to do it. I can barely lift my hand or squeeze Dad's back.

"Easy, Sam. Shep's okay. Esme's more okay than you are."

"Is Carl—"

"Arrested. He'll never hurt you again. It doesn't look like the DA will be able to bring any charges against Esme, even as an accessory."

A nurse comes rushing in, and within minutes the poking and prodding starts, and I couldn't mind if I tried.

My room is full of flowers and balloons and a big-ass card sits on a table across from me with Bowie's face on it.

The nurses bustling around me can't seem to understand why I'm laughing.

. . .

They let me out a few days later, and I spend the next few after that at home. That first blow to the head shouldn't have been that bad, but the attempted strangling on top of it apparently caused a small cerebral aneurysm, if there is such a thing as a small one of those. They had to put me in a coma after an emergency surgery. I haven't quite processed that yet. The incision is already almost healed, my skin busy knitting itself together while I slept.

I *really* almost died.

That I survived and don't seem to have lost brain function is a miracle to me. I'm still here. I'm still me.

There's a quiet peace to the house that is new.

I barely see Shep, and I can't blame her. She sends me a letter (a real letter) from her aunt's house telling me that she misses me and that she wants to spend my birthday with me.

I tell Dad I want to stay up all night on March 14th, and he seems to get that it's one of my *things* and doesn't argue. He calls Sky's and Aidan's parents and tells them he'll chaperone the all-nighter, and I think they're all so flustered by their kids being friends with a real-life Kid Who Lived that they don't even argue.

When March 14th arrives, I'm still tottering on my feet a bit. I've lost weight, and I hate how my muscles feel different. My clothes all fit too loosely. My binder barely even binds.

Shep shows up first, because I asked her to.

Dad retreats to his room, leaving us in the living room because I can only handle the stairs about twice a day so far. My head still spins when I move too quickly, and my body is weaker than a half-drowned chicken.

Sitting on our aubergine sofa, Shep also looks like she's had the life sucked out of her.

She hasn't made a move to touch me, and the void feels almost worse than my physical injuries.

"Who's going to talk first?" I ask after five minutes of silence.

Shep cracks a small smile at that. "I don't know. What do you say when your dad tried to kill your" —she fumbles over the gap in the English language for whatever I am to her— "your Sam?"

"I'm the farthest thing from a hobbit," I tell her.

"You know what I mean."

I do know. "I couldn't bear to lose my Shep, either," I say quietly. "That's why I couldn't tell you I suspected your mother of killing Billy—that's why I went over there alone."

She nods, but she closes her eyes tight for a second. "I wish you'd told me."

"I was terrified I was right and it would leave you with only Carl forever," I say.

Shep is quiet at that. Finally, she lets out a heaving sigh. "Oof. Yeah. Okay."

Then we're both silent for a long stretch.

"She feels so guilty," Shep says softly. "She's apologized so many times to me, so many times. She thinks she almost got you killed by texting my dad—she really didn't know he'd—she didn't know he was the one who murdered Billy. All this time, he just . . . pretended it was her to control her."

"Is she going to be okay?" I ask.

"God, I don't know. I wish my grandma was here. Abuelita would know what to do—though she'd probably murder Carl herself, so there's also that." Shep cracks a small smile that doesn't reach her eyes. "Next double family dinner's going to be awkward."

Oh, god. I glance toward the kitchen. Dad's . . . remarkably not mad about almost dying. As soon as we got home from the hospital, he just relaxed, looking the way I feel after taking off my binder when I've worn it way too long. Started humming Bowie's "Starman." I don't think he even realized he was doing it.

"Ready for me to win that weird-off?" I say shakily. Shep just nods. "Everyone who touches those shelves in my room seems to connect with Billy in some way. Dad immediately started singing 'Under Pressure' the first time—even you did it. 'Space Oddity,' though."

At her startled look, I give her a wry smile.

"Dad told me he smelled popcorn when I got home from the dance that night—*I* smelled it a bunch of times. I think—I think

Billy helped us. I don't know why or how it's possible, but I think he did." I make myself meet her eyes, half-expecting her to laugh.

But of course she doesn't laugh.

"That actually makes me feel better," she says, then sucks her lip against her teeth before blowing out a breath. "I think he needed you."

"Us," I say. "You cared before you knew I existed."

Shep glances up at the ceiling. "The house feels different now. More peaceful."

Those hastily boarded-up shelves we found in my room—we'll never know why someone decided to cover them. Maybe that was Billy's influence too.

I haven't told her about the card I found, and I do now, though I don't have it down here. Her brown eyes get wider and wider. She swallows a bunch of times, and I know she is thinking the same thing I have a hundred times: Carl killed Billy because he saw him as a threat. Competition.

"Do you think—" Shep breaks off, then laughs without humor. "It's stupid."

"I'm sure it's not," I say. "Can't be worse than my psychic fingertips or whatever."

She cracks a real smile at that. After a moment, she says, "Do you think Billy helped you find that card maybe—maybe because he knew my mom was suffering? That all this time she thought it was her fault?"

Oh. *Oh.* Her words bring a wave of pure emotion, and I can't even answer her, but she takes my hands in hers, and for a moment we sit there, silent. I don't know what's true, but I'd like to think she's right. Esme deserves to be free, after all this time. There was nothing she could have done to save him. I know that. I think Billy knows it too.

I look back to Shep and change the subject, since I think both of us will lose it if we keep traveling down this track.

"You and Sky and Aidan—I've never had friends like you before," I say. "Even with Lee. It was never—she was never the same. It's always been easier for me to get on with adults."

"Why?"

I shrug. "I've never been very good at humaning in general. Other kids always thought I was weird. Adults at least thought I was a novelty for being able to talk about history and random trivia. And being friends with dead-too-soon kids from the past was easier."

I can say that now. I get myself now.

"You are weird. But you're the best kind of weird." She tries to smile, but she looks . . . haunted.

She has dark circles under her eyes that look like they've been tattooed there. This is the moment I never thought would come, when my big secret would lessen a burden instead of adding to it.

"You know all those dead-too-soon kids?" I say.

"Yeah," she says. Although she really doesn't think I'm a freak, saying it out loud still sounds ridiculous.

"They all died before their nineteenth birthday," I say simply. "If it wasn't one thing, it was another. I took that inside of me. Like I couldn't escape it."

"But—" Shep splutters, looking outside as if something's going to come bursting through the window at me.

For a moment I'm touched by how quickly she jumps to believe some force exists to make fate happen. I shake my head with such certainty that Shep calms.

"No," I say.

She looks unsettled again, and now she does reach for me, scooting closer to take my hands in hers. "I can't lose you, Sam. Not now. Do you *want* to die?"

"I could have decided to just be . . . done. To rest."

"You had a choice."

"I had a choice. This time, at least."

I swallow when I think of Matthew Shepard in Wyoming, Brayla Stone in Arkansas, kids like me who had that choice ripped away.

Shep's hands are ice-cold on mine. "You chose to stay? Why?"

Her question nearly breaks my heart. "Remember what I told you that first time you came over? You asked me what I wanted."

She thinks back. I see her remember.

"You said you want to live."

I nod. "I want to *live*, Shep."

And then that wave of emotion is back, and I don't care if we're a mess when the others get here. She's in my arms, and her shoulders shake as she cries her relief into my chest. I pull her to me, cuddling down into the soft sofa cushions.

"I should have known about Dad," she sobs. "He almost took your dad from you. He almost—I should have known."

"Sometimes we're too close to know what someone is capable of," I say.

. . .

Sky and Aidan arrive an hour later, folding me into their arms in hugs that are almost too tight. They chatter at me, and I let them, my brain for once letting me just listen, refilling a well that ran dry in my short coma. Neither of them remarks on our tear-stained faces and puffy eyes.

"Expect a *brutal* apology from Blaise," Sky informs me. "She heard you almost got murdered again and had a 'come-to-Jesus' moment. Fessed up to putting those notes on your doors—and the zip tie in your locker—and got suspended. Frankel, I think, would have put her in the stocks if she could."

"And Dylan," Aidan adds. "He's the one who saw your file. He read what happened to you in Montana and was so distressed by it that he told a bunch of people . . . including Blaise."

I blink. "Dylan?" His weirdness must have been because he was feeling guilty. "So the school finding out—"

"A product of the grapevine and crush-tinged, clueless curiosity, not malice. Blaise covered the malice base all by herself, as I said." Sky's face is annoyance and amusement in one. "I actually was in the office when Blaise confessed to Frankel about leaving the note with the zip tie, and I thought I was going to see flames exploding out of the office door. Frankel tore Blaise a new one."

"How is Principal Frankel?" I ask, too stunned about Blaise owning her shit to pursue that line of thought any further.

"She sent you a card, actually," says Sky. He digs around in his duffel bag and hands it to me.

It's a birthday card, and I imagine her trying to figure whether to give me a birthday or a get well soon one.

You did what I've tried to do for thirty years. Thank you, Sam. Happy birthday. —MF

"She signed it MF?" Aidan asks. "What a BAMF."

I feel bad I ever suspected her. One of the first things I did when I got home from the hospital was delete every single image I took of her journal. I'm glad we didn't figure out how to read it.

There's one from Mr. Quach, too. I open it to see another note, and something falls out of the card.

342

We look forward to seeing you back at school when you're ready, Sam. My dad's asked if he can come by one day and meet you. No matter what you say to that, he thinks you're a hero. He asked me to give you this picture—it's him and Billy with their dates at homecoming in '88.

Shep has picked up the picture and is holding it as if it's going to vanish in her hands. She offers it to me. There they are, two grinning boys in black suits, looking like they are channeling James Bond. The two girls are Margie and someone I don't recognize, standing back-to-back and smiling just as widely. Margie's in a blue-green dress with enormous puffy sleeves. On the back of the picture is written: *Sang Quach, Billy Clement, Margie Frankel, and Willa Strong, Homecoming 1988.*

Sang Quach. I hope he's been out of the hospital for a while by now. I hope our stays didn't overlap. I pass the picture to Aidan, who takes it with careful fingers as reverent as Shep's.

"Ronnie and Jax also wanted to throw you a party whenever you're up to it." Sky nudges his duffel bag to the side and examines his fingernails.

The thought is a bit terrifying, partly for obvious past trauma reasons and partly because parties are parties. People and loud music and noise.

Then again, this is a party, and this is fine.

"Whenever I'm up to it?" I ask.

"Yeah, it's *for you*, doofus. They don't want to plan it till they know you won't keel over."

"Oh," I say. I look at Shep, and I know she remembers the story about Lee's party invitation. But the past isn't the future, and now I've actually got both. "I should have invited them tonight."

"Eh, you just got out of the hospital," says Sky. "And you're a Pisces. They'll forgive you."

343

"One other thing," says Aidan. "The town wants to have a memorial for Billy on his birthday. A vigil, I think. Principal Frankel is organizing it. One of my managers was talking about it at work—I guess Billy's parents are even flying in."

I look up to see Dad in the doorway. He coughs. "I was going to tell you about that, Sam. Margie—Principal Frankel—said no one expects you to go if you're not up for it, but—"

"I want to," I blurt out. "Billy's parents are coming?"

Shep looks like she's as shocked as I feel, and I grab her hand and squeeze it tight. I can't imagine she isn't feeling conflicted about seeing them face to face, but Billy's story has been so important to her. I'll reassure her—maybe Margie can help. Principal Frankel.

Dad orders us Chinese food at my behest, since I don't think I want to risk Dylan delivering pizza here for a while for my own mental health. And then Dad trots out a birthday cake far too big for fifteen people, let alone five.

We eat until our bellies are round and hurt from laughing, and then we settle in to watch movies through the night.

Sunrise is supposed to be at 7:28 a.m., and the plan is to watch it from the beach, even though it won't be rising over the Pacific. I've barely been to the beach here yet, which is sort of abysmal. I can't think of a better day to do something new, though.

There's one thing I need to do before we go.

I manage to get up the stairs to my barren room alone. A feat.

My laptop sits on the bedside table. I deleted the note I'd left for Dad the moment I got a chance, face burning at the knowledge that he narrowly avoided having to read it.

I log in to Tumblr, to the Letters from Andromeda account. Both Margie and I looked to the stars to process our pain.

I don't need it anymore, this shouting into the void. The anger I feel at Lee is gone. I don't know that I'd go as far as forgiveness, but I'm not angry anymore. This, the anniversary of my first-almost-getting murdered.

The moment I log in, I notice that someone's sent me a private message.

I open it.

Sam,

I blink back the shock.

I stumbled across this last week. I know I'm never supposed to contact you again, but I wanted you to know that you didn't deserve what I did to you.

I am so sorry. It doesn't make it better, but I donated half my college savings to the Trevor Project.

Lee

It's really her, too. The message is from her Tumblr, a blog she's kept up for years.

A soft footfall at the door makes me turn.

It's Shep.

"Hey," she says. "What's wrong?"

I show her the message. "I was just going to delete the whole Tumblr," I say. "Found this."

"Do you still want to delete everything?"

I hesitate. I don't want to talk to Lee. Ever again, really. I don't owe her anything. She knows she crossed a boundary by even contacting me. But I think I need closure.

I look at Shep, then pull up a reply.

I type two words. The first words I ever said to Dad—*thank you.*

My finger taps the track pad to send it.

Shep watches quietly while I delete the Tumblr. Lee should still see the message, but she won't be able to reply.

"You good?" Shep's voice is quiet in the predawn dark.

"Yeah," I say. "Are you?"

She lets out a shuddering breath.

"Yeah. I think I am." Shep sits by me on the edge of the bed. "What Aidan and your dad said—if Billy's parents are coming here—"

"What your dad did was *not* your fault," I say.

"I know," she says. "It's just—thirty years, Sam. Thirty years of grief without knowing where to put it. Without knowing who was to blame."

"That's just the thing," I say, thinking of the message I just sent off to Lee, knowing I didn't have to. I take Shep's hand in mine, raise it to my lips. I kiss it. "After all this time, now we can go on together. Everyone."

My room is quiet. That horrible tension is gone, and I don't think it will ever come back. But I still feel him here, feel Billy in this space we share. It feels like home.

"Let's go to the beach," I say, getting up.

On a flash of inspiration, I pull *Sam's Book of Half-Lived Lives* from under my bed where I stuffed it what feels like an eon ago. Shep smiles at me as we head down the stairs hand in hand, where the others are waiting for us at the door. Dad's showing the boys pictures of adoptable (full-grown) dogs at the local shelter—we're going in in a couple days to meet them. Dad is so excited, I practically expect him to sprout a wagging tail at any moment.

The wind is cold as the sky lightens around us.

Shep and I spread out a blanket on the dew-damp sand, and we all sit in a semicircle with our backs to the waves.

I look at Dad as I push my book into the center of the blanket. Everyone looks curiously at it, then at me.

"Remember when I said I need to just . . . know things sometimes, Dad?"

He nods.

"They're who I needed to know. Billy's one of them."

I look at Shep. She told me in her letter that the pages were in her dad's bedroom, and she had to turn them over to the police. I don't know if I'll ever get them back, but I can tell Billy's story now myself.

I open my book, my hand shaking.

No one calls me weird or morbid. Dad squeezes my shoulder as if to say, *You could have told me, Sammy*, and he swallows when he sees the title and again when he recognizes Brayla Stone's name. I think he gets why I decided I couldn't before now. I give him a crooked smile and let them page through my book, listening to them talk in hushed voices about the work I did. They seem somehow proud. Shep nestles closer to me.

"They'd be happy you hold their stories, I think," Sky says quietly, eyes glued to the page about Anum.

Dad passes around a thermos of hot cocoa, and the murmur of conversation fades as the sky turns from blue to gold with the light of the oncoming sun.

"Penny for your thoughts, Sam," says Sky.

"I've never been nineteen before," I murmur. I look at Shep, and she leans forward to kiss me, tears in her eyes. She scoots closer, pressing her shoulder to mine.

We look back to the horizon just as the sun breaks it.

I'm nineteen years old. I fought for this life and won.

My name is Sam Sylvester, and I've got a whole life to live.

ACKNOWLEDGMENTS

When I set out to write *The Many Half-Lived Lives Of Sam Sylvester*, I hadn't intended to write a YA. While I always loved YA, I'd been firmly ensconced in adult fiction for my entire career, but in 2017, in the wake of the Pulse massacre and the rise of Trump, Sam's voice caught hold of me. My one real guiding star in this book was to write the book I wished I had as a teen.

First and foremost, I need to thank my agent, Sara Megibow, for sticking with me through the past six years. We've had so many disappointments, and you've had my back when I wanted to quit. I couldn't be more grateful for the support you've given me in this business, which, despite progress, can still be heart-breaking for disabled, queer, and trans authors and readers alike—even more so for Black authors and authors of color in general. Thank you for fighting for me.

To Jes Negrón, the editor who originally acquired Sam's story, I also want to say a heartfelt thank you. Jes was my first literary agent back in the early years of my career, and as such, she was the first to champion my writing and root me out of the slushpile. It felt fitting that she would end up being my first advance-paying sale, and I am thankful every day to have such a good friend. I owe you several fruit baskets and a massive hug. Your steadfast belief in my abilities has sustained me on many of the Bad Days.

To Suzy Krogulski, my editor who came in to take Jes's place after her departure, I appreciate your patience and your willingness to talk things through. This book is stronger because of your notes, and I'm proud of what we managed in a global pandemic! Thank you for believing in Sam and their story.

While the book was written in 2017, it went through much of its editorial process in 2020 and 2021, and as such, I can't write acknowledgments without shouting out my communities online who provided structure, a coworking environment via Zoom (even across time zones and oceans!), and Discords and Slacks with enough emojis to articulate the myriad frustrations, fears, and unique tribulations of the past two years. As a habitual hermit who would have probably lost my already-shaky social abilities in my wee cat cave in lockdown, seeing friends' faces every day on Zoom helped me not completely get lost in my own head.

Two friends volunteered to give the book a lightning-quick read when I was deep in the Pit of Despair and couldn't see it clearly, so Jo Ladziński and Rekka Theodore also have my sincerest thanks.

Huge thanks to my friend Oliver Creutzner for generously allowing me to use his delightful analogy of bisexuality—we are all, indeed, allowed to enjoy pizza and pasta (and sandwiches!) even if we are currently eating mashed potatoes.

Finally, I want to thank the sensitivity readers who helped me make this book what I wanted it to be. Your kind notes were so appreciated, and any remaining issues after I implemented your feedback are mine alone.

While my experiences as a queer, non-binary, autistic person informed Sam's experiences, no one person's life encapsulates the entirety of a community. I hope that Sam is meaningful to those who needed them. Thank you for reading.